"That sounds great!"

Brayden breathes out his relief and his beaming, friendly smile grows somehow wider. Joy bubbles to the surface, and Jenner can imagine it dancing just under his skin, tingling with its intensity. Distantly, he wonders, were a hand grazed over Brayden's smoothly-waxed skin, what the goosebumps currently pebbling it would feel like. "I've got no problem with crowds. My, um." He shows the first sign of bashfulness, ducking his head and beginning to blush, the color rising up his neck to his cheeks.

He blushes, Jenner marvels. *So fucking adorable.*

"My friends back in Miami always call me on being a huge flirt. It's come in handy with tending bar."

"I bet it does." Jenner walks around the bar and returns to Brayden, folding his arms over his chest. Jenner is almost a whole foot taller than him. He towers over Brayden and tries to minimize his pleasure at this discovery, lest the possibly-worrisome and growing bulge in his pants gives him away. Scanning Brayden's body, Jenner debates his answer, and knows Brayden waits with bated breath.

"Please, I really need this job," Brayden says softly.

That does it. Having the lithe, sweet, beautiful creature before him literally *beg* decides Jenner then and there, despite lingering worries about Brayden's ability to deal with the non-female, non-flirtatious customers, especially since they're likely to be people who remember him.

Also recommended...

You may also enjoy these other ForbiddenFiction works:

Don't... by Jack L. Pyke
"Don't... open me." Three simple words that tease Jack, taking him places from his dark past. For Jack, BDSM is a way to resist his worst impulses. Yet, the stranger calling himself The Unknown seeks to use that to seduce him. As Jack slips further down into the abyss, two men hold the power to save him. Will it be Gray, the Master who knows Jack's every secret? Or Jan, the first man to give Jack a reason to hope? With deadly ghosts coming out to play, Jack may lose everything, even his life. (M/M)
http://forbiddenfiction.com/library/story/JP2-1.000134

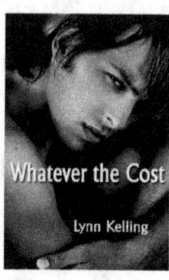

Whatever the Cost by Lynn Kelling
Liam and Jacen are roommates–and elite prostitutes working for a secret organization, The Company. They spend their lives making fantasies come true for spoiled, dangerous clients. In the midst of daily risk of emotional and physical damage, their friendship has been an island of sanity and safety. When The Company orders them to do a job a job together requiring them to cross the no-sex boundary that has kept them friends, Liam and Jacen must examine how they really feel about each other, and how far they are truly willing to go. Is this the life they want? Used to offering up their bodies without protest to the mercurial whims of others while fiercely guarding their hearts, the true meaning of love and consent is a challenge neither has ever faced before.
http://forbiddenfiction.com/library/story/LK1-1.000005

Bound by Lies

Lynn Kelling

ForbiddenFiction
www.forbiddenfiction.com

an imprint of

Fantastic Fiction Publishing
www.fantasticfictionpublishing.com

BOUND BY LIES
A Forbidden Fiction book

Fantastic Fiction Publishing
Hayward, California

© Lynn Kelling, 2013

CREDITS
Editor: Rylan Hunter and D.M. Atkins
Cover Design: D.M. Atkins
Cover Art: Photo by 7thlord at Dreamstime.
Mask Vector Icon by Freepik Production.
Production Editor: Erika L Firanc
Proofreading: Kailin Morgan and Aislinn

SKU: LK1-000109-02 FFP
ISBN: 978-1-62234-113-9

Published in the United States of America

DISCLAIMER

This book is a work of fiction which contains explicit erotic content; it is intended for mature readers. Do not read this if it's not legal for you.

All the characters, locations and events herein are fictional. While elements of existing locations or historical characters or events may be used fictitiously, any resemblance to actual people, places or events is coincidental.

This story depicts fictional BDSM; it is not intended to be used as an instruction manual. It contains descriptions of erotic acts that may be immoral, illegal, or unsafe. The characters are not models for the Safe, Sane and Consensual forms embraced by most current practitioners of BDSM. The author takes license with the use of BDSM for dramatic effect. Do not take the events in this story as proof of the plausibility or safety of any particular practice.

For my fellow ugly ducklings and hopeless romantics,
with love.

Contents

Chapter 1
Surrender

Roughly two-thirds of the way north, on a long drive straight from Miami, Florida to Robertsville, Pennsylvania, Brayden Clare stops at a gas station in Maryland to fill up. The middle-aged woman at the next pump stares openly at him while he pumps the gas.

That's just your raging self-consciousness talking again. You're projecting, being paranoid. She's probably staring at the massive, obnoxiously colorful surfboard wedged in the back of the Jeep.

He tosses his hair back out of his eyes and peeks, trying to make it seem like a natural, casually disinterested glance.

Nope, she's staring at me, he finds, and smiles politely.

"Hey. Afternoon," he nods to her. He has found, through much trial and error, that sometimes it's better to make the effort to confront life's awkward moments rather than pretend them away. Ignore them all you like, if they're there, they're there.

She hadn't expected him to say anything, he sees, as her eyes widen comically. Blushing and dropping her gaze, she giggles nervously, playing with her keys. "Um. Hi. Yeah, um…" Rolling her eyes at herself, she gives him a little wave and ducks behind her car, sliding back in behind the wheel. Through the window, he sees her cover her face with a hand.

Chuckling softly with sincere amusement, his heart becoming a little bit lighter, Brayden pulls the gas nozzle from the Jeep and finishes the transaction. Usually he's the furthest thing from cynical. It's been his greatest source of pride over the past four years, how he's slowly learned how to be able to smile, often, and mean it. It's the drive to his old home that's affecting him, turning him, mile by

1

mile, back into someone he has vigorously tried to no longer be.

His phone buzzes in his pocket, startling him slightly. Uncertain who could be calling, he fishes out the phone and sees from the caller ID that it's Andre. A tiny photo flashes on the screen, identifying him—dark brown skin glistening like chiseled marble in the sunshine, white smile beaming.

"I thought I got rid of you," Brayden says as he answers, lacing paper-thin annoyance into the words, thinking, *God, I'm glad he called.* It's proof that Andre is still thinking about him, that the act of leaving the state hasn't automatically removed Brayden from everything, and everyone, left behind.

"I'm not that easy to get rid of," Andre retorts. "As you know well. What state are you in? Besides confusion."

"Funny. Really. That's hilarious. I'm in Maryland."

"D'ya miss me yet?"

Brayden smiles. It's genuine and for the first time in two days, warmth sparks in his heart, melting some of the gathered chill. He gets back in the Jeep to finish the call.

"Nah, I'm good," Brayden teases. "How about you? Find someone to replace me?"

"Mm, might be a little tricky. There were some definite benefits to rooming with you…"

"You could always specifically ask for a slut when you advertise."

Through the surprisingly good connection, Andre laughs loudly. "Oh baby, don't you get it? What I like best about you is what a *reluctant* slut you are. That's rare. 'Specially in Miami."

"Mm," Brayden grunts. "Yeah, guess so."

There's a pause, and Brayden waits for it, Andre's insight, now that the joking has broken the ice. "What's wrong, Marsha?"

"Nothing's wrong. It's been a shitty drive. It's cold. Hey, did I leave my sandals there?"

"No, something is definitely wrong. You don't sound like yourself at all. Is this about—"

Brayden cuts him off. "I'm kind of dealing with a lot right now. Of course I'm stressed. That's all."

"You should tell them."

"There's nothing to tell. It was fun while it lasted but now I've gotta go back to reality and act like a grown-up. That's all."

"'It was fun while it lasted?' Are you seriously telling yourself that? This isn't some *phase* you're going through, Braydy."

"I disagree."

"So that's it? You're going to just pretend to dig on pussy for the rest of your life because it's easier than facing the truth?"

"I'm hanging up. Wh-why did you even call me? Don't you think I'm miserable enough right now?"

"I offered to make the drive with you," Andre says softly.

Brayden's face twists up as some of his tightly bottled emotion surfaces momentarily. Holding his breath until it burns in his lungs, he presses his fingertips to his eyes. He listens and tries to find the balls to hang up on Andre like he threatened to. Betraying him, his imagination supplies the fantasy of having Andre's massive form beside him in the Jeep, the sheer weight of muscle testing the shocks, Andre's bald head nudging the plastic roof. It's a wonderful thought, but it also makes Brayden queasy. He would never be able to let the different facets of his life bleed together like that. Andre is the past now. He's the city, with all of its heat, bustle, action and decadent freedom to act spontaneously without scrutiny or judgment. Nana and Emma are the future, even if they're also his small home town, full of ghosts and bad memories, where the name Brayden Clare will bear many specific labels, assumptions and expectations from the moment he shows up. He draws a line down the middle, right between them in his head, keeping them away from each other.

"This isn't who you are," Andre urges.

"Yeah. It is now. I'll call you soon." He hangs up and turns off the phone.

In retrospect, Brayden realizes how desperate he was when his big sexual epiphany happened. At the time, though, it was a whole other story. He was naïve, young, and uncomfortable in his own skin.

He knew Andre was bisexual, just as he knew that wrestling — watching it, doing it, thinking about it — was a huge, intensely secret turn on. The man-on-man, body-against-sweaty-body struggle for dominance unfailingly made his dick stiffer than any of his actual, hands-on attempts to get interested in girls. Even when Brenna James sucked him at the bonfire a few years back, he had to fantasize about the match he'd gone to see the night before just to get it up.

The wrestling aspect, therefore, played a big part in his epiphany, but Brayden also knew that the best way to lose some of his many inhibitions was to get good and drunk.

So, he got drunk. *Really* drunk. It was a Sunday night. Andre, a pre-law student, was doing class work. Brayden kept giving Andre beers, though. One after the other until Andre gave up the pretense, left the books behind and joined him on the couch instead. Then, Brayden got out the hard alcohol. One shot for Andre, one for himself. Over and over again. When Andre told him to slow down, Brayden insisted, calling it a long-overdue chance to blow off steam.

Things became unsteady — his body as well as his resolve to do or say something about the way he had been feeling. He accidentally spilled a whole glass full of tequila all over his chest and lap a few hours into the binge. Andre was laughing his ass off, telling Brayden he smelled like a liquor cabinet and looked like a wet dog, so Brayden took a shower.

When he reappeared, Brayden could see the change happen in Andre's expression. Freshly bathed, skin damp, dressed in only a small, white towel wrapped around his narrow hips, it was the most naked he'd ever been when alone with another guy, even if it was for innocent reasons. His lean swimmer's body was toned in all the right places thanks to long hours spent at the gym and in the ocean. The way Andre was looking at all of that exposed, suntanned skin was different than any look Andre had ever given Brayden before. It was darker, heavier, and full of intent.

"You're in my way, bro," Brayden warned, like he was picking a fight. He stepped to the side as if to go around, and Andre just slid sideways into his path.

"Oh, am I?" Andre countered, playing along as he always did. "What're you gonna do about it?"

All at once, Brayden was aware of their size difference and every single one of the eight inches in height that Andre had on him. Many years of training in the wrestling ring sang out in the thick, bulging muscles popping over the length of Andre's body, clad in only loose shorts and a sleeveless shirt. Used to having to look up at the majority of other men, the effect of having to do so in that situation—tipping his chin up to meet Andre's eyes—felt different in the same way Andre's expression did.

Awareness of his arousal made him panic with how stark his need was to hide it.

Brayden didn't consciously decide to charge at Andre, he was driven to it by his desperation. Andre stood between him and the closet where his clothes were. The alcohol made it seem like a great idea to try to sprint past the giant in his path in order to get to those clothes. Gritting his teeth, green eyes flashing with the fire of determination and madness, Brayden "Braydy" Clare tensed every muscle he had and growled as he ran at the man standing in his way.

Thank god the floor was carpeted with ugly, thick shag.

Andre clotheslined him, sending him falling flat on his back, gaping like a beached fish for suddenly hard-to-find oxygen. Angry, Brayden recovered quickly, scrambling back to his feet.

They grappled while standing up, knocking into furniture as they spun and cursed. Brayden struggled. Andre laughed, not mockingly, but in admiration for his much-smaller-friend's spunkiness. Noticing Andre's roughened breathing, proud to have caused it, Brayden kept up the fight.

Andre swept Brayden's legs. Then it was a floor match. They rolled and Andre let Brayden think there was a chance in hell for him before getting Brayden on his back and pinning him easily.

Andre was on top. He glistened with a thin sheen of sweat from the heat rather than the exercise. Legs like tree trunks trapped Brayden from the thighs down. One forearm like an overgrown python crossed Brayden's upper chest, pressing higher and higher until it was against his throat so that both of Brayden's hands were kept occupied trying to pry it off his windpipe in order to keep the air flowing into his lungs.

Andre wasn't lying down on him. There wasn't much contact at all between their middles. It was harmless, or so Brayden told himself, at first—they were just expelling excess energy and goofing off.

Except that wrestling always made Brayden hard. His cock had started to rise from the moment Andre started to look at his mostly naked body in non-friendly ways. Having Andre's warm, slick skin and firm body in his grasp, in addition to being overpowered so easily—it just intensified everything.

It made it so much better.

Hearing Andre breathe near his ear, feeling his larger body press him into the floor, it swelled Brayden's interest to dangerous levels. His dick was tenting the towel and he suddenly realized he couldn't move at all. He was very effectively trapped where he was.

He was fully erect and wearing a towel that was probably coming undone, likely to fall off at any moment, and Andre would see, would *know*.

Andre shifted to make sure he wasn't really hurting Brayden. There was a slight dip of his pelvis and that was it.

He felt it.

His hyper-intelligent brown eyes fixed on Brayden's face, studying it like Brayden was his homework now. Staring at the far wall instead of the massive man holding him down, his head turned slightly to the side, Brayden pretended that his erection hadn't just dragged against Andre's hip and said nothing. All he could do was wait for the inevitable backlash and tidal wave of humiliation to come crashing down.

Grunting and pushing upwards with his body, all of his limbs, he tried to dislodge Andre. He didn't say 'get off me' or 'enough'. He struggled, knowing it wouldn't do any good, or maybe, rather, *because* he knew it wouldn't do any good.

As if he was only trying to one-up Brayden's breathy, somewhat sensual little gasps and grunts by giving him something to really cry out about, Andre acted.

He reached down between their bodies and *grabbed*. Brayden's mind overloaded and shut down. Thick fingers wrapped around his erection through the towel's terry cloth. Engulfing the swelling flesh, Andre's hand tightened and slid over it.

There was nothing accidental about it.

Brayden froze. His expression was blank, his eyes stared at nothing. The only response was a slow rising blush as he stopped breathing and told himself there was no way it could really be happening.

With a shrewd gaze, measuring and judging every subtle reaction like the expert prosecute he would someday be, Andre tugged once, then let go only to reach lower and drag his hand up over the waxed-smooth skin of Brayden's inner thigh, pushing the towel up and out of the way.

Exhaling sharply through his nose as his breath refused to be held any longer, Brayden's lips sealed tightly together to hold in a moan. He tried to slip free somehow, but of course couldn't, which was precisely why he was so turned on in the first place. As Brayden tried to twist his hips, Andre's hand closed up around his genitals, getting a handful of his sac and his dick.

It was the very first time another man had touched Brayden like that and the effect was powerful. Twitching into the touch, unable to disguise a hard moan, his body vibrated with pleasure. Simultaneously, he needed much, much more, and also had to make it stop, no matter what. The chaotic clash of lust and horror made him lash out. Grabbing at Andre's left arm, Brayden clawed at him, denting the skin.

A voice in the back of Brayden's head told him to fight, to shout in protest, to do *something*, but as Andre gently fondled him, Brayden could only lay there and take it, shuddering. A warm palm dragged up the underside of his bare cock; it rolled over his balls, pressing them up against his shaft. Fingers played along his length, mapping it, feeling it thicken and jump at the attention. Then Andre simply cupped his hand around the head and applied gentle pressure. Fluid pulsed from the slit. Brayden grunted thickly and bucked, his back arching off the floor.

The whole time, Andre never stopped staring at his face with calm confidence and plenty of curiosity. Brayden felt the weight of that scrutiny, unable to look his friend in the eye, or even get close. A quivering exhale over parted lips provoked Andre to give him a tighter stroke, root to tip, using precome to slick the shaft. Brayden writhed and Andre only tightened his focus, watching his lips form a plaintive gasp, tugging again.

He gasped again and it wasn't with pleasure this time, it was filled only with all of the hurt Brayden felt.

Never had he felt that helpless, not with everything he'd gone through as a teenager. It was too tangible, too physical and intense. It was everything he usually tried so hard to avoid, bombarding him all at once.

Andre backed off just a little, right away, just enough, and Brayden's panic won out.

He rolled free.

"Where you goin'? Come on. B! Brayden!" Andre called, his voice filled with care and concern. Brayden hastily grabbed up the dislodged towel and scrambled to the bathroom, slamming the door shut.

They didn't talk about it or even acknowledge it happened for a full week afterward. Both of them pretended everything was normal. Everything was just fine. It might have been convincing enough to be true if not for the fact that all week long, Brayden wouldn't look Andre in the eyes. In theory, it might have gone on like that for much longer, maybe even long enough to become intolerable. It might have gotten bad enough that Brayden would have moved out, in search of a more comfortable living arrangement.

But it didn't go on longer than a week. The next Sunday morning, Brayden was staring out at nothing, his eyes half-lidded with drowsiness, his sun-lightened hair falling over the side of his face in soft waves as he lingered a little too long at the coffee pot. He stayed there like that, a weary, somewhat defeated statue, as Andre got closer and closer. There was no protest or search for escape as Andre got right up in his personal space to whisper in an ear, "It's nothin' to be ashamed of, you know."

The coffee sloshed in the mug as Brayden's hands started to tremble.

Andre plucked the mug free and set it aside before the steaming liquid could spill and scald. With nothing to hold on to, Brayden broke from his spell, answering the soothing words the only way he knew how. He elbowed Andre in the gut, catching him right under the ribs.

Sighing tiredly, Andre easily caught Brayden's arm. When

Brayden twisted away, Andre simply caught the other arm, too, spinning him in order to pull both arms behind his captive's back.

Panic — hot, liquid panic — washed through Brayden's body and he fought as hard as he could, but Andre simply moved them closer to the wall like he was prepared to hold him against it and wait out the fit until Brayden was ready and able to talk about what was happening. The left side of Brayden's face pressed to the drywall. Andre twisted Brayden's arms up higher behind his back, making his heart pound with frightening speed and force. Telling himself it was fine, it was under control, it was harmless, Brayden denied the truth. That was bad enough, but when Andre's knee slipped easily between Brayden's thighs, parting them, making him widen his stance, things turned a sharp corner and permanently altered their course.

Because then, Brayden moaned.

Heat surged under Brayden's skin, shooting out in twisting tongues of fire through his whole body.

A broken cry wrenched free.

Andre sighed by his ear, "Fuck."

Brayden pulled against the hold on his arms, but not to get free. The more he struggled, the tighter Andre clamped down on him.

"It's okay. I've got you. I've got you," Andre promised. In moments, Brayden, lips parted and eyes shut, couldn't move at all. His whole body thrummed with nearly electric energy.

Andre shifted his grip on Brayden's arms to one hand and reached his freed hand around, cupping Brayden's genitals through the thin cotton pants he had slept in.

His already gruff voice roughened with lust, Andre asked, "This what you want?" The flesh jumped at the words, but it was the only response he got.

"Or maybe *this* is what you want…"

Swiftly, Andre tugged the elastic-waist pants down in front, just enough for Brayden's cock to spring free. A hard, shuddering groan emitted from low in Brayden's throat as Andre took hold of him and began to stroke in long, slow squeezing pulls. Brayden's fight instinct kicked back in, but Andre was standing flush behind him and the more Brayden pushed back into him or tried to twist free, the quicker Andre's hand would pump and the more cruelly Brayden's arms would get twisted up behind his back.

Seething, blowing out every breath, Brayden didn't once say stop, just as he never stopped fighting. Soon his arms burned from the strain and his cock was like hot iron, riding Andre's loose fist. Grinding his forehead into the wall, Brayden growled. Andre began to jack him even more rapidly and with a whimper, Brayden bucked and thrust forward into each downward squeeze, riding counter to Andre's hand. Faster and faster they moved until Brayden was shamelessly rocking in and out of the fist.

He was right on the edge. His release was close enough to taste, ready to explode like spectacular fireworks from him in the best orgasm of his life.

But Andre let go of his dick, wrapping the arm around the front of Brayden's chest instead. Flushed a deep, dark red, Brayden's cock strained painfully up against his belly, slick with precome. His balls felt heavy and were drawn up tight.

"What the fuck are you doing?!" Brayden seethed in a needy, growled tone of voice that Andre had never heard from him before, rediscovering, at last, the ability to speak.

"What's the matter, Marsha?" Andre teased, intentionally using the nickname that he knew Brayden hated, a play on his more commonly used nickname 'Braydy'. Brayden bucked and twisted in his arms, pushing off from the floor with his feet, throwing his head back. He even pressed his ass back harder into Andre, but that only caused Andre's disturbingly thick erection to press snugly, and obscenely, between Brayden's butt cheeks. "Want me to let go?"

Nothing. No answer.

"Or do you want me to finish jacking your cock?"

Still no answer, but Brayden pulled so hard at his trapped arms that he whimpered with the pain. Andre nuzzled into the warmth of Brayden's neck, breathing him in.

"Ask me," Andre prompted.

Nothing.

"I'm not touching unless you ask."

Brayden pulled harder than ever on his arms and was probably about to dislocate his shoulders. In response, Andre reached down and directed a firm slap to the underside of Brayden's painfully swollen cock. "Stop it!"

Brayden gasped, writhing and still wordlessly trying to pull free.

Andre drew back and slapped again. Precome pulsed thickly from the slit. Brayden's eyes rolled as he blew out his next breath.

"You like that, huh? Say you like it. Admit it."

Not saying a thing, Brayden bit his lip and squeezed his eyes shut. Andre opened his hand wide and took hold of Brayden's testicles and shaft, squeezing them a little.

Brayden made a sobbing, breathless sound, doubling over, trying to draw his legs up. Andre relaxed his grip, then retightened it and pulled.

"Ahh! Please. *Please.*"

It seemed to be all that Andre needed. With two twisting, corkscrewed squeezes up Brayden's cock, he brought him off. After Brayden spilled thick and hot over his roommate's hand, he was let go and slowly staggered away to get cleaned up.

"Brayden," Andre tried.

Brayden just waved him off.

The talk they should have had never happened, because Brayden wouldn't talk. For the next couple of weeks, things continued and progressed down a dangerous path. Their friendship remained paramount, but it was never quite the same.

Then, at the worst possible time, the call came, the one that removed Brayden from Andre's life for the foreseeable future, giving him an out and letting him escape revelations only just beginning to bloom.

Sitting at a traffic light, only an hour from his hometown, Brayden looks at himself in the rearview mirror. His face is a classically handsome one, though he doesn't see it that way. All he can see is the boy he was, called pretty in mocking ways, always with laughter and sneers. Tucking a stray tendril of his shoulder-length brown hair, laced with sun-kissed streaks of blond, behind an ear, Brayden examines the person in the mirror, a stranger to him. Fear and misery sit right beneath the surface, in the glassiness of his eyes, in the pout of his lips. He wonders if he's running toward something or away.

The call came a week ago. Brayden could not ignore it, no matter how much he might have wanted to. His peaceful life on the beach was interrupted.

He quit his job as a lifeguard, gave Andre notice that he'd be moving out, packed his Jeep and prepared to migrate back to everything he thought he left behind for good. The years he spent growing up in Robertsville, Pennsylvania were miserable ones. They were all about survival. Survive school and the ravenous rumormill of that too-small town, escape, find happiness — those used to be his goals.

And he did. He did what he set out to do and he was so close to finding happiness. For the first time, things had finally started to make sense. It was a miracle, that elusive understanding. He got a real glimpse of it, like the twinkling of a star. Then it was snatched away as the dark closed in.

Because Brayden's Nana can't keep up with her bills anymore.

She admitted, humbly, to having a hard time providing for her ward, Brayden's young cousin, Emma Leah. There is no one else left who can help them, only Brayden. Lara's Brayden. Lara, who exists as more of an idea than a mother, or a daughter, though she is those, too. Brayden is Lara's son, but he is his father's son as well, and Brayden suspects it was the latter that got Nana to pick up the phone, and to hope. Even at twenty-two, he understands what it must have cost his Nana to do that much.

Chapter 2

Parrish Has a Project

Max shouts with exasperation, "You coming? Hey. Parrish! Are you coming?!"

"Hmm?" Jenner Parrish grunts in response to her pestering, too fixated on his prey to be bothered with actual eye contact. The tip of his index finger is pressed thoughtfully to his mouth. The gi hanging from his tall, tapered frame merely hints at the power contained within it, draping over broad, thickly muscled shoulders and biceps impressive enough to melt panties clear across the county. As he swallows and taps the seam of his lips with the finger, his naturally sunken cheeks hollow even more, framing the mouth nearly every girl that sees him wants to kiss, but, oh-so-tragically never will.

Begrudgingly admitting the sexy picture he makes, Max continues, "Yeah, your highness, I'm talkin' t'you."

Max, short for Maxine, lets the full force of a borrowed Staten Island accent, one she learned from her parents who were and will always be New Yorkers at heart, pour into her words. It has the effect she desires. Jenner Parrish smiles and shifts his gaze to look at her. She's down the hall from where he's lingering near the double doors leading to the indoor lap pool at the neighborhood YMCA.

"Hey babydoll," someone yells obnoxiously to her from the other direction. It's a voice she recognizes even as she shares a knowing look with Jenner and smiles bitterly. "You busy tonight? 'Cause if you're not, I can help you with that."

"I'm keeping her plenty busy, Todd. Thanks," Jenner answers for her, before she can decide exactly how she's going to disable the asshole she would bet a week's worth of tips is making lewd gestures behind her back for Jenner's benefit.

Todd Flemming is one of Jenner's old buddies from the football team—a beefy, square-faced fullback who couldn't find his ass with two hands and a flashlight. Five years later and it's the same bullshit every time, without fail. Their bodies get older by the day but for some, they'll always be in high school, making jokes about what a whore she is just because one of her ex-boyfriends from freshman year felt bitter about their breakup and started telling stories about her as revenge.

"I'm sure you will, Parrish!" Todd cackles, his voice echoing more as he walks away. "You fucking animal! Leave some leftovers for the rest of us!"

Receeding footsteps tell Max that the asshole is gone for now. She tries to let it roll off her back, as usual. It's not worth her time. Never is.

Jenner's dark, sapphire blue eyes fix on her, sweeping over her body, head to toe in an appraising way, maybe trying to see her the way that Todd and the other guys do, maybe just pretending to because he knows people could still be watching them, eavesdropping, and whispering. Though she's also wearing a gi, hers is tied to accentuate her ample breasts and tiny waist. Hand braced on one cocked hip, she tosses the inky black curtain of her hair back over her shoulder, eyes sparkling with wicked impatience.

"Hey, beautiful," Jenner tells her, "your Bronx is showing."

Though she was born in New York, she never got to experience life there. One day she's going to go back. Mimicking her parents' accent has always been a fun way to pretend she's not really from this awful little town, Robertsville, at all, but just a visitor, passing through on the way to somewhere better.

"You're my ride. Can ya get yer head out of your ass and get your shit already?"

She loses his attention. He looks back towards the pool. "Have you seen this?" he asks distractedly, pointing through the doorway.

Max sighs dramatically and stalks over, "What? What are we looking at?"

"That," he says, speaking low so that only she can hear, gesturing with a tilt of his head. Her gaze lingers on him a moment longer, though, and the way his short dark hair and naturally pale coloring enhance the sinister appearance of his stare. It astonishes her as much as it always has, the power Jenner has over people, able to intimidate men into fearing him, able to make girls swoon. As one of Jenner's best friends since second grade, and not even of the same sexual orientation as he is, she is constantly, and very annoyingly, unable to resist him.

She follows his gaze and sees....

"Jesus Christ," she breathes.

"Mm, maybe if he grew in a beard, but with a face that pretty, it'd be a sin."

"Who is that? He can't be from around here. No one has a natural tan that perfect. He doesn't even have *tan lines*. Does he?"

"No, I've checked," Jenner murmurs.

"Yeah, I bet you have."

The pair of them gape at the bronzed god climbing out of the pool, water cascading almost in comically melodramatic slow motion like they've stepped into a bad porno. It flows down over an impeccable swimmer's body, the muscles all long and lean and flawlessly sculpted, from the ripples of his washboard abs to his mouthwatering bubble butt barely covered by a teeny-tiny, itty-bitty suit. He tosses his long hair back, spraying water in a glittering arc, revealing the face of a model, with wide, captivating, brightly colored eyes. The suit is wedged in his butt crack, and when he uses a finger to pluck at the edge and momentarily peel back the edge of his super-small bathing suit to unstick it, Max notices Jenner zero in on the spot, even turning his head for a better angle, like it might help him see underneath what's barely keeping the man decent enough to be out in public.

Jenner sighs, "Do you know how *badly* I need to take a bite out of his ass?"

"I can imagine. But I'm calling it. He's mine. No way he's queer."

Jenner laughs maliciously, his bow-shaped lips curling. "Obviously you aren't paying attention. Look closer."

She rolls her eyes at him again and huffs. Humoring him, she endures the hardship of staring at the gorgeous newcomer a little longer. "What?"

"He doesn't have a single hair on his entire body. Well, you know, except for on his head but that goes without saying."

"So?"

"So, how many straight guys do you know that endure a full-body wax on a regular basis?"

"He's a swimmer! Swimmers wax. It's, you know, aerodynamic."

Jenner laughs again. She doesn't like it. It sounds too much like the way he laughs when they're not alone and he's pretending to be an asshole like everyone else.

"Stop that, I'm serious," she pouts. "Hey, I just thought of something. You know that weird light blue Jeep with the surfboard that's been parked on our street since the weekend? I saw it in the parking lot, *here*, when we pulled up. Surfboard, super tan, super hot swimmer...."

"No, it's not possible," Jenner scoffs, but slowly, doubt creeps into his expression. He starts to piece it together. "Hey, what's the name of the old lady that lives at that house?"

"Clare. Ms. Clare."

"Holy shit."

"What?" She watches, oblivious to the reason for Jenner's revelation as his mouth falls open with shock. "What?!"

He hisses, gobsmacked, "Do you know who that *is*?!"

"Who? The hotass over there? No. Why would I—"

"That's *Brayden Clare*. He was a year behind us."

She stares confusedly at Jenner, scanning her memories of time-faded faces from high school.

"I think I'd remember him if he looked like *that*."

"He didn't look like that in high school! He was..." Jenner gestures, mapping out an invisible body in the air before him with his hands "Short. Skinny. Pale. Pimply. Forgettable. Come on, you have to remember. That's the kid whose dad died. Those assholes always called him Cry Baby Braydy."

Now Max's mouth falls open, her dark lipstick outlining the perfect O it makes, "No fucking way! He... he's.... He got... taller."

"Taller? He's sex on legs. That's a little more impressive than a growth spurt. That's a *miracle*."

"Cry Baby Braydy isn't gay," Max protests, staring at him from across the pool again, with renewed, changed curiosity, comparing the past to the present. "They just said that stuff because he was small and girly looking."

"If he's not gay, he fuckin' will be after I get *my* hands on him."

Despite Max's repeated attempts, Jenner doesn't let her pry him away from the door to the swimming pool until Brayden exits, walking right past them as they quickly face the other way and pretend to be heavily in conversation with each other. Jenner stealthily follows him to the locker room, with Max singing quietly in his ear, "Someone's got a stalker!"

As Jenner stands at his locker, changing out of the gi while stealthily watching Brayden peel the tiny bathing suit off, Jenner actually gets dizzy from the sight of Brayden's bare ass. All of the blood in his head plummets south, as if it's decided that filling the hugest hard-on he's had in months is much more important than maintaining brain function. Lips parted around an unvoiced moan, leaning against the row of lockers, he helplessly stares at the dimples in Brayden's lower back and tries to fix into his memory the glorious sight of his perfectly shaped, perfectly tanned butt cheeks. It's only a glimpse before a towel hides the marvelous sight and Brayden absconds to the showers, leaving Jenner with a major case of blue balls.

Realizing that there's no way he'll be able to speak actual words to Brayden under the circumstances—it's not like Jenner can waltz right up to him in the showers without seeming a total pervert—Jenner makes some attempt to get control of himself and gets dressed.

He's silent as he meets Max in the hall and they head back to Jenner's truck together for the ride home. Max's worried, sidelong glances in his direction are mostly ignored but he has no doubt she can tell the types of thoughts capturing Jenner's attention so completely. They've been friends long enough to have been in this type of situation before. Jenner always reacts the same way, just as Max always reacts to his reaction the same way. It's a fucked-up wheel, turning them in the same circles. Part of Max's is to try to break the cycle. Part of Jenner's is to ensure she never does.

The drive is a short one. As they park in front of their house and get out of the truck, one of their elderly neighbors, Mrs. Thompson, who has owned her house since it was built fifty years ago, passes by, walking her miniature poodle. Mrs. Thompson spends most of every day sitting outside on her front porch, keeping an eye on every person, animal, car and house in sight as if she's been appointed sole responsibility for being the entire neighborhood watch. Jenner likes to combat this nosiness by giving her something to get excited about once in a while.

Max cheerfully calls, "Hey, Mrs. Thompson!"

Jenner smiles and waves, then gooses Max after circling the truck. With a squeal, Max jumps, giggling, shooting Jenner a look of playful accusation. Mrs. Thompson gasps with shock, staring at them.

"Think it might rain? Cloudy today, isn't it?" Jenner asks conversationally, chuckling as Max hurries out of range of Jenner's grasp. Once they're inside, Jenner instantly drops the act. His thoughts swing right back around to Brayden Clare. Their third housemate, Art Conner, is right there, looking the picture of his Irish heritage with his wild mop of curly red hair, thick red beard and millions of freckles, looming over Jenner's six-foot-four inch height by a few inches and nearly twice as broad. Art is eating an apple and leaning over the kitchen's center island, watching with narrowed eyes as Jenner stalks mindlessly to the fridge, grabs a bottle of water and tries to leave the room with it. Art's arm shoots out to block his path.

"Okay, what's going on? I know that look."

"Parrish has a *project*," Max tells him with a cat-like grin.

"Is this true?" Art asks solemnly.

Jenner doesn't reply; he just drinks his water and ducks under Art's arm.

The last time Jenner had what his housemates deemed 'a project' he had become set on rescuing an abused kitten from a nearby house, getting the owner brought up on animal cruelty charges and gaining a family member in the process. Pussy, a little white puff-ball of a cat, now lives up in Jenner's room and is intensely loyal to him. But the one sticking point of Parrish's projects is that he refuses to talk about them, preferring to keep everything — whether it's potentially embarrassing or not — to himself. He has never even acknowledged he *has* a cat, even when she's sitting blatantly cradled in the crook of his arm. Sometimes headstrong denial is the only road worth treading. If there is anything life has taught Jenner, it's that no matter what may be right there in front of people's eyes, they will believe any lie they're presented with, so long as you're confident and insistent enough about it.

As far as Max and Art are concerned, all of this denial is just a weird facet of Jenner's personality. He allows them to mock it to the extent that they do, knowing the teasing is not intended to be cruel, but to try, futilely, to draw him out.

Privately, one of his reasons for being so motivated to rescue Pussy was because of an incident when he was eleven. It was a hazy, lazy sort of afternoon, mid-summer. A group of boys from the neighborhood were riding bikes through backroads and unfenced backyards, looking for trouble. Jenner was with them because it was absolutely a case of 'keep your friends close, but your enemies closer'. From early on, he aligned himself with them, though he tried to keep to the sidelines and not get involved when things got rough. Most of them weren't so bad, but the nicer ones were notorious for eagerly going along with whatever rotten plan their headstrong, outspoken leaders came up with. Sometimes it was throwing rocks through windows. Other times it was harassing some of the smaller, more passive kids on their block. That afternoon, their target was a gentle, meek boy named Patrick, who owned a long-haired white kitten named Feathers and liked to play with her in their yard.

Someone yelled, "Look at that stupid cat! Hey Pat, what'cha got there?"

A kid named Mark snatched the kitten from Patrick's hands, saying, "Give it. Give it to me!"

Two other kids pushed Patrick back, and Patrick started to cry.

Mark, whose parents barely looked at him and only rarely remembered to feed him, laughed, "God, he's such a pussy!"

19

Jenner felt sick watching them toss the tiny animal in the air as a chorus of voices mocked Patrick's tears and egged Mark on. Patrick tried to get to Mark and take his kitten back, but there were too many boys standing deliberately in the way. A moment later, Mark kicked the kitten across the yard like a football.

After she landed, she didn't get up.

Sure, there were about ten different kids there, too many to take on all by himself, or with Patrick's help. It didn't matter that the numbers were against him. He did nothing, said nothing. Even if it was Mark who kicked that tiny animal, what happened to her was still Jenner's fault. He knew, deep down, that if he was truly worth anything, he would have ignored the fear of standing out in the wrong way and spoken up.

It wasn't long after that incident that he started to study martial arts. He kept telling himself that if he could become stronger, maybe the next time would be different. He would feel more confident, more ready to stand on his own. Strangely, no matter how long he studied jujitsu or how physically strong he became, that fear of standing out in the same ways that Patrick did never got easier to conquer.

Many years later, seeing a different white kitten — Pussy — locked out, shivering in the cold and starving, Jenner knew what to do. That he kept what he did a secret wasn't just for him. It was for her, too; to keep her safe from those who would kick her for being small.

Max and Art don't know about Patrick or Feathers. They weren't there and he's never spoken of it. But they know how he has always responded to unwanted scrutiny — whether it's regarding a white kitten or any other aspect of his personal life — closing off the more people pry. Since it's a given that Jenner won't say word one about his *new* project, Max tells Art, "You know the Jeep?" She cocks a thumb over her shoulder in the direction of the Clare house.

"The blue one? Surfboard?"

"Yeah. We figured out it belongs to *Brayden Clare*."

"So?" Art shrugs, unimpressed.

"He's that kid from high school whose dad bit it. Rough deal all around. Everyone gave him a hard time and then he vanished right after graduation. But now I guess he's back and somehow he's suddenly so hot, just the sight of him nearly made Parrish jizz in his pants."

"Okay, now I know you're fucking with me. Jenner's never impressed by anyone, let alone impressed enough to come in his pants."

"Well, that's why this is so very interesting," Max purrs. She leans against Art's bulk, letting him drape an arm over her shoulder, which makes a good armrest as she's more than a foot shorter than him.

"You two can stop talking about it now," Jenner tells them as he heads to the next room, calling back over his shoulder.

Max says, "See? What did I say? It's a project."

"Wow. You're right!"

"I bet he's standing at the window right now, waiting for Brayden to get home."

A second later, Jenner appears in the doorway, glares at Max and Art in a manner threatening enough to get them to immediately stop talking about it, as previously requested. It goes without saying that if they press the issue much further, they might mysteriously suffer side effects like waking up with one eyebrow shaved off. When Jenner needs to make a point, especially when it comes to his reputation, he does so without hesitation.

They give Jenner a few minutes' peace. Then Art seeks him out and finds him right where they said he would be, standing by the living room window, watching the Clare house.

"Lots of neighborhood gossip about that place," Art tells him conspiratorially. "I heard his mom was a real headcase, joined the Peace Corps after his dad bit the big one, even though she had a kid and all. The kid — Brayden — no one really knows what happened to him after that. Some people say he died, too, but you know, clearly he didn't. No one but old Ms. Clare lives there anymore. Well, her and some little girl. No one really knows what that's about either."

Standing at the window, mostly hidden from sight by the darkness of the house, Jenner wonders how many other houses along their street have eyes peering similarly from shadows, or more openly, in the ways of those like Mrs. Thompson. Watching the comings and goings of neighbors, assuming things, making up stories about

21

why and where and how; Jenner knows that's how the rumors are born. Once they spread, they become more powerful than the truth or the people being gossiped about. As Jenner knows well, if you're insistent enough about a lie, what's real doesn't matter at all.

A blue Jeep turns onto their road and slowly pulls into the driveway four houses down, on the opposite side of the street. Just because Jenner doesn't see anyone gazing out from behind curtains or blinds, doesn't mean they aren't there, watching along with him. Someone Jenner recognizes instantly, wearing what looks like a woolen sweater-jacket, gets out of the vehicle. Long brown hair catches the light on the cloudy, cold day, defying the weather, like Brayden brought a piece of the tropics with him when he moved back home.

"That must be him," Art says. "Wouldn't have recognized him, though."

Can Brayden sense it? Jenner wonders. Being watched and scrutinized, being judged — it's constant. His gaze mistrustfully sweeps the silent houses and darkened windows, wondering what stories about Brayden's homecoming boredom is breeding.

Jenner doesn't reply, but knows Art doesn't expect it of him. He's used to talking to Jenner without getting much back. Jenner has been defensive about so much for so long, it's doubtful he will ever be able to change his stripes even if he wanted spots.

Fate and nature have not been kind to Jenner, though it might appear otherwise. Sure, he owns his own business. He's good looking, and both his size and attitude get him attention from just about anyone whose attention he seeks. The trouble is, when everyone sees you a certain way, expecting you to act a certain way, it puts you in a box. Jenner's personal box is labeled "cold-hearted tough guy". He's a hardass bar owner who intimidates people into falling in line, whether he's actively trying to or not. Back in school, he was the quarterback of the football team. Extreme popularity meant he had expectations to fulfill if he wanted to keep being popular. He let those around him believe what he wanted them to believe, actively denying them the ability to suspect otherwise. What friends he had only liked him for his athletic ability and talent at charming the cheerleaders; they didn't really know him at all. Other boys feared and respected him. Girls found his elusiveness alluring. Seducing the unattainable Jenner Parrish became their challenge. Most days he felt like the idea of a person rather than an actual human being, with feelings and opinions.

Jenner's whole world has been diligently constructed with fabrications, every piece crafted so that his family, friends, co-workers and, previously, his classmates, knew only what Jenner wanted them to know. His realization about his sexual orientation came years ago, but he's still not out to anyone but his two best friends.

Jenner knows he's lucky that Max and Art have been able to prove themselves, gradually, painstakingly. When all of the pretending became too much, and it was confide in someone and vent, or go crazy, he'd told them. It's an admission he still regrets sometimes. Once light is shed on a truth, you can never pull it back into the safety of shadow.

After living in Robertsville all his life—and now running the most popular bar in it—Jenner knows well how quickly and easily rumors and labels spread. Whether you're at the supermarket, the local bar, or just getting the newspaper from your driveway, there's nearly always someone watching, commenting on how you're dressed, who you're with, or whose hand you're holding. He hears the whispers, feels the stares. Figuring that his personal life and activities are his own business, Jenner simply shuts out anyone who hasn't thoroughly proven themselves to him.

The current rumor swirling around Jenner, Max and Art is that their living situation and relations with each other aren't entirely platonic, but instead rather scandalous. Jenner knows he and Art are imagined to have wild, debauched sex with Max out of convenience's sake. Sometimes they play into it, especially at the bar when the liquor is flowing. It helps keep speculation off of Jenner's prolonged bachelorhood and Max's distaste for locals. Art simply doesn't give a shit. He can get all the women he wants anyway. It must be nice, Jenner thinks, to have it so easy. Jenner has never experienced what it's like to bring a date home, to introduce them to people or hold hands in public.

"Gonna make it more difficult that he's a towny," Art murmurs. "Plus he lives right across the street. Kind of awkward if he's a one-night-stand."

Jenner gives him an exasperated look. "If that's what I was after, I'd just go to Manse, wouldn't I?"

"You still go to that place, huh? So, what are you gonna do about Brayden, then?"

Jenner thinks this over, and grumbles morosely, "I don't know. I'll figure something out."

Chapter 3
Home Again

Brayden is able to get all the way upstairs to his new living quarters, a large enough bedroom for his needs on the second floor, without being noticed by his grandmother or his cousin. The room used to be his mother's when they moved in with Nana after leaving Dad behind. Years' worth of living is like heaviness in the walls. It's impossible not to feel memories echo back through years and years, making him feel like that overwhelmed kid he used to be.

Ever since the moment he crossed into town, passing old landmarks, places he's visited too many times to count, it's been like falling back in time, or being caught in a place where the year doesn't matter. Past, present and future are all tangled up together. Shrugging his duffle bag off of his shoulder and letting it fall with a soft thump to the hardwood floor, he digs out his phone and stares at the little icon indicating that he has a voicemail message waiting. It's from Andre, and it's been waiting to be retrieved for three days now.

He draws the silence of the eerily familiar room around him like a shroud and lets his misery soak deeper into his bones. The longer he's in his old hometown, the more days that pass, the more the old feelings take hold. The guy he thought he was in Miami — lifeguard, bartender, and friend-with-benefits — flakes off of him like a dried up, shedded skin. It's not just the weight of his childhood traumas pulling him down into a funk; he's mourning the future that could have been. All Brayden wants is to live up to his responsibilities and be left alone. He's not a kid anymore. He hasn't been a kid for a long time. Living in Miami taught him to be himself, unencumbered. He was outgoing in ways he never was before, but the pain of relinquishing so much of his own happiness so fast is making him bitter and withdrawn again. And the more he withdraws out of resentment at the turn his fate has taken, the more he feels like the old Brayden — tragic boy who was always too quiet because of the loss of his father and a lingering sense of the unfairness of it all. Now he's lost again, and the situation still stings, but he tries to tell himself he doesn't have to be that person. He can try to be better.

The doorknob turns slowly. He watches it rotate soundlessly from a few feet away and tracks the edge of the door as it inches just as slowly open.

"Hey, squirt."

Big green eyes — very similar in color and shape to his — get even bigger, startled at being discovered.

"Oh. Hi, Brayd. I was just, um…"

Emma Leah's small, feminine voice brings an unbidden smile to his lips and melts some of the hard shell around him. The phone is returned to his pocket and he waves her in. "Come on, it's okay. What's up?"

"Nothing. I didn't want to bother you. I just wanted to let you know that Nan's making fried chicken for dinner. You like chicken, right? You're not, like, a vegetarian?"

He shakes his head, his smile filling out, more of his true self coming through the fog.

"Oh. Good. 'Cause you look like you might be, you know… a vegetarian."

"Are you calling me a hippie? Just because I have long hair," he says with mock-offense.

"Shit no!" She claps her hand over her mouth as if to catch the cuss word and swallow it back down. Brayden laughs. In her smallest voice yet, she asks, "Don't tell Nan?"

Crossing his heart, he tells her solemnly, smile temporarily stifled, "No problem."

"So, did you find a job yet?"

"No," he sighs, shrugging off his jacket and hanging it on the back of a chair. "The Y wasn't hiring and it wouldn't have been enough pay to make it worth it anyway. It would have been nice to keep lifeguarding, but whatever. I'll find something else."

Emma Leah wanders farther into the bedroom, drawn to the huge surfboard propped against the far wall like a moth to a flame. She studies it, her light brown hair falling in a fine curtain of silk down her back, the lenses of her glasses catching and refracting fragments of sunlight filtering in through the window. The family resemblance is noticeable. They could almost be siblings. Brayden always wanted a brother or sister growing up. He always seemed surrounded by grown-up problems and grown-up drama without anyone with whom to sneak away and have carefree childhood adventures. He wishes, fleetingly, that the age gap between them wasn't so broad, and that he had Emma around when he was her age. This train of thought causes him to realize the way that she has been hanging around him whenever he's home, trying to talk to him or studying the fascinating things he brought up with him from Florida, which is practically a whole other planet to someone who has never been out of state.

She's lonely. Of course she is, living in this house, alone, not with her parents but an elder, a guardian and her only relative, besides Brayden. There is Lara, of course, his long-absent mother. Funny how he doesn't even count her anymore. Lara's become an afterthought.

That drags him down, makes him start to feel awful again.

Emma's tiny hand quests out toward the waxed-smooth surface of the board, not daring to touch, but getting close. It hovers there, like a bird.

"Maybe I'll teach you to surf sometime," he ventures.

Her head swings around, and she blurts eagerly, "Yeah?! That would be so cool! I mean, I guess we'd have to drive to New Jersey or something, and I've never heard of anyone surfing in New Jersey, but oh my gosh, it'd be so much fun. I'd love that. I mean, you don't have to. I know you're busy, but oh my gosh."

It's a good thing I'm here, he thinks, feeling the truth of it like a calming weight, anchoring him down, keeping his restless spirit tethered. *She needs me just as much as Nana does.*

"I'm really glad you moved in," Emma confesses shyly, as if reading his thoughts.

Taking her hand in his, small and delicate as a sparrow, he agrees, "Me too."

"You're her hero, you know," Nana tells Brayden with a knowing glance. He steps up to the counter. It's laid out with an impressive spread of food and all of the fixings for the chicken. The chicken sits in a bowl of buttermilk, fresh from the fridge. Beside it, his grandmother mixes flour, garlic powder and spices. A huge skillet waits on the stovetop.

"Nana, you really don't have to go to all this trouble."

"Nonsense. We haven't had a proper family sit-down since you got here. It'll be our celebration."

His head filled with the savory scent of spices, Brayden lets his gaze draw up to the second floor where he knows Emma is doing homework in her room. "Yeah, well, maybe if the parents in this family weren't so good at taking off when they shouldn't, we wouldn't be in this mess in the first place."

Ruth 'Nana' Clare, her grey-and-white streaked hair tied back, thick glasses perched on the bridge of her nose, slaps an open hand down onto the counter and lets out a tired sigh. "You should show more respect, boy. Besides, I like having my grandbabies here under my roof where I can make sure you're both safe and healthy. It's not a hardship, it's a blessing."

"If you say so," he allows doubtfully. "I just don't think it should fall to you to take care of us. We should be taking care of you."

"I'm not that old. Yet." Measuring him with a long look, after a moment she adds, "You are taking care of me. That's why *you're* here, isn't it? Instead of down on the beach with plenty of pretty young ladies to distract you."

"Nan," he groans.

"But I suppose we have our fair share of them up this way too. Maybe you'll meet someone nice. You seem lonely."

"*Nan.*"

"I'm just saying, you look like a kicked dog lately and I don't like it."

"Yeah, well, maybe I will."

"That's the spirit. You don't need to search the world to find happiness. Sometimes you just have to open your eyes and see what's right there around you, waiting."

The look she gives him as she says it underlines both of their feelings about his mother, Lara, and helps Brayden feel grounded.

"You smile more now. That's good. That's really good. You never smiled before. It's not natural for children to carry that much sadness in their hearts. I don't want you going back to those old ways. I want you to be happy here."

"Yeah," Brayden murmurs. "Me too."

With a sigh, she confesses, "I did call her, you know. Lara."

"Let me guess, it didn't do any good? Big surprise."

"Things are tough for your mother, and you know it. Don't be cruel."

"I was eighteen, Nan. She dragged me down there, to Florida, just to get away from all of the memories of Dad, here, and this town. But this was our *home*. I had no choice. But even *that* wasn't enough for her. What was I supposed to do when she got on that plane without me and crossed a whole ocean just to get more space? How is that fair? How is that fair, on top of everything else? She's the child now. *I'm* the parent. I'm twenty-two and I'm already more of a parent than she *ever* was."

He waits for it, knowing it was one step too far.

There is no anger, though, no additional slap of Nana's hand on the counter.

"Don't be mean," Nana entreats quietly, head bowed. "Meanness is what drove her from your father, before she lost him for good. Maybe you're just stronger than she is. Think about that. You've got part of Anthony in you. He was a *good man*, meanness or no."

Brayden wipes at his eyes, seeing flickers of ghosts out in the yard, playing catch, hearing echoes of old laughter, old arguments too. If he tried hard enough, he could recall some of those fights, which drove Lara, with young Brayden in tow, out of their home, looking for a new one. When times got tough, she took him and moved in with her mother instead, leaving Anthony behind, though he still came around. Anthony was determined to be a father for

Brayden, no matter where Lara's head might be.

Then the cancer ruined it all, every last shred of chance that it could get better, someday. It took him, and took him fast. All of that unfairness has been Brayden's supreme torment for as long as he can remember.

At least Nana understands some of the reasons for his heartache. He digs down deep to find a smile, and plasters it on. She returns it, encouragingly, with her fingers buried in the dry floury mix, sending dustings of powder floating through the air.

"Do you have any suggestions of where I should look for work?" he asks after clearing his throat. "You know the town better than I do now, and I'm having a hard time figuring out the best thing to do. I knew I should've gone to college. My skill set isn't exactly in high demand up here. And entry-level pay at the work I *could* get isn't going to take us far."

"Let me think it over. I have some ideas. Right now, put it from your head and go wash your hands. Oh, and grab an apron so you don't ruin your clothes. If you want to pull your weight around here you can start by learning some cooking skills."

"Yes, Nan," he grins.

Chapter 4

Help Wanted

"At least hire a goddamned maid, Parrish! This place is a pit!"

"Just like it is every day at ten a.m.," Jenner adds tonelessly.

"That's exactly my point," Max huffs. "I ain'tcher maid, douchebag. And yet, here I am, scrubbing the floor and scraping shit off the walls."

She leans heavily on the mop and glares at him; he's standing behind the bar with a soapy dishrag. Between the two of them, they're attempting to clean up to a minimal level of acceptability. The night before, there had been a big football game playing on the flatscreen installed over the bar and, as usual, the crowd got a little rowdy, more than a little drunk, and had trashed the place. At a little past midnight, it had even fallen to Jenner to forcibly remove a patron from the premises; his carefully-practiced jujitsu immobilizing techniques coming in particularly handy. Jenner can't bring himself to feel too put-out, though. The bar had made a killing. Pockets metaphorically stuffed full with cash, he knows keenly that drawing the customers isn't the problem. It hasn't been the problem in quite a while.

"You are my maid," he tells her with cool amusement as he works at scrubbing a nasty stain from the bar top. "That's why I pay you. Waitress slash bartender slash maid. That's your job description. Suck it up."

Her eyes narrow and he waits to see if he's pushed her patience too far this time and if, at any moment, she'll decide on a projectile to hurtle at his head. There are plenty of handy objects in grabbing range for her to choose from. For a few seconds it's a standoff. When he determines that her exhaustion is winning out over annoyance, he rewards her display of self-control with, "I have an ad in the papers. I have a sign on the window." He gestures to it helpfully. "It's just a matter of time."

She sighs, scanning the room, glancing longingly outside through the one window to the fresh air beyond and mumbles, "I'd appreciate a maid more than another barkeep."

"I think you'd have said differently last night," he says, thinking of the swarms of people crowding up against the counter, barking orders impatiently.

"Mm," she grunts. "There still coffee in the pot?"

"Help yourself," he smiles.

Max rests the mop handle against a table and heads back to the break room in the rear of the building. He watches her go and when she's gone from sight, he deflates, letting his own weariness show now that there's no one to see it. He wipes his forehead with the back of an arm. It's not something he would ever let on in front of his employees, but he agrees with them that they're pretty much just treading water. The prospect of another long day being short-handed and stretched thin makes him want to get out of there. The gym would be a good alternative; the gay fetish club, Manse, would be better. It's been weeks since he was last there. A submissive with a nose ring and a pretty-enough mouth had sucked him off in the club's recesses. He wasn't Jenner's type. He was too thin and too tall, but who cares when it's that dark and the heat and thumping music are more tangible than the human being on his knees, ready to service? Jenner decides it's time to go back, that a night of decadence, dominance and sex is what he needs to take his mind off of the things that plague him.

Drawing his phone from his pocket, he finds his calendar and checks the dates for an opening when he can get away without being missed too badly, not an easy feat when you own your own business.

The bell on the front door tinkles, catching Jenner by surprise. He looks up from the gadget cradled in his palm with raised eyebrows, wondering if one of the patrons from the previous night has come back to claim a lost item. God knows they stacked enough in the lost-and-found bin that morning—clothes, a wallet without I.D., two phones, one shoe, and a purse.

"Can I help you?" Jenner says it automatically, even as he freezes with shock. Because the person who has just entered his bar is possibly the last person he ever expected to see there. As someone who is well used to keeping the different spheres of his world spinning in perpetuity in their own orbits, never allowing them to overlap or collide lest it fuck up everything in the process, a sense of vulnerability washes over him.

Setting his jaw, swallowing around a sudden, thick lump in his throat, he masks his surprise and unease with a façade that is nothing but calm and confident.

Did he follow me here, Jenner wonders. *Was I too obvious? Does he know I've been watching him? Is he going to call me on it?*

Shards of crisp white sunlight glint through the dingy window decorated with unlit neon tubing proclaiming the names of beer and alcohol manufacturers. The light catches on long hair, making it shine like spun gold and Jenner wants to reach out and wrap a hand in it so badly that he feels it as an ache that twists his gut and throbs in his balls.

Cry Baby Braydy, Jenner thinks a little deliriously. *Don't call him that. Sweet Jesus, he's even more gorgeous up close.*

Gripping the bar's edge, leaning forward against it, a switch gets flipped in Jenner. He goes into predatory mode as his target, his *prey*, comes steadily closer, their eyes locked. Everything in Jenner screams at him to take, to plunder, to fuck, and it does so with such force that he gets lightheaded with the strength of the need.

But as Brayden approaches, something strange happens to his expression. Briefly, upon seeing Jenner, heartache so profound and poignant crosses Brayden's face, it makes Jenner feel like he must have just murdered Brayden's dog or something. He can't remember the last time he saw someone so distraught. It also makes Brayden look more like the boy he was in high school—forever grieving, tucked away in corners, trying to disappear.

Does he remember me? Did I do something to hurt him back then? Jenner frantically scans years of foggy memories, but can think of nothing specific linking him to Brayden.

With a sense of vertigo, Jenner witnesses Brayden replace the heartache with hope. The boy becomes the man. Sadness lingers behind green eyes, but it's infused with wisdom and resolve.

It takes Jenner's breath away.

"Hey, I know you," Brayden says with a grin that changes his face even more, softening the rougher edges. Captivated by the beauty of that brave smile, Jenner is more drawn in by the stubborn remnant of pain. "Varsity football, right? You were quarterback, I think."

Of all of the things to say in greeting, that it's high school Brayden mentions first makes Jenner smile. It's part reflex, part relief that he's not the only one still thinking on those terms. "Oh wow. Yeah, I guess I was. That was decades ago. Or it seems like it anyway."

Jenner can't stop staring at the rich caramel hue of Brayden's skin against the crisp, stark white of his button-down shirt, tucked neatly into dark jeans, adorned with a black leather belt. He tries to draw his gaze away from the exposed areas of skin at his guest's neck and along his bared forearms where the shirt has been rolled up to the elbow. Jenner's mouth waters at the idea of sealing his lips around the warm flesh, feeling the pulse beating under the skin.

Clearing his throat, Brayden raises and traps Jenner's gaze. The sweetness of his green eyes draws Jenner in and holds him. "I'm sorry, I don't remember your name."

"Parrish," Jenner blurts, offering a hand from over the bar. "Jenner Parrish. And you're?"

Cry Baby Braydy.

Stop it.

The secretly-treasured mental image of Brayden in the locker room at the Y—and his bare ass—fills Jenner's mind, uncalled for, sending a bolt of heat directly to Jenner's cock. He forces it away. Hard.

"Brayden Clare. I was a year or two behind you in school. You probably have no idea who I am," Brayden says, giving Jenner's hand a firm shake.

Oh, you'd be surprised, Jenner's inner voice provides. He tells himself, *Keep playing dumb. Don't lump yourself in with the assholes you've always hung out with. The best way to ruin your chances is to be-*

come the bad guy.

But it's probably useless, you know. He remembers you. He knows you were on the football team. Those were the guys who gave him that nickname. Those were the guys doing most of the laughing.

You're already the bad guy.

He resists, with effort, the urge to stroke the soft skin of the back of Brayden's hand with his thumb before releasing him.

If he thinks I'm cruel, maybe the best way to counter it is to show him, firsthand, that I'm not.

Or else he'll just peg you as a creepy stalker faggot and hate you even more.

Speaking over his exceedingly unhelpful inner diologue, Jenner asks, "What can I do for you, Brayden Clare?"

"Well, I saw you're hiring here and was hoping to speak with whoever's in charge. I'd like to apply for the position."

Position. I can think of a few interesting positions.

Stop it. Focus.

He almost literally shakes his head to clear it, willing away his growing hard-on.

Then Jenner smiles. It's calculated, laden with charm. "You're speaking to him. It's my bar. Or it is now, anyway. It's been in the family for years. I inherited it. Do you have experience bartending?"

"Yeah," Brayden says, still eager to please, to say the right thing. Jenner can see him making the effort, picking the right words, showing his interest in the job without going overboard and seeming desperate. "I just moved back here from Florida, and I had a steady gig at a bar down there. My day job was lifeguarding but it didn't always totally cover the rent. But yeah, I'm certified. I started as a waiter but they were training me to cover the bar, too. I took classes and I'm a really quick study. And hey, if there's ever a medical emergency, I'm a pro at CPR."

Jenner feels the fantasy coalescing: Brayden in a miniscule, almost-obscenely small bathing suit like the one he had on that day at the pool, running down the white sands, falling to his knees, tossing his golden brown hair back over a shoulder, leaning down over him and parting his lips.

He blinks and straightens. This could be a problem, if being around Brayden disrupts Jenner's ability to reign in his libido to this extent. How is he supposed to get any work done if a distraction like this is hanging around day and night? He considers telling Brayden the position has been filled.

But then selfishness wins out. "How are you with crowds? It can get pretty crazy in here. It's one of the reasons we have trouble hiring. But the pay is decent. Fifteen bucks an hour plus tips. We'd need you on a rotating schedule of days and nights. To start you'd be working a lot of weekend hours to give my current employees a break."

"That sounds great!" Brayden breathes out his relief and his beaming, friendly smile grows somehow wider. Joy bubbles to the surface, and Jenner can imagine it dancing just under his skin, tingling with its intensity. Distantly, he wonders, were a hand grazed over Brayden's smoothly-waxed skin, what the goosebumps currently pebbling it would feel like. "I've got no problem with crowds. My, um." He shows the first sign of bashfulness, ducking his head and beginning to blush, the color rising up his neck to his cheeks.

He blushes, Jenner marvels. *So fucking adorable.*

"My friends back in Miami always call me on being a huge flirt. It's come in handy with tending bar."

"I bet it does." Jenner walks around the bar and returns to Brayden, folding his arms over his chest. Jenner is almost a whole foot taller than him. He towers over Brayden and tries to minimize his pleasure at this discovery, lest the possibly-worrisome and growing bulge in his pants gives him away. Scanning Brayden's body, Jenner debates his answer, and knows Brayden waits with bated breath.

"Please, I really need this job," Brayden says softly.

That does it. Having the lithe, sweet, beautiful creature before him literally *beg* decides Jenner then and there, despite lingering worries about Brayden's ability to deal with the non-female, non-flirtatious customers, especially since they're likely to be people who remember him.

Loosening his iron grip on his self-imposed behavioral filters, he reaches out and gently hooks a finger around a stray fallen tendril of Brayden's long hair. It's even softer than he'd imagined. Tensing briefly at the contact, like he's bracing himself, Brayden bows his head slightly. The sunny grin vanishes.

"You'll have to do something about this."

"Oh. I'll tie it back. No problem," Brayden assures him, his gaze sharpening.

Jenner savors the moment just a little longer, having Brayden so completely at his mercy.

"Okay. You're on."

"Oh my god. Thank you! Thanks, Mr. Parrish, you won't regret this, I promise."

Grinning, biting his lip, Jenner says, "It's just Parrish. No mister required. Or Jenner, if you prefer."

"Okay. Jenner, then."

Jenner's lips curl into a purely wicked smile, his cheeks dimpling deeply. He rests a hand on Brayden's shoulder and gives it a squeeze. "Come on. I'll introduce you to a few people and get you set up with some shirts and a space to keep your stuff in the back."

Chapter 5
Temptations, Expectations and Tough Situations

Panic—raw, clawing, and gut-churning; that is what has seized Brayden since early that morning when desperation to get a good enough job to pay his Nana's bills had driven him to look for work at the town's most popular bar, Parrish Pub, even though in Florida he absolutely hated working as a bartender. He reviled the constant flirting, which only served to underscore how much easier his life could be if only he had any desire at all to carry through with the insinuations seemingly hidden within his interactions with the good-looking, well-lubricated women ordering beer after beer from him. On the off-chance that a guy flirted with him, the instant terror it provoked was much more powerful than any self-flagellation over knowing he wasn't heterosexual. Besides all of this, he was good enough at the job itself to get by, but it didn't matter. He despised the whole scene. The beach, open and relaxed and free of the constant reminders of how pathetically repressed he is, was always much more his speed.

But then he walked into Parrish Pub, and any relief he might have felt at facing and conquering his fears was instantly squelched when he saw who was there awaiting him, not only in employ of the bar, but the bar's owner—the person who would be his *boss*. It was the same sort of guy that loved to pick on him in high school, calling him Cry Baby Braydy, shoving him in lockers, calling him a fag and laughing when he cried; the same sort of guy that he had moved to Florida to get away from. Brayden didn't always get a good look at who was among the guys bullying him. They ran in packs and Brayden's goal was to always keep his head down. Even giving him the benefit of the doubt, Jenner Parrish might not have been one of the people that had actually taken part in his social torture, he certainly fits the mold. His body is taller, broader, stronger — hard proof that he can kick Brayden's ass around the block whenever the mood happens to strike. Even when you get past physical cues, Jenner exudes a brooding, cool, hardass demeanor. He's the testosterone-fueled man's man that Brayden strives to be but knows he never will. Not in this lifetime, no matter what he does or how much he exercises.

The impromptu interview goes well enough though, to Brayden's surprise. However, as he becomes more and more hopeful that he might actually get the job he needs so very badly, not only for the money but to give his new life some sort of meaning and direction, his panic shifts rather than dulls. When Jenner walks around the bar to face him, putting their bodies inches apart and displaying the almost laughable size difference quite starkly, Brayden sinks into a sense of low foreboding. The worst part of all is when Jenner touches Brayden's hair. Brayden waits for it, cringing — the snide comment about his appearance, the cruel laughter.

It never materializes. What it does do is to stoke the panic within him, giving it power.

And now he follows Jenner through the hallway, trying to grab tight hold of the strengthening knowledge that he did it, he accomplished his goal, but all positivity fizzles out as they get to the kitchen and Jenner's hand falls onto Brayden's middle back. Jenner ushers him along by the contact which quickly becomes the focus of all Brayden's thought and attention. Having Jenner's fingers on his back is like having a loaded gun pressed there.

They walk through the swinging door and stop on the other side. Jenner's hand moves, gripping Brayden's shoulder instead, halting him. Brayden suspects that Jenner doesn't even know that he's doing it, that maybe he's just a touchy-feely sort of guy, but the suspicion doesn't make it easier to bear. Brayden tries to focus on the even more massively huge wall of a man looming before him, with a shock of red hair and beard. It's a near impossible feat.

The base of his neck tingles sharply, sensing Jenner's nearness, inches away from Brayden's back, so close that if Brayden's hair wasn't hanging loose about his shoulders, he suspects he would feel Jenner's breath over the skin. The tingle shivers down his spine, lighting up the nerves through his back, shooting out to twist his stomach with queasiness, causing his testicles to draw up. The stark helplessness that threatens to consume Brayden in that moment is nearly unbearable. For a reason he doesn't even understand, tears threaten, swelling his throat, pricking at his eyes, but he denies them with effort.

He feels like they're there, in Jenner and Art — all of those people who seemed to know something he didn't, that saw him and knew just by looking that he was less than them, without as much worth in any sense. He was pitiful, pathetic, weak; not even fit to look them in the eye let alone talk to them. He hears them laughing, calling out, "Cry baby! Cry Braydy! Cry! What a fucking loser!"

You're not that kid anymore. Don't let them get the best of you. Don't let them win before you've even tried.

Jenner introduces the cook. His name is Art Conner. When Art shakes Brayden's hand, it makes him feel like a child in the company of *real* men. The glimmer of something in Art's face when they lock eyes draws Brayden out of his thoughts. He wonders if Art is remembering him from school. He acts polite and welcoming enough as they shake.

"You don't know what you're gettin' yourself into, man," Art says amiably. "You ready to work your ass off?"

"Hell yeah. I'm used to worrying about someone dying on my watch. My last job was as a lifeguard. I'll gladly bust my ass if the most I have to worry about on a daily basis is spilling drinks and bar fights."

"I hear that. Hey, you ever almost lose someone? When you were a lifeguard," Art asks, intrigued.

"Maybe he doesn't want to talk about it, huh?" Jenner tells him quietly.

This makes Brayden turn to look at the man behind him with wonder. Jenner's face is hard and set, warning Art off as Jenner seems to literally feel the tension the question brings out in Brayden's form. And just like that, the small display of Jenner looking out for him soothes some of Brayden's panic away.

Maybe this won't be so bad after all, he thinks.

"Yeah. I did," he says after consideration. "Sometime we should have a drink and I'll tell you the story."

"Definitely."

"Come on," Jenner nods, pulling Brayden away. "Break room's over here. I'll introduce you to our waitress. One of them anyway."

At the end of the short hallway and to their right is a darkened doorway. Through it is a dimly lit, long and narrow space with a small table and chairs to the left, and a row of lockers down to the right with a bench that runs the length of the opposite wall. A dark-haired, exotic looking young woman is quietly stirring a steaming cup by the coffee maker. At first, lost in thought, she doesn't hear them or turn when they enter. Jenner's low-pitched, slightly raspy voice breaks the silence as he says, "Maxine, this is Brayden. Ask and you shall receive. He's going to be helping us out."

Looking shocked, she drops her spoon into the cup. Then she takes her measure of Brayden from over a shoulder, her almond-shaped eyes sharpening with wariness. She scans both of the men before her, looking like she's trying to anticipate the punch line and figure out what the hell is happening.

"You're shitting me, right," she manages. "This is a joke."

From behind Brayden, Jenner shrugs, wearing a smug grin. "No joke. He saw the job notice."

"It's, um, nice to meet you, Maxine," Brayden says politely, floundering a little, but offering a hand.

"What's wrong with me?" Max laughs, looking suddenly insecure and tucking a loose strand of her black hair behind an ear. She glances down at herself and her dingy shirt and sweats. Shooting a pointed look at Jenner like it's his fault she isn't dressed to impress, she says, "I swear I don't usually look like such a hag. I've been trying to decontaminate the place from last night." She takes a step forward and gives Brayden a smile. He meets her halfway and she takes his hand. "It's a pleasure. You're a lifesaver for taking this job. I mean it, you have no idea. And it's Max, by the way. No one calls me Maxine."

"Your mother does," Jenner says, leaning in the doorway.

"Very nice to meet you, Max," Brayden says, his voice softening. This part is easy for him. He falls into his expected role easily, having had plenty of practice at it. He glances down her body, the way her full breasts fill out the old shirt, the way the sweats hang low on her hips, offering a glimpse of ivory, smooth skin just above the waistband. He lets her see him look and holds her gaze after she giggles and momentarily bows her head. "You know, you look familiar. Jenner and I were talking about high school. You didn't happen to—"

A few things happen at once. Max's gaze snaps to Jenner. Following it, Brayden notices that there's a possessive glint in his dark eyes at the sight of her and Brayden still holding hands and standing so very close to one another. Seeing their reactions, Brayden jumps to some conclusions. His newfound confidence falters and his panic sparks anew.

"Um…"

"Yeah, actually," Max says after an awkward pause, amusement lighting her face from within. "*Jenner* and I were in the same grade so I guess we did all go to school together. I don't think I remember *you* though. I know I would."

"Well, I've, uh," he flips his hair back, reclaiming his hand and slipping it into the front pocket of his jeans instead, "kind of changed a lot since then."

"Max and I have been BFFs since grade school, haven't we, Maxie?"

Brayden glances back and tries to interpret the look that passes between Jenner and Max, and the particular quality of Jenner's knowing smirk. It makes him suspect that there's quite a rich history between them, possibly intimate in nature, so he asks, "Are you two a couple?"

Max barks laughter. It's a free, rolling sound and its honesty makes Brayden instantly like her more. She returns to her coffee and takes a hesitant sip. "Oh Jesus H, that's hilarious. A *couple*."

Jenner scowls with such ferocity it makes Brayden chuckle. "So that's a no?"

"That's a *hell* no," Max assures him. "Parrish is like the older brother I never had. Which is why we get along so damned good, don't we, baby?"

"Max, Art and I share rent on a house nearby," Jenner tells him dryly. "Despite what you may hear to the contrary, the truth is we get so sick of each other, working and living together, the thought of romance is somewhat disgusting."

With the challenge posed, Max takes the bait and slinks up to her best friend, roommate and boss, rolling her hips seductively as she walks, pulling her shoulders back to emphasize her ample bosom, licking her lips wet. She advances toward Jenner like a cat in heat and brushes against his hip, dragging a fingertip down the front of his chest. Wrapping her petite, voluptuous body around his side, she teases, "Oh you don't really think I'm *disgusting*, do you?"

He rolls his eyes skyward and keeps his mouth firmly shut, remaining stiff and refusing to react to attempts at instigation.

"Mm," he hums. "A total pig."

"Oh, now, don't be mean," she *tsks*.

Unease exudes from Brayden in force. One glance his way and Jenner pries her loose, swatting her bottom to send her on her way back to her coffee. Then he straightens and walks to the lockers, inspecting the empty ones methodically and stopping in front of one.

"Okay. This one's pretty clean. Brayden, this will be yours. Keep your stuff in here when you're on a shift. Maxie likes to lock her purse in hers so that she doesn't have to worry about someone getting in here and lifting it, so I'd suggest that you use a padlock to secure any valuables you may have on you. Otherwise, it's a good place to keep a clean change of clothes or two. Oh, speaking of…"

He frowns and walks to the far end of the lockers where a stack of clothing is stuffed into the last one on the right. After sorting through the contents, he hands Brayden his selections.

"These should fit you. It's a week's worth of them. If you need more, let me know."

Upon scrutiny, the small stack of black items turns out to be cotton knit, collared shirts embroidered with the bar's name in white thread, the V-neck buttons closed. They're mediums which should fit him, though they may be tight. Brayden glances up at Jenner, feeling that cold tingle at the back of his neck again at the knowledge that the man has literally been taking his measure. Jenner probably wears at least an extra-large and even that is probably skin-tight over his broad shoulders and muscular chest.

"Thanks," he mumbles.

"Look," Jenner sighs, stepping up to him, face-to-face, and looming over him. "If you're up for it, we could use the help right away, starting tonight if you're available."

"Yeah," Brayden agrees, pushing past the sense of intimidation and grasping at the opportunity to finally make some real cash. "Of course. No problem. When do you need me?"

"Five to one. Eight hour shift. That work for you?"

"Yeah," Brayden grins, letting the happiness of gainful employment wash everything else away. "I'll be here."

"Fantastic."

"Jenner, I..." He can't hold Jenner's gaze, the intensity of the scrutiny too much to endure for more than a second. Looking down at his boss's feet instead, Brayden's hair falls forward. "I really appreciate this opportunity. Thank you."

"No problem," Jenner says, matching Brayden's hushed tones and Brayden can still feel him staring. A shiver races down his spine. "Welcome to the team."

Twenty minutes later, after dealing with some paperwork and getting formalities out of the way, Brayden is gone. Max lingers in the entrance to the tiny back office beside the kitchen, watching her roommate with a practiced eye. Jenner ignores her thoroughly, or tries to.

"He called you *Jenner*," she observes.

"It is my name," Jenner says snidely.

"No one calls you Jenner. I've seen you threaten bodily harm for less. Especially with new people. But I guess your little boytoy isn't totally *new*, is he?"

"Shut up, Max."

"You really think this is a good idea? You were obsessed with him when he was across the street and sharing a gym with you.

How the hell are you going to handle being his fucking *boss* without becoming a total psychopath?"

Jenner tents his fingers, elbows braced on the desk. He taps the sides of his index fingers against his lips, his focus on something far away—a glimmer of possibility, something to strive for, if only he can align the pieces in just the right way.

"He begged me," he tells her, the soft, thick quality of his voice telling her everything his words don't. "He looked into my eyes and *begged me* for this."

"You're hopeless, you know that right? I never figured you for a romantic."

Pain laces his expression. He has no reply. People don't figure him for a lot of things—being sentimental or vulnerable to loneliness and hurt feelings, or for someone just looking to trust and get close to something with true meaning without first scaring it off. There's always a buffer of space built of fear or respect there, keeping everything and everyone at a distance, trapping him in isolation. Whenever he tries to reach out, it just pushes them farther away.

I'm doing it again, aren't I? I'm pursuing someone who's going to run at the first sign that things aren't what they seem—that I'm not what I seem. It's all hopeless.

Why do I bother, anymore?

"Jenn, he's not gay," Max tells him tenderly, apologetically. "It's gonna break your goddamned heart to be this close to him every—"

"Leave it," he says sharply, interrupting her. "*Leave it.*"

"Okay. Okay, I'll leave it," she sighs, her fingers dancing along the doorframe as she retreats. "Just don't wanna see you get hurt."

When she's gone, he admits to the empty room, "Yeah, well, too late for that."

Chapter 6
What Jenner Needs

Jenner feels like he's sentenced himself to some form of endless water torture—dying of thirst when what he craves, what his body screams out for is right there, sometimes rubbing up against him in the close confines behind the bar. And no matter how badly he needs it, how very much it literally hurts, he cannot partake. The torment flays his nerves.

It's been a week—one week working alongside Brayden. The added help has eased all of their burdens and Jenner has to constantly remind himself that it's a good thing that Brayden gets along so well with the customers. Now, if only Jenner could solve the problem of his nearly constant raging hard-on, he might begin to be happy about the turn of events.

Jenner gathers the used, dirty glasses and wipes down the bar, catching snippets of the conversation of a couple of middle-aged guys bitching about their jobs and nursing pints of lager. He tries to focus but once again starts watching Brayden out of the corner of his eye. Brayden is leaning forward with both hands braced on the counter in front of him; his lean, toned arms tense and tightly encased in the black knit fabric of his short shirt sleeves. The top half of his hair has been pulled back and braided to keep it out of the way. White, perfectly straight teeth gleam as he smiles, then laughs at something one of the long-legged women seated on stools at the other end of the bar says to him. He charms them so easily. Jenner is captivated by it, how effortlessly Brayden lures them in and keeps them at a safe distance, helpless to get away but unable to get too close. But that isn't what keeps him peeking, stealing glances when he can be sure Brayden doesn't notice. For Jenner it's the details — the way Brayden's hair will curl around on itself as it falls over his shoulder, escaping the hair tie, the strength in the way he carries himself, and the deep well of dark sensitivity Jenner has seen lurking behind his eyes. He wants to puzzle it out; the riddle to whatever it is that pains Brayden, the cause for that buried ache that can only be sensed when Brayden is not consciously hiding it. It can't just be about the deceased father. That was too long ago to still be an open wound. Brayden isn't his puzzle to solve, though.

The crowd has thinned. Their bar is known for its free-flowing alcohol rather than its dinner fare. The offerings that Art whips up in the kitchen are more to absorb the booze than sate a real appetite, so as the after-work happy hour crowd disperses and the after-dinner drinkers have yet to arrive, they are blessed with a small lull.

"Hey," Jenner says, grabbing Brayden's arm to get his attention. The contact is like a surge of electricity that sizzles up Jenner's arm and simultaneously makes his dick stiffen.

Brayden turns to him, his customers temporarily forgotten, and looks up at his boss. For a split second, that heartache is there, close to the surface. Jenner tries to latch on to it, to draw it out even as his tortured libido tells him that all Brayden needs is a good, hard fuck or maybe a slow, intense blowjob. He can almost imagine how it would be, what it would feel like to be sheathed in him, or to taste his cock. In that fleeting moment, what he wants most in the world is to take one step forward, to trap Brayden against the wood of the bar, wrap a fist in his silken, gold-streaked hair and grind in one smooth drag against the perfect, rounded swell of his ass, tightly encased in jeans, and show him *exactly* what he does to Jenner just by existing. It would be easy. A tiny slip in self-control and it might happen despite what rational logic dictates.

"Yeah?"

The question snaps him out of it just in time.

Breaking eye contact, choosing to glance out at the emptying bar instead, Jenner says, "If you want to take a break and get some dinner, it'd be a good time for it."

Brayden shrugs, watching his boss carefully. "Eh, I think I'm good for a little longer. You can go first. Looks like you might need the break more than me."

That brings Jenner right back to focusing on Brayden and trying to determine what that comment could mean. But when he looks back, the mask is in place and he can see nothing in Brayden's expression other than what he wants to be seen.

"Okay then. Yell if you need anything."

"Will do." Close enough to touch, Brayden simply turns from him and once more leans over the bar, like he knows that Jenner is studying him but doesn't care. Eyeing the women, dressed in casual business attire — a-line skirts, high heels, ample cleavage and wearing plenty of makeup — Brayden says to them, "So, where were we?"

They giggle. One of them says, "Well, I *think* I was about to give you my phone number…"

Brayden leans in closer, saying under his breath to her, "And what would I do with something like that?"

"You'd call it," she whispers.

"And what would we talk about?"

"Oh, I have some ideas…"

Scoffing at the scene under his breath, Jenner pushes past his employee, his hip brushing against Brayden's ass, and storms off to the break room.

He prays that it's empty and it is. Once inside, he slams the door shut and thumps his forehead against it. Baring his teeth, wanting to scream and growl and rage, he does so silently. Drawing his fist back, he wants to release the punch and whale on the door, to vent his pent-up frustrations on something inanimate simply because he has no other option. It takes all of his will but he pulls the punch at the last minute, touching his knuckles to the wood's grain rather than hitting it so hard he breaks skin or bone.

He takes a deep breath, then another.

"Why did I do this? Why did I do this to myself?" Unsurprisingly, he gets no answer. "I should fire him. I have to fire him."

But Jenner knows he could never fire Brayden. That would be giving up and letting go and he intends to do neither, even if it kills him or drives him insane.

There's a soft knock from the other side of the door.

"What do you want?!" he bellows.

"Can I come in?"

Groaning loudly, Jenner takes a moment to compose himself, then stands aside to open the door.

He gestures at the small table, the picture of composure. "Have a seat."

"Chicken sandwiches. That okay with you?" Max says, holding two plates.

"Whatever."

With a sidelong glance at her roommate and employer, Max gently sets out their food and interprets the subtle cues he gives off.

"That bad, huh? We'll be a lot busier later. Less chance for vicious blue balls."

Jenner stalks to the door and closes it tightly. After thinking about it, he turns the lock before joining her at the table.

"You're the dumbass that hired him."

"Thanks for reminding me."

When he continues to hover, distracted and tense, she says, "Sit. Sit down. Go on. Talk to me about it. You'll feel better."

"Talk to you? You want me to talk to you about what's *bothering me*? Well okay. Let's talk." He pulls out a chair and straddles it, directly across from her. "Hmm, where should we begin? Oh. I know. While he's out there every night giving those women all of his attention, I'm the pathetic shit that can't stop wondering what kind of sex noises he makes, if he grunts or moans and whether his voice gets a little softer and quivers when he's coming. I can almost imagine it, and it makes me want to fuck that pretty smile right off his mouth. I want to know that, and hear it for myself. I *need* to know it—and the particular sound he makes when I stuff his hole full of my cock. I want to know that too. I want to wrap that fucking braid of his around my hand and pull on it while I ride him. And sweet Jesus, how *small* he is? How he has to crane his neck to look up at me and how easy it would be to overpower him, to just pick him up and move him, bend his ass over the bar or a table. His little body is just sick and tight and hard. Not too many muscles. He's not bulky; he's just sexy as *fuck*. What else? Oh. I stare at his nipples. A lot. While we're working. While people could *see*. They're hard quite often—his nipples—like his body hasn't adjusted to the colder weather. It makes me want to strip him butt naked and drag ice cubes all over his skin to see it pebble. Then I'd warm him back up with my tongue, but I would draw it out for *hours*."

"You've put a lot of thought into this," Max observes. "Do you usually think about the ways you want to fuck guys with this level of detail?"

Jenner licks his lower lip wet. "No. No, I'm pretty sure it's just him."

"Hmm. That's kinda unhealthy."

"Mm. Probably."

"You're his stalker, Parrish. You've become that guy."

He groans and covers his face with his hands, his elbows braced on the table.

She picks up her sandwich and considers Jenner's problem. "I know how to fix this," she says. "We need to get you laid. How long's it been anyway?"

"Too long," he grumbles.

"Well, there we go. Problem solved."

On Thursday night, a table full of his old football buddies is gathered in the back corner. For most of them it's a guy's night away from their wives and girlfriends, reliving the glory days while the Eagles and the Steelers play on the flatscreen. Jenner waits on them simply to spare Max the trouble, since he knows the kinds of comments those guys are likely to make about her. He catches a few of them looking at her and waits for the crude remarks that always materialize.

First, though, their conversation revolves around Brayden after they catch a glimpse of his nametag and they put the pieces together. It's a lot of discussion about how funny it is that just a few years ago, Brayden was shying away from them at school and now it's his job to serve them their beers, hiding away behind the bar like he's still scared of them or likely to cry if he gets too close. Whenever Jenner approaches the table, their voices become more hushed, the conversation interrupted with things like, "Hey man! Good game tonight! What's on tap again? Where's that little piece of ass of yours? She hasn't come over to say hi once!"

Jenner can't call them on the whispering about Brayden without making it weird for everyone, so he just monitors it all as best as he can from afar. He laughs off the comments made to him directly, answering questions about Max with sarcasm, things like, "George, you're just too much man for her to handle."

Which provokes one of the other guys to laugh and say, "You got that right! Look at that gut! She'd get lost in the rolls!"

Feeling like a referee in a game that has more rules every minute, the stakes devastatingly high, Jenner's gaze keeps drifting to the bar, and Brayden. Minute by minute he becomes more certain that what he needs is to get away and escape to another, safer world, one he knows well and which can at the very least relieve some of the tension keeping him on edge.

Chapter 7
Delights of the Masquerade

The rules of the masquerade, as stated on the website, are simple. Attendees must be male and dress in accordance with the role they are playing and the type of companionship they are seeking. For this one night, there are no shades of grey, no switching, and no questions. You either attend wearing pants and carrying some type of leash – chain, rope, leather – or you attend wearing a skirt or kilt and wearing a collar. If you're wearing pants, that marks you as a top and as a Master. Conversely if you are wearing a skirt, that distinguishes you as a bottom and a slave. If you see someone you like, and they're willing to participate, you claim them by hooking your leash to their collar. Once someone is claimed, they're off-limits.

It's to be held at Manse, a renovated mansion that now serves as a locally famous gay bar. Owned by the wealthy, eccentric and exceedingly bored David Davenport, Manse functions on most nights as a hang out for all of the area's gay community. On Saturdays, it's a different story. The local harcore BDSM devotees and enthusiasts are invited to meet and play in the dungeons. Saturdays are always a much smaller crowd, as Jenner can personally attest. David is always trying to lure in new blood by hosting events like the masquerade, which help newcomers transition into the lifestyle. Admittence to the events are by invitation only, but all you really need to acquire entry is to send an email through the website, introducing yourself and explaining what you're looking for. David and his staff run background checks, Jenner knows, as a safety precaution. If you try to give a fake name, you won't get in. The bouncers stationed at Manse's front door screening photo IDs against that evening's approved guest list make doubly sure of that.

Manse is a few towns away, but close enough for Jenner's purposes. He has made the drive regularly for years, studying the art of Domination under David on Saturdays or going on other nights to cruise for a hookup. It was easier when he was barely eighteen, so passionate about learning everything he could from David that he attended classes and private sessions alike with David and his submissive, Shea. But, once the full responsibilities of running the Pub settled firmly on Jenner's shoulders, that became difficult, if not impossible. Getting away to Manse on a Saturday was soon a laughable notion. Of course, by then Jenner knew who the subs were and could find them any day of the week, at Manse or with a single phonecall, whenever he was in the mood.

Now, weeks or sometimes months pass without a single visit to his old haunt, and David. He misses it even if he never could find the right submissive to partner with. Simply being known, being unquestionably welcomed and accepted, is the greatest luxury he has ever experienced.

After Jenner and all of his employees survive Thursday without incident, Friday, the night of the masquerade, finally arrives.

Jenner puts Art in charge of Parrish Pub after he leaves for the night at ten, closing the kitchen and reassigning the remaining staff to handle the bar. He uses the empty apartment above the bar to get dressed, a space Jenner has been trying and failing to lease out for months and has since taken to using as a crash pad. It's home to a small bed, some personal items of his own, and not much else. Clad in impeccably tailored black pants, heavy, steel-toed boots and carrying a leather leash, gloves and a hood to wear once he gets to Manse, he drives to the place.

Things are in full swing once he gets there. The parking lot is full, with vehicles spilling out and parked along the roads around the estate. As a long-time patron of Manse and personal friend of David's, Jenner knows some secrets and drives around to the back, easily finding a closer spot. To calm his frayed nerves, and begin to soothe away the accumulated stress of weeks, he lights a cigarette and lingers in the shadows cast by the full moon's light through towering maple trees and evergreens. Starlight glints from the stonework of the mansion, reflecting off of the leaded glass windows. Even from outside, he can feel the pounding music from the speakers all the way down to his bones. Closing his eyes, inhaling the smoke and opening his senses, finally, Jenner begins to relax.

At the sound of a door snapping closed, then footsteps, Jenner glances up to find David approaching him. With his perpetual smile fixed firmly on his face, David exudes all of the immense power he's ever had. Bombarded by the sheer force of the man's will and charisma, Jenner can't help but smile back. He has always loved David, who has guided and shaped the way Jenner practices the art of domination. Though David is of a more average height and therefore shorter than Jenner by inches, as well as less sizeable in sheer muscle mass, that has never seemed to make a difference. David's strength does not originate from his physicality. Brute force simply isn't his style. One look, one word, one gesture is all it takes for him to send men falling to their knees, eager to submit and serve.

Jenner has always admired that about David, and tried to learn from him the ability to hone other talents as a means of bending others to his will.

David walks up to Jenner, not stopping until they're breathing the same air and sharing body heat. Tilting his head back to blow a tendril of smoke up into the night sky, Jenner feels David caress the skin of his bare chest beside his nipple, below the edge of the makeup masking his tattoo. Instantly, the skin to skin contact causes Jenner's flesh to tighten, his nipple pebbling, his cock stiffening and just as eager for David's rapt attention.

"Good to see you," David says, smooth and easy, with that smile which first intrigued Jenner years ago, luring him into a world unlike any other. Though it's always there in some form or other, whether broad or slight, bold or subtle, David's grin has the ability to reflect many things – amusement, raw lust, pride, disappointment, scorn or threat, among many other moods and fleeting emotions.

Letting the cigarette, held between two fingers, fall to his side, Jenner holds in a breathless chuckle as David's crooked finger skims down the center of Jenner's body. So many memories of intoxicating pleasure and wild debauchery flood him. Just being near David has always keyed Jenner up, the promise of what's to come, if only he wants it enough to try to take it, there and tempting so strongly.

"Likewise," Jenner answers, holding David's intense, penetrating stare as that bent finger trails along the length of Jenner's swelling erection through the fabric of his pants. Many desires hit him at once, but the biggest one a curiosity about whether Shea is there somewhere, ready and waiting. Jenner has had Shea too many times to count, but always with David present, watching and guiding, and only with David's express consent, as well as Shea's. It's not Jenner's place to ask, though. If David is in the mood to watch his apprentice fuck the breath out of his dutiful, precious slave, David will say so, and arrange it. It's the only way it will happen.

The contrast between David and Shea is another thing that has always intrigued Jenner. Shea who is so unassuming, a blue-collar everyman who usually seems so awkward and bashful, who doesn't come from money and doesn't boast any great talents other than being able to submit to his Master's will so completely and spectacularly that as soon as he witnessed Shea and David together, Jenner has wanted that for himself. To have a submissive of his own, who yields so profoundly, trusts so utterly, and gets off on it as much as the Master taking him is the dream, the ultimate goal.

Seeing starlight catch on the silken strands of David's short, dark hair, styled so immaculately, the curve of his seductive lips, the glint of steel in his light green eyes, Jenner feels his body reacting greedily to every touch and stroke, and asks, "New blood tonight?"

David chuckles knowingly and takes firmer hold of Jenner's cock, which causes Jenner's smile to falter, overtaken by the ache and need.

After letting the moment draw out, witnessing Jenner's every reaction, David suggests, "See what you find." Squeezing just so, making Jenner's knees weak, David effectively reminds him how permanent his devotion truly is. "Otherwise, come find me."

Releasing Jenner, turning away and striding back to the house, David adds, "Have fun. It's been too long, you know. We've missed you."

Wanting to call him back, to beg, to please, to perform and indulge, Jenner sucks hard on the cigarette and throbs with the force of his lust.

"Fuck," he sighs, exhaling once David disappears inside once again.

An hour later, he's in the thick of it, with bodies all around him, men of all shapes and sizes. The heat of them, the collective musk and sexual energy, coupled with the pervading smoke, heavy bass and plentiful alcohol creates a richly decadent atmosphere. The Dungeon Monitors are out in force, he sees, patrolling the downstairs, watching to enure that the rules are followed and the guests are being safe. Since the place is full of many new faces, David must have brought in extra help to keep the crowd in check. With his leather leash wrapped around a fist, palming the metal clasp on its end, Jenner downs the last of his tequila and scans the crowd for a slave to take. He wants someone small and fit, but beyond that he doesn't care, as long as he gets off before he goes home. When it was renovated, some of the mansion's walls were knocked out on the main floor to open up the space, but even so there is still a seemingly endless maze of rooms to wander through, all leading off of the largest space, which holds the bar and the dance floor. He winds his way through all of them without finding what he's looking for and ends up near the front entrance.

The open front door is flanked by two imposing guys checking IDs and forbidding entry to anyone who doesn't make the cut. Just inside the entryway is a counter. Behind the counter, a third security staff member handles the necessary paperwork and financial transactions, asking guests to sign a consent and legal waiver and pay the cover charge. It's only once you get past the counter that you're truly welcomed inside.

The chill blowing in from outside has mostly cleared the area with the exception of a few sweaty slaves in tight miniskirts, cooling off in the draft. Some of them turn and try to catch his attention when they see him, his thickly muscled chest and arms bare and on display. They aren't his type, though, so after checking for the hundredth time the makeup covering the tattoo on his chest, which could be used to identify and out him, something he very much doesn't want to happen, he continues on his quest. He pauses when a figure rounds the counter, having paid the fee and cleared the security checkpoints.

The new guest slips in, quietly, trying to look everywhere at once, as if he doesn't know if he's in the right place or has permission to be there. Jenner gives the newcomer a furtive glance out of nothing but dull curiosity.

His heart stops in his chest.

There's no way, he thinks.

A heady wave of heat and keen, powerful excitement radiates out through his body. Senses sharpening, he zeroes in on the target. The noise, the smoke, the other people, they all disappear.

"Sweet fuck," he gasps. "Oh my *god*."

Go. Move. Now.

A fear sparks in his brain, bright, hot and specific. He has to move quickly. He might only have seconds.

Stalking across the twenty feet or so separating them, he unwinds the leash and finds the clip. Another Master is approaching, one he doesn't recognize. Jenner just barely manages to get there first.

"Hi," he shouts over the din.

The slave turns. The top half of his face is covered with a plain black mask, his long, golden-brown hair tied up in a knot at the nape of his neck. Jenner stares at lips he knows as well as his own by now, judging only from the hours he's spent memorizing them at the bar. He endures it with a longing ache while his subject measures him. Bright green eyes scan Jenner's bare, waxed-smooth chest, dark nipples, and washboard abs tapering down to narrow hips. This is the true test, Jenner knows unequivocally, and in that one second he experiences the cold bite of real dread. If he's found to be undesirable, he'll know right away and there will be no disputing it. Live or die.

"How about we get a drink first," Brayden says warily after seeing the leash held up in Jenner's hand.

Jenner only has to nod toward the two other Masters waiting behind him should Jenner fail to claim the prize.

Jaw clenched, bowing his head slightly, Brayden finally consents. He pulls at the metal loop fitted in his collar as Jenner latches the leash. A blush spreads outward from Brayden's neck, over his chest, and Jenner's mouth waters, wanting to feel the heat of it under his tongue. Cock swelling painfully, a hot, hard line inside the tight briefs he'd worn, he tries not to stare at the dark green woolen kilt hanging from Brayden's hips.

How?

Why?

Fuck.

The stark reality of having Brayden on a leash and leading him by it through the mansion to the bar sparks a torrent of questions that he knows he cannot ask if he wants to try to remain anonymous. Of all things, Jenner knows at the very least that he wants that. Anonymity is key. But, just the same, he wants to ask what Brayden is doing there, if he knows what he got himself into by coming to this place, dressed as he is; he wants to ask him if he's gay, or bored, or maybe just curious.

Tension on the leash, every slight tug a reminder of precisely *who* his slave is tonight, makes Jenner feel woozy from the sheer, spectacular possibilities unfolding before him.

Jenner almost makes the simple, stupid mistake of ordering Brayden a rum and coke with a slice of lime, his preferred drink, which Jenner of course only knows about from working with him. Catching himself, he instead orders two beers. In the distance, weaving through the crowd with ease, he sees both David and Shea. There are others there, too, the old blood, the ones he's indulged with, sometimes over and over again, or those who have simply watched. All around them, here and there throughout the old building packed full of secrets are the handful of men who know everything there is to know about Jenner Parrish the Master. He's been inside them or dominated others for their voyeuristic pleasure. The conflict between being at Manse, surrounded by such people who know such dangerous truths, while keeping Brayden, Jenner's private, primary desire, safely by his side, sets Jenner on edge.

The leash, the sly glances at Brayden's body, claimed at Jenner's side, slight wafts of the scent of him—it gets in his head, gets him high.

It's too loud for conversation, which is a good thing because Jenner is sure that if Brayden was to hear one more clear word from him, he'd figure it out and it would all end right there. Desperate to keep this, whatever this is, going long enough to maybe, possibly, get to have an anonymous (on his part) sexual encounter with the object of his obsession, Jenner watches Brayden drink his lager. Brayden is fixated solely on Jenner's body, ogling his muscled arms and pecs, avoiding meeting his eyes. That's a good thing. He downs the beer quickly and sets the empty on the counter.

"Okay, let's do this then," Brayden says with audible and visual nervousness.

For some reason, Jenner can't bring himself to usher Brayden along with a hand to his shoulder or back, as he usually would. Touching bare skin would be too much. He wants to save it until he knows he won't have to stop, that he can touch, fondle, grope and caress without limit or prying eyes. Instead, he keeps using the leash, drawing his slave away from the rowdier groups and toward the stairs climbing to the second floor.

When they get to the base of them, Jenner pauses, turns and asks, loudly, trying to alter the tone of his voice, "Are you sure? You want this?"

"Yes," Brayden nods.

The second floor is segmented off into many tiny rooms without doors. They find one right away. Music from the first floor is piped in through a speaker in the wall and it reverberates through the floor as well. They still have to shout to be heard.

The walls are wallpapered. Curtains hang on one of them, and Jenner would bet money that there isn't actually a window behind them, that it's only for effect, to make the room seem cozier than it is. A small bed with fresh, white sheets is the only furniture. They barely notice the inconspicuous waitstaff, dressed in black suits and masks decorated with an M for Manse, slipping in and out of rooms with fresh sheets and complimentary toiletries. The Dungeon Monitors are there, too, giving the guests their space but watching, always watching. The staff always does an exemplary job at tidying up after the guests, keeping them safe and staying out of the way whenever possible, which is one of the reasons why Jenner keeps coming back, even if more often than not, he doesn't find precisely the type of company he's been looking for.

But after a torturous dry spell, Jenner has found not someone merely passable, but the fantasy itself, claimed and willing to submit.

If you're dreaming and passed out on the furniture somewhere, he warns himself, *don't you dare wake up yet.*

From the minute they cross the threshold, Brayden's panic begins to flow freely and Jenner can sense it, like a predator catching the scent of pheromones. It's in the tension of his body, the wideness of his eyes, the sweat slicking his skin and the quickness of his breath. They stand in the center of the small room and when Jenner makes a move to come closer, Brayden flinches violently away.

Immediately, Jenner raises his hands, showing that he means no harm.

"Sorry. Sorry. I just. I don't. Do things like this. I...."

"It's okay," Jenner says soothingly, even though he doesn't expect to be heard. He waits for Brayden to turn and bolt.

Please. Please. Not yet.

Brayden's restless fingers find the leash, hanging now un-held from his neck, and he begins to play with it. Staring straight ahead, at a spot on the center of Jenner's chest near his make-up covered tattoo, looking like a dark bruise there, marring the otherwise flawless, porcelain skin, Brayden says, "Restrain me."

Jenner blinks. He takes a shallow breath. "What?"

"Restrain me!" Brayden says more loudly, shouting the words almost angrily, with defiance. So much defiance. "Do it!"

Eyes closing with near orgasmic pleasure in anticipation at the exquisite permission, Jenner moans and gathers his wits.

Brayden waits, tensed and wary like a cornered rabbit.

It happens quickly. With plenty of training at both martial arts and handling men's naked bodies, Jenner's hand darts out, grabs the leash, yanks on it hard. It sends Brayden sprawling forward in a calculated fall toward the bed, his hands shooting out to take the impact of his landing. Getting behind him, Jenner pivots, planting one foot, then the other between Brayden's as he bounces against the edge of the bed. Pushing him more forward so that he's forced to crawl up onto the mattress, Jenner then grabs each of Brayden's wrists and twists them up behind his back, using one hand to hold them. He unclips the leash and winds it around and around and around Brayden's overlapped wrists, tying them together.

Brayden is breathing so heavily and rapidly that Jenner becomes slightly afraid he's going to hyperventilate.

"Stop means stop. Okay?"

"Y-yeah."

The only light in the room is a faint flickering amber glow from a single wall sconce. It leaves them in almost full darkness with their back to the tiny bulbs. Shadows move at the periphery of his vision, as they're watched, observed by either the staff or other guests. He's not sure which but doesn't really care.

Wrapping a fist around the bound wrists, Jenner draws Brayden upright so that he's kneeling. His chest presses flush to Brayden's back and he can feel every breath, every tremor, and every glistening drop of sweat that trickles downward. His own heart racing, blood boiling hot, swelling his cock full and heavy, making his testicles throb, he inhales the scent of Brayden's fear and arousal. Its tang tickles his nose and Jenner growls with need. Hearing the sound as well as feeling it, Brayden shudders and twists but he can't get away.

Jenner finally allows himself to touch. He cups a hand over Brayden's navel, rubbing over the taut skin, feeling the hard planes of muscle, the gentle ripples of his abdomen. Exhaling sharply, Brayden lets his head fall back and to the side, offering his neck, his back arching gracefully. He's starting to become erect and must know his hooded companion can tell by the way his kilt hangs.

Jenner's hand, encased in butter-smooth black leather, rubs hard down over Brayden's right thigh, over the coarse texture of the kilt until it meets the soft downy hair covering Brayden's skin, just above his knee. Pushing up and under the garment, caressing back up the thigh, Jenner expects to find the barrier of underwear and when he doesn't, he moans thickly.

Still as a statue, Brayden swallows, his Adam's apple bobbing as Jenner's gloved hand begins to fondle his cock and balls. He gasps helplessly, then hisses, "*Fuck.*"

Nuzzling into the soft silk of Brayden's hair, getting high off of the light citrusy scent of his shampoo, Jenner runs an opened hand up the underside of Brayden's shaft, letting the weight of it fit in his palm. His own cock jumps and presses demandingly at the inside of his pants as Brayden whimpers and again tries to twist away.

Forcing his bound hands uncomfortably higher up his back, Jenner keeps his captive still. Pivoting his free hand, he closes his fingers around the fullness of Brayden's sac.

"Oh fuck," Brayden hisses, bucking once and rotating his hips. Jenner grabs hold and tugs, pulling the sensitive organs away from Brayden's body, then squeezing. Mouth falling open around a groan, Brayden writhes in Jenner's arms, getting harder, getting off on the discomfort.

It's better than Jenner's imagination hinted it could be—the sweet, scared, wanton sounds coming from the alluring creature in his arms, the very stark proof of Brayden's desire which Jenner takes tightly in hand and begins to stroke – it's heady and more intoxicating than the richest wine. He drinks it up, doing everything in his power to control his animal lust which demands that he *take* and *fuck* and *violate*. He needs to tread lightly, proceed carefully.

"Want you. Want you so fucking bad," he growls. Slowly, unhurriedly, he manipulates Brayden's cock, fingering over it lightly, tracing the vein pulsing under the silky skin of the shaft, over the bulbous crown, through the slick of precome weeping from the slit. Rubbing a single digit through the divot under the head, he triggers the small bundle of nerves there. Brayden ruts against his hand, seeking friction. "You like that?"

Brayden moans.

Jenner links his thumb and index finger in a ring around Brayden's dick, curling the rest of his gloved fingers around the shaft. He makes the grip tight enough to provide friction but remains motionless, forcing Brayden to do the work.

After one thrust, Jenner rewards his new slave by squeezing tighter when Brayden draws his hips back before loosening up again.

"Bend over." He punctuates the command by forcing Brayden's hands up, making him fold forward simply to take the pressure off of his shoulder joints. "That's it. Good. Just like that."

Jenner keeps him in place by holding firmly to Brayden's bound arms. His captive thrusts again and again, riding the leather encasing Jenner's hand. The movements are stilted, shaky and nervous but with the force of need for release behind them. Face and neck flushed a hot, dark pink, Brayden gasps and does as his body demands. His thrusts become smoother and quicken to a steady, sharp pace. He fucks Jenner's fingers and moans low in his throat.

For only a half-second, the hand, Brayden's fucktoy is temporarily gone. The back of the kilt gets flipped up. Moaning thunderously, Jenner watches Brayden's bared ass flex and clench with each thrust of his hips once the vessel of the gloved hand returns to reclaim his straining dick. Because both of his Master's hands are busy, for the moment at least, and he's only able to grope Brayden's backside with his eyes, Brayden relaxes. The tension eases slightly from his form, and he ruts and rocks against the hand circling his dick.

The sight of Brayden's firm buttocks clenching and dimpling with each of his rocks forward, the way his back arches so beautifully when he draws back, snaps something holding feeble control over Jenner's actions. He presses his clothed groin flush to the curve of Brayden's ass, letting him feel the hardness of his Master's cock, the interest instilled. It's both reward and threat. As Brayden gets closer and closer to orgasm, Jenner starts to rub off against his bound, helpless, beautiful slave's backside, driving pointed, needy thrusts against it.

Brayden gasps, panting, chasing release. He fucks Jenner's fist with abandon. Twitching and shuddering, his body convulses as he climaxes. He gapes, mouth working soundlessly as he unloads, coating the bed under him, and Jenner's glove, with his seed.

Every muscle is loose and pliable, easily moved, as Jenner braces Brayden's shoulders against the bed, grabbing him firmly by the hips and dry-humping his nicely presented ass.

Jenner growls and grunts, driven wild with primal need. He rides the crease, hands wrapping the sides of Brayden's cheeks and, with a sharp cry, comes in his pants.

The room spins. Emptied and sated in more ways than one, Jenner's hands act of their own accord, untying Brayden's wrists and freeing him. He hasn't yet found his tongue when Brayden struggles upright and climbs off the bed.

"Wait," Jenner gasps. "Wait, um…"

He turns to Brayden, and doesn't know what to say to keep him there, how to draw this out or hold on to it.

Brayden spares his Master one last look, both of them sweaty and breathless. His gaze drifts quickly from Jenner's masked face to his bare chest—specifically to where make-up had previously covered a small tattoo, a name written in script.

"Um. Thanks," Brayden mutters, smoothing down his kilt, fixing his mask, knocked askew.

"Wait! Please!" Jenner calls.

But Brayden passes through the doorway, now empty.

Jenner watches him slip away, into the hall, his heart breaking all over again at the dull certainty that he's just experienced what he craves so profoundly for the first and the last time.

Chapter 8

No Way Out

That night, Jenner goes to the apartment above the bar to sleep, rather than going home and risk facing Max or Art, not with what a mess he is in every possible sense of the word. He gets there exactly twenty-three minutes after Brayden had bolted from the room at Manse. As soon as he's through the door and stripped of the come- and sweat-drenched clothing, he climbs into the shower and jerks off to the memory of what happened. He knows he has to savor it while he can. What they've done that night will either remain his private source of psychological torture — a solitary oasis of happiness in the endless, parched desert that is his quest for love and meaning — or it will go spectacularly wrong and obliterate without prejudice every glimmer of fragile hope.

Either way, he's fucked. Violence or a more subtle breed of mental torment — pick your poison, we've got every flavor in stock.

After the shower, he subsists in a daze, as if the experience leached him of every last ounce of energy and interest in anything but existing. Confused as to how Brayden managed to elude their gaydar, Jenner can't even begin to process the motives and reasons behind what transpired at Manse. He almost tries to convince himself that he was with a stranger, anyone else other than sweet, sunny Brayden who seems to brighten the most when being charmed by an attractive woman. It would be much simpler that way, if Jenner had been mistaken and it wasn't Brayden at all — almost a blessing. He wouldn't have to live with the fact that he has to work with the man every day and be slapped with the chore of having to rub shoulders with him without letting on that anything odd has transpired. He should be happy to have had the chance to indulge the fantasy, but instead he's miserable — more so than he's ever been before.

The most likely explanation for what happened is that Brayden was looking to get off, just like Jenner was. Maybe he was curious and happened upon Manse's website. So he came, and went. It had nothing to do with Jenner or attraction, it was filling a need. Jenner knows what that's like. Almost every encounter he's had at Manse has been much of the same.

It was indulgence without any strings attached. Once, it would have been enough, but not now, not after all of the time Jenner has spent thinking and dreaming about Brayden. As much as Jenner might try to fool others, he can't fool himself. He wants more, to be with Brayden again, but the only way that could happen is if he confessed what he's done, lying to Brayden about not recognizing him, taking advantage of him rather than being honest. And that's the best way to ensure Brayden will never want to see Jenner again.

Starting the next day, Saturday, Jenner doesn't talk to Max or Art, his best friends in the world, let alone any other more casual acquaintances. He draws into himself and shuts off. Silently he cleans the bar, works on payroll in the back office and brushes off all attempts at conversation.

At three in the afternoon, Brayden comes in to work and Jenner locks himself in the office for a mini panic attack. He's only begun to recover when there's a knock on the door.

"Yeah?" he asks shortly without opening the door.

"It's me," Max calls. "Are the paychecks ready? I just wanted to lock mine up before starting my shift."

Jenner sighs and tries to rouse himself. He unlocks the door and opens it, eyes downcast. "Yeah, just gimme a sec to get it."

Reaching for the small pile of envelopes, he sees in his peripheral vision as Max slips in that just behind her is Brayden.

The blood drains from Jenner's face and for a moment he feels like he's going to puke up the salad he had for lunch.

"Hey, Jenner," Brayden says lightly, with a warm smile. Obscene memories overlay reality, perverting it. Visions of Brayden on his knees, exposed and wanton, distort the pleasant, composed version of the man standing before him.

A guilty, creeping tickle starts in Jenner's gut and he wishes for the Earth to open up and swallow him whole. He knows he should talk to Brayden about what's happened, but he can't. He won't risk losing Brayden entirely, even if it means having to lie to him every day for the foreseeable future. Feeling like the biggest asshole on the planet, Jenner lets the self-recriminations and self-hatred wash over him as he keeps his eyes trained on his desk, rifles through the paychecks, and murmurs, "Hey."

"Enjoy your night off?" Max asks obliviously. Jenner hadn't told her what his plans were; just that he was going out.

He shoots her a deadly glare to warn her off and doesn't respond otherwise.

Standing at the wrong angle to catch Jenner's expression, Brayden chimes in, "You went out?"

After a pause, he relents. "Yeah. I did."

"Oh yeah? Where to? I'm still kind of trying to figure out the best places to go after hours. My Nana's not really the best source of—"

Jenner interrupts with a clipped, "I'd really rather not talk about it. Okay?"

"Oh," Brayden says, finally catching on to Jenner's mood. "Sorry."

"It's... it's fine," Jenner sighs. "Here."

He hands them their paychecks.

Truly concerned, Max whispers, "Parrish, are you okay?"

He ignores this. "Can you two give the front another once-over to make sure we're good to go? I need Art in the back to ramp up for dinner. I'll be out to give a hand when I-I—"

Jenner stutters to a full stop at that, realizing what he's just said. A blush rises on his face and neck. The cold hard pit of dread grows larger in his gut because he never blushes. It's a sure sign of his guilt-riddled conscience. He tries to finish his sentence just to get them out of his office. "Give me a couple of minutes, all right?"

Brayden nods, frowning like he's trying to read between the words. It only stokes Jenner's alarm. Brayden says cautiously, "Yeah. Sure thing, boss."

Max stares at Jenner's uncharacteristic blush and his look of horror, and lingers.

"Please," Jenner growls.

"Yeah, okay," she says, finally, relenting.

When they're both on the other side of the door again, Jenner closes it firmly and turns the lock.

It's the longest night of Jenner Parrish's life. It lasts for eons rather than hours. Stuck tending bar right beside Brayden while Max waits tables and Art churns out food with the help of Jackson, one of their college-age part-timers, he just tries to last out the night. He and Brayden exchange words only to keep the drinks stocked and flowing. Thankfully, whereas Jenner's mood is in the toilet, Brayden is more chipper than anyone has ever seen him thus far. He charms ladies and gentlemen alike, his air of pleasant joy infecting everyone around him. Making a ton of cash in tips, he keeps everyone laughing and having a good time. He flips bottles to the *oohs* and *ahhs* of the crowd. He does shots with a bachelorette party that spends many hundreds of dollars at Parrish Pub that night that they might not have otherwise had Brayden's good looks and bright laughter not kept them there longer than they planned. None of the guys from the old high school crowd show up, giving Brayden even more reason to not hold back, letting his personality shine. In a distant sort of way, Jenner knows it should make him happy that he probably had some part in Brayden's good mood, but all it does is make him feel like a liar and a predator.

What does it matter if there are no patrons whispering about Cry Baby Braydy and snickering behind their drinks, when Jenner has taken advantage of him in a way no bully ever could? For years, he thought he was better than that, that when it was just him, alone, he would never choose cruelty and selfish pleasure over the well-being of someone smaller than him and much less able to defend himself. What Jenner did to Brayden was so much worse than tripping him in a hallway or calling him names for the amusement of the crowd. He violated a sacred trust.

Mid-way through the night, he runs into Max in the hallway.

She confronts him with, "What's going on with you? You're acting really squirrely, and—"

"Fuck off," he snaps, regretting it instantly. Too prideful to apologize, Jenner also feels like it's partially Max's fault that he went to Manse in the first place, looking to get laid at her suggestion.

"Jenner," she starts, taken aback.

Rolling his eyes at it all, he storms away and goes back to work.

The busier his hands are — pouring drinks, collecting money, restocking — the more the shame dulls. He gets lost in it, and soon the end of the shift is nigh. They lock up at one in the morning. In a semblance of apology for earlier he sends Max home rather than expecting her to clean up at all. Quietly but diligently, he and Brayden perfunctorily clean up the bar. Jenner tells Brayden he can take off but Brayden only shrugs and keeps going, muttering something about wanting to feel like he's earned his good tips. Jenner can feel Brayden keeping an eye on him but is thankful that he doesn't pry.

Once things are in order, Jenner goes to help Art finish in the kitchen and locks up the night's earnings in the safe. It's almost two when Jenner groans with weariness and shuffles into the break room to get his wallet and keys and head upstairs to bed.

"You look tired," Brayden observes.

Jenner starts with shock, having thought he was alone. Turning, he finds Brayden sitting on the bench across from the lockers.

"Brayd. Christ, you scared me. I thought you'd be long gone by now."

With a half-smile, Brayden says, "Yeah, I was on my way. Just started thinking about stuff and, I don't know. Guess I'm not in a huge rush to get back to that old room in my Nana's house. Need some time to unwind after work, you know? It's hard to do when you have to be quiet as a mouse or risk waking people up."

Undoing the clasp to the chain around his neck, on which is strung the key to his locker, Jenner says, "Mm. I can imagine. I know what it's like to crave privacy, your own space."

He gets the key and uses it to open his locker. In a swift movement, he twists his dirty, sweaty, black work-shirt up over his head.

"Look, I'm sorry if I was short with you at all earlier. It's just been one of those days. It wasn't..."

The words trail off. Brayden has suddenly gotten to his feet, facing Jenner, frowning and tensed with fear, his chest rising and falling visibly as his breath quickens.

"...personal," Jenner finishes lamely. "What?"

Brayden's eyes are locked to the tattoo above Jenner's heart.

A single word.

A woman's name.

Bette

Jenner follows the stare. Understanding blooms like a flower finding the sun.

"Fuck."

"It was you."

It's said softly, those three little words of accusation, but they cut Jenner deeply. The stricken paleness of Brayden's suntanned face tells Jenner everything. His expression, his hurt, is a perfect reflection of all of the boys like Patrick, who have become trapped in Jenner's conscience. Just one more person Jenner has wounded by not being honest and standing up for what he knows is right. He should have made Brayden's feelings the priority over his own and pulled Brayden aside privately to confess. His failure to show Brayden even that much respect just tells Jenner that he is, at heart, exactly the kind of person he has always secretly despised. He is cruel, and selfish, and hurtful. Brayden's green eyes dart side-to-side, his gaze skittering around once freeing itself from the tattoo, seeking the exit, an answer. In that moment, Jenner knows he has become Brayden's tormentor. He's not Brayden's boss, he's just the guy trying to make Brayden look the fool, knocking him down a few pegs and reminding him that he's not as strong as he hoped he was.

"I can explain," Jenner hears himself saying, wondering if it's true, if there's anything at all he can say to explain himself.

His mouth working, at first, Brayden makes no sound. He blinks, dazed, looking lightheaded, upset and overwhelmed. "No," he manages.

Brayden bolts for the room's one exit.

Jenner is ready for him, though. His training kicks in and he easily catches Brayden by the forearm when he tries to get past. In a terrible echo of the previous night, Jenner gets hold of Brayden's other arm as well and twists them up behind his back, putting any doubt that might linger to rest.

Brayden moans. The sound shakes Jenner to the soul.

But, unlike the previous night, Jenner is free of the hood and all is silent. There's no noise to hide behind. Every breath can be heard. Every gasp and whisper. Jenner's lips move against the irresistible soft cascade of sun-kissed hair by Brayden's ear and Brayden is barely fighting him, but Jenner can feel him trembling.

"*Please*," Jenner begs.

Brayden's skin pebbles under Jenner's palms. Though he tugs at his trapped arms, Brayden finds he is held tight. Eyes closed, barely breathing, he hisses, "You. You *knew*?"

"Of course I knew."

"You knew *the whole time*?!"

Sensing Brayden giving in to the raw, scraping madness of terror, Jenner hushes to him, "I'm not going to hurt you." Looping his right arm around Brayden's chest, Jenner holds him in a tender embrace and gently drags his thumb over the jackrabbiting of Brayden's racing heart. "I would never hurt you. I promise that you can trust me."

There's no verbal answer but Jenner is strengthened when Brayden is able to take one shaky breath, then another. He's calming down.

"Come upstairs with me and we can talk about this in private. We don't have privacy here. Max and Art have keys. They could come back if I don't return home soon. That's important to you too, right? Being discreet?"

Brayden makes a small, hurt sound low in his throat. His eyes are still squeezed tightly shut.

"I can be very discreet," Jenner promises, knowing Brayden will likely have bruises on his arms in the morning and trying not to become perversely aroused at the idea. "You're safe with me. If I was going to take advantage of you, I'd have done it already."

The realization of this sinks in, slow and deep. In that moment, as Brayden debates his choices, Jenner senses the distinct power shift between them, no longer simply employer and employee, or strangers meeting anonymously as Master and slave for one night of indulgence. Physically and financially, Brayden is trapped. Jenner feels the power that he has over Brayden. It thrums under his palms with the beating of Brayden's heart. Little Brayden is fully cognizant that the man towering over him is stronger, quicker, and could do literally anything he wanted. There is nothing that could be done to stop it. There are no beseeching words Brayden could speak or actions he could take to get him out of this if Jenner didn't want to let him go.

Jenner Parrish feels the precise moment when Brayden Clare becomes truly afraid of him.

There is no verbal agreement. Jenner gathers his things and Brayden, shell-shocked, follows him upstairs. They exit the bar and the door leading to the apartment is right there. Jenner unlocks the bolt and flips the switch for the overhead light. They climb the steps in silence and Jenner leads the way inside, flipping light switches as they go.

"I thought you lived with Max and Art," Brayden says with a hollow, emotionless tone, hovering by the exit.

"Yeah. I do. But I inherited this place along with the bar and I've been trying, unsuccessfully, to rent it. Lately, I've liked using it to be alone."

He drops his keys and wallet in the kitchen and returns to Brayden who retreats a few steps as Jenner gets too close. Determined, and now with first-hand experience with techniques that successfully calm Brayden down when he's looking skittish, Jenner advances, backing him up to the wall. Each step ratchets up the tension in Brayden's body, increases the volume of the desperate energy he gives off. When they are chest-to-chest with Jenner bearing down on him, Brayden seems on the verge of tears.

Calmly, slowly, Jenner guides Brayden's arms up, clasping his hands and holding them tightly to the wall. Fitting a knee between his thighs, Jenner draws it up snug to Brayden's crotch. His blush deepens but each subsequent breath becomes more even. Brayden stares at Jenner's chest.

"Who's Bette? A girlfriend?"

Jenner chuckles. "I'm queer. In case you hadn't noticed."

Brayden's lips pucker slightly. "Oh."

"Bette is my mother's name. And just like almost everyone else in my life, she thinks I'm straight."

For a long moment, neither of them say anything. Brayden trembles restlessly under Jenner's hold, refusing to look him in the eye. Jenner imagines that he's reliving it, the things they did in that room, only now inserting Jenner Parrish as his counterpart. Jenner gives him time.

"I didn't tell anyone I was going to Manse last night," Brayden whispers.

"Neither did I. It just happened. I saw you and I—"

Jenner stops himself abruptly, before he can let on more than he wants to.

"What? And you what?"

"And I," he sighs, "didn't want anyone else touching you."

Then he *knows* Brayden is reliving it. He exhales sharply and bucks, fighting hard against Jenner's grip, which only tightens, his knee grinding up into Brayden's testicles, drawing a hard grunt.

"Should I let you go? We can sit down and talk about this."

The particular phrasing of Jenner's words pierces the fog clouding Brayden's mind. For the first time since they walked into the apartment, he looks up at Jenner's face. Brayden shrinks back at the hunger revealed in Jenner's dark blue eyes, but perseveres. "I need this job," he confesses like a damned man.

"Fuck the job," Jenner scoffs. "This isn't about the damned job. I'm not firing you and I won't use this as any sort of leverage against you. This is strictly personal. Okay?"

"Okay."

"Good. Now. Should I let you go?"

It all catches up with Brayden, visibly overwhelming him. He sucks in a rough breath and holds it, blinking back tears.

Concerned, desperate to help and somehow make things better, but not sure how, Jenner lets him go but stays where he is. "Hey. Better or worse? Braydy, better or worse?"

"Worse," he chokes.

Jenner takes a backward step.

"Worse!"

"Okay, okay. It's okay."

Suspecting that seeing someone so much larger than himself looming over him, big as life, might be part of Brayden's problem,

Jenner turns Brayden to face the wall. Holding both of Brayden's wrists in one hand, Jenner traps them over his captive's head, against the wall, as if stringing him up by them and letting him hang there.

"B-better," Brayden murmurs.

Jenner reaches around and palms Brayden through his jeans. Closing his hand, grabbing hold, he rolls the flesh. It jumps and thickens with interest.

"Better?"

Releasing his handful for only a second, Jenner pops the fly of Brayden's jeans and slips his hand inside Brayden's boxers instead.

"*Jenner,*" Brayden gasps, his voice breaking on the first syllable.

They're skin to skin, with no glove between them this time. Fondling Brayden's cock, gently coaxing him harder, Jenner rasps, "Better or worse?"

Brayden moans.

When Brayden is fully erect, his dick straining up into the air and throbbing, Jenner lets go of it. Keeping his left hand locked securely around Brayden's wrists, Jenner begins to slide Brayden's pants and underwear lower on his hips, past the curve of his ass.

"You know I got off on watching you. That's what I wanted. That was my fantasy. And it came true. I came so fucking hard last night, seeing you ride my hand. I licked your come from the glove after you left."

"*Jesus.*"

"You tasted *so good.*"

Brayden shudders and writhes, becoming restless again now that his genitals and ass have been carefully exposed and, for what purpose, he doesn't yet know. Jenner stills him by bracing a knee between his legs, pinning the clothing puddled around mid-thigh to the wall and thereby further restraining Brayden. Once Brayden feels his range of movement restricted he calms again. Jenner makes mental note of it. Clearly, Brayden responds well to high protocol when trying to cope with stress. It was the same at Manse, when he asked for the restraints.

"How long have you been a slave? Who trained you?"

Brayden shakes his head, grunts, "No one."

Softly, soothingly, Jenner says, "I've been a Master for five years, and I trained at Manse, under a man named David, but I've never taken a slave of my own for more than a single night, because I hadn't found the right one. This'll be our second night together, slave. That means something to me. Now, my job is to take care of you and make you as comfortable as possible. You respond well to restraints. That's good. I want all of your focus on me right now. Nothing else. No one else. Can you do that for me?"

Brayden nods, gasping softly.

"I'm going to give you ways, in addition to the restraints, to lessen your stress. There are different levels of protocol between a Master and a slave. Low protocol is for the most informal situations. Most rules are relaxed, but the trust and respect remains. With Medium protocol, things are still casual, but the slave may wear a collar, be more aware of their actions and words. This is all high protocol. As my slave, there are rules you are expected to follow, or be punished. You're to keep your eyes lowered at all times. You are to speak only when I've asked you for a response, and you will address me with respect. That means 'Sir' or 'Master', not 'Jenner'. Stop means stop. If you're okay with this, answer by saying, 'yes, Sir.' If you're not okay with it, tell me now by saying 'stop'."

Bowing his head, breathing harder, blushing darker, Brayden hesitates before answering with a hushed, "Yes, Sir."

"Good. Very good. Just focus on my voice. Control your breathing. Try to relax your body." As Jenner gives him time to settle, letting the seconds tick by in order for Brayden to know things are under control, Brayden gets still and becomes very quiet, as if by listening hard enough he will be able to learn what's happening behind him.

"Now," Jenner says slowly, "my beautiful slave, I have a new fantasy." Jenner sucks his index finger to wet it. Reaching down between their bodies, he strokes through the crease of Brayden's ass. He finds his target and rubs in small circles over the tight, wrinkled knot with his thumb to begin to stimulate it, drawing blood there, taking his time.

Brayden shudders breathlessly.

With a twist, Jenner inserts his moistened index finger into Brayden's heat, impaling him on it. "Better or worse?"

Brayden's mouth works around a cry that, at first, sticks in his throat, then wrenches free. It breaks on the edges, sharpening into a whimper as Jenner withdraws the finger only to press it back inside and repeat the process.

First, Brayden holds his breath as Jenner finger-fucks him. Then he gasps in huge gulps when oxygen becomes necessary. Jenner glances avidly down between their bodies at the sight of his captive taking in the finger, savoring the velvety soft, clenched heat of his ass, stroking over his inner walls. Brayden is so small, Jenner imagines it could be difficult for him to take Jenner's cock, but he can't wait to try.

"Can you guess what my fantasy is?"

Breathing heavily and unevenly, Brayden rests his forehead against the wall in front of him. He arches his back, his spine curving beautifully as his hips tilt to invite each penetration.

He tries to shift his feet and rolls his hips forward. He twists slightly to the side. Jenner simply follows him, sometimes keeping the finger nestled deeply without moving it, letting Brayden feel the obscene violation of it, but then he always goes back to the slow, gentle, demanding strokes in and out.

The first touch of Jenner's lips to the spot just under Brayden's right ear sends a shiver outward through his body. Jenner skims his lips over the goosebumps. Brayden clenches up around the finger. Jenner presses a tender suckling kiss to Brayden's neck before teasingly scraping his teeth over the spot. It makes Brayden grunt and push back into the next inward thrust of Jenner's fingers.

"Stop means stop," Jenner whispers. "The bed'll be more comfortable for this. I'm gonna move you over there. Or, I can let you go. What would you prefer?"

The reply isn't immediate, or loud, or confident. "Don't let go."

Pouring every last drop of his passion into the words, Jenner groans, "I want you."

He withdraws his finger and, instead, reaches around to fondle Brayden and feel how hard he is. Brayden is fully erect. The entire underside of his dick is wet with precome. Jenner moans his lust and sucks one more kiss to Brayden's neck.

"Okay," Brayden grunts in surrender.

Chapter 9

Without Masks

Even with his eyes closed, Jenner's features are burned into Brayden's retinas with such clarity that the after-image of him is just as vibrant as the real thing. He had never given conscious thought to Jenner in a sexual role before. For Brayden, Jenner was everything to fear, everything that had power over him. His physical size, his position as boss, holding the financial reins of his employee's life, as well as the person he used to be, a popular jock to Brayden's awkward outcast, it all overwhelmed any other considerations.

But not now. Now all of that is pushed aside and Brayden helplessly tries to reconcile what happened at Manse with the newfound knowledge that it was *him*. It was Jenner.

It seems impossible. It seems like a distorted dream that he expects any moment to wake from.

Jenner.

Brayden sees him anew. Jewel-like, dark-blue eyes so fathomless in depth that he feels he could fall into them if he looks too long and with too much intensity. The small cleft in his chin; the particular bow shape of his lips; the dimples deeply denting his cheeks and the pronounced nature of his cheekbones all add up to create a visage extremely masculine but terribly beautiful. As Jenner holds his wrists in a vice-like grip and leads him blindly to the bed, Brayden realizes for the very first time that some of his fear of Jenner was due to attraction—an attraction so acute that it twisted around on him, like a snake with fangs bared, ready to strike. This is everything he's been avoiding, everything he couldn't face. And now it has him, quite literally. Escape is impossible, or so he tells himself.

It seems unbelievable, that Jenner has secretly desired Brayden, someone so beneath Jenner on the social ladder. For so long, Brayden wanted the kindness of his peers desperately. The idea of one of the popular guys showing any interest in him at all would have been laughable, at best a ploy to screw with his head and humiliate him in front of everyone else. The paranoid part of him whispers that maybe that's still the case. Instinct warns him not to trust Jenner, but the careful listing of rules, the explanation of protocol makes it easier to go along with it, letting the moment and the formality of Jenner's approach to sex instill some confidence that things are what they seem, despite it all.

Brayden's knees touch the side of the mattress. As Jenner guides Brayden's hands behind his back, trapping them there together, he leans slightly against the bed to keep upright. His jeans were hastily pulled back up by Jenner but they hang open.

There's a pause that draws out too long. Brayden feels Jenner's eyes on him like a caress. Fingers weave into the loose hair at the nape of Brayden's neck, scratching lightly over his scalp, causing shivers to shoot out under his skin. His lips part around a sigh. The fear is still there, but the gentle touches and Jenner's patience lull Brayden into a sense of security.

Discarded on the carpeted floor, Brayden sees through half-lidded eyes the leash that Jenner used to bind him at Manse. It links him to the sensations of that night, awakening them in memory.

Maybe Jenner sees him looking, because he asks, "What is it? What do you need?"

"You have the leash," Brayden says quietly, before adding, almost too softly to hear, "I want you to use it, Sir."

Jenner responds immediately, crouching to snatch it up, pulling the shirt off of him and using the leash to tie Brayden's arms in place, his loosely-curled fists resting in the sweeping curve of his lower back. Half-undressed, barely covered as the jeans begin to slip lower, held up only by the swell of his ass, Brayden waits for it, anticipating it – Jenner's touch anchoring him to the spot, the moment, and whatever combination of pleasure and pain it brings.

It doesn't come. He waits and waits, making him feel frantic, wanting to get it over with. Then....

"This is wrong," Jenner says, the tone of his voice changed drastically, distant and laden with doubt. "We need to slow down."

"What?" Brayden blurts. His eyes open and, tilting his head up and to the side, he seeks out Jenner, whose fingers caress through his hair. The tender sensuality of it stokes the heat of Brayden's desire and subsequently weakens the foundations of his self-consciousness. Searching Jenner's face, reading the uncertainty there, Brayden hears himself say, "You can't just leave me like this."

"It's too fast. I promised you we would talk about this. I—I shouldn't have presumed," Jenner says, struggling for the right words and Brayden can see his confusion, met with a situation probably unlike any he's encountered before. And, because he feels the same way, Jenner's confusion banishes Brayden's. It evaporates, replaced with empathy.

Brayden turns his cheek slightly into Jenner's hand, so that it brushes against the palm. Brayden begs him, "*Please.*"

The kiss happens quickly, surprising him. Jenner tugs lightly on Brayden's hair, forcing him to tilt his head back farther, and catches his mouth in a hard, urgent press of lips. Before he can think to react, grunting softly and marveling at the impossibly soft feel of Jenner's warm, full lips moving against his own, Brayden opens and Jenner pushes inside. Demandingly, Jenner licks over Brayden's lips and starts to map his mouth with his tongue. The twisting muscle teases, stroking, probing, tasting.

Struggling just to breathe, Brayden moans. Jenner bears down on him, taking everything. The sensations and intimacy are pure pleasure that rocket straight down to Brayden's dick. Every thought and doubt burns away with the heat of the kiss. Brayden lets Jenner use him, sucking on his lips, tongue-fucking his mouth, leaving him throbbing, tingling, and desperate.

Brayden could never have imagined it would be like this. Getting lost in the abandon, the lust, Brayden feels only relief when Jenner's free hand pushes the jeans out of the way and wraps Brayden's erection, tugging on it in a gentle but rapidly increasing pace.

Quickly, Brayden becomes frantic. Caught between the hand in his hair, cupping the back of his skull while Jenner kisses his breath away, and the one jacking his cock, it's all Brayden can do to vocalize his anxiousness into the kiss. Jenner swallows every sound, urged on, pushed full-force into the dominant role. He milks every keening grunt, every gasp and whimper. When Brayden begins to thrust sharply, counter to each tug, Jenner jacks him at a frenzied speed, leaving Brayden panting, pushed right up to the edge, hard as silk-sheathed steel in Jenner's hand.

"Stop!"

It hits Jenner like a slap. He stops immediately, releasing Brayden completely.

"What's wrong?"

"I thought you wanted to..." Brayden starts, unable to finish. Jaw clenched, he clears his throat and mumbles, "And I was about to...."

"Come? That's kind of the whole point."

The confession is a struggle. It begins as a bright spark of defiance that slowly darkens. If he typically acts innocent and unassuming, he doesn't feel that way in the slightest now. The timid, lost little boy, intimidated into shyness, is gone. All of his frustration—with his family, with the move, with Andre—it gives him confidence, makes him bold. The words sit on his tongue before he releases them, letting them do whatever damage they will.

"If you're just trying to placate me in order to get out of this, then let me spare you the trouble."

Jenner seethes. He grits his teeth and closes his eyes as he tries to master himself. It doesn't seem to work.

"Goddammit."

Spurred into movement, Jenner grabs a duffle that's been shoved under the bed by Brayden's feet. After a moment spent digging in it, he finds what he needs. He returns to Brayden, standing directly behind him. Pushing at the middle of Brayden's back, Jenner bends him sharply over the side of the bed and tosses a condom down beside him.

Brayden stares at it in disbelief, unable to look away. His breath catches, coming in fits and gasps. It's too late to take back what he's said.

In his peripheral vision, he sees Jenner squirt lube from a small bottle onto his hand. Then he pushes Brayden's pants and underwear down to his knees and nudges his feet apart as wide as they'll go. Impatiently, hurriedly, roughly, he rubs lubricant over Brayden's opening and twists two fingers up into him, smearing the cold gel inside.

"Ahh! *Fuck!*"

Brayden bends slightly at the knees, his hands curling into tighter fists, his short fingernails digging into his palms. He gasps into the bed at the cold strangeness of Jenner's fingers stretching him out. The fingers scissor apart, working the inner muscles of his sphincter loose with skill and expediency. Feeling the skin of his face and neck heat with a deep flush of embarrassment, Brayden endures the humiliation of it. He tries to be quiet and keep still but finds it difficult to manage. Just as the ache dulls, with Jenner's fingers pumping in and out of him, pushing in to the last knuckle, bending and corkscrewing on the withdraw, and his body slowly adjusts, Brayden feels a third finger press in beside the other two.

At Brayden's subsequent sharp whimper of pain, Jenner eases up, taking more care, but still just as impatient. He unzips and strokes himself while he preps Brayden for penetration.

"This better? I don't want to hurt you, I just want to make sure I can fit…you're so fucking tight."

Brayden tries to speak but all that comes out is a moan.

"Has it been a while?"

You have no idea, Brayden laments inwardly. He doesn't answer but tenses his arms and shoulders, straining against the leather tie as the bite into his skin soothes another, more elusive hurt.

Jenner squirts more lube onto his hand then favors Brayden with long, deep, slow thrusts with the three fingers. Clenching up around the invasion, pushing a little against Jenner's hand, Brayden is unused to being fingered at all, let alone stuffed as full as he is. Jenner's desperation to get on with the actual sex is palpable. It takes him over and Brayden submits to it, as terrified as he may be. The confident force of Jenner's need outweighs Brayden's confused misgivings.

Suddenly, Jenner stops touching him and lunges to grab the condom from the bedspread. The wrapper is ripped open with Jenner's teeth. He spits out the piece of foil and rolls on the rubber.

Brayden's panic ratchets up again. Focusing only on his breathing, Brayden feels Jenner take hold of his hip to steady him and senses the intensity of Jenner's stare on his naked body. With his bare ass up in the air, his hole feeling wet with the lube and tender from being manipulated by Jenner's fingers, Brayden is nothing but helpless and overwhelmed.

There's a wet sound as Jenner slicks more lube onto his latex-sheathed cock. He moves closer to Brayden, lining up.

"W-wait," Brayden stutters, petrified.

"Shh, it's okay. Slow and easy...."

The head of Jenner's cock gently touches Brayden's throbbing opening. It's obscene. Brayden grunts hard through the fear. With gentle, restrained pressure, Jenner begins to enter him. The small ring of muscle gradually spreads around Jenner's girth. Jenner pulls Brayden back onto him. Growling and shuddering, though he seems to hear Brayden cry out sharply and with evident pain, Jenner doesn't stop.

Then the widest part of him is in. The head catches inside Brayden as Jenner pulls back slightly, fitting just past the snug outer ring of muscle. Their bodies are joined. Jenner takes a breath and Brayden makes a low, sobbing moan against the bed which deepens and stretches out as Jenner thrusts in deeper, wanting to get farther and possess that much more of him.

With slow, shallow pushes, he works his way inside. Throughout this process, Brayden's fingers twist and splay in their bonds, clawing at the air. He tilts his hips to help ease the intense, burning ache of Jenner moving inside his ass.

An eternity later, Jenner is fully seated and Brayden is very quiet. A tear slides down his cheek and his lungs are on fire with the fight not to break and cry like the weakling he knows himself to be. This was a mistake, Brayden understands too late. Jenner was right. They should have stopped. It is wrong—whatever this is, by any definition. The misery catches like wildfire and spreads, making him question his whole identity. This is what he thought he wanted and it doesn't feel right. It feels *wrong*, so what does that leave him with? Who the hell is he if he's not this?

"Brayden," Jenner moans blissfully. "My *god*. Oh my *god*."

Turning his face into the bedding to hide it, Brayden wills Jenner to move, feeling impaled, stuffed too-full and slowly dying from it. The cock up his ass feels foreign, too big, a violation and nothing more, nothing pleasurable like he expected it to be.

Just finish, he pleads mentally, bleakly. *Just finish so that I can leave.*

But then, just as ripe sorrow begins to claw at Brayden's soul, Jenner begins to move again, withdrawing until the ridge of his cockhead catches on Brayden's rim. He thrusts back in with a long, deep dig. And he doesn't stop. He keeps moving, rocking in and out, caressing Brayden's hips and thighs, kneading his ass and when Brayden moans, it's with more pleasure than pain. He's shocked to hear it.

Encouraged by the promising nature of the cry, Jenner angles his next thrust and drags over Brayden's prostate.

Brayden jolts with the added stimulation, crying out with the bombardment of sensation.

Jenner chuckles and holds him still, using both hands as he rocks against the spot, making Brayden yell. He tries to seal his lips shut to hold in the cries, but it doesn't help. Shuddering in Jenner's hands, thick fluid weeps from his cock as Jenner pounds his hole, slowly making him crazy.

Reaching around Brayden's hip, Jenner finds his cock, curved up in a tight line against his belly, dripping wet. He squeezes up it from root to tip. Pushing into the touch, growling and sobbing with need, Brayden's senses are washed out in white fire. He climaxes spectacularly, shooting thick jets of come, fluttering in contractions around Jenner's cock still fucking his ass.

"Oh shit," Jenner hisses. His hips twitch against Brayden's bottom as he unloads, sheathed completely in him. "*Brayden.*"

Gasping, grunting and weakening, Brayden pulses in Jenner's hand even after he's spent, having just experienced the best orgasm of his life by far.

Quickly, Jenner unties the leather strap, freeing Brayden's hands which have gone numb and are turning purple he's been pulling on them so hard, cutting off the circulation. "Fuck. Your hands...."

Limp, numb and bloodless, Brayden's arms fall to his sides. Jenner hurriedly gathers him up, guiding him upright without yet pulling out. He brushes the sweat-streaked tendrils of hair from where they're stuck to Brayden's face and presses a soft kiss to his temple. "You okay?"

"Mm."

"Brayden," Jenner breathes, filling the name with affection. Brayden flinches subtly against the sweetness he hears in Jenner's voice, instinctively mistrusting it.

Pins and needles prick Brayden's skin from his elbows down to his fingertips. Jenner dutifully rubs the life back into them.

Woozy and lightheaded, Brayden chuckles, "Hell of a first kiss."

Jenner freezes. Even without being able to see Jenner, Brayden can feel the impact of shock and cold dread upon him.

"First with *me*. You mean first with me, right?"

Brayden is silent, and it says everything.

"No." Waiting patiently for the revelations to sink in, just as Jenner waited for him not so long ago — why Brayden was reacting as he was, why he was so tight, and the cause of his nervousness — Brayden sighs with resignation and humiliation. Staring across the room at one of the apartment's blank walls, Brayden gives Jenner time to catch up and tries to close off some of his own raw emotions out of self-preservation.

"Oh god. What have I done? You were a-a *virgin*? Oh my *god*. When you said you were new to being a slave, I didn't think... Y-you should have stopped me. Told me — "

Listening for anger, Brayden hears none, just remorse and shame.

"Hey," he interrupts, bristling at the concern. "I didn't want you to treat me like a virgin, okay? And come on, I'm twenty-two. It's kind of embarrassing to admit."

Jenner nuzzles against Brayden's hair with a sigh, wrapping him from behind in the most intimate embrace of his life thus far, holding on to Brayden, his skin slippery with sweat, and his body still full of Jenner's thick cock. Unable to truly process his reality, and how completely Jenner has him, Brayden grows slowly more accustomed to being so possessed.

"I'll never forgive myself," Jenner hisses.

Brayden overlays Jenner's arms with his own where they cross his stomach and chest. "I wanted this," he counters. "I didn't say no."

"But you've… you've been with girls, right?"

Again, Brayden quiets, unsure how to explain when he's never figured it out either. "It never felt right with women. It never worked. So no. I never… I mean, I assumed I wasn't into sex with girls because I was into men, but…."

"Jesus. What are you saying? How far have you gone fooling around with guys?"

"Well, my roommate in Florida gave me a blowjob once."

"Once?! Brayden!"

He realizes he's still waiting for Jenner to laugh at him, that part of the defensiveness is an emotional shield against the unavoidable repercussions from what he's just been a part of.

"I'm fucked up. I get it, okay?" He spits it out with mortification. "I was scared. I've been scared for so long, and I just wanted it to happen. I wanted to know without a doubt if this is who I am or not, but I couldn't ask for it. I don't know."

"Th-the ties. The restraints. Submitting. That's what those are about, isn't it? It's easier for you when you're just doing what you're told, when you feel so helpless. You can tell yourself you were *forced*."

No sooner have the words been spoken than Jenner appears to become aware of their positions and how very close they are in that moment. Like he's pushing Brayden away, or trying to rid himself of something unclean, Jenner tries to escape. Brayden grabs him before he can pull out, holds on to him, and forbids retreat.

"Don't? Please?"

He looks back over his shoulder at Jenner. Jenner glances down at the tear-tracks Brayden can feel drying on his cheeks, and knows his eyes must be bloodshot from trying not to cry. None of this helps him keep Jenner there. *I'm more trouble than I'm worth*, Brayden thinks miserably. *Now he thinks I'm gonna cry rape.*

But strangely, Jenner looks nothing but heartbroken. Squeezing his eyes shut, he doesn't protest. He lets Brayden keep him there, saying, "This is all my fault. I didn't want to hurt you. I would *never* want to hurt you."

"Why? Why do you even *care* if you hurt me or not? I don't understand."

Frowning, Jenner places a light kiss to the corner of Brayden's mouth and withdraws from him with a groan. The used condom is tossed away.

"Let me get you into the shower. I only have one clean towel but it's yours if you want it."

Thinking of the prospect of facing his reflection and cleaning the lube out of his ass, Brayden replies, "Nah, you can go first. I kind of just want to lie down for a minute and stretch out."

The hurt in the expression that briefly crosses Jenner's face tells Brayden that Jenner thinks it's an excuse to sneak out without an awkward goodbye. Nodding with sullen resignation, Jenner says, "Okay. Do you need anything before I go?"

Brayden shakes his head.

"Okay." It sounds like a dismissal, like goodbye.

When Jenner emerges from the bathroom not fifteen minutes later, Brayden is fast asleep, curled up on Jenner's bed. As Brayden lies there, unaware, for a long while Jenner simply stands where he is, watching.

Chapter 10

Consequence

Climbing out of strange dreams, Brayden awakens to find himself in a strange place. The knowledge of where he is is slow to come as he had been focused on the more physical, sensory details of what was happening after Jenner took him to the apartment above the bar to "talk", than trying to register the mundane aspects of the place. Beige carpeting, walls painted a soft sage color, and an overall lack of furniture or decoration other than the bed he lies on don't strike him as familiar at all as he opens his eyes. No memory or recognition sparks at first. With temporary amnesia, he realizes that his wrists sting with hurt and both of his arms, up to his shoulders, ache with deep muscle pain. The inside of his ass throbs and he feels wrung out, emotionally and physically. Sleep tries to lull him again, tempting him with the promise of a temporary reprieve from reality, but he denies it.

With effort, he turns from his back to his left side and sees Jenner Parrish, his boss, only inches away, seated on the ground. He's leaning back against the side of the bed, legs bent at the knees and feet planted squarely on the carpet. Though it's hard to believe, his eyes tell Brayden it's true. Jenner looks like he's been guarding Brayden while he slept. Brayden remembers suddenly, with gut-churning clarity, where he is and what happened right before he passed out.

I need to get out of here.

Initially, he's at a loss as to how to get himself out of his predicament. Brayden wishes he could disappear through the walls like a ghost rather than be forced to try to sneak out without waking Jenner, who appears to be sleeping soundly. Covert movement seems beyond Brayden's ability with his body struggling to overcome the new sorts of torments inflicted upon it. At the very least, it would require him to be able to get up off the bed and even that much is daunting given the pulsing, low ache in his rectum.

With effort, he sits upright. Rolling his head on his shoulders to un-kink his neck, flexing his arms, he starts to try to revive himself. The beginnings of stark bruises are rising on his wrists and he groans inwardly at the prospect of having to explain them to anyone who might see them — his Nana, his customers, his co-workers. Quickly, he pushes away the worrisome thought as it sparks new questions, specifically about whether he even wants to go back to work at the bar at all after fucking his boss. As soon as he had the consent form from Manse in front of him, the pen to sign in his hand, poised above the paper, Brayden knew he was making a choice. The dread had started then, as soon as his name adorned the waiver. It was yet another step along a dark, dangerous path that he'd started down as soon as he had Andre pinning him to the floor of his old apartment in Miami. Now things have gone farther that he ever thought they would, and where it all leads next he can't even imagine.

Looking around for his shirt, Brayden spots it crumpled on the floor by the corner of the bed. Carefully, he shifts his weight and swings a leg over the side of the bed. There's a blanket draped over him, and Brayden has no idea where it came from, has no memory of seeing it on the bed when he had lain down. Jenner must have covered him with it, he realizes, after he'd fallen asleep. Slightly uncomfortable with the mental image of Jenner doing that, the tenderness of the gesture, it adds incentive to get out and fast.

Move, Brayden tells himself. *Get up. Get out of there.*

Perched on the edge of the bed, he stares, sleep-dazed and weary, at his discarded shirt, while he's bombarded with flashes of memories from having sex with Jenner. The warm scent of his skin, the way he'd moaned Brayden's name, the steely thickness of Jenner's cock moving inside him, the needy caress of his fingers raking over Brayden's naked body.

Brayden is crusted in dried come and sweat and feels disgusting. His arms are sore from being restrained so tightly, the pain there only increasing the longer he's awake. Everything seems changed in him, inside and out. Nothing is the way it was. There was some small hope in him going into this that he would feel empowered by finally having sex with another man, and submitting completely. Maybe it would give him clarity of mind, he'd thought. But now that it's done, he's left lost again, adrift in a sea of emotion, regret, and vulnerability that he has no idea how to navigate.

He misses his parents.

He misses Andre.

He feels profoundly alone. Bitter regret threatens, rising up from somewhere deep down as he stares at the soft, waved texture of the close-cropped, nearly black hair on Jenner's head.

This person has something of mine now, he thinks. *No matter what happens from here on out, Jenner Parrish will always own part of me, and I'll see that in his face every time I look at him. Hell, any time I look at someone or someplace connected with him. It'll surround me.*

Just like with Dad, it'll follow me everywhere. Something else to haunt me. Just what I need.

You can leave, his mother's familiar voice in his head tells him. Seductively, she adds, *It would be easy — just grab your things and go. You could get in your Jeep and drive. No looking back. Go back to Florida or go somewhere new, somewhere where no one knows you at all. A fresh start.*

But then he thinks of Emma Leah, and how whenever Brayden is home she tries to be near him, sitting by his side on the couch, cuddling up against him as they watch television or telling him about her day at school over dinner at his Nana's table. There's a light in her eyes whenever she looks at him — a heady mixture of trust, love, devotion and pure innocence. It's one of the best things about his life, now. He has someone who cares about him that much, who needs him that much. And if he chickened out now, what would become of Emma? That light may not die completely, but it would surely darken and dim. She would pull away reflexively at the bite of disappointment, just as he'd done when his mother disappointed him, choosing the ethereal promise of her own dreams over her very real responsibility to her child.

I could never do that to Emma, Brayden knows. *I will never hurt her like that.*

If you don't go, you must stay, his mother's voice riddles to him.

That's what moves him, stripping away his tangled worries, clearing his head just enough to get him to his feet. Empty, turned inside out and despondent, he creeps to his shirt. Grabbing it up, he turns it right-side-out. The floorboards cooperate and in near silence, with a glance to the front door, he pulls the garment over his head.

When his face is through the neck of his shirt, he sees Jenner watching him from his seat on the floor. Arms braced on his knees, still but alert, Jenner holds him there with his eyes — dark pools of promise and secrets now shared between them.

Dread swells. Brayden's heart leaps up into his throat, beating frantically.

"Stay," Jenner beseeches him. "Please. It's not even dawn."

"M-my family expected me back hours ago," Brayden hears himself explaining with a clumsy tongue and stilted words. Already, he feels the awful urge to add the honorific of 'Sir', just to please Jenner, to use respect as a means to placate. "They might be worried. If I call to say I'm okay, it'd wake my cousin Emma."

Focusing only on whether or not he's forgetting anything and the quickest way to get out of there, the weight of Jenner's stare unsettles Brayden. Because for the first time, he has some idea what's behind it. It's not the first time Jenner has looked at him in that way, but never before did he suspect the particular manner of the man's interest.

Brayden goes to the door. Fully clothed but simultaneously completely naked while in the presence of the one person on Earth with a lover's thorough knowledge of him, Brayden itches to be alone and look for new ways to bury stark truths.

His hand is on the doorknob when his skin prickles with restless tingling; sensing Jenner has come after him and is now standing there, right at his back, mere inches away again. Resenting that Jenner so easily makes him feel like prey, Brayden freezes where he is, waiting, expecting to be touched without understanding whether he wants that or not. His scalp tightens, his mouth goes dry and his stomach knots.

Exhaling around the lump in his throat, he makes a soft sound.

Jenner advances ever closer. Brayden can feel the heat of him—his breath, his body—and fixes his stare on the curving lines of the wood grain in the door.

"You're scheduled next for Tuesday," Jenner says quietly, his deep voice a low rumble in Brayden's ear like the thunder before a storm. It's the same way he spoke when laying out all of the rules of protocol, reining in Brayden's anxiety with the skill of a professional. Brayden slips a little back into that submissive mindset, and worries at how much better it makes him feel, right away. "Will I see you? Will you come to work?"

Work, Brayden thinks with dismay.

"I don't know," he says honestly.

When Jenner next speaks, there's a plain urgency to it, as some manner of fear affects him. "This isn't anyone's business but our own. Even Max, Art—I won't say a word. I swear it."

That almost makes Brayden smile, but the turmoil churning in him squelches it. "I just don't know if I'm comfortable working for you anymore. Let me think about it. I can't think right now. I just need to go home."

"Okay."

Resignation. Finality.

Brayden turns the lock and pulls on the door. Jenner's hand darts out, pushing it back closed. Frowning heavily, Jenner turns Brayden around to face him and, before Brayden has time to react, surges in to kiss him one more time.

Brayden's lips part to voice a protest but then Jenner is on him, his lips silken and so very soft as they close around his own. It's tender and unhurried. It makes Brayden feel uncomfortably exposed and scared but it also thrills him on a level he doesn't even begin to understand yet. He kisses Jenner back but keeps his eyes closed.

"Please let me see you again," Jenner whispers against his lips.

But already Jenner has taken more than Brayden had in him to give, so Brayden pushes him away, slipping out the door and running down the steps in search of air and escape.

Ruth 'Nana' Clare is woken at just shy of four o'clock in the morning by the sound of someone opening the back door and entering her house. As her bedroom is on the first floor, at the rear of the building, she is easily roused by the faint noises. She pulls on her robe and seeks the source of rustling in the kitchen, staying to the shadows until she sees, for certain, that it is indeed her grandson, home at last after a long night out.

"I knew you'd get here sooner or later," she says, surprising Brayden. He stands by the sink, holding a glass and drinking water from the tap. The lights are all out, so all she can make out is his form in the moonlight.

"Jeez, Nan, you scared me!" He blows out a breath and adds, "Go on back to bed, I just needed a drink."

"You haven't had enough to drink?"

The teasing in her question is borne of curiosity, not accusation. As she flips on the small light over the stove in order to see him more clearly, he squints against the glare and mumbles, "That's not why I was out."

She stares at him, examining him from a few feet away. "Have a seat, child. You look like hell warmed over. I'll make you some breakfast."

"No thanks. I'm just going to head upstairs, I think."

His eyes are bloodshot and he seems sad to her. Trying to puzzle out why, she chances, "It's not drugs, is it?'

"No, Nana. I don't do that stuff. Really, time just got away from me. I was with a, uh, friend from work."

"Well, I'm glad you have a friend," she says softly. "Is everything okay?"

She hovers by one of the kitchen table's chairs, gripping the back of it. Hiding behind his curtain of hair, Brayden shrinks under her scrutiny. It's evident to her that he wants to be out of there, away from her questions, so like his mother, and also his mother's father, that it pains her. So many people that she has cared for and tried, somehow, to help, but they didn't want it, couldn't accept it. She has never understood the reasons why they kept their secrets, pulling away from her, slipping into shadow rather than choosing love and light. She stands her ground and does all she knows how to do — try to reach him, somehow.

"I'm guessing that's a no," she sighs when there is no answer. "What can I do to help? Just tell me. That's what family is for. At least in my opinion, which I know might not count for much."

Brayden's eyes skate around the room, and she tries to follow where they land—Emma's new backpack, sitting by the door and bought for her, recently, by her big cousin; the pantry, overflowing with food from the latest grocery run, also paid for by Brayden's salary from the bar; back to where he'd come from, past the back door and the world beyond.

He asks, "You're glad I'm here?"

That moves her. She steps forward and grabs up his hand, holding it in hers. He tries to inch away and get free of her, but she clasps his fingers and squeezes lightly. "I'm *grateful* you're here. You know that. Don't know what I'd do without such a thoughtful grandson. Now, what's this all about?"

He shakes his head, his face unreadable, like a mask. "I won't let you and Emma down. I promise."

"Good. I'm glad. We both need you here, you know that much, but maybe you need us too. You don't have to keep everything to yourself, sweetheart. I'll gladly listen if you want to talk. And if there's something bothering you, which it seems there is...."

He pulls his hand away. It slips free and he sets his glass by the sink. "I'm gonna jump in the shower and try to get some sleep."

Nodding slightly, she relents, watching him go. He hurries from the kitchen, up the stairs and away.

"You're here."

"So are you."

Max stands frozen in mid-step in the hallway of their house after doing a double-take at seeing Jenner in his bedroom, sitting on his bed and holding his cat, Pussy.

She continues to stare. Jenner doesn't blink, he only waits for her to say something else or leave him alone.

"I've been feeding her for you," Max tries, nodding at his pet.

When there's no response, she adds, "You're welcome."

Stroking the feline idly, Jenner's face is astonishing in its total lack of emotion. It brings him much contentment to watch Max try to puzzle him out and fail in the attempt. Complete control, always. When parts of his life fall into disarray, he reorganizes, strictly, the other areas to make up for it.

"Do we have a problem here? Did I do something to piss you off?"

"Nope. No problem," Jenner says with a quirk of his upper lip, dismissing the idea.

Not buying it but satisfied enough for the moment, Max hardens, concealing her feelings as well and sighs, "Whatever," leaving her housemate to his demons.

Jenner watches her go. Pussy starts to bat at a stray thread hanging from the sleeve of his shirt, rolling onto her back to get a better angle at it. Repositioning her with a glower, Jenner resumes his brooding.

It's been about eight hours since Brayden left the apartment and the passing of each one has only increased Jenner's sense of foreboding. But he has no idea what to do. In the moment, everything had seemed perfect. It was only afterward that Jenner's gloom had settled in, realizing Brayden had been a virgin, glimpsing the possibly dark motivations for Brayden's preference for bondage and submitting, fearing that the next time Jenner sees his new slave it will be to receive his resignation. That'll be it. Brayden will be gone.

You scared him off. It's your fault. You brought it on yourself.

He'd never want to stay with someone like you. He'll quit, vanish, and go searching for someone better. Someone kinder.

Pessimism is a cloud over his head, a defense mechanism. Beyond those negative instincts, Jenner tries to figure out if he's the bad guy in all of this. And, if so, how to set things right. It would be maddening to lose something so incredible, so soon after getting his first, decadent taste.

His phone bleeps in his pocket.

Cursing, he digs it out and answers the call only after registering the number on the ID.

"Yeah," he says, wearily. "Hey, Cal."

Callum Parrish, Jenner's older brother, is their father's son through and through. Callum tells Jenner, abruptly, "Mom's having everyone over for dinner. You should come."

See the way he talks to you? Your own brother? He doesn't care. He hates you, just like everyone else. You're an item on his To Do list. You're the role you fill, nothing else. Why do you even bother? If they knew who you really are, they'd despise you; shun you as a freak, a disgrace to the family. You're not the strong, proud, noble son; you're nothing but a pretty lie.

Logically, he knows it's just a sour mood, but lingering bitterness causes him to respond, "I've been great, actually, thanks for asking. The bar's doing really well and I met a swell girl. It might be love."

"Are you gonna give me a straight answer or should I take the obnoxious sarcasm as a no?"

"You don't want to meet her, then? I think you should. She has a sister. We could both get hitched and put all of Mom's worries about dying without grandchildren to rest."

"I'm sure you've got plenty of illegitimate kids out there, Jenny. Been tellin' the folks that for years."

He almost laughs aloud. With what sounds like genuine curiosity, Jenner says, "Huh. You think so?"

"Are we done? You can avoid us all again and we'll keep talking about you behind your back."

"I'm hurt that you don't miss me enough to try to convince me to change my mind," Jenner says, his voice dripping boredom.

"Sure, I miss you. I could do this all day. If you do change your mind, call the house. It would be non-shitty of you to come, you know."

"Yeah, I know," he sighs. There's some quiet sincerity in the words, enough to make Callum pause before hanging up.

"You aren't in real trouble, are you?"

"No such luck. Trouble might be an improvement."

Pussy's eyes fix on the glowing light of the cell phone. She meows at it.

"Is that a cat? When'd you get a cat?"

"What cat?" He scratches behind her ears. She purrs and nuzzles into the touch. He can almost hear his brother roll his eyes through the phone.

"Okay then. Later, Jenn."

"Yep."

He ends the call and slides the phone back in his pocket.

"Don't look at me like that," he scolds Pussy when she mewls at him, her eyes watchful and fur fluffed wildly. "If he wasn't such an ass I wouldn't have to be such a dick. It's a give and take thing."

She licks his hand, then leaps from his lap, padding silently away from the bed and out of the room. "I don't blame you. I'm not very good company, am I?"

The next few days find Jenner hiding from the memory of his night with Brayden by avoiding the apartment above the bar and retreating back to his primary residence. He barely speaks to Art and Max, though, and acts much more strangely than usual. Any desire to live up to people's expectations of him is gone. He can't bring himself to care about acting like he has it all figured out when bracing for such heartbreaking disappointment. They give him the space he seems to want. When he's out of earshot, Max and Art try to figure out what could be going on with Jenner's recent odd behavior at work and now at home. But he never gives them a clue, just leaves them with vague suspicions that it involves Brayden only because Jenner has been careful not to mention him.

On Tuesday morning, Jenner is in his office at the bar when the phone rings.

"This is Parrish."

"Jenner. Hi. It's me. Um, Brayden."

Stomach dropping to the floor, Jenner tries to play it cool and says, "Hey. What's up? You're calling so I guess that means...."

"I can't make it in today."

Jenner takes the phone away from his ear, pressing it, hard, into his forehead for a moment, before placing it back. Making a valiant effort to control his tone, he says, "I'm sorry to hear that. Is there anything I can do or say to change your mind?"

"I'm not quitting, I just need another day. I'll, uh... I'll be in tomorrow."

"Good. Good, I'm glad."

There's a pause.

"It's gonna be weird, isn't it?"

"No," Jenner scoffs.

"Liar."

Jenner laughs, despite himself. The jagged edge of tension dulls. It's the first time he feels like maybe it'll all work out anyway.

"Like I said, no one has to know," he promises. "And you'll be safe. From me," he clarifies. "Just give me a chance to prove it. I told you about the different protocol levels. This is all part of situational D/s. We could use mainly low protocol for when we're at work. That means it's my job to watch out for you, make sure you're okay and step in if needed to make any adjustments, but it would all be done with an understanding that those around us are unaware of the lifestyle. Privacy is key, but it's about balancing that with addressing your needs. Nothing happens without your consent."

"Jenner...."

There's a hint of torment in the way the name is spoken. Jenner gets chills, racing up his arms, his neck, down his back, and a low pit of heat begins to burn. All he can think of is everything he's experienced of Brayden—the taste of his skin, the sound of his moans, the gripping heat of him around his cock, but most of all his surrender and his trust—and everything he still wants.

"Tomorrow. Come to work."

A command. Unyielding. Demanding.

"Yes, Sir."

"Thank you."

Chapter 11
The Wrong Idea

Max sits with Jenner on the stoop in front of the door to the apartment above the bar smoking a cigarette; the sometime habit they use as their excuse to be outside in the cool, crisp morning air rather than inside cleaning up the smelly, stuffy main room. They pass the cigarette back and forth between them, watching pedestrians mill around on the sidewalks to visit the stores or get coffee and waving to those they recognize.

A florist across the street arrives for work. As she gets out of her car, parked nearby, she smiles their way and sighs, "You two make such a lovely couple!"

Max snorts with stifled laughter.

"Hi, Marla," Jenner replies. With a slight nudge of Max's side he says, loud enough for Marla to hear, "I should be so lucky."

"Damn right," Max murmurs with a glance up at him.

Marla pauses to ask, "Who's that new blond fellow working for you? Is that really Lara Clare's boy? I thought he was over in Africa with the Peace Corps or something."

"Yeah, that's Brayden," Jenner answers. "You'll have to ask him about it. I have no idea."

Max marvels that you can't tell at all from his voice how this type of thing—the casual prying, snooping and implications—royally pisses him off. He really should have gone into acting. It's a tragically wasted talent.

"Huh." Marla unlocks the shop's front door, keys jingling, and tugs it ajar. "Your bar is the last place I'd expect someone like *him* to work. You'd think he'd be over here asking *me* for an application!"

Oh shit, Max thinks. *Bitch, you went one step too far.* Sparing Jenner a sly glance, she sees something tighten like a coiled spring inside him. Gritting his teeth, the muscles in his jaw flexing, she watches him regulate a surge of anger with tempered control. Max rests a hand on Jenner's leg, a silent message to let it go.

With a wave, Marla slips through the doorway, calling. "Well, talk to you later!"

The door shuts behind her. Lights flicker on inside the store. Jenner finally meets Max's gaze.

"This fucking town," he sighs. She passes him the cigarette. He takes a drag, then passes it back. Rubbing his back, proud of his restraint, she knows it has always bothered Jenner more when the seemingly neverending stream of thoughtless, snide comments are made about people he cares about, as if it was commonly thought Jenner privately cares so little about people like Max, and now Brayden, that he would join in with the joke about how pathetic they really are.

And yet, despite his quietness and the fleeting flare of tense anger thanks to Marla, the air of raging bitchiness has mysteriously dispersed from Jenner as quickly as it materialized. He's not hiding in his office or avoiding Max. He's outside, socializing. The typical smart-ass, bring-it-on tone to his voice is curiously absent, but it's definitely an improvement compared to the past few days. He simply sips coffee from a Styrofoam cup, hunching forward around it, his free arm slung around Max's back as they share one another's company.

"Look," Max murmurs, motioning with the burnt-down butt towards the east. Moving through shadows cast by the buildings lining the street is a male figure. Steadily it approaches.

Other than stiffening subtly, Jenner doesn't react. He only takes another sip of coffee. Max places the cigarette's filter between her lips, free of stain or gloss for the moment—she doesn't bother getting dolled up for clean-up duty, no matter how cute her co-workers might be. Jenner's palm slides up and down her upper arm, the friction and radiating body heat from him more than enough to keep her comfortable.

"Morning," Brayden nods, stopping in front of them. There's a bag slung over his shoulder. Max catches Jenner staring at it as he grunts hello.

"Welcome back. Long time no see," Max smiles.

"Aw, you missed me?"

"Never." Blowing smoke out in a thin plume, her smile remains. She drops what's left of the cigarette into a bucket of sand by the door, crushing it out. "I'm just sick of having to cover for your ass, Clare."

Brayden chuckles, his eyes darting quickly to Jenner, then away. Freed of her excuse to be outside, Max stands. Jenner's arm falls away and he stands after a moment's hesitation. Feeling the building tension between her male co-workers, Max wonders if Jenner is pissed off about Brayden's prolonged absence. She breaks the heavy silence, saying, "So, I guess we should go in and get started, huh?"

Glancing again at Jenner, perhaps expecting a reprimand about calling out from a shift without any notice, Brayden says, "Sure." But when she turns and goes inside, he doesn't follow, choosing to wait for Jenner instead.

Jenner clears his throat. "Thanks for coming in."

"No problem."

Neither of them moves. Max squints confusedly at them from the doorway.

Jenner steps up beside Brayden and claps a hand onto Brayden's back. As Max speculates whether Jenner has been acting weird out of fear that Brayden was going to quit, because he finally caught on to Jenner's constant, creepy staring, Jenner says, "Enough slacking off. There's work to do."

"What are we, your slaves?" Max calls back.

Brayden chuckles, but awkwardly, like he doesn't think it's funny at all. They head inside. Behind her Jenner asks Brayden, "Need some coffee?"

"Yeah, coffee'd be awesome."

A moment later, they get to the break room. Brayden unloads his bag, securing it in the locker. Max ties her hair back from her face, still keeping an eye on the boys. Jenner gets out a fresh cup and passes it to Brayden, stepping aside to give him room to get at the coffeepot. Grabbing the bucket of cleaning supplies, Max gives up the guessing game, leaves them and goes to get started on the usual morning detox.

When Max is gone, Jenner locks eyes with Brayden. As soon as he does, he instantly regrets it, because he sees in Brayden barely concealed, amorphous, shifting need behind a sheen of normalcy. If that's all there was, there wouldn't be a problem. The trouble is that there's also terror and helplessness. It makes Jenner want to kiss away all of the confusion, to leave Brayden nothing but breathless and wanting. He's not sure if he should impose some rules for Brayden to play by, or if, should he try to, that would be the one step too far, pushing Brayden over the line and scaring him off again. They need to talk about this. Come to a more formal agreement, but now is not the time, nor the place.

Chest rising and falling, Brayden bears the scrutiny as his gaze shifts lower to Jenner's lips, like he's waiting for that kiss. Reflected in the brightness of his eyes, the terror begins to outpace the need and lust, so Jenner steps back, folding his arms over his chest.

"There's a lot to do. The morning deliveries should be coming any time, so come out when you're done with the coffee. Or bring it with you. Just don't leave it on the edge of a table. Max is liable to knock it with the mop handle or something."

"Sure."

With a nod, Jenner turns to go. He feels the tension break as soon as his back is turned. Right on Jenner's heels, Brayden takes a deep, filling breath, exhaling heavily with a groan.

The day is a busy one, for which Brayden is thankful. Since he's working a split shift along with Max and Jenner, he goes home for some sleep and a meal after tackling the morning clean-up, then returns later in the day. When he gets back to the Pub that evening, it's already filling up fast. Brayden and Jenner man the bar, keeping the drinks flowing, with Jenner making the occasional sprint to the kitchen to check on things there. Apart from an unsettling but small and containable grease fire, there's a reasonable level of excitement to keep things from getting boring. The worst thing for Brayden about bartending at Parrish Pub is the way that people smile at him. Those smiles are always because of one of two things, since everyone in Robertsville sees him through the lens of a decade's worth of local gossip. If the customer is a woman, they might be smiling at him with obvious attraction. He's become an expert at detecting it, the intent there as they compliment him, trying to lure him in when he has no interest in being lured. He can't let them know that, so he has no choice but to play along. It can be exhausting, but it's not as bad as dealing with the other sort of smile.

If the customer's a towny, which ninety-nine percent of them are, then they know about his parents, or think they do. They've heard stories about "that Clare boy". So, they smile at him, knowingly. Those smiles are like a bad coat of paint. You can see right through them.

A few times that night he gets, "You're Lara's boy, aren't you?"

To which he answers as he always does, smiling back, "I guess I am. Can I get you anything?"

The key is to direct the focus back to getting them drinks. No matter what they say, that's what he keeps in mind. Usually, persistent curiosity brings additional questions — which are always worse — like "Whatever happened to her anyway?", "Is it weird to be back here, after what happened to your dad and all?" or "Where've you been all this time? California? San Francisco?"

Then, sometimes, they laugh, like the joke is on him.

The insinuations are a constant, which is why he likes it when it's frantically busy. If he can't stop to listen to the questions because he's got drinks to pour and money to put in the till or orders to take as the crowd roars with a multitude of voices around them, that's the best scenario he can hope for. A sorority descends on the place, packing the bar and as many tables as they can claim. He gets a lot of the first kind of smile from them. Because not all of them are townies, he gets none of the second kind of smile, so he lingers with them. At one point he helps them set up some body shots. They try to get him to do one off of one of the girls, chanting his name and giggling, but, hyperaware of Jenner's presence, he declines persistently. "It'd get me in hot water with the boss," he explains, which isn't really untrue anyway.

By closing, everyone is exhausted. Max locks the door and Brayden folds her petite body up in a platonic hug born out of their shared relief.

"I hope it's slow tomorrow," Max grumbles, her arms wrapped around Brayden's shoulders.

"Bet you got good tips," Brayden tells her, smelling the fruity perfume of her hair.

"Yeah, but my feet are killing me."

"Want a foot rub?"

Max pulls back, looking hopefully up at him. "...Really?"

"Yeah," he shrugs.

"Then hell yes. Count me in."

He chuckles as she grabs his hand, dragging him toward the break room. Letting his guard drop at last, after hours of calculated politeness, he's just glad to be alone with people who won't give him a hard time.

By the time Jenner and Art join them, with Jenner drying his hands on a towel and Art making a beeline to his locker to get his gear and get gone, Max is stretched out on the bench, leaning against the far wall, her feet propped on Brayden's lap as he massages them.

She moans. Art, not stopping or caring to look, digs for a clean shirt. With disinterested playfulness, he says, "What's going on in here?"

"I love Brayden. He's awesome," Max sighs.

"Take your foreplay somewhere else, please."

"It's a goddamn foot rub. Asshole," she frowns, swatting at Art's backside before he moves out of range, having found the shirt he was looking for.

"I'm sure it is. Give 'er hell, Braydy," Art calls back, pumping his fist into the air.

"Will do, man."

"You just gonna stand there and watch or what?" Max asks Jenner, who is lingering in the break room's doorway.

"Oh, am I supposed to join in? How's it go again? I haven't seen this porno in a while. The burly bartender walks in on the slutty waitress and the blond himbo and—?"

"Hey!" Brayden complains. "Who are you callin' a himbo?"

"Oh, I meant it in the best possible way," Jenner grins. "But please, don't let me interrupt. You seem to have a knack for making Maxie moan."

"You know it, baby," Max purrs. Reluctantly, she pulls her feet from Brayden's lap. "Thank you, I totally owe you one. You're my hero. But I'm gettin' the hell out of here before the slave driver thinks of something else for me to do."

"You know, now that you mention it..." Jenner says thoughtfully.

"Nope! No fuckin' way. I'm out," she says. Max grabs her purse, slips on her shoes and bolts from the room. "Later!"

"Bye, Max," Brayden shouts amiably.

"What do you think? Too obvious?" Jenner asks after they hear the front door open and close heavily.

"That you wanted her gone?" Brayden shrugs. "You really don't like it when I flirt with her, do you?"

Now it's Jenner's turn to shrug, his expression unreadable, even as he smiles.

"I'll leave you alone. See you tomorrow." Jenner begins to leave.

"Jenn!"

He pauses, but doesn't turn, keeping his back to Brayden.

Getting up from the bench, Brayden sighs and pushes his hands down into his pants pockets. Then he steps slowly toward Jenner.

"You still staying upstairs?"

"I could be if you want me to."

Brayden takes a steadying breath, nervously pushes a tendril of hair behind an ear and says, while looking at his feet, "Maybe tomorrow, after work, we could go up there and, you know. Talk. Or something."

Jenner pivots, facing him, blue eyes searching. "Tomorrow?"

He starts forward. Brayden flinches away. Frowning at this, Jenner takes two quick steps forward and Brayden almost falls over his feet trying to back away.

"Are you afraid of me?"

"...No. Yes. I don't know."

His back to the lockers, Brayden has nowhere else to go. As an experiment, Jenner keeps walking forward. Brayden inhales sharply and holds the breath, squeezing his eyes shut. He can feel it when Jenner is right there, chest-to-chest with him, looming over him.

"Kiss me," Jenner asks.

"I can't."

"Why? Why can't you? Explain it for me. Or is it that you don't *want* to kiss me?"

"It's not that simple."

"Of course it's that simple."

"It's not for me."

When nothing else is said, Brayden opens his eyes, seeing Jenner taking a long look down Brayden's body. Brayden's hands are out of his pockets now and splayed at his sides on the metal of the locker doors. His jaw is set in a stubborn, proud line.

Restless, frustrated and slightly dejected, Jenner demands, hissing between his teeth, "What do you want from me, huh? Do you want me to fuck off? You said you want to talk, whatever that means, so I'm a little confused here."

"You know what I want."

"Clearly I don't! You're playing some game here and not telling me the rules. Is that what you want? Rules? I told you about some rules that could make this easier on you, but we don't know each other well enough for me to make assumptions about what you're expecting. You made me wonder if I forced myself on you, and ran out of my apartment with hardly a word but now you want to come home with me? What is this? Do you want to be my slave? Do you just want to get off? What? You need to *tell me*. You need to *explain*."

Brayden's brow furrows. His lips stay sealed. Jenner's hand shoots out, and wraps around Brayden's throat. Instantly, both of Brayden's hands come up and take hold of Jenner by the forearm as he tries to pry him off. "Stop," he gasps.

Jenner immediately lets him go. After a long pause, when Brayden says nothing, does nothing, he tries again, but this time he gently brushes Brayden's cheek with the back of his knuckles.

Brayden flinches away, turning from the touch just as ferocious-ly as he had when his throat was grabbed. "*Stop.*"

Heart-rending anxiousness flickers in the quirk of Brayden's lips, the set of his eyebrows, the tenderness hurting more than the violence. And, slowly, Jenner begins to understand.

"If I held you down right now and kissed you, would you kiss me back? Would you call me Master and beg for more?"

Brayden's breathing quickens. Color rises to his neck and cheeks, spreading.

"Do it and find out."

Jenner breathes out a soundless laugh. "Wow. Okay."

"Do it," Brayden nearly growls, egging him on when Jenner backs off. "*Do it.*"

"No, I don't think so."

Eyes opening, aggravated, Brayden wants to scream as Jenner takes another backward step, and Brayden is unable to make him-self bridge the distance between them. "You don't understand!"

"Explain it to me."

Brayden growls. Throwing up his hands he says, "Fuck this."

He opens his locker and grabs his keys but leaves the bag. He walks around Jenner toward the exit. As much as he wants Jenner to grab and hold him, forcing Brayden to submit, he doesn't do it. He doesn't even try. Jenner lets Brayden go, out the back door and into the night, showing him he needs to make his own choices in order to get what he wants.

Chapter 12

The Talk

Twenty-four hours later, Brayden and Jenner are sitting in two fold-ing chairs in the bare living room of the apartment above Parrish Pub. Jenner had brought the chairs from home, knowing that the lack of seating (not counting the bed) could be a problem if he in-tends there to be actual talking instead of "talking".

The day had been strained. Max got her wish and it wasn't busy at all, leaving her plenty of time to wonder at the awkward, strained silence between Brayden and their boss. It had led her to ask Jen-ner, again, for an explanation. Unsurprisingly, Jenner completely avoided her questions.

It all adds to Jenner's stress. Not only does he have Brayden to figure out, but he has to tip-toe around his best friends. And he doesn't want Brayden to know that Max suspects, for fear of push-ing him into quitting. That leaves Jenner to play referee while trying to manage his own feelings about the complicated situation.

Max went home early in the night, but Art waited around to give Jenner a ride back to the house. Jenner didn't know whether or not to take Art up on the offer. Surely, Jenner figured, Brayden had changed his mind after giving Jenner the cold shoulder all god-damned day and would choose to go home rather than prolong their shared torment. But, to Jenner's surprise, Brayden did not tell him to fuck off. Instead, he gave Jenner a peculiar, pointed look as he retreated to the break room, saying within earshot of Art, "I need a minute to get my shit together if you two are taking off. Need me to lock up?"

It was an opening — an opportunity to linger.

Pleasantly amazed, Jenner replied, "No, I'll wait." He turned to Art and told him to go on home without him. Art asked if Jenner was sure, said that it wasn't a problem to hang out for a minute, but Jenner insisted. Now, with Art long gone and possibly commiserating with Max, Jenner wonders if Art is going to join Max in her meddlesome curiosity, concocting god-knows-what theories behind his back.

With a heavy sigh, Jenner slouches forward in his folding chair, the emptiness of the room uncomfortably focusing attention on its limited occupants. He asks, "You want a beer? I can grab a couple from downstairs."

"No, thanks. Serving drunks all day kind of kills my taste for it."

Brayden is sitting back in his folding chair, his arms wound around the sides, his hands gripping the thin back legs like he's trying to convince himself he's shackled to them, or at least this is what Jenner imagines. It makes Jenner wonder if he's been judging Brayden harshly, if he's seeing things clearly or merely reacting to phantoms projected by his own frazzled mind.

Jenner nods, hands laced together, trying to be patient.

"So what did you want to talk about?"

With a somewhat reticent glance, Brayden tries, "Are you still pissed at me?"

"What? No. No, of course I—" Jenner stops, wiping a hand over his face. He couldn't help noticing that Brayden has brought his mysterious bag upstairs with him, the one that had traveled to work yesterday and has been stowed in Brayden's locker downstairs. Now it's sitting over by the wall. Its presence is very distracting.

"You asked me what I want from you," Brayden says, filling the space left by Jenner's abandoned explanation. "I might have an answer. I'm still trying to figure it all out, but I wanted to ask you the same thing. What do you want from *me*, Jenn? Honestly. Is it just about sex? Is it about bossing me around in the bedroom and getting your rocks off on how helpless you can make me?"

Brayden's choice of nickname only amplifies the nature of their relationship, and especially because, for a reason Jenner does not even understand, it doesn't bother him. But if anyone else called him Jenn, it definitely would. What is it about Brayden that makes it all right? Why doesn't it set Jenner on edge to hear the feminine endearment on Brayden's lips? What does it portend for where this is all going?

With a sigh, pushing his musings aside, Jenner admits, "Right now, I just want to understand what happened and what your motives are."

"Why do you care?"

"I don't know. But I do."

"This is about more than keeping me employed at the bar, and getting free access to sex whenever you want it?"

Thinking of David and Shea and what they've been able to have together, Jenner says, "What I want isn't just about sex. I think you know that. You've known that since Manse. I want you to trust me so that we can explore that type of... dynamic. It's not about bossing you around. It's about mutual trust and respect. It won't work otherwise."

"Say it," Brayden prods. "Humor me. Spell it out. Please." It's barely a whisper and Jenner can see his breathing quicken with anticipation.

"Okay. I want to dominate you, to become your Master and have you consent to be my slave. It would be a formal agreement between us, with clearly defined rules for safety, different levels of protocol which would be used at my discretion, determined by your needs and the situation. But, I need your active participation and to feel like you *want* this. You should want to kiss me, without being commanded or expected to do so. You seem unable to give me that. I want to know why. If you don't trust me, or desire me like that, then none of this is going to work."

"It's not you. Or just you. It's who you *are*—the type of person that you are."

"What type of person am I?" Jenner demands, starting to get defensive despite efforts to the contrary. It's clear that Brayden can hear it in his voice. The pushier Jenner gets, the more Brayden shuts down. It only makes it harder for Brayden to voice his thoughts, but Jenner resents the burden of having to be nothing but calm and diplomatic when he's in emotional chaos. Telling himself that he needs to trust, too, Jenner tries to put Brayden's wellbeing before his own.

"You-you're bigger than me. Stronger than me. Faster than me. And you're one of *them*. One of those guys that always had everything they could ever want in high school and weren't afraid to take it. I had *nothing* in high school. I still don't."

"High school? What the hell does this have to do with high school? That was years ago! We didn't even know each other then."

"It has everything to do with it," Brayden says morosely, gripping the chair, avoiding eye contact. "I've been trying to understand what I want, but it gets mixed up in my head sometimes. With Andre there was some separation because he wasn't part of that time in my life. I wasn't 'that poor Clare boy' to him. I was just me. No labels. It was different than it is here. He didn't expect me to act a certain way, it was about getting to know each other on our own terms. But he was also my friend first and that made it harder in a different way. It didn't feel right. Whatever. It doesn't matter. Not anymore. I left him in Florida. Now there's you. I do want you. Maybe I should have recognized it earlier. Like, as in *before* I had sex with you and let you... whatever. Yes, at first I just wanted you to use me. It wasn't personal. I was just hard up, I guess. Looking for something it seemed you could give me."

"But what does this have to do with *high school*?" Jenner demands.

Brayden gives a stony, unblinking stare. "Don't pretend that you don't see it, that you don't hear what they all say about me. I'm not stupid, or blind, and you aren't either, so can we stop acting like it doesn't happen? The customers, the people in this fucking town, they respect you, without a second thought, because you're Jenner Parrish, the quarterback, the golden boy. I'm still just that weird kid with the weird parents. Maybe I haven't moved on as much as I thought I did, okay? That whole span of years was a nightmare. It was awful in every way — my family, school, my utter lack of friends. People talked about me, and what had happened. Called me names. They still do. They do it every day."

Jenner tries not to let on, but his usual success at masking thoughts doesn't seem to manifest, because a faint sneer curls Brayden's lip after he glances Jenner's way.

"You know all about it, don't you?"

Jenner grits his teeth, yells inwardly at himself not to look away, not to even think about it. Brayden gets slowly upset, the pain washing out the fury for a moment as he owns it, accepts the weight of it all.

"They called me a cry baby because I was upset a lot. I was *upset*. My father died in the blink of an eye, when I was already feeling bad about him and my mom splitting up, before I could apologize or say goodbye and if that wasn't enough, I was treated like I had the plague, by the whole fucking *school*. Then they'd talk about my mother, how she'd lost it, how she was crazy. Is it really such a shock that I was a virgin? Huh? Everyone avoided me! Everyone except...."

Jenner waits, but Brayden's eyes lose focus. He falls silent. "Except who? Brayden, except who? What happened? Did someone...." Suspicions and glimpsed truths light Jenner's murky confusion, clearing it away, replacing it with rage. Layers of memory, of supposed friends mocking Brayden, bullying him, echo in his mind. Jenner knows what bullying can lead to when things cross a line, when no one keeps things in check. People get hurt. People like *Brayden* get hurt. "Someone hurt you."

"Are you kidding? My *life* was hurt. *Everything* hurt. It was just more of the same, until it wasn't. I was bullied all of the time. I got used to it. But it... I don't know. This one time, it was different. They thought it was all a joke. Pick on the little guy. You know. Happens in every school, everywhere. It just happened to be me, and it just happened to go too far." He stops, dropping his gaze to his lap.

"Brayden," Jenner coaxes. "Tell me. Now you have to tell me."

"Three guys from the football team," he blurts, speaking in short, stilted sentences. "Got me alone in the locker room. Pulled my shirt up over my head so I couldn't see their faces. Wrestled me to the ground. One held my arms and another sat on my legs. They strung me out like that. The floor was really cold. Anyway, the biggest one, the one in charge... that was John. I recognized the voice. He was saying stuff like, 'Maybe we should make sure he's not just a faggot. Maybe he really is a girl.' Then they pulled my pants and underwear down. He, uh, touched me. For a while. It didn't hurt.

It was pretty much the opposite of hurt. Then they got spooked by a sound, thought it was the janitor and took off. That's it, except it screwed me up. A lot. I kept... I kept wishing they'd do it again."

"John who?"

Brayden breathes out a jaded little laugh. Hair falls in front of his eyes as he bows his head. "Maybe I should have taken you up on that beer."

"*John WHO?!*"

Out of the chair, fists balled up tightly, Jenner seethes.

"It's all right," Brayden tells him, too coolly, with too much resignation. "It's not even about *John*. So what if they touched me and held me down? So what? All it did was help me learn some things about myself. Shit I tried to ignore until Miami... and Andre."

"I will *find them.*"

Brayden gives him a moment, then says, "Now who's stuck in high school? Don't you get it? It wouldn't help. What could you even do? Threaten some guy out of nowhere? Get the cops called on you? Start more people talking? I only told you so that you would know why. Why I can't...." He rubs the heel of his hand into his eye socket and sighs. "I like you, Jenn. You're a good guy. Problem is, I know what you're capable of, and how much I'd let you do. I get off on being taken by force. It's hard for me to accept that enough to willingly put myself in your hands, because if I start to care about you, I'll never get better. Shouldn't I be trying to get better? It's not healthy to want to be made to obey like that, to like hurting just to hurt, to feel, to *belong*. I'll just keep letting you make me do these, these *things,* and I don't know. I don't know anymore."

"Let me help."

"How?"

"I don't know. I'll figure it out."

Brayden shakes his head. "You should be with someone who isn't fucked in the head."

"You're not—" Jenner stops, forcing himself to calm down and try again. "I told you already. I care. I've... I want you. And I want to help. But you have to let me *try.*"

Now, Brayden does laugh, not bitterly but with real amusement. "We sound ridiculous."

"I don't care!" Jenner says, trying not to laugh with Brayden, because he's right. They are ridiculous. Both of them. Completely. "God, I want to hurt them. I want to hurt them for scaring you a-and *touching* you. I'd rip them apart with my bare hands."

Those guys, the ones who hurt Brayden, who scared him in a way that has echoed through years and years, making him question himself like he is — those are the same guys who were Jenner's friends. They could be regulars at the bar. They could have been there that very night, watching Brayden from across the room, smiling to themselves at the memory of terrorizing him back in the high school locker room. It makes Jenner sick. All of it makes him sick.

Jenner knows he looks angry. He's furious. Brayden just stares at him with something like awe, his small, near-constant, easygoing smile playing over his lips. "Wow. I don't think anyone's ever been this upset for me, *ever*. You do give a shit, don't you?"

And, just like that, Jenner is on him. Pulling Brayden up out of the chair, Jenner holds him, but gently. Wrapping Brayden in his arms, Jenner feels Brayden's instinct to fight and escape kick in. Brayden pulls back against the hold and Jenner simply keeps him in the embrace, his parted lips dragging over the silk of Brayden's hair, the rich scent of him intoxicating.

"Let go," Brayden asks, afraid. "Jenner, let go."

"I promise not to hurt you. Stop means stop. Always. No matter what. Do you believe me?"

"I-I don't… yes. Yeah, I believe you."

"Do you trust me?"

Brayden pushes at him and twists, but Jenner keeps holding on.

"Do you *trust me*, Bray?"

Jenner leans back, searching for a glimpse of Brayden's face. He presses a kiss to Brayden's temple, then his cheek, then his mouth. Pale terror is all Jenner can see at first. But then the kiss reaches through that instinct. Brayden starts to kiss him back, very tentatively, feeding off of Jenner's passion.

"No one hurts you anymore. No one. Please, trust me," Jenner whispers over his lips. Their mouths seal together and Brayden drinks in the urged words. Slowly, Jenner starts to let him go, holding Brayden less tightly, but the kiss goes on.

When they break, Jenner sees the realization spark in Brayden's eyes that he trusted without even being aware of deciding to.

"Thank you," Jenner smiles.

Shaken and speechless, Brayden holds on to Jenner, drawing strength and reveling in the freely given, abundant affection. Jenner lets himself care, lets it show, and the more he does, the more Brayden is drawn in. That's the key, Jenner realizes. They both need to conquer their fears, and take what, until now, they've been unable to take.

Chapter 13
In the Moonlight

"What's in the bag?"

In the dead of night, the two men walk down the sidewalks. They're a few blocks from Brayden's house. Jenner offered to walk him home and, after minimal protest, Brayden agreed. The decision really had nothing to do with whether or not Brayden wanted Jenner to accompany him home, but what other people might think. After thinking it over, Brayden concluded that with most of the town asleep, it's probably the safest time for him to be strolling in public with a male lover. Less chance of being caught, and have people witnessing how happy it makes him to have Jenner, in all of his possessive glory, by his side.

Brayden lifts the bag an inch from where it hangs on his shoulder, his thumb hooked underneath the strap. "This? Nothing."

"Liar."

Seeing the smile in Jenner's dark eyes, Brayden fights against a rising blush.

"Oh my god," Jenner chuckles. "It's your overnight bag?"

"Shut up," Brayden scowls, self-consciously. "It's a...you know...towel. Clean clothes. Toothbrush."

"It is your overnight bag!"

"No! It's just in case. Last time I went to your apartment I had to walk home with lube dripping down my inner thighs."

"So you *were* expecting to get laid. Why didn't you tell me sooner, like before we left?" He nudges Brayden's side, smirking. After a moment of hesitation, Jenner reaches out and tucks the curtain of golden brown hair behind Brayden's ear for a less obstructed view of his face. The tenderness in the gentle touch causes a riotous reaction in Brayden and results in an even deeper blush. It thrills and terrifies in equal measure that Jenner is driven to touch him like that, and Brayden's nervous shyness grows. His tongue feels heavy and awkward in his mouth, making speech seem impossible. He starts to focus more on his feet so that he doesn't trip and fall on his face.

"That explains the towel and clothes," Jenner continues. "What about the toothbrush?"

"Um, so my breath doesn't reek?"

"Trying to impress me. I like it. Or is it in case I tell you to suck me off and you have to go home to Nana with cock breath?"

"Holy shit, I can't believe you just said that."

Jenner chuckles wickedly. "Avoiding the question. I think that means yes."

"It does *not* mean yes," Brayden says, not meeting Jenner's eyes.

"So it means no?"

Silence descends, filled by crickets and the soft footfalls of their steps on the concrete.

"Whatever," Brayden mumbles.

"Well, next time you come over, I think I'll have to make sure you have a reason to use that toothbrush."

"You're ridiculous."

"*You're* ridiculous," Jenner counters. "How do you even still have a tan? It's been months. Do you really go to a tanning salon?"

"If I was still in Florida, I wouldn't have to," Brayden says in his own defense. "I could just lie out naked on my balcony like I used to."

Feeling the full force of Jenner's stare, Brayden pulls him out of the way just as Jenner almost walks right into a telephone pole. With a belly laugh, Brayden watches Jenner try to keep a closer eye on where he's going. His dark, lust-filled eyes flick to the side every few seconds to watch for more poles.

Jenner finally retorts, "If you were still in Florida, you'd still be a virgin."

"A tan, warm virgin."

"Seems you've taken care of the tan thing. I can take care of the warm virgin thing."

"Apparently."

They walk a little further without more conversation. When Brayden chances a glance at his companion, he sees Jenner's far-away look and chuckles.

"What?"

Brayden grins, "I can tell what you're thinking."

"No, you can't."

"Yes, I can. You're wondering if I really did lay out naked on my balcony."

"Well, you just don't strike me as the exhibitionist type. What if your neighbors were watching?"

Brayden shrugs. "So what? I have a nice ass."

"Oh, I know," Jenner assures him. "Eh, I guess with that ridiculously small bathing suit of yours I could see you just going nude. Doesn't really hide anything anyway."

Immediately, Brayden comes to an abrupt halt, also stopping Jenner with a hand to his chest. They're only two blocks away now. "Whoa, whoa. What? How do you know what my bathing suit looks like?"

Now it's Jenner's turn to be shy. Cursing under his breath, he hides behind a hand with which he rubs his brow and admits, "Maybe I saw you at the Y. Swimming."

Mouth open with shock, Brayden asks, "When? I haven't been back there since...."

"Before you started work at the bar," Jenner says reluctantly.

Processing this slowly, Brayden doesn't move to continue home. Jenner folds his arms and waits as he's stared at.

"And you were *watching me*? You knew who I was before I asked for the job?"

"No, not really. Maybe a little."

"Jenner!"

"What? You're hot! Of course I looked."

"You're incredible."

"Thanks."

"That was sarcasm. Did you only hire me because you thought I had a nice ass?"

Jenner takes a minute to think about this one. His delay only causes Brayden to suspect the worst.

"Holy shit!"

"Okay, that *may* have been part of it," Jenner allows, "but I was really swayed when you asked me so nicely for the job and told me how much you needed the work."

"And then you made the move on me at Manse," Brayden says, putting it together.

"I had no idea you were queer before that night. I swear to god."

"Would you ever have told me that it was you if I hadn't seen the tattoo and figured it out on my own?"

"Does it even matter? You did see it. It happened. I'm glad."

"Yeah, because you got some."

"You know," Jenner says, very intentionally derailing the line of questioning. "You never told me what you want. *I* have been quite clear, I think, but *you* on the other hand...."

Brayden turns and keeps walking, quickly. Jenner jogs to catch up.

"Well?" Jenner presses. "Will you be bringing the bag tomorrow night? Should I get a bigger bed? Or maybe a St. Andrews cross and selection of floggers?"

After licking his lips wet, Brayden swallows, eyes fixed on his rapidly approaching home.

"Let's wait and see, shall we? I'd hate to spoil the surprise."

Jenner steps in front of him, cutting him off. "Tell me what you want."

Amazed as ever at how much Jenner makes him feel like a dwarf, since he's eye level with Jenner's throat when they are facing one another, Brayden hesitates. Then he answers, but it's too quiet to hear. Jenner prods him to repeat it.

"I want to trust you," Brayden says, a little more loudly. "I want to belong somewhere. I want to be wanted, and not just for sex. I want to be wanted completely and belong... to you."

Hooking a finger under his chin, Jenner tilts Brayden's head up so that he can look into his eyes.

"Will you submit to me? Will you agree to be my slave? As your

Master it would be my absolute responsibility to take care of you, in every way. Not just when it comes to sex. Taking care of you in every sense of the word would be the focus of all of my efforts. Whatever you need—pleasure, pain, comfort, support—I would give it to you. All you would be asked to do in return is obey me, and trust me, *implicitly*. You would never be made to do anything you didn't want to do. Stop always means stop. You would belong with me. You would be mine." When Brayden's eyes slip closed, Jenner adds, "Look at me, Bray."

Warily, devoid of all the lighthearted humor that has filled their walk, Brayden gives him a miniscule nod.

"No, say it. You have to say it."

"Yes, I'll submit to you. I'll be yours. Your slave. Happy?"

"Not until you are, too."

Brayden tries to turn away from him, so Jenner acts, bearing down, catching his lips in a soft kiss, holding his jaw to keep him there. Jenner takes the kiss a little deeper, a little harder. The hand on his jaw slides to cradle the back of Brayden's head, the fingers splaying in his hair, keeping him still. Jenner hungrily licks back over Brayden's tongue. His other hand, Jenner clasps to Brayden's lower back, the arm wound tightly around as he easily pulls their bodies flush together from hip to chest. Tangled up in Jenner's arms, Brayden opens wider to the kiss, his lips softening, kissing Jenner back and surrendering.

Only when there's no fight or stiffness left in Brayden's posture does the kiss end and Jenner release him.

"People could be watching," Brayden murmurs, folding his arms self-consciously. His lips are throbbing slightly and the taste of Jenner is on his tongue.

"People can kiss my ass. And it's the middle of the night."

"I thought you valued privacy and discretion."

"I do. I value you more."

Brayden can't help but smile, his spirits soaring with excitement for everything Jenner has promised, outpacing any trepidation that might try to drag him back down. When he bites his lower lip to try and hide his gladness, Jenner's thumb brushes beside where his teeth dent the skin.

"Don't. That's one of my rules, too. No holding back. When it's just you and me, I demand honesty. Always."

Letting his lip slip free of the bite, Brayden is rewarded with another soft, quick kiss, and a murmured, "Better," from his new, smiling Master. "Much better."

They're in eyesight of Brayden's home and quickly reach it. With butterflies in his unsettled stomach, Brayden doesn't know how to say goodbye. Hands in his pockets, shuffling his feet, head bowed, he says, "I don't know if I'm ready for this. It's just a lot to wrap my head around."

"We can take it slow. We'll go at your pace. No pressure. And this isn't just a hobby for me. It's a lifestyle and I take it seriously. I've been trained on how to do this," Jenner tells him softly. "For years, I studied and apprenticed with an expert. The owner of Manse, David, well, you could say I've been a pet project of his. He taught me how to be a Master, the techniques, and the trust. All I've ever needed is the right person to be my counterpart, my slave. I've been searching for you, waiting for you, Bray, for a long time. All I'm asking for is a chance to prove myself, and that no matter how we may have found each other, or who we used to be, that you're safe with me and that this can be amazingly rewarding for both of us. I'll take care of you. I'll take care of everything."

Brayden glances up at Jenner, remembering how confident he had been at Manse, how comfortable he had looked wielding that leash and wearing his hood, navigating the mansion and crowd with ease. No wonder he looked like he belonged there. Brayden imagines that's the same way Jenner walked the halls back at school, like they were his halls, his rules, his people. Jenner belonged there, too, in ways Brayden never did. It's both terrifying and thrilling to have this chance to become part of Jenner's world of belonging. It seems too good to be true.

"Okay," Brayden says. "I'm yours." Starlight reflects in Brayden's eyes and, unbeknownst to either of them, part of Jenner's heart is given away forever.

"Thanks for the company," he tells Jenner, shyly. "Walking me home and all." Brayden looks to the house, remembering how his grandmother was so easily roused the other night. He prays that

Jenner doesn't kiss him again, lest she be watching.

"My pleasure. Go get some sleep."

"Yes, Sir," Brayden says with a crooked smile. "See you at work?"

"Yep. Don't forget your bag."

Once Jenner rounds the bend in the road and disappears from sight, Brayden finally turns, ready to head inside. Shared secrets and promises buzz around his head. Already he feels different. Though his life may have just taken a wild, unexpected turn, he knows at the very least, it will be one hell of a ride.

Chapter 14
Crash

Outside, heavy rain falls in sheets. It pounds against the earth, the house, and the plastic roof of Brayden's Jeep. Though it's morning, barely any daylight is visible. The clouds and relentless rain have washed it all away.

Thunder crashes loudly. Brayden glances up at the ceiling, listening to the pattering on the roof. He's glad that there are still a few hours until he has to go out in this dismal weather and walk to work. He would be soaked to the bone if he went now.

As soon as the thought of driving to work instead occurs to him, he banishes it. The walk is something he needs — that few minutes of space to distance the facets of his life, shedding the persona of the dutiful grandson and cousin with each step, the closer he gets to the bar and Jenner. It's a ritual preserved from his adolescence, when he chose to walk to school rather than ride in the bus. Then it was the many ways his father was absent that led Brayden to seek quiet and a reprieve from the whispers and secretive, judgmental glances of his peers. He was the boy whose mother ran from his father before the cancer made it worse, the way cancer makes everything worse. No matter how old he is, the comforts he needs seem to remain the same. Even a monsoon can't dampen that.

Sitting up on his bed, he folds his legs and grabs his phone from the nightstand. Through the wall to his left, in Emma's room, the radio is playing. The volume has been turned up loud enough to drown out some of the storm and, therefore, reverberates through the rest of the second floor of the house. Blanketed in all of the noise, Brayden feels safe — hidden.

In his mind, he forms the image of a person — someone he loves, someone he misses and likely will not see again for a very long time. Aware that it's the coward's way, that he could dial the phone and actually speak to them instead, he doesn't. Instead he begins to speak to this person as if they could already hear him, pretending to confess his biggest secret.

"I guess you know that I've been lonely. How could I not be?"

He keeps his voice lowered, lest Emma hear him during a lull in the radio station's airplay.

Brayden continues, "I met someone. Someone who cares about me. I imagine introducing him to you. It plays out in my mind and it goes a different way each time. You like him. You hate him. You hate me for being with him. And it's not what you think. I've given him a part of myself that no one else has ever had. He's my lover. He makes me happy. But no one knows. No one. And I just want to *tell you*. I wish I could tell you. Maybe someday."

Thumb skating over the tiny, slick screen cradled in his hand, Brayden wishes he was brave enough to make that call. But since he isn't, where hope and acceptance should grow in his heart, a dull pit of ache hardens instead and becomes heavy, weighing him down into that old loneliness again, despite Jenner and everything he has given Brayden.

Sometimes it's just not enough in the face of all the lies.

"I wish you could accept me for who I am, and be here to tell me that it's okay. That *I'll* be okay."

Of its own accord, without deciding to, his thumb awakens the gadget, bringing it to life in his hand. It glows brightly in the dim room. In his contact list, he finds the person he's been envisioning. The picture glows out at him, the expression happy, tempting.

He does it before he can second-guess the decision, and types out a message:

I miss you. I wish you were here.

Then he clicks send and lets out a held breath. He imagines the message floating out into the storm, over rivers, lakes and miles and miles. It travels to its recipient in his stead. Brayden feels safe in the knowledge that he couldn't call it back even if he wanted to.

The sky shines. The world below it is covered in amorphous mirrors. Puddles like glass multiply the available sunlight, making the world new.

Brayden lies on his bed. His pants are unzipped. His right hand is pushed down inside the front of them, hooked around the root of his flesh.

Thinking of Jenner, whom he'll see in minutes, once Brayden finally leaves to start his shift, he fantasizes about what the night will bring, especially after everyone else leaves and it's just him and the one person capable of taking anything from him. Jenner has so much power over Brayden, it makes his head spin and his cock hard. Jenner makes someone forever forsaken, unwanted, and abandoned feel crucially needed and absolutely possessed. More than anything, Brayden wants to beat off thinking of Jenner — his body, his mouth, the irresistibly dominant force in him — and imagine Jenner sucking or fucking him.

But the house is quiet. The rain has stopped. The radio is silent. Anyone could be listening.

In that moment, Brayden hates his life, that he's living in this little house with people he can't be honest with nor have privacy from.

He wills his erection away, even as his libido betrays him. Pulling his hand out of his pants and away from his stiffened flesh, he stretches the arm up over his head instead and grabs onto the mattress' top edge, reveling in the torment of denial. Slowly, he begins to convince himself that Jenner has tied him to the bed like that, strung him out to endure the sensations. Wanting that so much he can taste it, Brayden is wracked by a shudder of need. His skin flushes hot, tingling with pure want.

A young girl's laughter shatters the fantasy like glass.

"Dammit," Brayden groans, sitting up.

Emma's voice carries through the wall as she breaks into a song. It's the dash of cold water that he needed.

Struggling to his feet, pulling himself together, he feels nothing but trapped in his life, desperate to get free.

After a long, miserable morning doing errands and driving around in his truck in the pouring rain, Jenner pulls into the driveway of the house he shares with Max and Art. He parks and grabs the shopping bags from the passenger seat.

It's only when he opens the car door and sees the Audi parked on the street out front that he realizes he has company awaiting him.

Time to play your part. Places, everyone! Places! Better know those lines because the show must go on.

Dread creeps into him, turning his stomach, twisting it up. He tries to ignore the reaction and walks to the front door.

This is who they need you to be. Get over yourself and humor them. It won't kill you.

As soon as he's inside he hears, "Well, it's about time."

"Cal," Jenner sighs. His brother, Callum Parrish, steps up to him. Callum has been waiting in the living room. There's no sign of Art or Max. "What are you doing here?"

"You blew off dinner last week. You're acting like a child, and it's unacceptable." Dressed in a carefully pressed, light blue button-down shirt and designer, tailored grey pants, Callum walks up to Jenner, cocky as can be, smiling at his younger brother's discomfort. "Family is the most important thing. Where would you be without your family? I'll tell you — you'd be a friggin' bum. A jobless, pathetic bum. So how about you show a little respect to your mother and make an appearance this Sunday, huh?"

Biting back his initial retort, trying to master his temper, Jenner twists his hand in the handles of the plastic bags. They begin to cut into him and he welcomes the pleasantly distracting, small pain. "Sunday is my only guaranteed night off. I have other plans."

"Plans?" Callum scoffs, folding his arms over his chest.

He's a few years older but a few inches shorter than Jenner. Callum inherited the brains; Jenner got the looks and charm. With a master's degree in finance, Callum pulls in six figures at his job at an international pharmaceutical company. He'd passed on the family inheritance, choosing to follow his own path rather than devote his life to a small town bar.

That choice paid off. It has brought Callum success. The lucky recipient of Callum's hand-me-downs, Jenner feels his older brother acts superior to him. Callum enjoys showing off his wonderful life to his comparably pathetic sibling, so Jenner doesn't try to get close and build a relationship there. No matter how often Callum shows up or calls, as if on some level he is reaching out to Jenner, trying to rein him in as even Jenner pulls away, Jenner denies him. He keeps that wall firmly erected lest Callum find out some of his younger brother's weaknesses to use as ammunition against him.

"Who do you have plans with? What, do you have a hot date?"

"Yes," Jenner deadpans. "I have a date."

"What's her name?"

Jenner doesn't respond; he gives his brother a level stare. In theory, he could go to the family dinner, but he would much rather keep the night open to possibly and preferably spend with Brayden instead.

"Okay, what's she look like, then?"

"Blond and tan," Jenner says, letting on that much, allowing his brother to draw his own conclusions. And really, it's not a *total* lie. Some of the honesty in the reply must show in Jenner's face, because Callum bites — hook, line and sinker.

"Oh yeah?" Callum says with an eager smile. "A blonde, eh? Nice. You could always bring her, you know."

"Not likely. Was that all, or — ?"

"Yeah. That was all. But if you don't show your face at home next week either, you'll be hearing from me again."

"Lovely."

Jenner ushers his brother out, quickly closing and locking the door behind him. Eyes closing with weariness, he stands there a moment longer with his back to the house, unaware of Art lingering a few feet away in the doorway to the kitchen, having heard the whole exchange.

"So, you're dating Brayden? That's the only tan blond you know."

"Fuck!" Jenner spins, turning to face Art, going suddenly pale with his alarm. "That... you...."

"It's fine, Parrish," Art soothes, hands raised to show he means no harm.

"I'm *not* dating...."

"Brayden," Art finishes. Jenner is so flustered, it's clearly a lie.

"Yes. No! It's... I was just telling Cal what he wanted to hear."

"Then why do you look freaked out?"

"I'm not freaked out," Jenner argues, his eyes too wide, his stance too tense.

"Dude, I'm not judging. I'd just like you to be honest with us. We're your friends and you've been acting like—"

"I'm not dating Brayden."

"So you're just fucking him?"

The casual, crude implication at Brayden's expense hurts, the question like a calculated punch from a blindspot. Jenner is absolutely sick of it—the jumping to conclusions, the labels and thoughtless ways that people get put down just because it's easier to assume than to ask for truth. It doesn't matter that it's Art, not when he sounds like all of the guys Jenner has had to tiptoe around for most of his life, just to get by, guys who still make jokes at the expense of others. To them, all Max is is a slutty piece of trash. Jenner's just a meathead. Brayden's just a spineless weakling from a family of screw-ups. Who are they to judge? Do they really have their own life so figured out? Rage blazes so suddenly and so hot in Jenner that Art recoils slightly, knowing he's gone too far. Jenner crosses the distance between them—a good ten feet—in the blink of an eye. When he's nose to nose with Art, seething, Jenner spits, "*You don't talk about him like that.* Do you understand?"

"Y-yeah, man," Art says quietly, stammering just a little.

"You don't talk about him *at all*."

Jenner is strung so tight, it's clear he's just barely keeping it in check, and for no reason but the sake of their friendship. If it was anyone else, other than Art, they'd already be incurring Jenner's accumulated wrath over his frustrations with the town, with Callum and the comment about Brayden.

It draws out another long moment in perfect, absolute silence. Art doesn't even breathe.

Then, Jenner seems to realize what he has already implied

through his reactions. Pivoting on a heel, he leaves Art behind and retreats upstairs.

"Parrish, wait!" Art calls after him. "We should talk about this! Parrish!"

Just a few moments later, there's a light knock at Jenner's door. From out in the hall, Art says, "Hey, I have Puss. Your cat. The one you won't talk about. She looks thirsty and her bowl is in there, so…."

Opening the door a few inches, just far enough to grab his cat from Art's hold, Jenner appears, stone-faced, to reclaim his pet. He tucks her in the crook of his arm, where she instantly curls happily. Her laughably disheveled white fur is a perfect counterpoint to Jenner's fuming, dark seriousness.

Before Jenner can literally shut him out again, Art says, "Look, I'm sorry. No offense intended. I mean it."

Jenner holds his ground, not backing down but also not closing the door, yet.

"I mean, this is a good thing, right? Max and I have been wondering what's up with you and this explains it. You don't need to hide from us, man. We're not gonna be assholes about it."

Slowly, Jenner softens as concern for Brayden outpaces everything else. When Art encounters Brayden at work, there could be fallout if Art was to let on what he now suspects.

With some apprehension, Jenner asks, "Don't say anything to him. I promised I wouldn't say anything to you or Max. No one's supposed to know."

"No problem," Art assures him. "I won't say anything."

"And don't treat him differently."

"How long has this been going on?"

"Not long. Long enough."

Art stares at Pussy, cradled so gently and carefully in Jenner's arm. Idly, he scratches under her chin, making her purr.

"So, it's serious? Between you and…?" Art leaves it hanging rather than say the name. "I've just never seen you act this way before over a guy. I didn't even know he was *gay*."

"We're done talking about it, okay? Let it go."

"Sure. Sure, man."

"Thank you."

Only a few hours later, they're both at work, along with the person causing all of the commotion.

When he knows Brayden or Jenner are least likely to notice, Art slyly observes them together. He's a little fascinated at the notion of Jenner being so devoted to someone like Brayden, who didn't even register for Jenner in high school, even with all of the talk of Jenner's little obsession with the guy.

They thought it would always be unrequited. Brayden is a private, yet friendly and smiley person who spends much of his shift flirting with female patrons right under Jenner's nose. It makes the concept of the two men being involved with each other seem near impossible for Art to comprehend.

But, the longer Art watches, the more he picks up the subtle things, like how Jenner is always aware of what Brayden is doing, and is right there to offer help if any seems to be needed. On any other day, Art would just chalk it up to Jenner being a good boss. Now, he suspects there's more behind it. If Brayden gets little more than a fleeting glance when he's turning on the charm for a woman ordering a drink from him, maybe, Art suspects, it's because Jenner knows nothing would ever come of it—that it's all an act. But it also makes Art wonder what else Brayden has been lying about, if he's managed to keep his homosexuality under wraps so well and for so long. It's quite a feat to sleep with your boss under everyone's noses, with no one suspecting a thing.

From the shadows of the hall between the kitchen and the main room, Art sees Jenner pass behind Brayden, putting a hand on his shoulder to warn of his presence. Brayden shoots Jenner a smile from over his shoulder and, just for a second, Art can see it—the connection between them. It's there, then it's gone.

Max weaves her way between tables and clumps of people, tray in hand. Unsure whether to tell her what he knows, Art holds his tongue and resolves to keep it to himself a little longer. It's what Jenner would want.

At the end of the shift, Art is unsurprised when Brayden lingers in the break room long after everyone else has gone home. Retrieving his things from his locker, Art only has to take one look at Jenner's face to know he's being dismissed.

"Catch you later, then?"

"Yeah," Jenner nods. "Thanks for staying to clean up. I'll walk home."

"Cool. Later Brayd," Art waves. "Take it easy." "Thanks," Brayden smiles. "You too."

Hesitating just a moment longer, watching big, bullheaded Jenner and the much smaller Brayden with some unease, Art overcomes the urge to say something he shouldn't. While hoping he doesn't regret it later, he leaves them alone and goes.

Once Art has left, Jenner seems to savor the silence of their long-awaited privacy. Brayden watches him take a deep breath, exhaling heavily and letting go of hours of built-up tension. The shift hadn't been too bad. There was one incident as he was collecting money from a pair of guys he vaguely recognized, but whose names he couldn't recall. They were about his age, maybe a year or two older. As Brayden took the cash for their beers, he could have sworn the guy muttered "faggot" under his breath, especially because of the way he was smiling when Brayden glanced up at his face. Maybe it was his imagination. Paranoia. He didn't say anything to them, or Jenner, and he doesn't intend to. It's not the first time it's happened and it won't be the last. Sometimes it's best to just let it go.

It did set him on edge, though, bracing for more, for worse, unable to relax for the rest of the night.

Taking another deep breath, blowing out the stress, he sees some of the defensive harshness begin to leave Jenner's expression now that he, too, can just be himself again. Brayden doesn't know exactly what he wants; just that he has to get out of the bar and he can't go home to Nana. Not yet.

"Grab your bag. We're going upstairs," Jenner says in a voice suddenly lust-roughened and impatient.

"Sure," Brayden acquiesces. Glad, tired and nervous at the same time, his stomach flips.

For Brayden, being in Jenner's presence has become like being in the presence of a loaded gun with the safety off. It sets him on edge in different ways than their patrons do and it's exhausting to endure for long periods of time. Longing to let his guard down, to crawl into bed and sleep, he has just enough leftover curiosity and sexual energy from his afternoon fantasy to get him to go upstairs with Jenner when beckoned.

Their new arrangement of being Master and slave doesn't feel real yet, and he doesn't quite know what to expect or what will be expected of him, if anything. Beginnings are difficult with most things in life, though, as Brayden knows well. He has always been able to adapt with every shift, every change or loss. This is just one more thing to get used to, but with Jenner, the possible rewards are greater than anything Brayden has been offered before.

Moving like he is in a trance, Brayden leaves the bar. They make the slow climb upstairs to the apartment above. He sets his duffel bag down and waits as Jenner rifles through his own black bag that was waiting on the kitchen counter when they walked in. From it, Jenner pulls a bottle of scotch and two shot glasses. After filling them both, he brings the glasses over to Brayden and hands him one.

"You came prepared," Brayden jokes to ease his own jangling nerves.

"You have no idea," Jenner smiles, and in such a way that it affects his companion on a gut-deep level. Lifting his glass in a toast, Jenner clinks the edge with Brayden's, saying, "Cheers."

"What are we drinking to?"

"You. Tonight."

"Mm, cryptic."

"Not necessarily. I think you know exactly what I mean. Unless you're too tired and would prefer to rest?"

Brayden responds by throwing back his shot, wincing only a little at the burn as it slides down his throat. With a sly, amused gleam in his dark eyes, Jenner drinks his shot as well, then takes the glasses away to the sink.

Jenner returns to Brayden's side, standing before him and running his hands over Brayden's arms; down, then up to his shoulders. For a moment, Jenner's hand wraps the side of Brayden's neck then shifts farther to cup the back of his head, tangling in his hair before sliding down again. The touches rub new life into Brayden's weary body. The unvarnished truth is that they're there for one reason, and they both know it.

Easily reading the building resistance in Brayden's posture, in the bunching of muscle under his hands, Jenner says to him, "You have a decision to make. Three options: we can finish off that bottle and talk; you can kiss me, right now; or, you can get down on your knees, eyes lowered, and ready to obey."

Brayden lets out an uneasy chuckle that dies off quickly. He closes his eyes to block out the overwhelming sight of Jenner's hunger.

There is no internal debate. There's only one answer, really.

Grateful for the scotch, Brayden gives in to his tiredness — from fighting what he wants, from hiding who he is, from working so hard with little reward.

He falls to his knees. His fingers interlock behind his back, for his own comfort and no other reason.

"Who am I?" Jenner asks.

"Master," Brayden answers, his head bowed.

Immediately, Jenner caresses the side of Brayden's face, praising him with a reverent, "Good. I'll take care of you. I'll take such good care of you...."

Chapter 15

Held Fast

Brayden has no clear awareness of crawling to the bed, led by Jenner, or of climbing up onto it. There are explicit commands, which he follows without much consideration. Jenner reminds him of what is expected — respect, absolute obedience, total submission. The span of long minutes is a wash of white, blazing anxiety that bleaches all thought and sensory input of meaning or sense. What keeps him going — the only thing — is the soft jangle of metal and scuff of leather from the cuffs in Jenner's hand and the promise of Brayden's imagined reward. He wants the cuffs desperately enough to follow all of the rules, whatever they may be.

Gradually, as Brayden lies down on the mattress, he starts to pay attention to the details. The hug of the leather can be felt around his left ankle, then his right as they are each bound and chained to the bed's frame by Jenner. Once his movement is restricted, Brayden's heartbeat resumes a more normal pace, allowing the pulsing of blood under his skin to calm and dull its roar.

He's manhandled slightly as his shirt is removed, leaving him bare-chested. With that done, Brayden actually sighs in relief as his left arm is guided up towards the headboard. Anticipating the strong grip of leather like he enjoys from the ankle cuffs, he is surprised into opening his eyes as he instead feels soft fabric being wound around his wrist. When Jenner takes Brayden's right arm as well and begins to affix the supple tie to that also, the pleading question in Brayden's eyes becomes too stark for Jenner to ignore.

"It'll be more comfortable," Jenner explains.

"Fuck comfortable!"

"Trust me," he urges, adding in a snarkier tone, "I'm able to tie a knot, you know."

"But I can slip these."

"Mm," Jenner grunts, continuing his work without further comment.

"Jenner," Brayden says in annoyed complaint.

"No. Until I say the scene is finished, you are under high protocol. You will address me as Sir or Master, only. Are we clear?"

"Fuck."

"That's not an answer, slave," Jenner warns.

With a harsh exhale, apprehension clawing at him, making him writhe, Brayden murmurs tightly, "Sorry... Sir."

"Breathe. Stop means stop. I've got you."

With a tug and a snap, the length of black, butter-smooth cloth is snugly knotted, wrapping both of Brayden's wrists, pulled now above his head. The tie is looped around a rung of the headboard.

"Okay, try to get out. Go on."

Brayden yanks at his arms, the muscles bunching.

"It's stronger than it feels," Jenner tells him with a smirk when Brayden is unable to get loose. "And easier to untie if you don't behave."

"You wouldn't," Brayden frowns, quieting his struggles.

"Sure I would. Try me. Call me Jenner one more time and see what happens."

For the first time, Brayden realizes that Jenner has slipped the jeans off of him at some point before the ankle cuffs were attached, leaving him bound in only his boxer shorts. Quickly he becomes self-conscious.

Graceful and fluid as a cat, Jenner mounts Brayden, straddling him where he's bound to the bed. Jenner's knees are braced beside his captive's hips, his hands planted by Brayden's armpits.

"Shit," Brayden hisses, closing his eyes as his nerves get the best of him once more.

"Are you gonna behave for me, slave?"

Jenner dips his hips, thrusting deliberately in a slow drag against Brayden's crotch.

Brayden grunts, his mouth working in a struggle to form a

sensible answer. He snaps his mouth shut to muffle the sound as it twists and deepens before managing a moment later, "W-what are you doing?"

"That's not an answer." Jenner *tsks*, applying a soft kiss to the line of Brayden's jaw. Finding his captive's left nipple, Jenner pinches it and tugs. "Maybe I should untie you if you can't follow simple direction."

"No!"

"No what?" Jenner sucks another kiss by the edge of Brayden's lips and continues to rut in a slow rhythm directly against Brayden's barely covered, swelling cock. The unhurried pace is just enough to tease, not enough to give relief, but gets Brayden fully hard fast. Plus, the intensely hot sight of Jenner undulating and dry-humping his crotch, on top of the soft kisses and nipple play takes Brayden right apart. He tries to keep his mouth shut to hold in his moans, but knows his torment shows plainly on his face in the quirk of his lips, the tilt of his eyebrows and furrows in his brow.

"No, uh, Sir."

"Are you going to behave for me, slave?" Jenner asks again.

"Yes, Sir."

"Good," Jenner smiles, pleased. With his left hand, Jenner reaches up to cover Brayden's eyes and slinks lower to take the nipple he's been playing with between his teeth instead of his fingertips.

Brayden's lips soften around an unvoiced moan as Jenner's hand masks his vision. The moan wrenches free when warm, silken lips, then the points of teeth bear down on the sensitive nub. Jenner kisses the stiffened, dark circle of Brayden's nipple, flicking it with the tip of his tongue. Then he bites down on it and Brayden instantly thrusts up against him.

After a moment, Jenner pulls his lips away from Brayden's nipple in order to ask, "Shall I bind you further?"

"Yes. Yes, please. Sir," he adds as an afterthought.

It doesn't take long before Brayden has a cord strung across the breadth of his chest, above his nipples but under his raised arms. When a blindfold is added, too, Brayden relaxes more than ever. Every muscle in his body unclenches, all care wipes from his mind. He just breathes, savoring the bite of the cord and fabric and leather into his flesh, keeping him in place.

"Good?"

"Really good," Brayden agrees.

Though he doesn't tell Jenner, the position is part of Brayden's profound pleasure. Lying on his back as he is, it would make it difficult for Jenner to penetrate him. With that off the table, at least for now, Brayden knows that whatever happens, it'll be something he can handle.

Stretching, testing his limits, Brayden surrenders, safe in the dark, shackled and tied, kept and tamed. Jenner stops touching Brayden, but he's still right there. As time stretches out, Brayden realizes that Jenner must be observing him. His gnawing self-consciousness grows, but it only adds to the enjoyment. Testing the ankle cuffs, Brayden tries to close his legs, but can't. He's hard and embarrassed by it. As he wonders if Jenner is looking, and *where* Jenner is looking, Brayden's dick jumps, straining against his boxers.

Then, feeling warmth, his senses sharpen. Detecting a nearby presence, he anticipates, then feels Jenner's touch. It drags up the inside of his right thigh. It skitters over the bottom hem of the boxers and drags feather-light over his testicles. It traces more deliberately the line of his shaft, the shape of the crown. Inhaling through his nose, Brayden holds the breath, waiting.

He doesn't have to wait long. What Brayden assumes must be the velvety softness of Jenner's lips dragging open-mouthed kisses up the center of his abdomen to his chest, makes him suck in his stomach reflexively. Mouthing over Brayden's pecs, Jenner finds his nipple again, teasing it alternately with his tongue and teeth — pleasure and pain. Brayden responds to both, arching into the pain, shuddering with the pleasure. Jenner rewards him by plucking a small clip from his pocket, pinching the clip's end to open its jaws wide, and closing them around the stiffened nub of flesh.

A small, almost unnoticeable smile turns up the ends of Brayden's lips. He twists slightly as Jenner moves to the other nipple, his hand simultaneously skating down Brayden's pelvis to close over his cock through the boxers.

"Dirty boy," Jenner grins. Brayden bites at his bottom lip, his back arching when the second clip snaps shut. He tries to thrust against Jenner's hand. "Look at how much you love this now that you don't have to pretend you don't."

A damp spot forms on the front of the boxers as Jenner milks precome from Brayden, teasing his erection without giving relief. Seeing that he's ready for more—distracted by the miniscule pain from the clips tweaking his nipples—Jenner eases Brayden's underwear down a few inches to free his genitals.

"I could do whatever I wanted to you right now...." Settling lower on the bed between Brayden's spread legs; Jenner kneels in the limited available space. Brayden can feel him there; the rough fabric of Jenner's jeans rubs the insides of his bare legs. But now that he's exposed, Brayden's fear ratchets up again, squelching new-found joy and abandon.

"You're all right, Bray," Jenner says softly, as the smile is instantly gone from his slave's lips, replaced with a hardened expression and a furrowed brow. A deep blush heats Brayden's skin as bonds become a hindrance rather than a luxury. "It's just me. You're safe. I would never hurt you. All I want is to make you feel good. And stop still means stop. Okay?"

For a moment longer, the stubbornness holds. Jaw set, body tensed, Brayden debates his answer, then nods stiffly, "Yeah, okay."

"Take a deep breath," Jenner coaxes, stroking Brayden lightly with a hand. "In. Hold it. Good. Hold it. And let it out. Do it again. In...." He reaches up and twists one of the clips. Brayden lets some of his air escape in a nervous laugh. "Hold it." Leaning down, Jenner sucks a dirty kiss to the tip of Brayden's cock, steadying it at the base.

Brayden hisses a muttered curse and twitches. His head falls back, his neck elongated, arm muscles tight and bunched.

"Hold it..." Jenner, moaning, licks a long wet stripe up the underside of Brayden's cock. "And let it out."

Whining softly, low in his throat, Brayden remains tensed, but quiet, his frown remains but a good amount of his fear has dissipated.

"I'm gonna suck you," Jenner promises. A condom is rolled onto Brayden, changing his expression, bringing new expectancy.

"You want that?"

"Yeah. Yes. Yessir," he murmurs, each word a struggle.

"Relax."

"Trying."

"Try harder." Jenner braces a hand on the bed by Brayden's hip. Right before taking Brayden into his mouth, Jenner adds, "Well, maybe this will help."

Even through the condom, Brayden can feel the moment when Jenner puts his mouth on him, feeding him back along the wet, restless muscle of his tongue. Jenner closes his lips around the shaft and sucks. The sensation and—maybe even more than that—knowing that it's Jenner pleasuring him, banishes most of the lingering, remembered whispers and laughter, telling Brayden that it's *bad* to want it, that there's something *wrong with him*. He tunes into nothing but the way Jenner sucks on the tip of his dick, then takes a deeper, longer pull.

Unable to hold in the whimper of desperation and longing that it brings out, Brayden has no choice but to voice it and let Jenner really see how helpless he is.

His cries seem to drive Jenner on. Sucking the thick, stiff, hot column faster and deeper each time his mouth lowers onto it, Jenner helps distract Brayden by fondling his balls. Tremors of coiling pressure build in Brayden, and the proof of his enjoyment urges Jenner to quicken his pace. He sucks Brayden all the way to the root. Brayden's hips snap, pushing to get deeper and fit himself, impossibly, completely in his Master's throat. A choked moan slips from him and his body undulates. Jenner gives him plenty of suction as he pulls off.

"P-please." Brayden begs when Jenner's mouth is suddenly gone.

"Don't worry, I'm not done yet." Jenner moves on the bed. It shifts and squeaks. "I'm gonna use a toy on you while I suck you, to help you loosen up and enjoy this."

Brayden gets very still, tenses back up.

"Do you trust me?" Jenner asks, squeezing in a twisting motion up Brayden's saliva-wet shaft, reminding Brayden of what he's given so far.

"Yes, Sir," he admits, in a small voice.

Brayden hears Jenner using lube. His boxers are tugged lower. When wet, slick fingertips prod at the junction of his legs and between his cheeks, Brayden knows what's coming. Jenner rubs in small circles around his opening, stimulating the area, possibly trying to get him to relax and unclench. Initially, it doesn't work at all. Brayden tightens up to keep Jenner out.

"Keep breathing," Jenner says in his most aggravatingly soothing voice. "In…" He presses the tips of two fingers into Brayden who chokes off a breathy cry while inhaling. Parting readily around Jenner's questing fingers, Brayden feels invading thickness slide easily into his ass as plenty of lubricant gets worked into him. He bears down. Jenner sighs heavily and kisses Brayden's hipbone. The fingers push even deeper and Brayden whimpers loudly. "…and out," Jenner finishes with undisguised, raging lust in the words.

The fingers are reluctantly withdrawn. The cool, firm, narrow tip of a toy touches Brayden there instead. He gasps, though trying to maintain deep, even breaths, and whines softly as the object penetrates him, and hears Jenner growl with need. Suddenly, Jenner's mouth is wrapping Brayden's cock again, sucking him in. Immediately, Jenner sets a quick rhythm and, very slowly, presses the tapered butt plug further, working it gently in and out, trying to nudge it deeper on every push.

It drives Brayden crazy. He tries to move his legs, and can't. He clenches around the violation of the toy and writhes, bucking into Jenner's mouth, but he's mostly helpless to do any more than that. He's completely at Jenner's mercy.

The plug stuffs him full. The dull ache from the stretch adds an obscenely delicious layer to his pleasure as Jenner blows him. Just when he thinks the toy can't get any wider, it does and Brayden forces his body to relax enough to let it in, knowing that Jenner is determined to get it in him anyway.

The widest part yet breaches him, and he cries out. The sound provokes renewed urgency in Jenner's ministrations. Jenner pushes at the base of the plug, nudging it, jolting Brayden. Past the thickest part, it narrows before flaring back out in order to stay in place. Jenner rubs Brayden's rim, stretched smooth around the toy, gripping that narrow ring and locking the plug in his ass.

Jenner hums his pleasure, sucking him up and down a few more times before pulling off and letting Brayden strain up, his dick curving tight to his belly.

Stripping the condom off, Jenner jacks Brayden to completion. The hand pumping him is coated with lube and slides easily, squelching loudly. Knowing Jenner is watching him, and how obscene he must look, Brayden initially fights his climax but gets quickly overtaken. Surrendering, shuddering, flushed and with abandon, he comes, painting the ripples of his abdominal muscles in hot streaks of milky white.

"Fucking gorgeous," Jenner moans, smearing the fluid around, playing with it as he strokes Brayden through the aftershocks. "You're just so fucking gorgeous."

Chapter 16

Trust

While Brayden is dazed, Jenner moves quickly and purposefully.

He removes the nipple clamps, adding more sensation to Brayden's already overtaxed system. The flesh throbs and aches. Jenner lets him enjoy it, using it as an effective distraction while he unfastens the ankle cuffs one at a time.

Then, just like that, Brayden is unbound from the chest down. Jenner slides the boxers from Brayden, leaving him completely naked. Jenner, quickly undressed, wearing a condom, gets in position as Brayden fails to catch on to what's happening. Brayden's legs get bent back, hooked over Jenner's shoulders as he kneels and bears down on Brayden's smaller body, folding him in half. With a twist, Jenner pulls the plug out, eliciting a long, shuddering moan from Brayden.

Thrumming, determined, driven, Jenner sheaths himself with an unrelenting, needy push inside Brayden's heat. Growling and gasping at the brutal grip of Brayden's compact body on his cock, Jenner caresses Brayden everywhere he can reach—along the outsides of his legs, up his sides and arms, over his throat. He releases the cord binding Brayden's chest as well, leaving him with only the wrist ties to keep him down.

Brayden gasps, pleading, "I-I can't do this."

There's so much self-hatred in the words. Brayden is convinced he's not brave enough, or strong enough.

"You're *so beautiful*, Bray, I just want you to realize that," Jenner urges. "You're incredible and there's nothing wrong with wanting this. I want you, just like this. I want you so badly I can't breathe

141

from it. I need you. I need you with me, right here. Right now."

Jenner draws back and presses in again, riding the clenched muscles, folding Brayden more completely and trapping him with the weight of his body rather than the bindings.

"I've still got you, see?"

"Y-yeah. Yeah, okay," Brayden tries. Attempting to breathe, he groans at each tug and rut. The blindfold and the silken fabric around his wrists are what keep him sane. He's clinging to those like a lifeline, but it seems like Jenner can tell, which is why they haven't been removed.

The harder Jenner presses down on him, pinning him to the bed, the easier Brayden's breaths come, and the more he enjoys getting fucked. So he goes with it. Jenner catches Brayden's mouth in a kiss, tongue-fucking him roughly as he thrusts. The smell of come, sweat and sex fills Brayden's senses, it's intoxicating. Jenner chases his orgasm with Brayden gasping, grunting, sweating and grinding down against Jenner's cock. Suddenly, Jenner pulls at a strategic place on the ties holding Brayden to the headboard.

The fabric comes loose, sliding from Brayden's arms when he tries to pull on them for reassurance and finds no resistance.

But before he can protest or react much at all, Brayden is enveloped in Jenner's embrace.

He grabs on. A rush of excitement washes over him as he listens to Jenner moan, grunt and sigh, knowing that Jenner is coming undone only because of what Brayden is doing to him, that it's him and no one else that drives Jenner to such frenzy.

With a trembling thrust and a held breath, Jenner comes, holding tightly to Brayden's smaller form. Brayden's arms are tangled around Jenner's neck and back. Impatiently, Jenner nudges the blindfold back, revealing Brayden's eyes. Jenner looks deeply into them, hidden from his sight for so long, and Jenner's searching look, his gentle concern, hold Brayden there more completely than anything else.

They kiss again, and it's slower, softer. A moment later, Jenner pulls back slightly. With the pad of his thumb, he dries the tracks of wetness leading from his lover's eyelashes, cascading over each cheek. It causes Brayden's gaze to dart away with shame.

Burying his face in the sweat-streaked golden waves falling over Brayden's shoulder, inhaling his scent, Jenner asks quietly, reverently, "Did I scare you? If I did, I'm sorry."

Wrung out, sated, Brayden feels turned inside out, like he's exposed too much once more. It's a comfort to know that Jenner seems worthy of his trust, but still, he's left unbearably uncomfortable with how vulnerable he's been made. The instinct to run and escape is so powerful that for a second the fight kicks in. Brayden tenses up and suddenly starts to push wildly at Jenner, attempting to get free and dislodge the flesh impaling him.

"Shhh. Shh, it's okay. Hey! It's okay. Relax."

Jenner tightens his hold. In the process he rocks his hips forward, reminding them both keenly of their positions and who has the dominant place. A tremor shakes Brayden to the core and for a long moment he lies perfectly still, swallowing a soft, hurt whine.

Pressing a kiss to Brayden's jaw, Jenner again hushes him, kneading a handful of the side of Brayden's ass, then caressing up to his side, "Relax, Bray."

"Let me go… get cleaned up…."

"No," Jenner replies shortly. "You'll go when I'm ready."

He draws back, thrusts in, his eyes half-lidded and drunk on the pleasure. Brayden's lips part around an unvoiced moan, so Jenner does it again.

"I want you to stay with me tonight," he starts.

"The bed's too damn small," Brayden complains logically.

"I'll buy a new one."

"What? *Now*?"

"Smartass."

Swiftly, so swiftly it shocks Brayden, but thrills him at the same time, Jenner withdraws and flips Brayden over. He turns Brayden onto his hands and knees, bent over in front of where Jenner kneels. With his right hand, Jenner strips off his used condom and, with his left, fills Brayden's fucked-out and rubbed-raw hole with three fingers. Without thinking about it, Brayden pushes back onto the hand. After tossing the rubber, Jenner braces Brayden with a hand to his lower back as he fingers him. Brayden breathes sharply through his nose, rocking repeatedly back onto the hand, riding it.

"Goddamn it," Jenner curses, ogling the sight. He guides Brayden into a rhythm, forward and back, rubbing over his sweet spot just right to keep him going. After a few minutes of that, Jenner instructs, "Touch yourself. Do it."

And he does. Brayden starts to jerk off while he fucks himself onto Jenner's hand, biting back half-whimpered moans all the while.

It just happens. Jenner follows the commands of his body. His fingers pluck free of Brayden's ass and, with a tilt of his hips, Jenner's broad cockhead fits at the wet ring of Brayden's opening. With a gruff, throaty cry, Jenner enters him again, with nothing between them this time.

It's dirtier and quicker than the first time. Jenner drives into Brayden's ass at a fevered pace, the cradle of Jenner's hips slapping his cheeks. Grabbing handfuls of Brayden's flesh, alternately spanking him and yanking him back onto the full length of the cock stuffing his ass, Jenner gets off hard. When he spills his seed, he does so directly into Brayden's body.

"Fuck! I'm an idiot," Jenner snarls, realizing too late. "Bray. Babe, come on. Let's clean you up. *Fuck*."

His legs unsteady, unsure they're going to hold his weight, Brayden glances back as he straightens up. He sees Jenner's cock pull out of him, slick with semen and no condom.

"Oh."

"I'm gonna take care of this, okay?" Jenner immediately assures him, though visibly panicked. "We'll get tested. I haven't been with anyone in a long time and I don't have anything that I know of, all right?"

"Jenn, it's fine. Really," Brayden tries to say. Pins and needles prick his lower half as the blood rushes back into his limbs. He gets off the bed and Jenner is right there, steadying him, walking him into the bathroom.

"No, it's not *fine*. I know better than that. I'm not an idiot, I... *fuck*!"

"Jenn." Brayden looks up at him, calmly. He lays a hand on Jenner's chest. A deep frown of self-recrimination creases Jenner's brow. His normally sunken cheeks are even more hollowed as he clenches his jaw.

"I'm so sorry," Jenner manages. The apology is thick with emotion and anger.

Slowly, without any of the sort of worry making Jenner anxious, Brayden focuses only on his own concerns and says, "Look, can you gimme a minute to clean up before we deal with this?"

It seems to snap Jenner from his thoughts. The panic in his eyes fades as he blinks and peers down at Brayden's timid determination to clear him from the bathroom.

"No, this is my mess. I'm cleaning it up."

"What? No, Jenn. Jenner...."

But it does no good. Jenner doesn't look like he's in any mood to be convinced of alternate plans and, just like with anything else that happens between them, Jenner has the size difference to do what he wants and carry it through. He finds a douching bulb in the medicine cabinet and approaches Brayden with it, taking him by the arm and moving him over to the toilet.

"You're kidding, right? Jenner, *please* let me handle this. I'll figure it out, okay?"

Unmoved, Jenner fills the bulb with warm water from the tap. Brayden stares at it with horror. Then Jenner is turning him towards the wall and positioning him so that he'd straddling the toilet. Getting Brayden in place with minimal effort, Jenner holds him there with a hand wrapping the back of Brayden's neck.

A perverse shiver of excitement snakes in Brayden's gut as Jenner's voice, raspier for his bad mood and stern enough to make Brayden's cock twitch feebly with interest, says, "I'm going to put the nozzle in you and I need you to clench around it. Tight as you can. Gotta keep the water inside, okay?"

Brayden stutters around a protest as Jenner does just that, plunging the narrow tip into Brayden's come-slick anus. The grip of Jenner's hand on his neck, the heat baking from his naked body inches behind Brayden, it turns him on. Humiliated as he is, it's still hot as hell.

"Tighten your ass up. You ready?"

Brayden nods stiffly.

Jenner squeezes the bulb. The water rushes into Brayden's body. He feels uncomfortably full of it. When the bulb is empty, Jenner says, "Okay, I'm going to pull it out now. Clench up, tight as you can."

He frees the nozzle and tosses it into the sink.

"So, you're leaving for this part, right?"

Brayden listens for a reply, but the only one he gets is the feel of Jenner pressing up flush to Brayden's back, his long, thick arms wrapping Brayden from behind. A large hand cups over Brayden's abdomen, filled with fluid, sticky with spend. Another hand fondles Brayden's mostly flaccid member then lower, rolling his balls.

Right by Brayden's ear, Jenner murmurs, "I've never taken anyone bareback before. It was incredible. You felt *so good* and the thought of you filled with my seed, *dripping* with it...."

Jenner fondles further back, behind Brayden's sac to the trickles of semen running down his inner thigh. With Jenner pressed up against his back so snugly, Brayden can feel his lover's dick fight to rise. It nudges him like a promise. Brayden's arms shoot out to brace against the wall and he stays clenched tight as a vice. Jenner takes Brayden's earlobe between his teeth, nips and tugs. Brayden's eyes roll back with a blissful sigh. He tilts his head slightly to allow greater access.

"You're *mine* now," Jenner whispers. "I've *marked* you. Wanna get down on my knees and lick your thighs clean...."

Brayden arches and moans, having long forgotten that he wanted Jenner to leave.

With a firm hand, Jenner grabs Brayden's shoulder and forces him down, sitting him squarely on the toilet seat.

"Let it go," Jenner commands, not releasing him.

Brayden doesn't want to, but it's become near impossible to keep his ass shut, so he simply stops fighting it. His feeling of degradation blooms anew but then he hears Jenner turn on the water in the shower and the hand is gone from his shoulder. Using the moment's reprieve, he quickly cleans up and flushes. No sooner is he back on his feet, than Jenner is turning toward him and gesturing to the parted shower curtain.

"After you," Jenner says with dry amusement.

"You're a thorough son-of-a-bitch, aren't you?" Brayden retorts. "And kind of a voyeur. *Sir*."

"*Kind of* a voyeur? I'm waiting." Jenner raises his eyebrows expectantly.

With a chuckle and a shake of his head, Brayden gives in with a slightly sardonic, "Yes, Master," for which Jenner rewards him with a hard swat to his backside on his way over the edge of the tub.

The shower is soothing, sensual, and one of the more relaxed intimate moments between them thus far. Brayden tries to claim control of the bar of soap, but Jenner easily snatches it from him and does the washing, scrubbing and rubbing over every inch of skin with eager hands. He even hand-washes Brayden's hair. When finished, Jenner cleans himself off.

Noticing a displeased quirk of the lips when Jenner washes his own hair, Brayden calls him on it.

"Oh, it's just getting too long," he explains.

"What, your hair?"

"Yeah."

"So?"

"So I don't let my hair get this long. I should have gotten it cut last week, but I've been too *distracted*. I wonder whose fault that is?"

"You should grow it out. Who cares? I like long hair."

"Yeah," Jenner grunts, falling curiously silent.

"What?"

"Nothing."

"No, tell me. What's the big deal?"

With a slightly dramatic sigh, Jenner sets down the soap and fingers through his hair, twisting the strands. "I have curly hair, okay? And I hate it."

Brayden smiles, lighting up. "Really?"

"Yes. And I'm not talking a 'fro. It's full-on, big, chunky curls that turn into ringlets if it gets too long. It's a nightmare and my curse. So, I keep it shaved short enough without it looking like I'm about to enlist."

Taking a step forward, Brayden closes the gap between them. He bites at his lower lip, imploring Jenner with a look. "Grow it out for me? Please?"

"Oh, you've *gotta* be kidding me. *Now* you turn into a flirt? When it comes to me looking like a fucking girl?" He reaches past Brayden and shuts off the water. "No way."

"Please," Brayden begs, pressing his palms together in supplication. "You owe me for the bareback, right? Grow out your hair and we're even."

Jenner stares at him, then breaks into a laugh, "You're ridiculous. It doesn't work like that."

"Says who?" Brayden's fingers trail up and over to Jenner's right nipple, drawing circles around it as it stiffens from both the cold and the stimulation. Then he pinches it between two fingers and twists. Fresh heat blooms in Jenner's eyes, his breath coming heavier. Brayden, encouraged by the reaction, dips his head only slightly and curls his tongue. He licks over the peaked flesh that's right in front of his mouth, suckling briefly on it. He drags his teeth over Jenner's nipple then sucks again, harder. When his hand falls between Jenner's thighs, for the very first time touching him there, his fingers skitter nervously over the softened flesh. The response in Jenner is even more dramatic.

In the blink of an eye, Jenner grabs the arm Brayden is using to grope him, slams him back against the bathroom wall and holds him there. Just as the wind is knocked out of him, Brayden feels Jenner's mouth crash into his. It takes him a moment to catch up as Jenner's tongue sweeps over his and he swallows Brayden's groan. But then Brayden is kissing him back, licking into Jenner's mouth to taste him.

He's dizzy when they break and empowered with a newfound knowledge of how easy it is to turn Jenner on.

"So, about that bed."

"Tomorrow," Jenner promises breathlessly, leading Brayden back into the bedroom.

"Seriously?"

"Yeah. Seriously," he nods. "If you want to take the bed tonight, I'll sleep on the floor. Or on top of you."

"Wouldn't put it past you. Are you sure? I could just head home. It's not a big deal."

"I'm sure. Stay. Please."

With a tickle of excitement, Brayden succumbs to temptation and nods. "Yeah, all right. Let me just go get my bag."

Chapter 17
Practical Problems

"This is stupid."

Brayden senses Jenner's mild aggravation when he replies, "Are you calling me a pussy? You are, aren't you, because you can't seem to let this go. I'm fine sleeping here."

Lying on his side at the edge of the bed, Brayden looks down at Jenner lying on the floor. His makeshift bed is padded with a spare blanket and pillow. Brayden props his head on a hand. "Okay, you're fine. It's still totally stupid."

"Let me ask you something. I've been meaning to ask and don't take this the wrong way since clearly I, um, *enjoy* your stature," Jenner starts. Raising a single eyebrow, Brayden waits to see where this is going. "But if you were a lifeguard and had to rescue someone my size, how the fuck would you manage that? Especially someone as big as me who's near drowning and might pull you under out of sheer panic. I've seen how people react when they're in that situation. It's dangerous."

"Hell, yeah, it's dangerous," Brayden allows. "But I did just fine. It's all in the training."

"Did anyone ever pull you under?" The answering silence says it all. Jenner scans Brayden's face, seeing the hard, pressed-thin line of his mouth and the way he avoids eye contact. "I'm glad you don't do it anymore."

"It's an important job," Brayden says in his own defense.

"Doesn't mean you need to risk your own life for strangers. You never answered my question."

"How I would save you?"

"Yeah."

After considering his response as much as the possible implications of Jenner's intense concern for his well-being, Brayden says, "I'd come up behind you so that you wouldn't see me or where I was. It'd be harder for you to take me down. And it's not just the person you're rescuing that's the danger, there's also riptides that'll just pull you right out to sea. If it got really bad, maybe I'd dunk you or slap you to snap you out of it, like, 'hey, I'm here to help you,' you know?"

"Can someone sue you for injuring them while you're trying to save them?"

Brayden shrugs, "There's those Good Samaritan laws that protect trained emergency workers from stuff like that."

"How bad was it?" Jenner asks quietly. Brayden lies down on his back, staring up at the ceiling, aware that Jenner can't see his face at that angle. "When that person pulled you under?"

"I don't know. I'm still here, aren't I?"

"Bray...."

"Let's just say it's a good thing there was a second lifeguard on duty that morning."

"Jesus. What about the other guy that was drowning?"

"He was fine. He was standing there when I woke up coughing up rank saltwater."

Vaguely wondering what time it is, as Jenner's place is without clocks, Brayden buries the memory, or tries to. He's surprised when he feels Jenner, who has sat up, touch his hand. Flattening it to the bed, Jenner presses their palms together, weaving their fingers.

"Why'd you do it? What's the appeal, especially after something like that happens?"

Keep from losing people, he thinks. *Keep them safe, any way you can. Keep them here. Keep them from slipping away, because they always slip away.*

"People have a duty to help each other," Brayden tells him quietly. "Why else are we here, living these lives, if not to at least do our part? I'm a good swimmer. And I guess I have that drive to contribute. Made sense to me."

They both stare at their intertwined fingers. It's the first time they've held hands. "I'm proud of you. I couldn't have done it. Given up so much, so selflessly. But I'm glad you did."

Brayden realizes that they aren't talking about lifeguarding anymore. He gazes over at Jenner, whose blue eyes are open with everything in him laid bare, reflected in their depths. Something cold, hard and jaded is hiding there, fighting for dominance with the warmer, more vulnerable part of Jenner's essence. Jenner shifts, moving closer to where Brayden's head rests upon the bed. Leaning down over him, Jenner brushes the hair back from Brayden's cheek. Brayden savors the heat and nearness, the electric charge in the skin-to-skin contact. Then, Jenner bends closer, his lips softening, eyes closing, and waits.

A moment later, the butterfly-light touch of Brayden's first freely-given kiss brushes over Jenner's mouth.

"'Night, Jenn."

Despite his assurances to Brayden about the sleeping arrangements, Jenner does not sleep well that night on the hard floor. He gets small snippets of rest, but wakes frequently between dreams of being caught in a tidal surge of something much less tangible but even more powerful than water. It engulfs him, consumes him. He's trapped and tangled, turned upside down. Though he could try to fight it, could fall prey to panic, he instead gives in and lets go.

His frequent waking turns out to be in his favor, though. Sometime around mid-morning, after finally falling truly asleep around dawn, there's the faint sound of someone fiddling with the front door's locks.

"Shit," Jenner curses, struggling to a sitting position, then to his feet, favoring the knotted muscles in his sore back as he does. With a fleeting glance at Brayden, who is wearing only a clean pair of boxers from his cherished duffel and tangled up in the bed sheet, fast asleep, Jenner hobbles out of the bedroom towards the sound from the door.

He's almost there when the door opens, but gets caught when it's only an inch or two ajar, snapping the chain lock tight.

"What the sweet hell...?" he hears as a familiar voice curses softly.

"Yeah, gimme a sec. Hold on," he says, pushing the door closed again and taking off the chain. With it freed, he stands aside and waves his guest in. "Ma. Hey. What a surprise."

Bette Parrish, a handsome woman from whom Jenner got his good looks and his curly, black hair, if not his height and size, looks Jenner over from head to toe, clearly disapproving of his state of undress, clad in boxers and nothing else. She asks, "What are you doing here?"

"Oh, late night. I came up here to crash instead of going all the way home. I was just getting dressed."

"Mm," she hums with doubt, trying to look past him, down the hall to the bedroom. He shifts over to block her view, smiling sweetly.

"Let me just finish up. We can go get some breakfast," he suggests with what he hopes is believable enthusiasm.

"A mother can tell when her boy's just woken up, you know. I wasn't born yesterday. Go on. Get some damn clothes on," she sighs, shooing him off.

"But uh, why are *you* here?"

"Well, I didn't know you were using the apartment. I have a friend from my book club that's looking to rent and I was going to take some photos of the place to show her. Maybe you'd finally have a renter! Though you would lose your crash pad," she adds with a sideways glance. Sliding the heavy purse from her shoulder, she sets it on the kitchen counter and begins to rustle through it, not even a little oblivious to her son's flustered state which is swiftly edging towards panic. "...Pants?"

"Yeah. Yeah, pants," he agrees, rubbing warmth into his arms which are suddenly covered in goosebumps.

Almost too quietly to hear, the bedsprings creak from the rear of the apartment. Jenner pales. Excusing himself, he jogs out of sight.

Once in the bedroom, he closes and locks the door. Brayden is sitting up in bed, wide-eyed. He mouths, "Who's that?"

Jenner, exponentially more freaked out than Brayden has ever seen him before, stands frozen in the middle of the room. "My mother," he whispers. Rubbing a hand over his shock-slack mouth, he tries and fails to figure out what the hell to do.

Brayden gets out of bed and starts to look for his jeans. When he finds them, he pulls them on one leg at a time, keeping an eye trained on Jenner. "Fire escape?"

Rolling his eyes, Jenner hisses, "You're not going out the fire escape. I don't even know if that ladder works anymore, anyway."

"There's only one little bed in here," Brayden points out. "What's she going to think?"

"Goddammit," Jenner groans. "Okay, fire escape."

They walk to the window. Brayden grabs his duffel and stuffs his shoes inside it, but by the time he gets to the window and Jenner, he reads the scowl on his lover's face and blurts, "What?"

"This thing looks like a deathtrap. It's rusted all to hell and I'm not making you jump from the second story down to asphalt." Frantically, he scans the room, settling on the closet.

Brayden sighs, "Seriously, dude? Must we live the cliché?"

From the hall, Jenner's mother calls, "Honey, who are you talking to?"

"Oh, for the love of God," Jenner complains, praying for lightning to strike just to have an excuse to not deal with the situation at hand.

"It's fine. Let me handle it. Moms love me," Brayden assures him.

"I was just *fucking you* a few hours ago," Jenner says quietly through gritted teeth, jabbing a finger at the bed. "Don't you think she'll be able to sense that?" He sees something from the corner of his eye. One of the ankle cuffs is still attached to the bed. Muttering another prayer under his breath, the panic close as ever now, Jenner hurriedly detaches it and holds it up for Brayden to see, proof that they're doomed.

"Trust me. It'll be fine," Brayden says soothingly, gesturing widely with his arms. Quietly, he mouths to Jenner, "When a mother's son has a male friend stay over, she doesn't *immediately* jump to the assumption of fuckbuddy, you know."

Not buying this at all, Jenner covers his face with his hands and takes a deep breath before going to find his own pants.

While Brayden double-checks that there isn't any more visible sexual paraphernalia scattered about, Jenner slides his makeshift bed to the far wall, putting more space between it and the bed than there had been. Then, resigned to his own personal hell, he opens the bedroom door, leading the way.

His mother is there in the hallway and only sees Brayden after a moment or two, as she's distracted with trying to figure out her camera's settings. When she does look up, faced with two young men rather than just the one, she blinks and says, "Oh!"

"Ma, this is Brayden. He bartends for me and crashed here last night, too." Jenner steps aside to let Brayden past as he holds out a hand to shake with Mrs. Parrish.

"Ma'am, nice to meet you," Brayden says with his friendliest, warmest smile, the one that makes it seem — to Jenner at least — like he's radiating the sun itself, he glows so much.

Helpless but to smile back, Bette takes the offered hand. "Oh, I didn't realize..." She glimpses the blanket and pillow on the floor beyond the boys, and tsks. "Are you kidding me? You made this poor child sleep on the floor, Jenner Parrish? How could you?"

"Mother..." Jenner starts, weary with it all.

"Nope. Don't give me your excuses. Come on, let's get out of the hall." She ushers Brayden out to the main room, murmuring with disapproval, "And you don't even have a crumb to offer him to eat."

"I have an entire bar full of food downstairs —" Jenner starts, but is cut short with a hard look. "Ma, about the renter. I was thinking of moving in here myself. I'm staying over so frequently lately, it's simpler than traveling across town to get to my bed when I can just come upstairs."

"What about the rent? The potential income?"

"I'm sure Art and Max can find someone else to take my room at the house. I can handle doing without the rental income. At least for now. It doesn't have to be permanent." He chances a glimpse at Brayden, whose expression is unreadable.

"What do you think about this, Brayden?" Mrs. Parrish asks with an undecided sigh.

"Uh, I think if it gets him to splurge on a few more pieces of furniture and a loaf of bread, then I'm all for it."

"When you inherited this, it was supposed to be an asset, not your home," she presses.

"I know," Jenner tells her. "I know you want more for me, but this would make things easier. Plus, I like my privacy. I don't have that at the house."

For a moment, he slips and glances at Brayden's bare chest. Brayden's nipples are darker than usual, with faint bruises from the clips and from Jenner sucking on them. It's sexy enough to wipe all rational arguments from Jenner's mind. Forcing himself with effort to look away from the objects of his distraction, he clears his throat and tries to keep his eyes trained only on his mother. But he feels Brayden looking back at him now and it makes heat rise under Jenner's skin—the secret they share, the way they're both lying to conceal it from his mother.

Bette is muttering, "I don't know," and wandering about the space as she thinks it over. In flashes, Jenner remembers what Brayden's skin tasted like. He wants to suck on Brayden's bruised nipples some more to see what sounds it would get him to make. But then he realizes that Brayden's sphincter must be stretched out still, looser from taking the plug and getting fucked twice and, horribly, Jenner's cock stirs with interest, ready for round three. Out of his peripheral vision Jenner thinks he sees Brayden smiling, but that could be his imagination running away with itself.

Jenner wanders behind the counter in the kitchen, wanting a solid barrier between himself and his mother and Brayden.

"How long have you been working at the Pub, Brayden?"

"Just a few months, ma'am."

"Oh, call me Bette, please. I'm not a ma'am. You like it there?"

"I do, yeah," Brayden nods, bubbling with barely concealed amusement as he watches Jenner shoot invisible daggers from his eyes in his desperation to get his mother out of the apartment.

"And you two are friends? You must be. Jenner has always had limited patience for most people, except for the very few he keeps close."

Sighing heavily, Jenner idly traces the ridge of his brow. He's bent over the counter and just waiting for it all to be over at this point.

"I heard that," his mother tells him.

"Well, he must not hate me too much if he let me crash here," Brayden answers.

"Or I do and it was just your consolation prize for working into the dead of night for your slave-driver boss," Jenner says, dripping with exasperation. "Are we done? Mother, if you'd like to stay, I'll go get some food and walk Brayden out."

"I suppose," she relents, but sounds unsure of the decision. She packs up her camera, stuffing it low into her purse. "Though I think it's rude of you to not also invite your friend."

"He's not my —" Jenner starts, then stops abruptly. "He was on his way out anyway. He's expected at home. He's got a shift in a few hours and I doubt he wants to spend his free time here."

"Brayden, let me apologize for my son's poor manners," Bette tells him. "I promise you, I raised him better than that."

"No problem, ma'am. I mean Bette," Brayden smiles.

"Come on," Jenner says to Brayden, putting a hand on the dipping curve of Brayden's bare lower back to hurry him along. Something in the gesture catches Bette's eye, but Jenner is too determined to escape to pay much attention. As the two walk to the door, barefoot, Brayden with his bag, Jenner's hand slides and shifts, but stays right against Brayden's skin.

"Nice to meet you!" Brayden calls back to Mrs. Parrish with a wave.

"You too, Brayden!" she returns, watching Jenner pull the door closed after them. "Hmm."

It's not the chill in the weather that has Brayden shivering as he walks home, dressed now in shoes and a warm shirt as well as pants. He can feel the tingle in his lower lip from where Jenner had kissed him in the stairwell, then bit the flesh before licking over the hurt with the tip of his tongue. Brayden can hear the remembered growl of Jenner's fevered words as he'd mouthed against Brayden's ear, careful not to touch him other than to grip his left nipple between two fingers and twist. He had arched into the touch, his smile dying, replaced with something else, something darker, and Jenner asked if Brayden was sore, if it hurt. With a tight nod, his hand braced on Jenner's arm, Brayden gave his answer.

"Do something for me," Jenner said. He pulled something from his pants pocket and slipped it into Brayden's hand. It was the two, tiny clips used on him the night before. "When you get home, put these on. Leave them on for twenty minutes before you leave to come to work, but come early and meet me here."

"Jenn," Brayden gasped, brow creasing with delicate lines as Jenner twisted the abused flesh the other way.

"I need to fuck you," Jenner nearly moaned, his parted lips skimming over the shell of Brayden's ear. "Tell me you want it." He rolled the pad of his thumb over the hardened peak of the nipple, felt Brayden shudder.

His control breaking, Brayden took a half-step backwards, leaning against the wall behind him. Jenner's hand slid up wrapping around Brayden's throat, his thumb caressing the soft skin just under his ear.

"Tell me."

"I want it. Please fuck me, Sir."

With a swallowed moan, Jenner let him go, unable to meet his eyes. Brayden struggled into his shirt and shoes and nearly bolted to get away.

He slows more the further he gets from the building, gradually feeling more certain that he wouldn't be followed or seen. The throbbing in his nipple is what he focuses on, but it isn't enough. To think that Jenner knew it wasn't enough is incredibly arousing. He gave Brayden those instructions to keep him tethered, like part of him is still there, chained to the bed. Brayden will do as asked and attach the clips to his sore flesh, but he will also forbid himself relief and keep himself from masturbating, like he wants to already. He will save himself for Jenner, waiting to feel Jenner's thick cock filling his ass, pounding into him, and if he's good, and Jenner approves, maybe then Jenner will let him get off.

With the fantasy firmly fixed in his mind, Brayden heads home.

Chapter 18
Brazen Brayden

Later that afternoon, Jenner excuses himself and leaves the bar for a break. A few minutes later, Max sees Brayden cross in front of Parrish Pub on the other side of the street, walk right past and avoid the bar entirely. She turns to Jackson, who is helping her restock the bar.

"Hey, is that Brayden?"

Jackson glances up after setting a few bottles on the shelf. "Um, where?"

But Brayden is gone from sight. "Never mind," Max sighs.

Outside, Brayden crosses the street, waving to Marla, the florist, who's busy appraising her window displays, but not too busy to shout hello and watch him go past. He jogs in a straight line to the door of Jenner's apartment, feeling like many sets of eyes are on him, making a wide circle around the entrance to the Pub though knowing it might not do any good anyway. He checks for onlookers, sees Marla is back to admiring her windows, and slips quickly inside. Hurrying up the steps, his breath coming quick and not only from the exercise, he knocks twice on the heavy wooden door.

"Finally," Jenner groans. He opens the door and pulls Brayden roughly inside. Impatiently, Jenner pushes his guest up against the wall just beside the doorframe. When Brayden almost grabs the hem of his shirt, then hesitates, Jenner urges him on, saying, "Take it—take it off. Come on."

Brayden looks everywhere—the windows free of curtains or blinds for privacy, the kitchen where Bette had been not hours before—but into Jenner's blown-black eyes as he twists the shirt off.

No sooner does it clear his head, than Jenner is moaning, "Fuck." Then he's on Brayden. Gripping the slightly swollen, tender pink flesh of Brayden's left nipple between his knuckle and thumb, Jenner dips his head and closes his silken lips around the dark, bruised circle.

"Oh my *god*," Brayden gasps, palming the back of Jenner's head, his fingers combing through twists of black hair. The pointed tip of Jenner's tongue flicks at his sore flesh. His teeth scrape, his lips graze, then he sucks, making Brayden cry out.

Part of him suspected that maybe Jenner was kidding about the quick fuck and the nipple play before work, especially after having the time and space to get a clearer head. But Brayden figured he'd go with it just in case it wasn't all bullshit, despite his reservations and self-doubt. Now he's glad that he did.

On the walk over, he'd been distracted, and not just by the countless neighbors waving or saying hello from front porches, sidewalks and passing cars. Andre had called right after Brayden put the merciless clips on his nipples, lying on his bed in his room. He'd let the call go to voicemail and listened to the message after. It was a warning of sorts. One of their mutual friends, Enrique, is passing through the area on his way to New York and is going to stop by to see Brayden, probably that afternoon. Enrique wants it to be a surprise, which is why he hasn't called Brayden himself, but Andre, knowing how much Brayden dislikes those kinds of surprises, figured he'd call ahead.

Brayden tries not to think about it. Enrique has been known to flake out on plans, so it might not happen anyway. Maybe it's just something Enrique told Andre in passing and never meant to actually do. And besides, Brayden has more pressing things on his mind, like how hard Jenner is making him. Fingers tweak his sore nipple and he breathes out a choked laugh because it hurts but in a really, really good way. Instinctively, his hand goes to his fly, impatiently undoing the button, pulling at the denim to give his aching cock some room.

With a grunt, taking over, Jenner swats Brayden's hand out of the way and shoves his own down inside Brayden's underwear instead. Brayden tenses at first at the sudden foreign contact but then relaxes into it as Jenner bites down on his throbbing nipple.

"God, you're so fucking hard," Jenner moans. On the walk over, Brayden had worried that people would be able to tell just by looking at him that he was aroused. Maybe, somehow, they would be able to tell that he'd been wearing nipple clamps of all things, and that he was on his way to Jenner Parrish's apartment to fuck around. Hearing Jenner call him on the stiffness of his dick makes Brayden feel slightly guilty. Nonsensically, he worries that Jenner will throw open one of the windows and shout down to the pedestrians below, 'Hey everybody, Brayden Clare really gets off on sore nipples!'

Jenner straightens up, letting go of Brayden just long enough to get his pants opened too. Pulling out his cock, Jenner flattens Brayden to the wall, coming right up against him and taking both of their dicks in hand, squeezing them together. Brayden's mouth falls open and he thrusts, shuddering, against the silky hardness of Jenner's cock.

"You did it, didn't you? You used the clips like I asked. Your nipples are so hot and sensitive. The blood is right there, beating under the skin. I can taste it. Makes me want to tie you to the bed again and fucking dry hump them."

Brayden chuckles dizzily at the mental picture of that. His dick pulses precome in Jenner's fist. "Kinky."

"You fucking want it, don't you? You want me to come all over your chest and lick it clean."

Grunting, gasping, wishing there were curtains or maybe a secret underground tunnel linking their living spaces and allowing covert travel back and forth, Brayden tilts his chin up, pulling Jenner down into a kiss. "Fuck me," he begs, wanton and horny. "Fuck me, Master."

Jenner's eyes flash dangerously. He gets very still, very fast and, after a pause, seems to make a decision. Digging something from his back pocket, he rips open a condom wrapper with his teeth and spits out the piece of foil. Brayden exhales his relief.

But then Jenner rolls the condom on *Brayden*.

"What are you...?"

Jenner sinks to his knees in front of Brayden. Opening his mouth wide, pushing his tongue forward, he swallows Brayden's cock.

"Dammit," Brayden hisses, holding Jenner's head in both hands, bucking into the wet heat of his mouth, even as disappointment threatens to engulf him. Like a creeping itch, his nerves start to jangle and clang. It feels wrong. Since he's not held down or bound, his instinct is to deny the pleasure Jenner is giving him. Part of him wants to push Jenner off and run. But then Jenner does something with his tongue that makes Brayden double over nearly in half, curling around him, still holding on as Jenner's head bobs and sucks. The word stop is right there, ready to be spoken.

It dies in his throat, strangled out as Jenner grabs him by the balls and tugs so hard that it feels like he's trying to pull Brayden's testicles like overripe grapes.

"Ahh, fuck! Dammit!" Brayden tries to find the air and he can't and Jenner still sucks him, taking him all the way into his throat. It drives Brayden to buck and fuck Jenner's mouth, the needs of his dick totally disconnected from the instruction of his brain. The ache that exploded in his balls blooms, burns and slowly fades, thumping with his heartbeat.

Jenner gently rolls Brayden's sac in his palm, soothingly. After a minute or two, Brayden is able to straighten up, leaning back against the wall again, panting and riding Jenner's mouth, with slight pushes. One of Jenner's hands cups Brayden's ass possessively, and he's close, *so* close. Black flowers blossom and spread across Brayden's vision. His head falls back. His moan, long and low, reverberates in the open space of the empty apartment.

Right on the edge, he plunges over just as Jenner twists the tip of his middle finger up through Brayden's pucker, breaching him as he comes. Unloading into the condom with a grunting cry, Brayden chases in, in, in over Jenner's tongue, caressing his hollowed cheeks.

Brayden is only dimly aware of Jenner stripping off the condom and wiping him clean with a towel. An inner battle begins to clash in his head. He has to make his own choice, and now. Jenner pulls Brayden's underwear up to cover him and that's it. That's all Jenner is going to give, so Brayden decides.

Feeling intensely self-conscious about it, he palms Jenner's dick and gives it an experimental squeeze. "Bray," Jenner sighs, sounding like he's talking to an impertinent child. He grabs for Brayden's wrist, pulling his hand away.

"Let me," Brayden asks.

"No."

"Why not? Is it against the rules?"

Before he can chicken out, Brayden goes to his knees. Circling his fingers around the root of Jenner's erection, Brayden licks over the head, tasting the salty tang of precome.

"Condom... Bray..." Jenner gasps, but it's a losing battle. He says the words like a man who has lost his grip on language entirely as Brayden takes a few long licks up the underside of Jenner's shaft, up over the head, across the weeping slit. "Jesus fuck..."

Wrapping his lips around the head of Jenner's dick, Brayden sucks. The condom is forgotten. Jenner is tense at first, but then he thrusts into Brayden's mouth like he's fighting not to. Brayden gags a little. Jenner pulls back, far enough that only the head is between Brayden's stretched lips, then pushes right back in, but more slowly, more shallowly.

"You're killing me," Jenner groans. "Fuck..."

Brayden smiles a little and his chuckle of pride vibrates through the cock sliding bare on his tongue.

It's hesitant and very obviously the first blowjob Brayden has ever given, but, knowing that, it only makes it better for Jenner because it feels like he's defiling Brayden's purity again. That's a turn-on he can't even pretend to deny.

Jenner stares down his body at the sight of Brayden on his knees, holding Jenner's dick, trying to suck on it and take each thrust without choking—his eyes watering, breathing through his nose, nostrils flaring. Jenner runs the pad of his thumb over Brayden's stretched-out lips, wet with saliva, and cups his jaw. It's perfect. It's better than he ever dreamed, and Brayden gave him this freely, without orders or expectations, which is the best part.

But then something surprising happens. As Jenner is lost to everything but the wrap of Brayden's tongue around his cock, the kiss of his lips around the shaft, the wet slide and push, he feels Brayden's fingers pulling Jenner's boxers and pants down farther, down to mid-thigh. Then both of Brayden's hands cup Jenner's bare ass. They grope him, kneading the muscle. Exploring further, Brayden traces down the crease of Jenner's ass.

Jenner growls, grabbing his lover's head with one hand, squeezing up the exposed part of his shaft to hurry things along with the other, but Brayden's hand shifts again. He folds it around Jenner's balls, fondling, tickling, and pulling gently.

Jenner closes his eyes and feels everything, every touch, as his climax creeps up on him, ready to explode into Brayden's willing mouth. It occurs to him that he should pull out before that happens, but then even that bit of rationality dissolves as Brayden's exploring fingers quest even farther, touching back behind Jenner's testicles, over the smooth patch of skin there, rubbing over it firmly enough to elicit a gasping cry.

Jenner goes still, defeating momentarily the need to rut and fuck as Brayden traces his asshole, marveling at Brayden's brazenness. The pad of Brayden's fingertip comes to rest at the center of the ring of muscle after making small circles around the spot. A sound escapes Jenner's lips—half gasp, half protest—but it's formless, incomprehensible and Brayden presses harder. Jenner pulls out and squeezes rapidly up his shaft, knees going weak as white fire explodes behind his cock and he comes. Coaxing Brayden's jaw open, Jenner comes on his tongue, his lips. Rasping out a breathless cry as Brayden buries a fingertip shallowly inside him, Jenner clenches around it.

"I can't... can't believe you.... The audacity.... You little slut. Stand. Stand up," Jenner gasps. Trying to recover, he pulls Brayden to his feet, turning him toward the wall.

The fire of Jenner's astonishment seems to only feed Brayden's confidence. With a cocky little smirk, he plants his hands on the wall as Jenner pushes at the center of his back with a deliberate hand, bending him over. Jenner grips Brayden's pelvis and draws it back.

"You," Jenner rasps, spanking the side of Brayden's bare ass with an open hand, delivering a hard slap, making the flesh jiggle. "Will ask." Another strike, even harder, making Brayden gasp.

"Permission." Each slap punctuates the words, hard and sharp. "To touch me there."

The last blow is the hardest of all. Brayden yelps, hanging his head, hiding his face. Jenner steps closer, holding him in the position but breathing over the back of his neck, putting his bare flesh flush to Brayden's exposed skin, rubbing up against Brayden's flushed, spanked ass. Brayden is like a statue, waiting, braced for more. That's good. Jenner knows he needs to encourage that obedience and respect. He needs to stop letting things casually slide by. He should have been able to stop Brayden before things went that far, but libido had recklessly overridden sense.

"Yes, Master. I'm, 'm sorry...."

Another hard slap. After a pause, it's followed by five more.

Brayden gasps, then swallows the sound, pressing into the touch as Jenner roughly kneads Brayden's enflamed right buttock.

"That's for not asking permission to suck me, and doing so without protection."

"Sorry, Sir. Sorry."

Jenner drags opened-mouth kisses up the back of Brayden's neck, around to his jaw, and Brayden moans.

Somehow, they compose themselves. Brayden washes his face and hands at the kitchen sink, eyes downcast. He notices with furtive glances that Jenner looks like he was just hit by a train. He appears dazed, dizzy and dumbstruck. His hair is slightly rumpled, his clothing askew.

"Slut," he accuses again, watching Brayden at the sink.

Brayden just smiles. "It's just... you're so *easy*."

His fear skips up a notch at the cool warning in Jenner's expression. But that's just how he likes it. The only thing better than the sudden spanking Jenner gave him is the threat in his blue eyes that there's another one coming his way, and soon. He has a feeling, too, that the next one will be even more intense.

"*Brazen little slut*," Jenner says, forming the words deliberately.

"Yeah? What are you gonna do about it, *Sir*?"

Drying his hands, Jenner glances around the barren space, looking like he's making a mental tally of all of Brayden's insolent remarks and actions.

Almost too easy, Brayden thinks. *How many pushes will it take before he pushes back? Guess I'll find out.*

"So are you really gonna get furniture?"

"Furniture? Like a spanking bench? Yeah, it's an attractive idea."

"I mean it."

"So do I. I can't believe you begged me to fuck you."

Brayden looks at him squarely, not backing down.

"And you shouldn't have done that—blowing me without protection. It's bad enough I penetrated you without a condom, but then..." Jenner sighs. "Tomorrow morning, we go to the clinic. Together."

"What, are you going to come pick me up at home so we can go get tested for STDs? Maybe pop in to say howdy to my grandma and cousin first?"

"I could. But I'm having a new bed delivered this afternoon. You could always stay here."

Jenner gives it a moment to sink in as a subtle, victorious smile flickers over his lips. Brayden's rebellious humor evaporates. His gaze darts to the door, remembering that they're both expected down at the bar to start work. They'll be showing their faces to people who spend time with them daily, who know them pretty well, and doing it right after sucking each other off and screwing around right over their heads.

"What are we doing?" Brayden says, dazedly, cold fear scraping the words raw. "What the fuck are we doing?"

Jenner sighs and steps into Brayden's personal space. Taking Brayden's face in both hands, Jenner looks down at him and tells him steadily, "You need this. So do I. And the rest? Fuck it. It's none of their goddamned business. This is private. This is about you and me. Master and slave. That's all. Okay?"

Brayden nods, but feels unsure.

"I can tell that this is all causing you stress, so *I'll* handle it. I'll handle everything, no matter whether it's just us, alone, or around others. You're mine. My responsibility. My slave. There's nothing for you to worry about. Nothing at all. At work, it'll be low protocol, unless I tell you otherwise. If we need to talk, and step away for a moment, you go to my office, close the door and kneel."

"Okay," Brayden agrees, feeling a little better with a clear framework in place.

"You trust me?"

"Yes, Sir."

Jenner traces the curve of Brayden's lower lip, causing his eyelashes to flutter closed. Softening to the touch, Brayden kisses Jenner's finger. When Jenner presses it into Brayden's mouth, between his lips, Brayden licks the tip, and sucks gently on it. He hears the sharp intake of breath from Jenner, and it makes his stomach flip giddily.

Jenner kisses his temple. "Good. Come on."

Brayden leaves first, after Jenner ensures the coast is clear. A few minutes later, Jenner follows.

Chapter 19

Suspicion

Brayden is in the break room. If she presses her cheek to the wall, Max can see him from her place in shadows of the hallway. She can hear him, too. As he paces, cell phone to his ear in the otherwise deserted area, totally unaware of her presence, he holds his forehead in one hand.

"Just give Nan the message, okay, Em? Please? I'll see you tomorrow. Okay? I promise. We can see a movie or I'll help you with homework. Whatever you want."

Aggravated but hiding it fairly well, he sighs heavily but silently. Turning sharply on a heel, he paces back the other way. Max stays perfectly still so that he doesn't notice her watching him.

She had heard Brayden ask his young cousin to tell their grandmother that he wouldn't be home that night. It seems like the chickenshit way out to Max, not telling his grandma directly, but that's just her opinion. And Max also knows why Brayden won't be home. He's spending the night at the only other place he could be spending the night—Jenner's apartment. Of course Brayden hasn't come out and said as much, but she's seen the both of them sneaking back and forth from the place more than once.

"I know I've been gone a lot lately, and I'm really sorry, Em, but I'll make it up to you." There's a pause and Max watches him closely—the way his face falls and eyes dart. "I've been spending time with a friend. It's important to me. Yeah, maybe sometime you can meet them. Okay? Thanks, Emma. Love you too."

Brayden hangs up and groans.

Peeling away from the wall, Max walks into the break room.

"Hey."

Looking up sharply, Brayden stares at her, mistrust flickering behind his eyes. "...Hey."

"Everything all right?"

She knows she could call him on it, the tryst with Jenner, the sneaking around, but something keeps her from doing it.

"Yeah," he says shortly. "Excuse me."

Without another word, Brayden pushes past her, hurrying back out into the bar before she can so much as blink.

All afternoon, Brayden watches the bar's front door like he's expecting someone, and hardly hears anyone that tries to talk to him, other than the patrons. His mood is sour and he seems to make a concerted effort to not get too close to Jenner, proximity-wise. The two hardly make eye contact. Max knows because she looks for it. It makes for a tense, uncomfortable atmosphere for just about everyone.

At one point Max finds Art in the kitchen and pulls him aside to tell him what she suspects after overhearing the call and noticing the sneaking around.

Art gets a strange look on his face as he listens to what Max has to say. When she's done, he confesses, "Jenner told me that something's going on with him and Brayden. He said to keep my mouth shut about it."

"What do you mean? Like they're messing around? As in the way Jenner likes to mess around with guys? Oh my god...."

Art drops his gaze. Max knows all about Jenner's trips to Manse, and his affinity for BDSM. It's been going on for years, ever since high school, when she started to find things like leather hoods, shackles and sex toys stashed in his car and his room. She called him on it, and he said he was learning how to be safe and wasn't out to hurt anyone, himself included. A nervous edge creeps into Max's voice. "Should we say something? Maybe if we just clear the air and tell 'em we know and we're fine with it things can go back to normal."

"We can't just out Jenner and Brayden," Art whispers. They're tucked into a corner of the room behind a rack of supplies. "Jenner made it pretty damn clear that it was none of our goddamned business whatever it is he's doing with Brayden. You know how he gets. If we push too hard or at the wrong moment, he might fire our asses and just never speak to us again."

"He wouldn't do that," Max scoffs.

"Wouldn't he?"

"They're just, you know, dating or something, right? What's the big deal?"

Art laughs, softly, shaking his head.

"What?" Max frowns.

Regaining some of his composure, Art scans Max's face. "It's none of our business, Maxie. Capice? Just do me one favor and keep an eye on Brayden."

"What do you think I have been doing?" Max hisses, annoyed.

"Well, good. Keep on doing it then. And if he starts acting weird or you're worried about him, then we'll say something."

"Worried about him how?" Max thinks of the phone call she'd overheard only an hour or two ago, and the way Brayden had brushed her off after.

Art searches for the right way to say it, and the longer he does, the more concerned Max becomes. "Well, Jenner's a big guy, right? A heck of a lot bigger than Brayden. He's intense. He likes kinky shit. He gets paranoid that people are going to find out he's gay and into BDSM, that his precious reputation would never recover. And he's been obsessed with the kid. You've seen the way they get around each other, the looks they give each other. Seems like a dangerous combo to me, but I could be wrong."

Max remembers how Jenner has always dealt with stress and peer pressure. He hasn't always hung out with the nicest people. Max and Art were a few tiers down from him on the popularity scale. Jenner was always at the top, and he liked it that way. Being popular and a big deal on the football team, sometimes he acted like more of an asshole than she knew he was, just to make it look good for everyone watching. She's seen him stand by and watch someone smaller than him get picked on, ridiculed or tormented, acting like it was fine, like it was funny, only to get upset about it in private, later. As the years have gone by, and Jenner has only gotten bigger, more skilled at defending himself, more immersed in alternative lifestyles, the lines have blurred. Is he still the guy who feels bad for the losers, berating himself for not speaking up or stepping in, or is he someone else now? Someone who's gotten so good at looking the other way and making excuses for bad behavior that he's still acting the tough jock to Brayden's helpless outcast even when no one's watching? If Jenner ever turned that corner, maybe thinking it's the only way to get Brayden in bed, Brayden would have no way to defend himself. Max has been alone with plenty of guys who were a hell of a lot bigger than her, who had specific goals in mind, driving every word, every touch. Sometimes they got so caught up in what *they* wanted, that they stopped seeing her entirely. In those moments, she was an object, not a person, and it was dangerous — very much so.

Hating that she's doubting her best friend, she asks, "You think he'd hurt Brayden?"

"We're the only ones that even suspect they're up to something. It's not like Brayden's got a huge support system here. And how many times have you heard Brayden say how badly he needs this job?"

"Fuck," Max gulps. The blood drains quickly from her face. She starts to dart away, toward the bar. Art grabs her arm to keep her there.

"Settle down."

"But he *is* being weird! Brayden won't even *look* at Jenner. And he never seemed gay to me before. What if some bad shit's already happening? What if Jenner's, like, blackmailing him into having sex? Or worse?"

Art's reaction isn't what Max expects it to be. He gets quiet and drops his gaze.

"What? What is it? You know something, don't you?"

Max swats him, but he doesn't move or react.

"Art!"

"Brayden has, um, bruises. A bunch of them. They're on his wrists, arms and chest. I saw them when he was getting changed."

Again, Max tries to bolt for the bar, seething, "Goddammit!"

"Hey!" he barks at her, then lowers his voice to a growl. "Jenner's not a bad guy. The kind of guy who would do that to Brayden? That's exactly who Jenner's been defending you from for years."

"You sound like you're trying to convince yourself," Max says, getting upset. "All of those guys? The ones who still grab my ass and joke about what a slut I am? Those are his *friends*."

One of her ugliest memories surfaces, of Jenner trying to throw one of Max's old boyfriends, Austin, out of the bar. Austin had been drinking, but he wasn't drunk. He was talking a little too loudly, and a homophobic slur wove into the conversation. To this day, she has no idea if Austin actually said it, or if it was one of his idiotic friends. Max had no chance to mediate. One moment they were sitting at a table, the next Jenner was dragging Austin out of the building and into the road. Granted, Austin took the first swing, but Jenner didn't just hit back, he *kept* hitting back.

Finally, Art was able to pull him off of Austin, but it was too late. There was a concussion, broken teeth, a broken jaw and a broken relationship. A lot of guys stopped wanting to date Max after that, even if they were from out of town. Their reputations had spread that far. But even if they knew nothing about it, one trip home to see Max's housemates was all it took. They were intimidated by Jenner and her close friendship with him. Maybe she should have killed the friendship then and there, after the brawl with Austin, but she didn't. She's stuck by Jenner even if part of her has never forgiven him.

Though Max understands how much Jenner resents having to live up to his friends' and family's possibly unresasonable expectations of him, and having to lie about being gay, the fact that he's never been able to let anything go makes her afraid that one day, he'll hurt someone else like he did with Austin. She imagines all of that anger turned on Brayden, whom she likes, and likes in not just a friendly way. She's been hoping for more with Brayden. The thought of him giving himself, his body, over to Jenner to idly fuck and smack around for the sake of a stupid job—it makes her sick.

Maybe her feelings for Brayden are clouding her judgment. Maybe she's totally got it wrong, but if she doesn't...

"If he's really doing this... I'll kill 'im," she growls.

"Jenner's a lot bigger than you too, you know. You didn't see how violent he got when I confronted him about Brayden. You can't say anything, to either of them," Art warns. "Let me do it. I can handle him if he picks a fight over it. Got it?"

Max's eyes widen and fill with unshed tears, shaken with the idea that her best friend could secretly be a rapist.

"Got it?" Art presses when she doesn't reply.

"Yeah. Yeah, I got it. I'm sure it's nothing, and it's all a big mis-understanding," Max says. It sounds like a lie. She yanks her arm free and leaves him standing there. Pushing angrily through the kitchen door, she exits into the heavy gloom of the bar beyond.

Chapter 20

The Trouble with Assumptions

The more Art watches Brayden—the tiredness written in his posture, the strain on his face, the way he's careful not to look directly at Jenner unless he absolutely has to—the more convinced Art becomes that something bad is going on there. It's all too easy to imagine what the consequences might be if Jenner got as frustrated with Brayden as he'd gotten with Art. Brayden, who's a foot shorter than Jenner and a hell of a lot smaller in mass. Even if it was about lust instead of anger, it still came down to using physical intimidation to take control and make things go a certain way. Once Art consciously attunes himself to the energy crackling between his co-workers, the easier it is to feel it. The tension between Jenner and Brayden is so intense it's like it has its own physical presence.

At the first lull in customer demands, Art walks up to Brayden where he's restocking behind the bar a few feet away from Jackson. Brayden gives Art a sideways glance from the corner of his eye, but says nothing.

"Hey, can I talk to you a minute?"

"Sure," Brayden murmurs without turning or stopping what he's doing, "What's on your mind?"

"Um, actually, can we talk in the break room?"

Brayden freezes and Art can see that he's sensed something. Brayden's hackles rise. He says to Art, "I'm a little busy right now. Maybe after I finish with this, okay?"

He's blowing me off, Art realizes. "This is important." *More important than restocking the damn shelves*, his tone conveys.

Brayden looks up at him, understanding, and says, "What's this about?"

Art's eyes flick momentarily toward Jenner at the far end of the room and away. Brayden sees and looks instantly stricken. "Excuse me," he says, pushing past Art and walking quickly around the bar, toward the exit rather than the break room. Brayden runs from the prospect of speaking privately with Art about Jenner and it confirms every single one of Art's suspicions.

Brayden heads for the door, ready to walk away, even if he's in the middle of a shift, even if he has no idea where to go or what to do. Art is watching with a mysteriously unhappy expression. Jenner is watching, too, but before Jenner can react, before *any* of them can react, the door opens just as Brayden gets to it.

A young Latino guy with a buzzed-short mohawk and tattoos creeping up his neck from under the collar of his shirt walks through the door. It seems like everyone in the bar stops what they're doing, falling silent, watching as the newcomer and Brayden lock eyes.

"Enrique," Brayden says, stopped in his tracks. He's stunned, feeling trapped or caught.

Smiling hugely, laughing, Enrique closes the gap between himself and Brayden to give him an enthusiastic hug. He claps Brayden on the back and lifts him a little off the ground. "Damn, it's good to see you."

"I can't believe you came," Brayden says, trying to extricate himself from the hug as he's kissed soundly on the cheek. He can feel everyone in the bar staring at them, listening to every word, jumping to their own conclusions. In his peripheral vision, he sees them whispering to each other, nodding their way. Being so on display is like wearing a straightjacket, and his panic spikes.

"Had to see you, B. Did Andre tell you I was coming? That sneaky bitch."

There are people everywhere—filling the bar, spilling out onto the sidewalk.

"Hey, come on. We can talk back here," Brayden says. The weight of everyone's stares—a roomful of them, but Art and Jenner's most of all—makes him feel even smaller. Like all of his secrets, his whole private life is about to be exposed; he shrinks in on himself and grabs his friend by the arm, dragging Enrique hurriedly back toward the hall leading to the break room.

They get there with Brayden leading the way, not letting go. Brayden turns to find that Jenner and Art have followed, past and present colliding. The dread begins to strangle him. He fights for air as everyone's attention remains fixed solely on him. It's just like it always was in that damn school, with everyone always looking at him—the loner, the weirdo with the fucked up parents who never talks to people—and their hushed conversations, judging, making assumptions about things they know nothing about. It was never like this in Miami. There was no baggage, no history to feed the rumor mill. The gossip and whispering may not be about his mother and father anymore. Now it's all about Jenner and everything that's been happening behind the lies and closed doors. But it feels the same. They'll all keep bearing down on him until he breaks, or runs.

Why did I come back here, and give up anonymity for this? Why did I sign on for this again? It's a nightmare. No wonder Mom left and refuses to come back, for any reason, not even for me. They never stop. It never stops.

"You have a guest," Jenner says expectantly.

Brayden closes his eyes to block them all out, feeling a little light-headed with the degree of his fear of the truth being laid bare—all of his sins, shames and failings. "Yeah, this is Enrique. Jenner. Art." He gestures to each person in turn, waiting for Max to show up. Another awkward moment later, she does and the darkness grows for Brayden. "And this is Max."

"How do you know Brayden?" Max asks, extending a hand.

"My pleasure," Enrique says personably. "B, baby, sit down. You don't look so good. I'm a friend from Miami. Haven't seen or heard from this guy in months, so I had to stop by and see how he was doing." Shaking Jenner and Art's hands in turn, Enrique smiles at each of them, then turns back to Brayden. "You cool?"

"Yeah, it's just been one of those days."

"Or maybe it's this shitty weather," Enrique says, sitting beside him at the table. "What you need is a full day of sun and surfing.

You'd be good as new."

"That would be sweet," Brayden agrees with a tired smile. "I fuckin' miss the ocean, man. This cold weather's killin' me. But the company is good."

"We miss you, B. I think all of Florida misses you. But Andre most of all."

Max asks, "Who's Andre?"

For a second Brayden's brain locks up as he hurries to say something before Enrique can, and possibly out him. "He's a friend."

"Brayden's old roomie," Enrique says. He pulls out a phone before Brayden sees or can stop him. With a few taps at the screen, Enrique pulls up a photo that he displays for the others. Max slides over a chair and takes the phone from Enrique after asking with a glance for permission to do so.

Brayden hunches forward, staring down at his lap as one by one, Max, Art and Jenner look at the picture of the dark-skinned wall of a man with his arm looped companionably around Brayden's shoulders. They're at the beach, with Brayden in a wetsuit and Andre in trunks, his muscular build on display, glistening in the sunshine.

Brayden can sense Jenner's eyes on him. That's why Brayden is looking everywhere but back at him. Part of Brayden listens in as Art asks Enrique how they met and Enrique tells them about clubbing and bonfires at the beach. He doesn't participate and knows that Enrique is a good enough friend to guess at some of the reasons why.

Ten minutes later, Brayden has had all he can take of the conversation about his former life as they skirt around the fact that he was fucking around with Andre sexually. Max has gone to lend support to Jackson with minding the bar but Art and Jenner linger.

"'Rique, can we pick this up later?" Brayden asks. "I get off at eleven tonight if you want to meet up then."

"Sure, bro. Call my cell. We'll figure it out. Sorry for dropping in on you like this, but I had to take the chance."

"No problem." Brayden hugs him, unable to meet his good friend's big brown eyes filled with concern.

They head out into the hall and Brayden watches from there as Enrique leaves through the front door with a wave, but it's like

Brayden is moving on instinct alone. He's lost in his head, heart pounding, his skin too tight, ready to lash out at anyone who touches him or looks at him funny. He needs to get out of there. He needs to get out of the bar and just go as far and as fast as his legs will carry him, all the way to goddamned Florida if possible. This was a mistake, he realizes. All of it—every moment since his Nana asked him to move back here.

A hand falls on his shoulder and he instinctively throws an elbow back, not even thinking about it. But the arm is caught before it connects, twisted painfully until the sharp twinge in his shoulder muscles wakes him up a little.

"My office. Right now," Jenner's voice growls in Brayden's ear.

Neither of them notice Art and Max watching on from the kitchen as Max gives him a food order. They see Jenner easily block Brayden's thrown elbow to the gut and pin his arm without thinking about it. They see the subsequent pain evident in Brayden's expression and how Jenner manhandles him into the small office.

"Art, wait," Max calls as Art follows after them. But it's too late.

"Just watching out for Brayden," Art tells her as he goes, "I'm trying to give Parrish the benefit of the doubt, here, but this has gone far enough."

"Got it," she says softly.

"Go help Jackson. You stay out of it."

In the office, Jenner closes and locks the door behind them, switching on the radio to drown out their voices. He pulls both of Brayden's arms behind his back, pushing them up until the muscles are strained to their limit, and shoves Brayden forward, face-first against the door. Trapping him there, Jenner uses all of his body weight to keep Brayden in place.

When Brayden fights, pressing back against Jenner with his shoulders, his feet planted on the floor and scrambling for purchase, Jenner isn't moved an inch. He just stares calmly down at Brayden's flushed face, blond hair whipping Jenner's neck. Brayden grunts hard, pouring all of his pent-up energy into trying to get free of Jenner.

It's better not to let Jenner in—to let *anyone* in. Brayden loved his father honestly and profoundly, with his whole heart, and all that ever got Brayden was pain. It was bad enough when their family was torn in half when his mother left. Brayden hadn't even processed that loss when his beloved father's absence became complete, irrevocable. He was gone before Brayden got to really say goodbye. He hadn't meant to break his father's heart, to banish one of the best, purest things in his life. The excruciating sadness in his father's eyes while he was sick and dying, alone in that hospital room without even the comfort of Lara at his side, holding his hand—Lara who couldn't face that pain, even for Anthony's sake—is Brayden's burden to bear. He remembers his one, last visit to his father in that hospital room, with Nana, and the horror of the truth his mother was trying to shield him from.

The truth is always a horror.

All of his terror of being nothing but what everyone else deems him to be—not a man at all, but the sum total of his faults and failings—bursts to the surface. All of his anger at having to keep secrets from everyone from his own mother to his best friends, at having to lie and being unable to enjoy his life without shame, funnels into him bucking against Jenner's larger, solid body.

"Come on, slave. That's all you got? Shake me off. I want to see you try. This isn't trying. This is just pathetic."

This riles Brayden anew and he cries out, sounding desperate. Pushing off from the floor and back from the thick wooden door into Jenner's muscular chest, Brayden tries. But Jenner just twists his wrists more sharply. Brayden's shoulders scream and he gasps sharply, the right side of his face flush to the door's flat surface.

"Lemme go," he snarls.

Let go before I hurt you, too. Just let me go.

"No, I don't think so," Jenner says smoothly.

Brayden's arms, shoulder to palm, hurt so badly that tears spring to his eyes, but he's not done. Jenner knows it before Brayden does. Planting his forehead against the door, Brayden uses that as extra leverage. His feet slide on the linoleum floor, squeaking. Jenner eases a thigh up between Brayden's legs, spreading them. It makes Brayden shudder with lust to be faced with proof that Jenner is determined to make him stay, to make him feel and face things he can't on his own, even if they're scary. Even if they hurt.

His chest heaves. His skin tingles everywhere. The spot on his forehead that he's grinding against the door starts to burn with agony.

"Stop it. Turn your head. Now." When he doesn't do it instantly, Jenner pushes Brayden's arms impossibly higher. It's fear that they might just break from the strain that gets Brayden to give in. He turns his face to the side and tries to catch his breath, whimpering as he gasps with the ache. "Better. Isn't that better?"

Jenner's knee moves against Brayden's crotch in a slow drag that gets Brayden to spread his legs wider without being asked. Sweaty, hot to the touch, hair stuck to his face in places and breathless, Brayden revels in the helplessness.

"Are you hard right now?" Jenner asks. "Filthy whore. Is that how I should treat you? Huh? As my *whore*?"

The pain in Brayden's arms is stronger than his ability to listen to what Jenner is saying, but he gets the drift. When the thigh grinds against him again, he tries to rock against it, counter to the movement. He mumbles something, but it's unintelligible.

"Sorry, what was that?" Jenner asks, leaning in so that his lips are right by Brayden's ear, making his skin pebble and his stomach flip.

"Said *yes*," Brayden hisses.

"Yes what?" Jenner purrs, lips moving against the shell of Brayden's ear as he eases his arms down, rubbing up them as Brayden flexes his hands.

"Yes, *Sir*."

"I'm sending you upstairs. Obviously you aren't capable of handling work. You're a danger to yourself and I won't tolerate it any longer," Jenner says softly.

"Please let me finish my shift," Brayden says through gritted teeth. "I'll be fine. I need the pay."

"Fuck the pay. I'll pay you for sex like the whore you are if you're that hard up for it. You get on your knees on my bed, spread your cheeks and I'll take it from there."

It shouldn't turn him on to be spoken to like that, Brayden knows on some level, but it does. A hard shudder rips through him.

Jenner feels it.

"I'm not your kept boy," Brayden argues halfheartedly.

"You are now. Compose yourself, then march your ass upstairs. We'll talk about this later."

Pure pleasure, a heady wave of it, washes over Brayden at hearing that he doesn't have to explain his reactions, everything clamoring for attention in his brain and heart. Jenner understands without Brayden needing to say a word. He's not casting judgment. He's forgiven Brayden already, without question. More than that, he's giving Brayden an out. He doesn't have to linger in an uncomfortable situation. If he chooses to trust Jenner, and how much Jenner cares about him, Brayden can lose himself there, in the safety of that. He doesn't have to be alone anymore, but can just go upstairs, and face his issues later, with Jenner at his side, fighting for him. It's intoxicating.

"Thank you," Brayden moans. "Thank you, Sir."

Jenner steps back, seeing everything. Power and confidence exudes from Jenner, making Brayden feel completely at ease. It's okay to be weak and damaged because Jenner is strong. Brayden waits for his breathing to regulate. Then he smooths his hair, straightens his clothes, and waits for the throbbing of his erection, hot against his leg and held there by his tight briefs, to dull to a manageable level.

With a nod he tells Jenner that he's ready.

They shut the radio off and open the door. Jenner leaves first, checking to make sure no one is there to give Brayden a hard time as he makes his way to the break room for his things. He gets three steps from the office doorway when the punch thrown by Art connects with the side of Jenner's jaw.

Stepping out from behind a stack of shelves, Art draws his fist back as Jenner grimaces. Jenner's hand goes to his face as he gives his friend an incredulous stare. Art cocks his arm back for another hit, but Brayden barrels out of the office.

"Stop!"

Art throws the punch but Jenner's ready for it and bobs out of the way in plenty of time. While Art straightens, Jenner hits him in the gut, driving some of the air from Art's lungs.

"Stop it!" Brayden yells. He moves to get between them.

"Don't protect him!" Art bellows.

"What the hell is wrong with you?!" Jenner shouts, trying to get around Brayden.

"Get away from him, Braydy," Art warns. "I'm not letting this fucker lay his hands on you anymore."

"What do you think is going on here, exactly," Jenner demands, licking blood from his teeth.

"Jenner. Don't," Brayden begs, gone from flushed to pale again, too fast. "Please. Art, it's none of your business."

"It *is* my business now. I saw the bruises. I heard him in there with you. I heard everything—the way he threatened you. I heard him hurting you. I heard you *beg him* to stop. It stops now. I don't give a shit if you are my friend, Parrish, or my boss. You don't get to treat him like that."

"Oh my god," Brayden groans, hiding his face in his hands. "This isn't happening."

"This isn't your fault," Art tells Brayden.

"You don't know what you're talking about," Jenner spits. "You have no idea."

"Oh, I think I do."

"*Jenner*," Brayden pleads, turning to him. "Please don't."

"It's too late," Jenner says. "He thinks I'm using you as my own personal punching bag or some shit."

"Worse than that and you know it," Art seethes. And that's when Jenner puts it together. As Brayden looks on, Jenner's face lights with dismayed realization. Brayden wants to deny all of it, every part.

"What we do is our business and no one else's. We don't owe you an explanation," Jenner says. "Fuck off."

"No. Brayden, come on. Get away from him. He's probably got you brainwashed, thinking you have to do what he says or pay the consequences."

"This is so fucked up," Brayden moans, his head throbbing. He wanders away from both of them, sitting on a large box placed against the wall a few feet away.

Murder gleams red and ready in Art's face. It becomes quite apparent that he's not going to let this go.

Lowering his voice as much as possible, Jenner hisses through his teeth, "I am not raping him. That's not what this is. You don't get to assume you know what's going on here after eavesdropping on part of a private exchange through a closed door."

"I can't do this. I can't." Brayden says, giving up, unwilling to be a part of the argument after they've thrown the word 'rape' out there. He bolts for the exit, pushing past Max when she appears.

"Fuck. Brayden! Bray, wait!" Jenner calls, but when Jenner starts to run after him, Art growls, "Oh, no you don't," and punches him in the stomach, doubling Jenner over, sending their worlds tumbling into chaos.

Chapter 21

Pain

Holding on to the pain grinding like shards of glass under the skin, using it like a lifeline leading him to safer ground, Jenner climbs the flight of steps to his apartment. It had taken an hour of solitary work, but he'd managed to close the bar by himself after Max and Art took off, leaving him bruised and bleeding in both literal and figurative ways. There were a few other members of staff left but Jenner told them to go home too, preferring to do the job himself and avoid the awkward stares and silence.

He could have defended himself against Art's attack, but was strangely unwilling to. After all, Art's intentions were pure, if misguided. With his best friends thinking Jenner capable of such terrible acts, the punishment seemed warranted. He let Art lash out because it felt like a crucial wake-up call. Maybe, after everything, Jenner really has been the bad guy in all of this.

It's not even seven o'clock, but he didn't have enough people to keep the place open and wasn't up to it anyway. The wounds on his face, the nauseous ache in his belly from being kicked by Art's solid boot, it's nothing compared to the hurt to his ego and the defenselessness he feels, with no idea where Brayden could be, or what he must be thinking. Then there's the problem of what he's going to do about his business if half his staff have gone permanently AWOL. If he wants to mend things with Max and Art, he needs to expose much more of what he's promised Brayden, and himself, to keep secret.

On the second to the top stair, Jenner pauses, leaning against the wall with his shoulder. His head feels like it's been stuffed with cotton. His fingers fumble at the keys in his pocket. After a minute, he gets hold of them and slides one into the lock only to have the door swing right open before he can turn the key.

At first he doesn't know what to make of it. Then he wonders if he's been robbed.

That'd be a perfect way to end this day, he thinks, *to have my door busted open when there's nothing in the damn apartment worth stealing anyway.*

Readying himself for a fight, without anything resembling the energy he would need to kick someone's ass right now, he calls wearily, "If you're still here, I called the cops, and I have a black belt in jujitsu, so... yeah."

Jenner pushes the door opened and leans on the doorframe, clutching his side.

"What're you gonna charge me with? Failure to have some balls and be a man?"

His head turns so fast that Jenner gets a blinding twinge in his neck. Wincing, he squints at the figure in the shadows.

"Jesus, Jenn. Look at you."

Brayden is standing in the kitchen, arranging groceries on the countertop. Jenner doesn't know what to say except, with awe, "You're here."

"Of course I'm here," Brayden sighs. Leaving the random bottles, boxes and produce behind, he walks up to Jenner. He stares up at Jenner's face, evaluating the bruises, maybe looking for signs of breaks or more serious injury. Jenner won't meet his eyes, but hobbles past, his hand still pressed to his left side. "Are you okay?"

"Fine."

"Art did this?"

Oh, I've had it coming for a while, Jenner thinks, but says nothing. *You can only behave like a dick for so long to those closest to you before they turn it right back on your ass.*

Jenner makes it to the freezer and digs out some ice. Brayden watches him wrap the ice in a dishtowel and press it to his jaw. When Brayden starts toward him, Jenner turns his back, bracing a hand on the counter.

"Have I been out of line with you?"

"What," Brayden blinks. "No. What are you talking about?"

Rolling his eyes, Jenner tries to gather his wits, but the fuzzy feeling won't pass.

"Art has no idea what he's talking about," Brayden tells him. "I was just... I guess I was afraid to tell him about us. But I should have. I should have just gotten over my shit and stood up for you. I'm sorry. I'm so sorry. Come on and lie down," Brayden coaxes. "The new bed is here. I put some sheets on it, just, you know, to keep busy. I stopped at the market down the street for this food, too, so that we'd have some basics. Do you need more ice for your ribs? Should I take you to the hospital?"

"You should go," Jenner says quietly. "Get away from me."

"No," Brayden frowns. "No way."

"All of this sadomasochism, making you my slave, taking my orders, is it really so far off from what Art was saying it is? The safe-word is supposed to keep things in check, but if you're not in the right frame of mind to know when to use it, I should know better than to start anything with you. I *have* forced myself on you. Maybe I am the bad guy."

"Art needs to get his head out of his ass," Brayden says sharply. "He's delusional. I mean, don't get me wrong, it was kind of a trip to have someone like him standing up for me for once instead of knocking me down for being different, but you know how this started just as well as I do. I was the one wearing the collar. I chose you at Manse as much as you chose me. Don't kid yourself."

"You were miserable today. Don't try to deny it. The whole thing with Enrique. That picture of you and Andre. You were happier there, in Miami."

Brayden smiles suddenly, but it's dark, bitter. His subsequent laugh is even more so. "Shut the fuck up, Parrish. You have no idea what you're talking about." He grabs Jenner by the elbow and yanks him toward the bedroom.

Jenner shakes him off.

"Go *home*, Brayden."

"Go lie down before you pass out!" Brayden shouts.

For Jenner, it flips a switch. Everything falls away, everything but his anger.

There's a pause where everything stops. The air is thick, almost solid. Neither of them breathes. Then, Jenner moves, and he moves faster than Brayden would have thought possible given the exhaustion and pain reflected in his lover's eyes. Jenner gets hold of both of Brayden's lower arms, brings them around and up, twisting them to cross behind his neck, forces him over the edge of the countertop and kicks his feet apart.

"This is what you want? Huh?!"

Jenner's voice is rough with fury, gravelly with emotion, and it makes Brayden's skin prickle, every hair standing on end.

"You think I'm *hurt* and *fragile* right now, but I will *always* be bigger than you. I will always be *stronger* than you and *quicker* than you. I know how to disable a man. I know where the weak spots are, how to bind you, ways to hurt you. Whatever I wanted to do to you, I could, and you wouldn't be able to fight back even a little."

Brayden hears. His wrists, crossed at the nape of his neck, are held so tightly in the grip of Jenner's left hand that both hands begin to go numb. The edge of the counter presses into Brayden's gut, unyielding, and he can't even get his feet flat on the ground. The heat radiating from Jenner is powerful and, even without seeing him, Brayden can feel how big he is, how it's nothing for him to disable Brayden like this. This is *easy.*

"I might have a cracked rib," Jenner tells him in that same gruff, raspy tone. "I've been punched in the head a few times, so I'm not thinking too clearly right now, but guess what? I'm not some helpless little *fuck* that you need to handhold. I'm something you should *fear.*"

Blood pounds in Brayden's ears. His heart hammers in his chest. Brayden tries to suck down some oxygen. He focuses on that, just inhaling, his mouth slack against the cool granite. An intense shiver races down his spine.

Brayden's pants are forced down. The button fly pops as the fabric strains, pulling against his thighs. The air of the room is chilly against his bared skin when Jenner yanks the pants farther out of the way, and Brayden is overly conscious of the black briefs pulled tight over his ass, of Jenner's enormous, solid body bearing down on him, immobilizing him.

"J-Jenn…" he tries, but then Jenner's right hand pushes under the waistband of Brayden's briefs, pulling the elastic against his pelvis until he's just waiting for it to snap. Two dry fingers twist up into his body, and Brayden wheezes around a gasp, without enough breath to quite manage anything more.

"Am I helpless now?" Jenner growls. "Am I someone you want to *save*?"

Grabbing a bottle of vegetable oil from the counter amongst the scattered groceries which Brayden bought for them, for this place, *their* place, Jenner pours some on his hand. He inserts the slicked fingers back into Brayden, reaching deep.

There is no escape. Brayden's face feels like it's on fire with the force of his shame, because against all odds, he's not disgusted by Jenner's behavior. Brayden's *enjoying* this, not enough to get hard, but enough to not say stop. This isn't his Jenner; it's the town's Jenner, the don't-you-dare-fuck-with-me Jenner that Brayden was afraid of as soon as he first walked into the bar, needing a job and having to ask one of their old school's most beloved for it. There's something empowering about facing that version of Jenner, at last. Head spinning, Brayden continues to focus solely on dragging shallow breaths in through his nose. The fingers pull out, and he moans, because it's not over yet, not by a long shot.

There's movement behind him, but the hand on his wrists only holds tighter. Brayden's hands are limp, bloodless. Then he feels it, the engorged column of flesh that nudges between his cheeks. Jenner's only half-hard but he presses forcefully enough to breach Brayden anyway, drawing a low, grunted sound from him as he's entered.

"Tell me, *Brayden*, is this love?" Jenner snaps his hips, and Brayden squeezes his eyes shut as tightly as he can as he fights not to cry, hating himself for not even wanting to try to convince Jenner to stop, choosing the pain as his punishment for abandoning Jenner to his beating, and for abandoning other people too, all of those years ago.

Bending closer, so his lips are right by the side of Brayden's face,

Jenner says it again, as he violates the only good thing in his life, "Is *this* love?"

He wraps Brayden's hip in one hand and pushes steadily into him. Brayden's mouth works around a soundless yell. A tear slips down his cheek.

Sobbing, Jenner moves Brayden's arms. He takes them down from behind Brayden's head, stretching them out over the counter in front of them instead. Jenner lays him out, bent sharply at the waist, and holds Brayden down. Jenner tugs slowly out and thrusts back in.

Brayden scrambles a little when reentered. All he can hear is weeping — Jenner's weeping. His tears patter down onto Brayden's fevered skin.

It takes Jenner a while to realize he's not hard at all anymore. He's so disgusted with his behavior that he's wilted any twisted interest there might have been to start with.

Jenner is utterly unable to look for long at the irrationally peaceful expression on Brayden's sweet face, like he has accepted this as something deserved. Brayden's sun-lightened hair is pushed back from his sweat-damp neck, his eyes closed, trying to catch his breath. Jenner pulls out and tucks himself away, backing out of the kitchen.

He leaves the room and goes to the bathroom. Kneeling in front of the toilet bowl, he waits to be sick, certain it's coming, feeling the bitter taste of vomit rising in his throat.

An uncertain amount of time later, he is still kneeling there on the tile and shivering. When arms encircle him from behind in a gentle embrace and Brayden hugs him, Jenner chokes on his tears. They're too thick to wrench free and he strangles on them, wanting to die.

Only half aware, he lets Brayden guide him to his feet and out to the bed where he lays down, curling up on his good side. Brayden covers him with a blanket and lies down next to him. Jenner folds his body around Brayden and keeps him close while salty rivers burn tracks down his face.

Time slips by in large, smooth spans, like silk through fingers. When Jenner wakes, Brayden is still there, in his arms.

"Oh *god.*" Jenner gasps, the horror of what he's done rising like the sea inside his chest once more. "*Bray.*"

Brayden turns in Jenner's arms, brushes the tears from Jenner's face.

"You should have left," Jenner tells him. "You should leave. I'm worse than those... those *bullies*. What's a schoolyard bully compared to how I just treated you? Art was right. You were right. You need to go."

"Art beat you because I left you there. I abandoned you because I was too afraid to admit that I love you. *I did that.* Me. I left like a coward and let your best friend use you as a punching bag. I did *nothing* to stop it."

Sounding strange in his own ears, like someone else — small and afraid — Jenner says, "I didn't mean for it to go that far, to hurt you like that. I raped you."

It feels good to say it. It feels like a way he can effectively push Brayden out of his life for good. It'd be better that way for both of them. Safer.

Brayden is visibly unaffected. He looks back into Jenner's eyes, steady and calm. "No. I didn't say stop. I submitted to my Master's will. *I trust you*, Jenner."

Screwing his face up around his disgust, gritting his teeth, bearing down so hard that he wills something — some vital internal organ — to burst and end him, Jenner sucks in a harsh inhale and battles fresh tears. "I didn't *let you* say stop!"

"You wanna hear what 'stop' sounds like?" Brayden says smoothly, his voice a caress. He draws in a lungful of air, his chest expanding around it, and roars the word, right in Jenner's face.

Jenner doesn't even flinch, but all of the care wipes right off of his face, leaving it blank, empty.

"*That's* my fuckin' safeword. Did ya hear that?"

Gathering Brayden in his arms, Jenner hugs him, breathing in the scent of his neck, using him as an anchor, stroking his hair.

"You may be stronger than me, but you can't outsmart me,"

Brayden says calmly, always calmly. Maddeningly so, especially when force is involved. The pain pacifies him more than words or promises ever have. "Everything you do, it's because *I let you* do it. My eyes are open."

"What's wrong with us?" Jenner asks fearfully. "My god, Brayden, what the hell is wrong with us?"

"We're just a good match, is all. I love you. I trust you to hurt me."

Jenner's eyes close over tiredly.

"I was terrified in Miami. I wasn't even honest with the first person I ever let get past all the fucking excuses. I used Andre to get off but I *never* trusted him, and I never trusted my friends. Not enough, at least. It was pathetic. Maybe it would've gotten better, but I doubt it. It wasn't until I got here and you knocked me on my ass, turned me inside out, that I felt like I finally made sense. I don't make sense unless I'm with you."

Brayden pulls back, enforcing his confession with a search of Jenner's face for understanding and acceptance. Jenner, more regretful than ever, tells him softly, "I'm a sadist, Bray. That's not going to change. I thought it would be better if I scared you into hating me. Then you wouldn't have to out yourself, or take a chance on me like you are. You could go and start over without me."

"I know," Brayden says, unaffected, unfazed, like he's just glad that Jenner's finally caught up. "I'm not going anywhere."

"Max and Art think I'm a monster. I have no idea what to do to fix this."

Drying Jenner's face with a wad of tissue, brushing it tenderly, Brayden says, "We'll think of something."

Chapter 22
For What It's Worth

The next morning finds Jenner covered in bruises that wrap large spans of his torso. The inner fire that usually keeps him going has been blown right out. He doesn't want to deal with anything that has happened.

Brayden, on the other hand, seems wholly unaffected by the events of the previous day. If anything he's left stronger for it. He brings in breakfast for both of them and serves it to Jenner in bed. It's proof for Jenner that maybe Brayden was right, that he's been the one pulling the strings all along, and Jenner's just the puppet.

After the coffee has been transferred from their paper cups to their bellies, Brayden sits cross-legged, tan and vibrant beside a sickly, miserable and pale Jenner. Sounding like he's been working up the courage to say so without it coming out forced or hesitant, Brayden declares, "We have to tell them. Max and Art."

"You don't owe them that," Jenner says wearily. "It'll be better if I just fire them and move on."

"Don't be a jackass," Brayden scolds. "They're your closest friends. They obviously like me enough to kick your ass in the name of preserving my honor. I mean, really Jenn, who does stuff like that? Putting themselves out there for someone they barely know, expecting nothing in return? If anyone deserves the truth, it's them. No argument. It's decided."

"Who are you trying to convince?" Jenner snaps, then quickly bites back some of the attitude. "Even if we tell them we're together now, it doesn't explain why you were bruised and what Art overheard yesterday. Hell, if *I* heard someone saying that shit to someone I knew, I'd probably kick their ass, too."

Jenner scratches at his empty cup, eyes downcast. "You were supposed to meet up with your friend last night. I fucked that up too, didn't I?"

"I called 'Rique. He understands. He's the one that showed up without warning. He can't expect me to drop everything in my life to just spontaneously hang out. It's fine. Hey. Jenn."

Jenner looks up with a weary sigh. "I didn't use protection. Or prep you. Have you been bleeding? Did you check your underwear and the toilet for spotting?"

Fierce color blooms on Brayden's cheeks, and for the first time, he can't meet Jenner's gaze. "I'm fine. I checked." It sounds like a lie.

"There could be tiny tears. We're going to take it easy for a while so that your body can recover from any damage. And we're going to the clinic as soon as I'm dressed."

"Really, I'm fine," Brayden says adamantly.

"It's not up for discussion. I'm telling, not asking."

Brayden groans.

"And if I gave you anything…" Jenner can't finish the sentence. Imagining the possibilities prohibits speech. "I couldn't live with that."

Brayden gets off the bed, rolling his eyes. "God, you're so fucking dramatic sometimes. Relax."

"Relax?! I could have just given you a death sentence and you say 'relax'." Jenner struggles to a more upright position and swings his legs over the side of the bed with a grimace of pain. "The only way I'd get laid, up until very recently, was with random submissives at Manse. I never even asked their *names*. God, everything about me is poison to you!"

Walking back to the bed, Brayden holds Jenner's chiseled jaw in his hands and places a kiss to the top of his head where the hair is growing in a little more every day and starting to curl up at the ends. "Whatever is meant to happen will happen. Worrying about it will do shit for us now. So, *mellow out*. It's all good."

"Fucking hippie."

Brayden laughs. "Come on. I'll find you some clean clothes."

Three hours later, Brayden has used up all of his bravery and bravado. His good mood is gone. He's off in his head, now that Jenner isn't there to keep him present and alert. Hurting in places and in ways he's never hurt before, feeling violated from the questions and the tests at the clinic, he's never craved an out more in his life. Even at the clinic there had been people in the waiting room he recognized. Friends of friends or customers or people who know people who know him. No one said anything to him directly, but he got a few nods of greeting, and Jenner had too. It was the worst possible time to be made to feel self-conscious about who he was with and why he was there. If only he had his own place, he could hole up with a big bottle of something abrasive and mind-numbing, and say screw the world for a little while.

Instead, he's standing in his grandmother's kitchen, listening to the shrill soundtrack to some cartoon playing in the living room and thinking with annoyance, *isn't Emma too damn old for cartoons by now anyway?*

What he should be doing is resting. But if he goes upstairs, he'll really have nothing to distract him from everything that's causing him stress. It's better to stay downstairs and be pleasantly pissed off about inconsequential things like the noise pollution.

"You're home," Ruth observes, shuffling into the kitchen while favoring her good hip. She drags out a chair and settles into it like it pains her.

"You okay, Nana?"

She waves the question off. "Sit with me. You look worse than I feel. Is there something going on with you I should know about? Anything you wanna talk about?"

Perking up with suspicion, Brayden holds his grandmother's tired gaze, trying to give nothing away. When he moves over to one of the free chairs, deciding how to explain and what to explain, he doesn't realize the stiffness that's evident in his walk, or the bruises that are becoming more visible on his arms.

"I'm fine," he says. "Just had a long night."

"You can talk to me, you know. I've been around long enough

to have heard it all."

Brayden laughs, as unaware of his sneer as he is of the careful way his bottom connects with the hard wooden seat. Taking a sip of the glass of tap water he's carried over, he resolves quietly that maybe it'd be better to go on upstairs after all. At least no one is there to question him.

His Nana continues to observe him.

It's been a few months since Brayden first showed up at her door, having sacrificed his freedom for family's sake, but at least then there was the hope of good intentions and positive thinking. Undoubtedly, there were ways to contribute and make a difference in the lives of his loved ones, and that got him through. It put a shine on his outlook. Now, the shine is gone, eaten up by a nagging hollowness brought of too much suspicion and mistrust. It casts dark circles under his eyes, chews at his soul. And there are the injuries to consider as well.

"My girlfriend, Mary," Ruth starts, slow and steady, but watching, always watching, "is having some trouble with her diabetes. She doesn't have the best medical coverage, so she goes down to the clinic that's a few minutes' drive from this end of town."

He tries to seem unaffected by this news, looking back at Ruth with a question in the shape of his eyebrows. Unconsciously, he slumps a little in the chair. There had been a few older ladies at the clinic, he can recall.

"She saw you there. Called me a few minutes before you got home, telling me about how you were sitting in the waiting room, along with a male friend. She said the two of you looked a little guilty about something, though she couldn't say what."

"There was a...." He scrambles for a reasonable excuse, feeling caught like a rat in a trap. His voice roughens and it deepens as he tries to sound confident. "A fight. At the bar. Last night. I tried to break it up."

Turning the glass of water in his hands, which tremble very slightly, he lowers his eyes to the tabletop. "I got caught in the middle. One of the guys pulled me out and held me back so I wouldn't get hurt." He holds up his wrist, indicating the bruises. "We were there to get looked at, just in case. But we're fine. I'm fine. Like I said."

"Brayden...."

"It was a bad night, okay? My... my friends got hurt and it shouldn't have happened, but we've got it under control. I'm just tired, and I'd really like to just go get some rest if it's all the same to you."

"You would tell me if there was reason to worry about you, wouldn't you? Hmm? You've been acting funny, like you're always on edge or angry. It's not like you." Already, he's standing, but she lays a hand, soft as a whisper, over his and gives it a squeeze. "If that bar isn't safe or if you're in some kind of trouble...."

"Nan."

"The job isn't worth your health," she insists, sounding worried.

"These things happen," he sighs, pulling out of her reach. "I stepped in because I have friends there. It's important to be there for people who count on you."

A tinny crash and wild, exaggerated *boings* and *bonks* sound from the television set in the next room. Frowning in the general direction, Brayden feels the intensity of his grandmother's stare. "You're a good boy, Brayden. But don't run yourself into the ground for the sake of others. That goes for me and Em too. If being here isn't agreeing with you, we'll figure out something else. I can tell that you're unhappy."

"God," he groans. "Nan, don't. This isn't about you and Emma Leah. And it's not even about the bar or the fight, it's... it's...."

"Is it about Max?"

"What?" Brayden knows for a fact that he's never so much as mentioned Max's name to his family. "How do you.... What are you talking about? I...."

"A girl—a very *pretty* girl—came by the house earlier this morning asking after you. She introduced herself as Max and seemed, well, *distraught* when I told her you hadn't come home last night. But she wouldn't say why. She left her phone number, asked to have you call her when you showed up."

A slip of notepad paper with ten numbers scrawled in flowing cursive script, written in purple ink, is slipped from his grandmother's pocket and slid across the table towards him. Picking it up,

Brayden stares in disbelief at it.

Ruth says, "Your friends are always welcome here. Max or who-ever. I'd love to meet them, get to know who you're spending time with. This is your home too, now."

Brayden grunts, distracted, half-listening.

"Well, go on. Get some rest."

"Th-thanks. Nana." Brayden says haltingly, taking his water with him as he hobbles stiffly from the kitchen.

"You're welcome, sweetheart," she says softly as he rounds the corner and disappears from sight.

Chapter 23

Enough

The phone only rings once before it's answered with a brisk, breathless, "Hello?"

"It's Brayden. I can't believe you came to my house." There's a pause and he can tell it's due to a complete loss for words, so he continues. "Jenner doesn't know I'm calling. I need to explain some things to you and Art. You need to hear it from me, and I need to say it before anyone else gets hurt."

"*You're* the one getting hurt, Brayden," Max says angrily. "Jesus, the more I find out, the worse it gets! Please tell me you weren't with him. Your Nana said you didn't come home last night. Just how stupid are you?"

"I was with him. He's a wreck. No thanks to you guys. And no thanks to me either." Brayden takes a deep breath and says it before he chickens out. "He didn't want me to come out just to save him from getting his ass kicked, or even to keep from losing his best friends. No one knows I'm... except him. No one. Jenn and I have been together for a while now. And it's none of anyone's business what we do in our personal lives, or our bedroom. I appreciate your concern, but really, I'm a big boy and I can make my own choices. I don't need you or Art protecting me from my own boyfriend."

"He was hurting you," Max tries, scrambling for an argument, audibly dumbstruck by the confession. "There were bruises. And Parrish... he said things, Art told me...."

"What can I say, Max? I like it rough. You know Parrish. He's into a specific type of guy. Guess what? I'm his type."

The silence on the other end of the line is so thick he doesn't

197

even think Max is breathing. Or else she's hung up on him.

Brayden continues, "We're gonna be stopping by to get some more of his things, so we'll talk more then. In the meantime, think about what I said."

He hangs up and drops the phone. Sitting on the floor with his back propped against the side of the bed and his knees drawn up to his chest, Brayden rests his arms on his legs and lets his head fall back against the bedding. The ever-present, ever-growing panic crawls up his gut to his throat, constricting his windpipe until his lungs burn. He wishes, more than anything, that Jenner was there with him. Jenner would understand. But calling Max was something Brayden had to do himself.

Across the street, diagonal to where Brayden is suffering through his panic attack, Max's ear is warm with the fading sound of Brayden's smooth, low voice, confessing to her that he's been getting fucked by Jenner for a while, and that he likes it rough. A tingling heat sparks between her thighs, thinking about that, imagining it. The tingle grows into a needful ache as her imagination provides obscene mental images of Jenner and Brayden.

"Who was that?"

Max nearly jumps out of her skin. Art stands in the doorway to her bedroom with Jenner's kitten tucked into the crook of his arm. Max clears her throat and forces her thoughts back on track, even as her fantasy provides the imagined sound of Brayden's moan when Jenner bends him over and stuffs him full of his cock.

"Whew, uh..." she laughs giddily. "It's funny, that was, uh... Brayden. Seems someone's been a bad, bad boy."

After she tells Art everything that Brayden said, Art stares blankly at her, waiting for the punch line that never comes. "You don't really believe that, do you?" Absentmindedly, he scratches behind the kitten's ears. She purrs appreciatively. "Brayden's clearly covering for him. Parrish probably threatened him if he didn't put our minds at ease."

"I don't know," Max says doubtfully. "He was pretty convincing. And, I mean, Parrish is an ass but maybe he's not *actually* a psychopath. Maybe it is just the S&M stuff and they're both into it?"

"Bullshit," Art over-enunciates, guarding the small white kitten the way he's trying to guard Brayden. "You don't treat people you care about like that."

"Maybe Jenner does," Max shrugs.

Back in his bedroom, still sitting on the floor and enjoying how uncomfortable the position is, Brayden can't seem to find the motivation to get up or do much of anything besides sit there. When he hears someone walk up to his door and slowly push it open, he barely registers it.

His cousin moves into the room, her wide eyes magnified adorably by her glasses, making her look like a cautious squirrel. They measure each other without saying anything. Brayden marvels at how old she looks, scolding himself for always thinking her a child, but he can't muster the energy to put on his façade any longer. He lets her see how wrung out he is, and how scared.

"Can I help?" she says in her soft little voice.

"C'mere," he sighs, patting the spot on the floor beside him. She springs into action and swiftly sits, tucking her body up close to his. It's an instant comfort just to not be all alone, even if there's no real way that Emma can help.

"You look scared. What do you have to be scared of?"

"It's kind of hard to explain." He imagines his Nana — or worse, his mother — seeing him with Jenner's arm slung protectively around his shoulders, or holding his hand. That's a scary thought. He imagines Jenner kissing him in full view of everyone in the bar, and that's just as bad. But at the same time, it makes him angry that he can't easily have those basic public displays of affection with the person he's involved with. Looking down at Emma, Brayden tries to remember what it was like to be her age, and can't quite manage it. She seems so delicate, helpless — the physical embodiment of Brayden's mental state.

"Do you ever get scared?" he asks her, thinking of schoolyard bullies and peer pressures.

Emma thinks it over, biting at her bottom lip. She leans forward, elbows braced on her skinny, folded legs, her curtain of golden brown hair hanging beside her face. "Yeah," she says matter-of-factly after a while. "I get scared sometimes of what would happen to me if Nana ever got sick or died."

Turning slightly to face her, Brayden scoops her up in an arm and kisses the top of her head. "Emma Leah," he frowns. "Girl, I'd take care of you."

"Why? It's not your job. I'm not your kid. I'm not even your sister."

"Yes, it is my job. We're family. We count on each other. It's what we do, no matter what."

"What about your mom," she counters with determination and wisdom far surpassing her years shining behind her eyes. "Do you count on her?"

Vaguely, he knows that Emma must have heard about their past, and the way his mother walked out on all of them, leaving him alone in the world. He's living Emma's nightmare.

"We can't change who people are," he says sullenly. "We can only try to accept them."

"Are you in trouble?" Emma says in a tiny voice. "Because you don't look good at all and I don't want anything bad to happen to you. I need you. Don't go away, all right? Please?"

"I'm not going anywhere, girl," he tells her with a gentle hug. "I'm not gonna ditch you like my mom did to me. That's not what this is about."

"Then what is it about?"

"I'm sorry, I can't tell you. At least not yet. Maybe someday. Okay? This is something I have to figure out on my own first."

She searches his face. When she decides she doesn't like what she sees, she throws herself at him, hugging tightly to his chest, pressing her face there. He wraps her in his arms and somehow it allows him to climb back out of his own head. Emma is real, and solid, and he's scaring her. That's something he can't abide.

The doorbell rings later that afternoon, when the sun is sinking low, grazing the edge of the horizon. Brayden assumes that it's one of his Nana's friends from church or the neighborhood stopping by to nose around and see what this business is about her grandson going to the medical clinic. He's sitting on the couch beside Emma, helping her think of ideas for an essay assignment from her English professor when Ruth calls from the foyer, "Brayden! You have company!"

Max, he thinks. Detangling from Emma and her schoolbooks, Brayden stands and shakes his hair back over his shoulders, pushing some irritably behind an ear.

"Coming!"

He prepares himself for the defensive, ready to say whatever needs to be said when he sees not Max's petite shape waiting in the doorway beside his grandmother, but a much, much larger one.

"What the hell are you doing here," he says automatically as his blood turns to ice in his veins. He can't reconcile it. The instinct to run from revelation is almost overpowering. He stops advancing and instead takes a step backward.

"Brayden Clare, I am taking no responsibility at all for your poor manners. What a way to greet your friend! Please, won't you come in," Ruth says, gesturing into their home with a welcoming smile. "It's so nice to meet you. Brayden so rarely introduces his friends to us."

Jenner Parrish, almost as tall as the doorframe, his shoulders nearly as wide, makes no move to squeeze himself through. In a moment of irrationality, Brayden sees his lover as a human wall, ready to grab and take him prisoner, to force him to confess all of the ways he's been a disappointment to the very people he most wants to hide them from. He imagines Jenner staking his claim to Brayden like a Neanderthal, dragging him off by the hair or mounting him right in the hallway. Even the back door doesn't seem promising, as Jenner has already displayed how much faster he is, his reflexes that much more honed.

Someone touches Brayden's lower back and he almost yells in surprise. Then Emma fits herself against his side, her arm circling his back, and asks curiously, "Who is it?"

Taking a deep, calming breath, trying to regain his composure, Brayden uses his cousin as an anchor and wraps her little shoulder with a hand. One look at her face and he knows she can tell he's scared, and that it's the newcomer that's caused it. Mainly to derail her suspicions, Brayden finds his voice at last and says shakily, "This is Jenner Parrish."

"Parrish for short." Jenner smiles charmingly, taking Ruth's hand in greeting. "You must be Ms. Clare." He turns slightly to the girl hiding herself under Brayden's arm. "And Emma Leah."

"Parrish is my boss. At the bar," Brayden finishes stupidly.

"And a friend," Jenner adds.

Brayden blushes a dark, deep red.

"Oh, then I can ask you directly," Ruth says to Jenner. "Is everything okay over there? We heard you all had some trouble last night."

The stark bruises on Jenner's face are proof enough of this, though no one says so.

"Yes, ma'am," Jenner says in his suave baritone. "Right as rain. We've got everything under control. I'm just sorry that Brayden was involved. It was a friendly scuffle that got a little out of hand."

"Well, okay then. Better safe than sorry. Please, come in. Can I get you anything?"

Bowing his head, Jenner barely glances Brayden's way before answering, "Thank you for the invitation, but unfortunately I can't stay. I stopped by on my way to see a mutual friend and was hoping Brayden would want to join me."

The constant, low ache that Brayden has had in his rectum all day long from the rough sex the previous night suddenly intensifies. Clenched, tensed and awkward, he grabs a jacket from a hook on the wall and gives Emma's arm a brief squeeze in goodbye.

"Yeah, come on," Brayden mutters, pushing past Jenner without looking at him. He feels Jenner's hand on his back as Brayden passes, with Jenner stepping aside to let him by. The contact is startling, like being nudged with a hot poker. It causes Brayden to flinch slightly.

"Thank you. Have a nice evening," Jenner tells them.

"Give us a call if you're going to be late!" Nana tells Brayden, shaking her head in disapproval of Brayden's attitude and giving a wave.

They're no more than halfway down the path to the sidewalk when Brayden hisses under his breath, "Quit touching me!"

Jenner simply waves farewell over a shoulder and keeps his right hand firmly planted between and just below Brayden's shoulder blades.

"Since when do you think you can tell me what to do?" Jenner returns, just as quietly. "And I don't recall giving you permission to

call Max for a chat about your *boyfriend*, either. Seems to me someone needs to be reminded of his place."

Brayden's face is so hot he can feel sweat beading on the skin
from the force of his blush. At first he clams up, unable to respond
with the appropriate, submissive reply or even find the balls to remain defiant. When they're a few houses down the road and Jenner's house nears swiftly, Brayden knows it's now or never, that
something needs to be said before they get there and he has even
more drama to deal with.

"She came to my house. I had to do something. And I felt like
she might be more likely to believe me if I confronted her without
you. Sir," he adds after a pause. They've stopped and Brayden is
hyperaware of how massive and displeased Jenner is beside him.
He's just as aware of being outside, in full view of the entire street.
Anyone could be watching.

"That doesn't change the fact that you didn't ask for permission
beforehand. This involves both of us, my privacy as well as yours.
You acted out of turn."

"I'm sorry," Brayden hears himself saying a little breathlessly.
The very real presence of Max and Art's home looms before them.

"If we're telling them the truth, we need to do it the right way,
and tell the *whole* truth," Jenner says. "As long as we're in there, it'll
be medium protocol. That means I'll be doing the talking. If I want
you to say anything, I will tell you so. Are we clear? They will not
have permission to speak to you directly. That's how it works. They
go through me. If they speak to you without my permission, you are
not to answer them or even look at them. You don't need to kneel,
just to stay by my side. Those are the rules."

Brayden nods. He still feels unsteady, but less scared. The rules
Jenner has laid out help him get a grasp on the idea of walking up
to the door and facing Max and Art. His relief is reflected in his expression and Jenner's fingers caress in a gentle arc, back and forth
over his skin through his shirt. They're right out on the street and
anyone could be watching—Nana, Emma, Max, Art, or any number
of neighbors or passers by—but the soothing touch is like a private
promise from Jenner to Brayden. It makes his cares about the rest of
the world fade away.

"This isn't about either of us being gay. This is about them accepting our lifestyle. There's a big difference. There's nothing here to be ashamed of."

The words, so plainly spoken, are like cooling waters over a sunburn.

"I love you," Brayden tells him urgently.

They're out there for anyone to see. It's not safe. Brayden can see how badly Jenner wants to kiss him, but he holds himself back, for whose sake, Brayden doesn't even know. But briefly, Jenner's hand comes up and brushes tenderly over Brayden's cheek.

An older man who lives down at the end of the road walks past with a Doberman on a leash, looking at them with a tight-lipped frown. Someone else a few houses away walks down their driveway to pick up a newspaper and they seem to linger, like they don't want to miss a chance to snoop. The man with the Doberman pauses by a mailbox as the dog sniffs the spot and Brayden can sense his displeased stare.

Jenner and I are standing too close. The way he's touching me isn't right. Not to them. But it shouldn't matter to me what they think, so why do I feel this way?

The doubt makes him feel queasy and ashamed of something that should be only wonderful and celebrated.

Jenner's hand falls away, like Brayden's 'I love you' and the gentle touch never happened.

Very softly, his expression perfectly composed and inscrutable, Jenner says, "I love you, too. More than you know."

The walk up to the front door takes an impossibly long time. It feels like many sets of eyes are on him. Paranoia is like fingernails tickling up his spine. To cope, Brayden shuts down and puts himself in Jenner's hands. They stand on the front porch. Jenner's hand has been on the center of Brayden's back since they left his house. It's there now — possessive but not overly so.

Jenner could just use the key to open the front door, but he rings the bell instead. Moments later, the door opens and Art is there, intimidating and huge. Distantly, Brayden wishes he had smaller friends.

Jenner's hand is on Brayden, screaming 'this is mine.' The

downward cast of Brayden's eyes and the innate submissiveness in his stance is evident, with his hands tucked in his pants pockets, his long hair falling over his shoulders as he bows his head. The ugly bruises on Jenner's face along his jaw, put there by Art, are stark and unmistakable.

As the moment draws out too long, a lot of things seem painfully obvious. Most of all, maybe, the way Brayden can't help but turn slightly into Jenner's touch when his nerves start to get the best of him, seeking comfort.

Silently, patiently, Jenner waits for Art to make the first move, but his eyes are trained on something quite small hiding at Art's feet. When Art says nothing after minutes have passed, Jenner reaches out with his left hand, palm-up.

Slumping slightly with resignation, Art scoops the cat up from the floor with both hands, careful not to let it scramble free or slip through his large fingers. He hands it over to Jenner, setting the feline on the outstretched palm. Immediately, the cat scurries up Jenner's arm and curls into a ball against his chest, where it knows it belongs. Brayden glances over. A small, amused grin curls his lips, there and gone.

"Sorry about the face and all," Art grumbles. He gestures lamely at his own jaw, then clears his throat, folding his arms over his chest.

"Can we talk? Inside?"

"Sure. It's still your house too."

Art steps back inside. They follow and go to the living room to stand around awkwardly, but at least they're out of the sight of anyone else that's on the street or peering from windows.

"Is Max here?" Jenner asks softly, probably, Brayden supposes, because the house is so quiet and any louder tone of voice might be misconstrued as aggression. That's not how they want to start this off.

"Yeah," Art says, matching Jenner's hushed tone. Then he bellows, making Brayden jump, "MAX!!"

"Jesus," Brayden gasps, forcing his heart back down out of his throat. Jenner gives him a sideways glance, takes his hand and weaves their fingers together.

Ducking his head, hiding behind his hair, Brayden tries to will himself invisible.

"What is it?!" Max complains, jogging into the room, sounding aggravated at being yelled for. When she sees the three of them, she stops, deflates, and mumbles, "Oh."

Without missing a beat, she turns to Brayden, opens her mouth with an upraised finger, but before she can make a sound, Jenner cuts in. "We all know that you and Brayden spoke on the phone and what was said. I didn't bring Brayden here so that he would have to defend his sexual orientation to the two of you. We're here to clear the air regarding our chosen lifestyle, since you seem to have enough of a concern about it to resort to violence. Obviously, I think I speak for all four of us when I say that who we are intimate with is no one else's business. But since you have expressed concern for Brayden's wellbeing, we are here to confirm that he and I are in a sexual relationship with a clearly defined, *consensual* power dynamic. If you overhear me giving him orders, that's why. If you see marks on his body, it's because I put them there *with his consent*. If he ever has reason to need your help, with anything, I'm officially giving him permission to come to either of you." Jenner looks directly at Brayden as he says this. "Agreed?"

Brayden clenches his jaw and nods tightly, mumbling a barely audible, "Yes, Sir."

"Louder, please. This is important. They need to hear you clearly."

"Yes, Sir," Brayden manages with a little more volume.

Tentatively, Brayden raises his eyes and sees Art squinting doubtfully at them. Max's expression is unreadable.

"Brayden," Jenner asks. "Do you have any need of help right now? Do you have anything you'd like to say?"

It's not a question of safety, but of judgment. They're both judging him, Brayden knows, and it feels like high school all over again—the old pain, soul-deep, flares up, all-consuming. It's all pointless. Futile. They'll never understand. Who he is, *what* he is, will never be okay. He turns toward his Master, hiding his face against Jenner's arm. Brayden's breath hitches and Jenner sighs, wrapping Brayden in what is unquestionably an embrace radiating with love and sweetness.

Jenner holds Brayden to his chest and hushes him, "This was too much to ask of you. Let's go. We'll forget the whole thing, okay? It was a bad idea."

Brayden turns his face up to Jenner, craning his neck, his vision blurring with unshed tears. He sinks back into that feeling of childlike fear and innocence, like the world is against him and trying to take everything that matters away; his father, gone; his mother, gone; his lover concealed behind self-made walls, unreachable. Each absence tears Brayden apart a little more. And his so-called friends stand by, drawing their own conclusions about everything.

Jenner's expression colors with anguish and he seems to forget to be so guarded. He forgets where they are or what the rules are. He just kisses Brayden with the force of all of the love in his heart.

They break apart when Brayden feels the cat rub its head against his stomach. He takes her carefully from Jenner and presses a kiss between the tips of her ears. "Hey, pretty girl."

Jenner slings an arm around Brayden and begins to guide him from the room without bothering to favor the others with a single glance. "Come on. Let's go home."

"Wait," Art says, his voice heavy. "We were wrong." He exchanges a look with Max. She sighs and runs her fingers back through her hair. "Brayden, I'm sorry if we made you think you had to justify your choices to us. We were just really worried about you."

Unable to look in their direction at all, Brayden cuddles Jenner's kitten and gazes out the front window instead, towards the awaiting sunshine and freedom from confrontation.

"You're really in love, aren't you?" Max says with awe. "I can't believe we didn't see it. Well, maybe I didn't want to see it. God, I feel stupid. Parrish…."

Jenner's eyes flash dangerously at her. "I'm sorry, but I have to make preserving Brayden's privacy my priority. I need him to feel comfortable at work, and after you both attacked me without even bothering to ask me about this first, when you *know* where it is that I've always gone to find partners…."

"You're firing us," Max realizes.

"For what it's worth, we can be discreet," Art tells them. "You're absolutely right that it's not our business and, honestly, I would rather be there so that Brayden has someone he can go to if he needs to. Sure, I want to keep my job but, Parrish, after all these years... you know you can trust our word, man. I give you my word that this stays between us."

"Yeah. Me too," Max adds.

"It's not up to me," Jenner replies with a touch of regret. "Not anymore. This isn't about me."

Brayden is astonished by Jenner's words, proof of how much Brayden means to him. There they stand, with Art and Max taking in the sight—Jenner with two treasures in his life held protectively against him, the brazen dare in his stance and expression, waiting for them to think less of him for being made vulnerable, and determination to wear his heart on his sleeve anyway.

"I'm really happy for you, Brayden," Max tells him, filling her words with urgency. "You deserve to have good things in your life, because you're one of the sweetest, most pure-hearted guys I've ever met and I'm just sorry you felt like you couldn't trust us not to hurt you. But if you've got Parrish here fighting for you, then you ain't got nothin' to worry about, eh?"

He's still unable to reply, waiting for the other shoe to drop and someone to laugh, for it to turn into a big joke, because it's going too well. It can't be this easy. There has to be a catch.

"And that kiss was fuckin' hot, by the way. I can tell what you see in each other, just, you know, speaking as someone else who digs penis."

Brayden laughs unexpectedly, and looks over to Max at last. "Nice," he chuckles.

She shrugs. "What? It's true. Art's probably just confused by the whole thing."

"Hey man, that just means there's more pussy available for me. Less competition. It's all good."

The cat meows, loudly, and Jenner says, "Not you, baby," ruffling the fur on her head. "Different pussy." Brayden flashes a smile up at Jenner, his eyes sparkling.

"I trust you guys," Brayden says after a moment's thought. "I don't want you to lose your jobs over my self-consciousness."

"Hey," Jenner whispers to him. "It's my business. It's my call."

"You said it was *my* call. I'm making the call. Sir."

"Are you sure, babe?"

A thrill races down Brayden's body at the use of the endearment used in earshot of other people. That's something he could definitely get used to, Jenner showing just how much Brayden means to him for anyone to see, feeling like he belongs to Jenner, letting others know that.

"Yes, I'm sure," he says confidently. Jenner cups Brayden's face in a hand, leans down and places a soft kiss to the corner of his mouth.

"Okay." Turning back to Art and Max, Jenner says, "You can keep your jobs. As long as you keep this to yourself, that is. And I mean *all* of it."

"No problem," Art nods.

"Absolutely," Max echoes.

A short time later, Jenner and Brayden are up in his room, packing up some of Jenner's things to move to the apartment, including all of the supplies for the cat.

"I can't believe you named her Pussy. Or, well, I can," Brayden smirks, shooting Jenner a sideways glance.

Jenner's not smiling, though. He's still on the defensive. "I want you to promise me that the first time you're getting uncomfortable or they step out of line, you'll tell me, immediately."

"Yeah. Okay. I promise."

"I'm serious."

"I can tell. I get it. Okay. Yes."

Jenner steps up to him. Wrapping Brayden's golden hair in a fist, Jenner yanks gently on it. It forces Brayden's head back slightly as Jenner leans down closer, breathing him in. He rubs up over the side of Brayden's neck, chasing the touch with a scrape of his teeth then sucks a rough kiss just below Brayden's ear. "Yes, what?"

"Yes, *Sir*," Brayden moans. His eyes close over in delirious pleasure.

Chapter 24
Playing by the Rules

"It really is adorable when you get nervous like this."

"I-I should go down there and help. It's loud, and loud means customers. I can handle customers."

"Lie down on the table."

For a long minute, it's a stand-off. Arms folded across the broad span of his chest, Jenner looks straight down at Brayden, who has to tilt his chin way up to meet Jenner's gaze. When Brayden straightens up and tries to stretch his spine, even rolling his weight forward onto his toes to give himself an extra inch or so, Jenner visibly represses a smile.

Heart beating fast, all of his internal warning systems blaring, Brayden tries, "Don't you have a business to run?"

"I gave you an order," Jenner says with that cocky fucking grin, with the dimples. It makes Brayden frown. He shifts his weight again, onto his right leg, and tosses his hair back over his shoulder. The tip of his tongue snakes out, just touching the center of his upper lip. Jenner warns, "Stop procrastinating, bitch."

"You said you were giving me a break," Brayden reminds him, nodding once for emphasis when all Jenner does is glare with those dimples.

"Is this defiance?" Jenner scoffs, laughing softly, but from the corner of his eye, Brayden sees Jenner's bicep jump as he flexes it threateningly.

It is clearly defiance, in addition to an intense case of nerves. It seems their relationship has progressed enough for Brayden to be able to stand up for himself a little, which is good. He still really stands no chance against Jenner's iron will, though.

Brayden does trust Jenner, his Master, and will happily submit. The thing is, he's still not able to make that last leap of faith, and walk freely over to the table, even when ordered to do so. He's waiting for Jenner to push him into the act, to force it upon him and take the responsibility of owning his desires away from Brayden. The thrill of being taken, being passionately claimed, is still much more alluring than being shameless about wanting to submit. Brayden is comfortable getting high off of Jenner's lust for him. It's safer. It takes him away from feeling like the shy, awkward boy, stepping out of his comfort zone and putting himself out there for the most popular guy around..

Sighing, Brayden pushes his hand back through a wave of sun-kissed tresses, gathering the hair from where it spills over his forehead, holding a handful of it. "No, Sir."

"Lie down on the motherfucking table."

"But, why? Maybe if you explain it, first, it'll be easier for me to—"

"You don't get to ask why. See, this is why we need to go over the rules."

"While I'm chained to the table?"

"Yeah," Jenner agrees, mocking, like Brayden's being a dumbass.

Thinking stalling might help, or at least buy him some more time, he asks, "Where's Pussy?"

"Probably down in the bar, getting hammered."

Brayden squints. "I meant the cat."

"What cat?"

"Fuck you."

"Oh, no. Fuck *you*."

"Is that what I am, now? I'm the Pussy? When someone asks about me, you deny my existence?"

Of course he's denying you, a cruel voice whispers. *Everyone denies you sooner or later.*

Drawing him from his paranoid thoughts, Brayden realizes that all humor has gone from Jenner's expression, instantly. It's a scary thing to witness.

Brayden stops breathing. His heart rate skips up even more.

Then he's knocked sideways and he has to put his hands out to brace his fall as he goes careening into the doorframe. Thankfully, he gets hold of it just as Jenner grabs him by the hips. The top half of Brayden's body falls forward until his arms, tense, push back against the wood and halt his momentum, but his lower half isn't going anywhere. Jenner's groin grinds in a firm drag against the crease of Brayden's ass. All Brayden is wearing is a pair of cut-off cargos. Winding a hand in the cascade of Brayden's hair, twisting it up to the nape of his neck, then pulling on it, Jenner forces Brayden's head back, keeps his iron grip on his hipbone, and leans close to say, "You want me to own up to this? To *everyone*? Put you on that leash you like so much and make you crawl up to Nana's house as my slave for confession? We told Max and Art and you fell the fuck apart. You getting brave on me, Bray? You got a taste of what it feels like to show people what a slut you are for my cock, how well you take your Master's orders and now you want more?"

Oh god. Oh god. Oh god.

All of the muscles in Brayden's upper body are strung out—his legs slightly spread, arms knotted with lean cords, his shoulders, back, and waist bare and on display. Every inch of him Jenner plays with a twist and a tug. Not wanting to provoke his Master any more than he has, Brayden tries to be still but at the same time ease the strain on his scalp.

I just want you to need me, he thinks, hiding his expression from Jenner. *I want you to be proud of me.*

"You're *mine*, slave. Not theirs. Got it?"

"Mmm," Brayden grunts, keeping his face turned away so that Jenner doesn't see the strange mix of happiness, hunger, trepidation and futility he feels. Part of him will always be saying he's not enough, that it will *never* be enough. If he gives himself completely, freely, to Jenner, it'll kill Brayden should Jenner decide he's disappointed and abandon him like Lara did. The need to instead feel *owned*, feel *kept*, is powerful.

"Answer me," Jenner growls with a yank of warning.

"*Yes*. Got it, Sir."

"Do I need to put your ass on that table myself, slave?"

"Yes, please, Sir," Brayden murmurs, tears sliding down his face.

It's done quickly. Jenner picks him up, carries him a few feet and lays him down on the long, low wooden table—thick and rough-hewn. They've placed it in front of a recently-purchased couch, under the overhead light in the apartment's main living space. Brayden can feel the vibrations through the floor from the chatter and noise in the bar below, reverberating up through the wood of the table. The light hanging from the ceiling is too bright and he squints against it, but then Jenner puts a mask over his eyes, making it tight. Comforted by the darkness, Brayden starts to relax. Once his ankles are chained to the table's legs, and his arms, bent back over his head, are cuffed together and chained to the other end, he relaxes even more.

Jenner moves around the apartment, turning on music and checking his phone for messages from downstairs to make sure he's not needed for the moment. His soft footsteps are tracked by Brayden, blindfolded, who turns his head this way and that as he strains his ears to catch every sound. Returning to Brayden once he's done, Jenner stops to enjoy the sight of his bound lover's sun-bronzed skin, his lean swimmer's physique, his artificially lightened hair, then sits on the couch, facing Brayden.

Jenner reaches out with his left hand and places it gingerly on Brayden's stomach, taut because of how he's strung out. Brayden sucks his stomach in at first. That's mostly instinct, bracing for anything. Jenner simply caresses him.

"We're going to have to get used to people knowing," he starts, stroking up to Brayden's left nipple, which pebbles, dragging stiffly under Jenner's touch. "And seeing it in their faces when they look at us... all of the things they imagine we're doing together."

Brayden's nostrils flare. Jenner rubs back down to his captive's navel, then farther, popping open the button on his shorts. Brayden exhales sharply when Jenner reaches inside.

"One of my new rules for you is that no one touches you, no matter what protocol, where we are or what the situation is. No one but *me*." This last part is said while Brayden's cock is closed up quite snugly in Jenner's fist, and he pulls gently on it like he was just doing to Brayden's hair.

"That means no hugging," Jenner continues. "No friendly pats on the ass. No foot massages. None of it. If someone else instigates it, you put an end to it, fast. Nod if you understand."

Brayden, breathing heavily through his nose, nods with vigor. Jenner keeps pulling on Brayden's dick while his free hand guides Brayden's shorts down in the other direction, until they're at mid-thigh.

"Better. Much better," Jenner says avidly, taking in the glorious sight held captive and presented to him. "I meant what I said about giving you a break. But just because I'm not gonna play with your ass doesn't mean I can't play with you in other ways. You'll just have to be patient, because I may have to go downstairs now and then."

"Shit," Brayden curses under his breath, wriggling as Jenner fondles his balls. Even with Jenner's promise to behave as far as penetration goes, the fact that they were both cleared at the clinic for any sexually transmitted diseases means that a lot more is on the table than used to be, so to speak.

"You couldn't have chained me to the bed if you were gonna take off?" Brayden complains.

Jenner laughs. "What's the matter? Uncomfortable?" He strokes lightly up and down Brayden's dick, getting him hard, watching him fight it—the teasing touches and the fact that he's totally on display.

Another benefit of making a trip to the house and having most of the day to bring things to the apartment is that now Jenner has all of his sex toys to play with. He has a few of them ready at his side. Taking one in each hand, he asks, "Lady's choice, sweetheart. Is it gonna be the feather or the flogger?"

"What?" Brayden blurts gruffly, his face now reddened from the stimulation between his legs. It's kind of adorable, Jenner muses.

"Simple choice," Jenner repeats. "Feather..." he drags it lightly up the underside of Brayden's erection. "Or flogger?" With his other hand, he swats at the upper inside of Brayden's left thigh, right beside his balls.

"Seriously?"

"Seriously."

Jenner begins rubbing the flogger back and forth over Brayden's testicles with a knowing, mischievous grin that Brayden can't see.

"Feather!"

"Are you sure?" Jenner asks. He drags the flogger up his captive's shaft, over the head, and back down.

"Yep. Really sure."

"You know, I was *really* hoping you'd say that."

"Oh no."

Jenner laughs. "I had to order this feather from a very specific vendor. It's unique, and I haven't gotten a chance to use it yet. The last time I offered to try it out on a slave, they chickened out."

"Dammit," Brayden swears, testing his chains.

"What's your safeword? It should be something you're not likely to shout accidentally, like 'stop'. Something that's more... well, safe."

First letting out a growl of frustration, Brayden settles down eventually and grunts, "Pussy."

"You're not changing teams on me, slave? You've had pussy on the brain all night." Bound at both ends, blind and exposed, Brayden tests his range of movement as his breathing becomes more erratic. "So, your safeword is pussy?"

"Yes, Sir. What's wrong with the feather?"

"There's nothing *wrong* with it at all," Jenner says easily, as smooth as melted butter. He tickles the soft edge of the plume from Brayden's navel up the center line of his body to his neck, up the underside of his chin, over his pursed, bow-shaped lips. "See?"

"If I beg for you to stop fucking with me, will you? Sir?"

"I appreciate your candor," Jenner smirks, trailing his toy back down. "I really do. Please, try. Beg for me, baby."

"*Please* stop fucking with me," Brayden pleads, wanton and earnest.

"Mmm, but I love to fuck you over, Bray. What's my incentive? I already have you helpless on my coffee table. It's basically my wish come true."

"I won't use the safeword if you're straight with me. How's that for incentive?" The edge in his voice tells Jenner he's getting close to freaking out.

"Fine," he laments, turning the feather over in his hands. Using the opposite end than he had been, he drags the feather's shaft over Brayden's bare hip. "Feel that?"

"Yeah," Brayden says shakily.

"The feather's shaft is made of sterling silver. It's very, very thin and carefully weighted. The end is tapered to a dull, rounded point, and it's about an inch and a half long. We okay so far?"

"Mm-hmm," is the hesitant answer.

"Good. Do you trust me?"

"Of course."

"Even after my behavior last night?"

"You told your friends about us, for me. Something you've never done before for anyone. I trust you."

Hanging his head, nodding to himself, Jenner says, "Okay. Then I will warn you that this is going to hurt, but in a way I promise you'll enjoy. I've done it myself, while apprenticing, so I know first-hand. We still okay?"

Brayden tenses, pulling on his arms, elongating his neck. Veins pop and he breathes in fits and starts. Then, gradually, he relaxes and asks, "Can I have another chain or strap? Over my chest? Please?"

"Yes. One moment."

Jenner gets up and walks from the room. Far off, possibly from the cabinet's toe kick where she seems to like to hide, Pussy the cat mewls. With the sound of leather running through Jenner's hands tickling his ears, Brayden appears to sense Jenner's return with every inch of his body. With exquisite care, Jenner wraps the strap over Brayden's upper chest and under the table to secure it.

"Better?"

"Yeah. Thank you. Feels nice."

It prohibits more movement. Jenner is quite pleased to see his slave enjoying bondage so much. With each inhale of breath the wide leather band pulls tight.

When Brayden seems even calmer, Jenner lifts Brayden's penis delicately with his fingertips. The feather's shaft is lubed. It's a urethral wand designed to reach just deeply enough to ease Brayden into the feeling of being violated in a new way. Dragging the lube-slicked pad of his thumb over the flushed, silken head of his lover's penis, pulling gently at the slit, Jenner says, "Concentrate on your breathing. You're gonna feel pressure."

"What... what are you —?"

Touching the tip of the feather's narrow end to Brayden's open-ing, Jenner allows it to ease slowly in. Brayden gasps violently and fights with impressive strength, but he's not going anywhere. Not even a centimeter of the metal shaft is inside his penis, but Jen-ner holds it there, letting Brayden adjust, watching his reactions. Brayden whimpers and grunts, turning redder in the face. The flush spreads down his neck and across his chest. His knees and thighs quiver. Jenner's baritone voice hushes, "More."

"No!"

The feather goes deeper, and Brayden cries out, then bites off the sound. He's suddenly sweating, Jenner notices, and shaking more, with his whole body, with each breath. "Beautiful, Bray.... You're doing so well. Just a little more."

With a gentle twist, an inch of the silver shaft is sheathed in-side Brayden's cock, the feather arcing with a white puff of soft-ness up from it. Jenner gets it where he wants it, then lets go, set-ting Brayden's member gently against his pelvis. Caressing over his body, everywhere, Jenner soothes him.

"Maybe next time I'll use a thigh spreader. It would keep your legs more immobilized," he ponders. With a tight, almost unnotice-able nod of his head, Brayden concurs, and heat swells in Jenner's core, his dick hot and hard against his leg. Standing, straddling the table, Jenner leans down over Brayden and plants his hands on Brayden's thighs, gripping and holding them down. Brayden moans thickly with pleasure, pushing back against Jenner's grip on him. In the clench of his jaw, the sweat dripping down his temples, the cords in his neck, the twitch of his cock, Brayden screams his lust and Jenner's gaze is glued to it. Knowing the hurt, the wonder-ful discomfort, the lusciously dirty violation, Jenner marvels at his slave's ability to enjoy the torment.

Needing to touch, to explore further, Jenner moves to kneel beside the table and lets go of Brayden's legs, even though it makes Brayden frown with disappointment.

But when Jenner licks slowly up Brayden's swelling, hot, throbbing cock, up to where the feather disappears into his body, Brayden moans wantonly. He thrusts, trying to get more contact with Jenner's tongue, so Jenner does it again, and again, tasting him, stroking him with the wet muscle of his tongue. Then he gropes at Brayden's scrotum, drawn up tight to his body. "What do you think?"

"Good," Brayden grunts hoarsely, straining at his bonds, but now out of greedy desire rather than fright. Jenner rubs up Brayden's thigh, past his hipbone to his waist. Brayden tilts his hips up in invitation. Taking hold of the feather with spectacular care, Jenner pulls it slowly out. Brayden's mouth falls open, his pelvis canted off the table, chasing the feather as it withdraws. Then Jenner lets gravity draw it back inside, the deepest it's gone yet, and Brayden shudders, breathing rapidly, his hands in fists, his arms hugged to the sides of his head as he battles the sensations.

Unable to stop himself, Jenner kitten-licks Brayden's dick until he's right about to come, with Brayden making desperate, muffled sounds, like he's trying as hard as he can not to enjoy this as much as he is.

Jenner stops licking. He stands up and moves away. "I'm gonna go downstairs to check on things," Jenner warns. "I won't be long."

Kneeling at Brayden's head, Jenner dials his own number with Brayden's cellphone. Then he unfolds Brayden's fingers, placing the phone inside them. "You know where the send button is? It'll call my cell if you need me."

"Mm," Brayden grunts, nodding, unable to speak, still shuddering. Jenner leans down over Brayden's face, kissing him upside-down on the mouth. As soon as Brayden feels Jenner's lips, he opens to the kiss hungrily, chasing Jenner's mouth, tongue-fucking it with a growl.

Jenner breaks away only after his jaw aches and his lips start to go numb, and before he can't bring himself to leave.

Chapter 25

Obedience

Palming his house keys and grabbing his phone, Jenner leaves the apartment and locks it up tight. Too impatient to care what state he's in, he takes the stairs down two and three at a time, bolting to the bar like a charging bull. He pushes through the front entrance. Max and Jackson call out hellos to him. The place is half-full, enough to keep them busy but not more than they can handle without breaking a sweat. By the door to the kitchen, Jenner corners Max as she grabs a tray laden with two large, steaming baskets of chicken wings and makes for a table where a couple of women wait patiently with mugs of beer.

"Hey," Max says distractedly. "How's it going?" Then she's past him and placing the food down on the customers' table with a big smile, asking if there's anything else she can get for them. A second later, she's back in front of Jenner. "What's up?"

"How is everything?" he counters without answering. "Any emergencies I need to know about?"

"Nah, it's been pretty cool tonight. Knock wood," she huffs, catching her breath, putting her hands on her hips, from which is draped a short apron, the pockets stuffed with pads and pens. She adjusts her bra under the black uniform shirt with a sly glance around.

Her gaze swings back to Jenner, who nods, "Great. Yeah. Great," and that's when she really sees him for the first time since he walked through the door.

"What the fuck? Are you okay, Parrish?"

Flustered, pink-faced and wild-eyed, Jenner just stares at her.

"Me? Yeah. Fine. Great." His eyes flick up to the ceiling of their own accord. He digs out his phone and looks at it expectantly. "So, things are good? You need anything before—?"

Max slaps Jenner's left cheek with an open hand.

All he does is blink at her stupidly.

"Wow," she marvels. "That's incredible."

"You hit me," he says.

"Why are you here? He's upstairs waiting for you, isn't he?"

"It's my bar. Who?"

"Loverboy?"

There's no snarky reply. Jenner just glances again at his phone. "I'm gonna check the kitchen. Call if anything comes up."

"Other than your dick, you mean? Sure thing, boss."

Jenner grunts and turns, walking away.

"I like you much more when you're getting laid!" she hollers after him. "Good job!"

Doing a circuit of the kitchen, seeing that everything is running smoothly enough in there, Jenner doesn't slow down or linger. He's ready to get out of there and go back upstairs when he sees his brother Callum walk into the bar with a date.

Jenner comes to a full stop just before he steps out into the bar's main room and becomes visible to Callum.

"What is he doing here?" Jenner grumbles, turning right around and making for the back door instead. The last thing he wants in that moment, with a raging boner and a head full of intentions for Brayden, is to run into his brother, for Christ's sake. So, leaving via the back, Jenner circles the building and pushes through the door to his apartment before he can be spotted. Climbing up is more difficult than walking or hopping down the stairs had been. It's a slower ascent than he'd like, but once he's at the door, he swiftly unlocks it and gets inside.

As he secures the deadbolt, he hears, "My fucking phone's been ringing. And I dropped yours… the cat walked by, rubbed against my fingers and…."

Blind with lust, homing in on his captive through the tingling of his every nerve-ending, Jenner kneels by Brayden's head and caresses over his chest.

"Are you okay? I'm here now. What do you need?"

"Just don't leave again," Brayden rasps. Pressing up against Jenner's hand as it slides down to his navel, tilting his hips in invitation, wanting to be touched, Brayden grows restless. "Take it out."

"You're quitting on me?" Jenner teases, shifting around to the couch, sitting there instead. He moves his hand to hover over Brayden's erection and the feather nestled inside. Barely skimming the skin, he lets Brayden feel him there through the heat of his hand and lightly grazing touches. Brayden thrusts, rutting against Jenner's palm.

"Just take it out."

"Why?" Jenner asks, "Is it too painful? Are you in agony?"

Lifting Brayden's cock, Jenner takes the shaft of the feather between his thumb and index fingers, getting a good grip on it. He holds Brayden by the root with his left hand. Slowly, Jenner draws the feather out, just a little. Brayden clenches his jaw, comes up off the table, both of his arms flexing, pushing his ass off the wood beneath him. Roughly, he breathes through his nostrils. Jenner pulls more of the wand free. For a second, he hesitates, watching Brayden's anticipation grow. Then, Jenner relaxes his grip, allowing the feather to feed slowly back into him. Brayden breaks out in a wild moan.

"You know, this doesn't seem like agony to me, Bray. It does hurt, right? I mean, you do have a metal object stuffed up your cock."

"Yes, it hurts," he growls.

The feather plays in and out, rotating, tugging, and filling him up. Brayden's cock is swollen and a dark red, stiff and hot in Jenner's grasp, the soft white of the feather a shocking contrast. Jenner pets the plume, and feels a heady rush of pleasure at the way Brayden reacts, feeling Jenner through the object, all the way deep down into his groin. He writhes when Jenner strokes back down, from feather to flesh.

"How does it hurt?"

"Enough. It hurts enough."

"You want it to stop?" Jenner dips his head, sucks a kiss just under the ridge of Brayden's cockhead, causing him to gasp. Jenner does it again a little lower and licks the spot. "Hmm?"

"I want to *come*," Brayden complains.

"Well, that's different, isn't it? Pain slut...."

"*Please*."

"It's a shame, really. You're strung so tight right now. All I want to do is fuck your brains out... stuff you full, front and back...."

"Mm," Brayden hums, restless again. He pulls at his legs and arms, alternately trying to rub up against Jenner and trying to twist away from his teasing touches.

"Let's go over a few more of my new rules. Then... maybe..." Jenner squeezes up Brayden's length, strokes down, then back up, setting a rhythm.

Brayden laughs brokenly; then grits his teeth as he throws his head back. Hips chasing Jenner's hand, the feather pushing gradually out, Brayden gulps down air by the lungful.

"Do I have your attention?"

"Y-yes, Sir."

Jenner's hand falls away.

"Don't stop," Brayden nearly sobs.

"You go tanning, am I correct?"

"What? What does that have anything to do...?"

"Answer the fucking question, slave," Jenner growls, giving Brayden's dick a light slap.

"Yes! Okay! Yes."

"Tanning bed or spray?"

"Um... uh, bed? In Florida I'd lay out, but—"

"That stops. Now. I won't permit you to get skin cancer because of vanity."

"You've gotta be kidding me."

Jenner pumps Brayden's stuffed shaft, squeezing tightly, keeping the feather in place with the tip of his finger.

Brayden growls against the discomfort, then yells, "FUCK!"

"Does it seem like I'm kidding?" Jenner says calmly. "You can get sprayed if you really want to, but if I don't like it, that's gonna stop too."

Even with half his face masked, Jenner can tell that Brayden is frowning at him. "Yes, Sir."

"I want you healthy. I want you sticking around for quite a long time. You know, so that I don't get bored. And I don't like the idea of you lying naked in some seedy tanning bed. Are we clear?"

"C-clear. Sir. Crystal."

"Good," Jenner nods. "Also, let's talk about swimming."

"Swimming?! Can you take the stick out of my cock first?"

"Don't talk back. It's not cute."

"Fuck your cute!"

Jenner chuckles. He resumes stroking Brayden, using two fingers pinched around the feather to keep it still. When Brayden is sweating and trembling, so very close to release, Jenner stops again. "As I was saying... you swim every day?"

"In the... the mornings... when I can. I try to go..." The rest gets lost in a choked moan.

"Okay. Here's the deal. I'll arrange my schedule so that we go to the gym together each morning. I'll do my thing, you do yours. But you are not to go without me. I've seen you swim. Next to fucking naked, letting them look at you, getting off on the attention. Don't you?"

"No," Brayden protests.

"Liar."

"It's... aerodynamic...."

"Fuck your aerodynamic," Jenner grins. "Your ass belongs to me now. I control who gets to see it. Not you. You can swim, but only when I'm in the building, so that if anyone acts *inappropriately*...." Teasing the tip of his index finger back over Brayden's sac to his hole, Jenner rubs in circles around it until Brayden tries to spread for him. "I can deal with that myself. Agreed?"

"Mm-hmm," Brayden grunts, his voice lilting. "A-a-agreed. Sir."

"Slut," Jenner whispers.

"Fuck me," Brayden pleads, made wanton by the pain, blindfold and bondage.

"No."

"*Please.*"

"*No.* One more thing." All over the caramel-colored expanse of Brayden's chest and around his pinkish-brown, hardened nipples is a light dusting of golden chest hair. Jenner scratches through it, leaving pink lines in the wake of his short nails. He tries to pull at it, but it's too short to get hold of. "Who waxes you?"

"Shit," Brayden groans, focusing on the play of Jenner's fingers on the hair beside his nipples. His chest rises and falls more quickly. "Me. Or someone at a salon a few miles from here. I guess you don't approve."

"What do you think?"

"Goddamn, you're a control freak."

"You say that like you're surprised. Or disappointed. You're *mine*, slave. That's true whether you're actively spreading for me or not." Catching Brayden by surprise, Jenner yanks away the blindfold, letting it fall to the floor. "Look at me and tell me that you wouldn't get off on having me pour hot wax all over your body. I've noticed you wax everywhere. Chest to ankle. Arms. Legs. Groin. You like to be slippery as a fish. I'll let you choose. Au natural or you can lay there, princess, and let me do you. *Look at me.*"

There's real embarrassment in the tightness of Brayden's expression. He refuses to look at Jenner, so Jenner hooks a finger under Brayden's chin and lets his silence speak of his determination for obedience. With a slight roll of his shining, wet eyes, Brayden reluctantly gazes up at his Master.

"Is it just for swimming?" Jenner asks softly.

"No, Sir," Brayden confesses so quietly Jenner has to strain to hear.

"Louder, slave."

"No, Sir," Brayden repeats more forcefully, but now with defiance like he's waiting for Jenner to be cruel, like they're just teenagers at opposite ends of the popularity spectrum. Part of Brayden will always see him like that, Jenner realizes. No matter how old they get. His gaze darts to the side as he blinks tears away.

"This isn't something to be ashamed of," Jenner tells him.

Brayden turns his head sharply away from Jenner.

"Talk to me."

"There isn't much that I'm not ashamed of, and you know it. Hearing you call me on it…" Brayden shakes his head, closes his eyes and seems to recede back into his own head. Just by paying attention to small cues like the furrows in Brayden's brow, the delicate crinkle of his eyes as he squeezes them shut, the pace of his breathing, Jenner can tell Brayden is going to a dark, bad place.

"Brayden..." Jenner beckons, trying to coax Brayden back to the light.

"Don't you know how hard it is to hear you call me on all of this stuff? How you make me feel, all the time? I'm not strong. I've *never* been strong, but I still have to pretend like I am, for my family, for my job, for everyone who thinks that they know me and doesn't. But you... Ever since you've done this to me... made me weak... made me want to be nothing but yours... It's so much harder to pretend and it's not fair. It's easy for you to point out all of the ways I'm screwing up, isn't it? Because no one's pointing out things about you that you don't want them seeing or talking about, are they? You're still the one who automatically gets respect, without trying. But you're ashamed too," Brayden accuses. "Scared of your family finding out you're queer, of everyone in town knowing. They'd look at you and know what you do with me. They'd *talk*, the way they already talk about *me*. You try to hide it, but all of that fear doesn't go away even if you try to act like this is about me, like I'm the only one who needs to admit they've been wrong. I know I'm a freak. I've *always* been a freak. Well, surprise, Jenny, *you're* a freak too. At least I only hurt *myself* instead of the people I *love*."

Jenner sneers then stifles it, knowing what this is, that it's Brayden pushing back. After all of the rules, all of the changes in his life, and finally, after Jenner's test of Brayden's loyalty, daring him to think Jenner cruel and heartless, to leave and give up on them, Brayden is fighting back. He's shackled to a table and baiting his Master's anger, daring him to unleash it.

"Come on!" Brayden shouts angrily, curling forward a little, as much as the bonds will allow as he eggs Jenner on. "Come on! Do it! *Do it!*"

Grabbing Brayden by the balls, pulling on them hard enough to make him chase up off the table to relieve the strain, Jenner tugs sharply then squeezes. Brayden's nostrils flare and he shudders with pain. With his other hand, Jenner begins to stroke Brayden's cock. It causes Brayden to whine back in his throat. But then he barks, "MORE!"

"You want more?"

Jenner steadies Brayden's cock and the feather, making sure the wand is fully embedded, and begins to pump his penis, hard and fast. Brayden lets out a ragged yell that sharpens quickly. He tenses from head to toe, trying to shake Jenner off, but Jenner doesn't let go or stop.

"No. FUCK. Oh god..."

Softly, calmly, with all of the deep-seated regret from seeing others in pain and saying nothing for so long, Jenner finds his voice and says, "I know who you are. I know how this feels. I know that you're scared. I know that you trust me. I know that you love me. I know it hurts. I know it's a lot. But despite the fact that so many people have failed you, *I will not fail you*. I'm not going anywhere, Bray, and I'll say it as many times as you need to hear it. I'm yours."

Brayden convulses violently, his eyes rolling up. With a whimper he thrusts hard against Jenner's hand. Swiftly, Jenner pulls the feather completely out and it's chased by a thick milky jet of spunk as Brayden comes with a cry of excruciating bliss.

A tear falls from each of Brayden's eyes, squeezed from the corners as he stares up at the bright light and ceiling rather than look at Jenner. Vocalizing the torment of sensation until he has no air left in his lungs, he's strung tight as a bow until Jenner swallows him down, sucking Brayden to the root.

A fresh yell wrenches free. Brayden's hips twitch up into the soft, hot, gripping, wet suction of Jenner's mouth but Jenner pulls off only to wriggle the point of his tongue into the stretched opening in Brayden's dick. Brayden moans hard. His skin beats with the rhythm of his pulse as it pumps out every drop left in him and Jenner licks it away. Flushed and tensed from his fingertips all the way down to his toes, Brayden's body sings as he battles through the orgasm. It's there in the quivering clench of his stomach, buttocks and thighs. Jenner's tongue wraps him, his cheeks hollowed out. After a few more deep pulls, Jenner sucks the sense from Brayden's mind.

The cuffs are opened, but Brayden doesn't know what to say and can't move. He's stiff and boneless at the same time. If he had more energy, he might have protested when Jenner scoops him up in his arms and carries him from the table back into the bedroom, laying him out on the bed. There, the blood is rubbed back into Brayden's lower legs, arms and hands. When he's comfortable, Jenner wipes him down and dries him off.

"Rest for a while," Jenner tells him. Brayden realizes that Jenner is intentionally ignoring the demands of his own body, refusing himself the release he seeks probably as some sort of penance after putting his lover through so much.

"Yeah, okay," Brayden says, curling up to a seated position then sliding from the bed to his knees in front of Jenner.

"Bray..." Jenner sighs wearily.

Stubbornness gazes up from the depths of Brayden's deceptively sweet eyes as he laces his hands behind his head, pressed against his long, golden brown hair. Glistening with a post-coital flush under his warm bronzed skin, naked, willing, he licks his lips wet and opens them in a wide O. Tongue pushed forward, Brayden gazes up readily at Jenner, giving permission.

He doesn't have to wait long. With a hard grunt, Jenner pulls out his cock and feeds it into Brayden's mouth. At first, Brayden struggles to take it, but when Jenner grasps the sides of Brayden's head under the jaw, and begins to move himself in and out, it gets easier.

Brayden lets Jenner lead and take what he needs, while doing his best to make it feel good. It thrills him to give Jenner such pleasure, after being so overwhelmed by the decadent freedom Brayden experienced on that table. To have Jenner so intimately, to give over to him so completely—it's incredible. Wishing he had more experience to work from, Brayden tries to anticipate what he thinks Jenner would like, trying not to gag when the thrusts get harder and deeper. Tears stream freely from his eyes, nose and lips. Jenner stares down at him, visually groping his conquest.

With a gasp and a grunt Jenner unloads, holding Brayden still as he startles, his brow furrowing as he struggles to swallow the huge load of come dripping down his throat.

"Come on, that's it," Jenner coaxes, caressing Brayden's cheek and the side of his neck as it works around his girth. "Good. So good...."

Once spent, Jenner pulls back, watching Brayden suckle just the head. He falls from between Brayden's lips, just before Brayden moves to hide his face against Jenner's thigh.

"I love you," Brayden rasps hoarsely, grateful for everything Jenner has given him — pleasure beyond his wildest dreams, safety and understanding. Their bond has been strengthened by the fact that Brayden said such things to Jenner, trying to provoke him, wanting Jenner to hurt him with either pain or abandonment, but Jenner didn't rise to the bait and stayed steadfast in his devoted care. Never before has Brayden been able to be so completely, brutally honest, to purge the dark thoughts simmering in his head and be subsequently accepted, darkness and all. He feels that he owes Jenner so much for that gift alone.

Jenner clutches Brayden to him, then falls to his knees as well and closes him up in a close hug. "Love you," Jenner whispers back. "So much."

Brayden's hands grip Jenner's back with trepidation and trust.

"Everything's gonna be okay. You'll see." Jenner's strong hand cups the back of his lover's head as he breathes Brayden's scent into his lungs. It makes Brayden feel wanted, like he's perfect just the way he is. And that's amazing.

"Okay," Brayden nods, choosing to believe it, as impossible as it may seem.

Chapter 26

Misbehaving

The couch thrums with the noise seeping up through the floor. Slouching back into the cushions, flicking aimlessly through the channels on the TV, Brayden keeps shooting glances at the phone on the table he's so recently been shackled to, waiting for it to ring. Jenner has already called once since going downstairs twenty minutes ago, trying to talk Brayden out of staying up to meet Enrique and go to sleep instead.

It hadn't worked. Brayden craves some contact with his old life and the people in it, as well as the person he had grown to be before everything changed on him. It's inconsequential that he's exhausted, sore and not feeling very sociable. Enrique had wanted to meet at a bar or cafe, but Jenner forbade it, and Brayden wasn't up to travel anyway.

There's a knock on the door and, without getting up, Brayden shouts, "Come in!"

"B-man, you in here?" Enrique calls, peeking inside the apartment and looking around. It's still mostly empty, sparse with only a few pieces of furniture and no decorations.

"Yeah, over here, dude."

Brayden stands, grimacing at the stretch and movement. He has to stop himself with effort from cupping his crotch. He's wearing a soft, worn pair of light grey sweatpants and a white cotton shirt. Hair stringy wet from being washed, it falls around his shoulders, dampening them.

"Did I wake you?" Enrique smiles with a confused tilt of his eyebrow.

"Nah, man. Just trying to be comfortable. Have a seat. There's beer in the fridge if you want it. Please, help yourself." Hooking a finger around the opened bottle he has in front of him, Brayden takes a swig and settles back down into his spot on the couch with a small groan. "Sorry about blowing you off before. It's been a little crazy around here."

"No worries," Enrique says, hesitantly going over to the fridge. Brayden urges him on with a raise of his eyebrows, gesturing to the kitchen. "Yeah?"

"Yeah, go on. Apologies for not being a better host and all of that."

"You okay?"

"Yeah, just a little um... banged up. Been a rough day."

"Oh yeah? You wanna talk about it, or...?"

Brayden dismisses the offer with a wave of his hand, pushing his wet hair back from his face with a slightly nervous gesture. After finding a beer and popping the cap off, Enrique joins him on the couch.

"To warm weather," Enrique toasts with a raise of his bottle.

"I'll drink to that," Brayden sighs, tapping the necks together.

"So, is this your place, Bray? It doesn't really feel like you," Enrique wonders, glancing around at the barren, dark, cavernous rooms.

"Nah, I'm living with my Nana and cousin Emma Leah a few blocks away. Most of the time, at least. I stay here, too. It's owned by the same guy that owns the bar...." He leaves it hanging there, watching Enrique from the corner of his eye to see if he makes the connections.

Then he does and his eyes open wide with surprise. Enrique turns his hat around so that the brim faces backwards and leans forward towards Brayden.

"That big gorilla lookin' one with the black hair and the cheekbones?" To help clarify, he sucks in his cheeks, puckers his lips and frowns a little, doing his best impression of Jenner.

Brayden laughs wildly, clutching his stomach. Drawing one leg up onto the couch cushion, holding it there by the knee, he curls his bare toes around the edge and lets his legs fall open. Resting his head back against the padded seat, his smile lingers. "Jenner. Parrish if you're nasty."

"Oh man," Enrique marvels. "For real? You're staying with *that* dude? He's like the polar opposite of you. He's so… tense."

A fleeting expression passes over Brayden's face that Enrique doesn't catch, and Brayden hides the rest behind his beer, thinking that Jenner might seem much less tense if Enrique met him now.

"Wait a minute." Enrique kicks off his sneakers and turns to sit cross-legged, facing Brayden. "You're dressed in pajamas…"

"…they're *not* pajamas…."

"And you just took a shower. There's one bedroom from what I can tell, and I don't see a blanket or pillow for this couch."

"I don't sleep on the couch," Brayden says quietly, looking down at his hands wrapping the bottle.

"The fuck, bro? There somethin' goin' on with you and the gorilla or what?"

Brayden can feel Enrique looking at him in a whole new way, and hates the flush of embarrassment that colors his skin. "He's a good guy. He… takes care of me."

"Takes care of you like 'takes care of you'?" The question is accompanied by a brief mime of fellatio. Brayden rolls his eyes and slumps farther down into the couch. "No *shit*," Enrique says with awe. "You got yourself a *boyfriend*, B?"

"It's not… we don't use that term. It's… different than that."

"Big spoon. Little spoon… you're the little spoon, aren't you?"

Brayden wipes a hand over his face, then drinks deeply of his beer.

"*That's* why you look fucked over. 'Cause you are, aren't you?"

"'Rique, quit. Please."

"You're not queer. Is this your experimental phase or what? Gorilla-curious? Oh Jesus, Mary and Joseph, if Andre found out about this shit, he'd be in the car driving here, *tonight*."

Brayden's expression falls. He scoots higher on the cushion, his small body folded up even smaller, and opens his mouth to cut in.

"Wait a minute. Did you and *Andre*—?"

"We might have screwed around a little. It didn't go that far. But please don't tell him about Jenner. *I'll* tell him."

Enrique shifts closer, his interest piqued. "No shit? How far did it go?"

Brayden shoots him a warning look.

"He could take you *apart*, B. You're so little!"

"I resent that," Brayden tells him, and leans forward to set his empty beer bottle on the coffee table.

"Wow," Enrique says appreciatively, settling back into the couch, tipping back his beer. "This is amazing. Does anyone even know?"

"No. Nobody knows. Not my family, not Andre. Nobody. Except you and two of Jenner's friends from the bar, so please, keep it to yourself."

Enrique squints at him, measuring, wary. Waggling his bottle at Brayden, he remarks, "You said he takes care of you. Does he? Looks to me like Sugar Daddy took a piece for himself tonight. I hope he gave something back, too."

Brayden doesn't know how to answer that, or if he even wants to. The phone rings, saving him from having to deal with it just yet. He reaches for the phone, presses a button and puts it to his ear. "Hey."

"Is he there?" Jenner asks on the other end of the line.

"Yeah," Brayden answers, glancing at his guest. "He's here."

Enrique puts his drink down and does his impression of Jenner again, this time also puffing out his chest and flexing his arms. Brayden waves a hand dismissively at him and tries to ignore it.

"I don't want him staying long. You need rest. I'll be back as soon as I close up."

"I really should go home tonight," Brayden says quietly into the phone, turning slightly away from Enrique.

"Why? There's no point. It's late. You should just move in with me and simplify things. I'm sure Nana would understand your desire for privacy. It wouldn't change your ability to provide for them."

"Can we talk about this later?" Hiding behind his hand, Brayden masks his amazement that Jenner asked so offhandedly to live together.

"Promise me you'll go to bed soon. *Our* bed."

With barely any sound at all, Brayden tells him, "I promise. Okay."

He says goodbye and hangs up. The phone falls to his side, bouncing on the cushion.

"Whoa."

"Don't start," Brayden warns.

"What was *that*? He totally checked up on you like you're his bitch."

"Maybe I am his bitch. You got a problem with that?"

"What happened to you, B? This is a little fucked up. It's like I don't even know you anymore." "You know me," Brayden sighs. "You just didn't know all of me."

Jenner's cat appears and pounces onto the arm of the couch, prowling up toward Brayden and curling into a ball near his shoulder. Brayden reaches back and scratches behind her ears, making her purr.

Enrique asks, "Who's that?"

"Pussy. Jenner's."

"So he likes 'em small and fluffy, huh?"

Brayden frowns and playfully shoves Enrique's shoulder. They watch the TV quietly for a few minutes, saying nothing. Then Enrique wonders aloud, "So who do you think's gonna win the fight?"

"What fight?"

"The one that's gonna happen when Andre finds out that primate's buttfuckin' you."

Dumbstruck, Brayden stares at Enrique, his mouth fallen open. "I can't believe you just said that."

"Don't even play like you're so shockable, Sugar Baby. You wanna tell me why you're so 'banged up'?" After one look at Brayden's reddening face, Enrique scoffs, "Yeah, didn't think so."

Once Enrique leaves, with a sworn promise not to divulge their conversation to anyone, even Andre, and to keep in touch for more juicy gossip, Brayden goes to bed and sleeps through the night until the alarm goes off the next morning.

The shrill beeping is cut off when Jenner swats blindly at the nightstand. With a groan, they get up and, as neither of them is in a perky mood, quietly get ready to go to the gym. Coffee is brewed, clothes are shrugged on. Jenner has what he needs, but Brayden's suit and gear is at his grandmother's place so they need to stop there on the way.

Brayden approaches the back door. Though Jenner seemed willing to wait in the car, he suddenly appears at Brayden's back.

"Changed my mind," is his excuse. "I'd like to see your room, where you've been staying. Is that okay? If it makes you uncomfortable...."

Remembering all of the times he fantasized about having Jenner sneak into his bedroom to secretly screw around, Brayden feels like fate is giving him a chance to prove he's brave enough to follow through in reality. Not that they're going to screw around. Having Jenner in Nana's house, in Brayden's room is challenge enough in itself.

"You're going to behave, right? If you come with me, you have to behave," Brayden warns. When Jenner just smiles, Brayden says adamantly, "I mean it."

"What're you afraid of? We're just getting your stuff. No big deal. They already met me, and I can behave respectably. I am housetrained, you know. And maybe if Nana sees what good *friends* we are, she'll happily agree to you moving in with me."

Brayden thinks it over, relents and, just before opening the door, points warningly at Jenner's smirk. Jenner draws an X over his heart and loses the grin.

They enter the kitchen, find it empty, and pad softly through it toward the stairs.

"Well, there you are. Good morning," Ruth says from a seat by the window, newspaper unfolded in her lap. It occurs to him that from there, she has a good view of the driveway and the road stretching in both directions. Who knows how much she's overseen so far?

Brayden can't conceal his unhappiness at being caught and he flounders for what to do.

"Ma'am," Jenner nods.

"We're headed to the gym. I came by to get my things," Brayden explains.

"You're moving out?" Ruth says with feigned surprise.

"No," Brayden sighs. "My swimsuit." He feels a nudge from Jenner at his back and, before he can think twice, he adds, "But I've been thinking about moving in with Jenner since I spend so much time over there anyway. That way I won't be barging in at all hours here. I'd still stop by as much as I could to help Em with her homework in the afternoons and all. It'd just be a better… sleeping… arrangement."

"You boys must be close to want to be in each other's hair night and day. You won't get sick of each other after working and living together?"

"Oh, I'm not worried about that," Jenner smiles. "Brayden's pretty easy to get along with and he hasn't complained about me so far."

Clearing his throat, growing pale, Brayden stutters, "N-nothing is final, it w-was just an idea."

"I want whatever makes you happy," she tells him. "Don't let me keep you if you've got places to be. Emma's getting ready for school, so you won't be waking her if you go up."

"Thanks, Nan." Brayden is up the stairs before she can say any more and Jenner follows after a pleading over-the-shoulder glance from Brayden. He'd much rather have Jenner where he can keep an eye and an ear on him.

"You're afraid to leave me alone with her." Jenner smirks as Brayden pushes him into his bedroom and closes the door after they're inside. "Why on Earth would you be nervous about that? I refrained from copping a feel during the chit-chat, didn't I?"

"Jesus, you're not going to do that at work, are you?"

"Oh, come on. Max and Art aren't going to care if I give you a handy in the break room now and then. Hell, Max might even stay to watch," Jenner ponders. "You know, that's not a terrible idea…."

"Can you keep your voice down?" Brayden hisses. "These walls aren't exactly soundproof!"

"So," Jenner asks, with a deceptively innocent expression, "You don't want a hummer before we go? I kind of want to christen your sweet little bedroom while we're up here. Defile it just a smidge. Leave some cumstains on the ceiling. Do you think you can shoot that far? *I* think you can, especially after — "

The hand Brayden instantly claps like a vice over Jenner's mouth muffles the rest, so Jenner mimes it. Making a circle with his thumb and index finger, he inserts the middle finger of his other hand into it, working it in and out, then withdrawing and mimicking a large spray.

"It's not cute," Brayden hisses.

"Fuck your cute," Jenner retorts through Brayden's palm. When the tip of his tongue snakes out and licks, Brayden gives it up and lets go. "Tick tock."

"Yeah yeah."

Moving around the room, opening doors, stuffing a few things in his gym bag, Brayden tries to be productive with Jenner standing there, big as life and twice as horny, in his grandma's guest bedroom. Brayden is just about finished getting his things when Jenner steps over to the door and quietly locks it.

"What—"

Jenner gestures for him to be quiet, putting a finger to his lips.

"My cousin—"

Jenner closes the distance between them so that they're standing chest-to-chest. Jenner's right hand raises, open, in a 'wait' signal. An upraised digit crosses from Jenner's lips to Brayden's.

"Open your pants."

"No way," Brayden scoffs. Pivoting his hand, Jenner seals it more completely over Brayden's mouth, prohibiting further speech.

"Open your pants, slave," he repeats slower and more adamantly.

Gaze glued to the door, Brayden reluctantly obeys, sending a prayer for mercy up to whatever gods watch over deviants and liars. Jenner eases Brayden's penis free and examines it while Brayden blushes furiously and preoccupies himself with stifling a massive panic attack.

"Does it still hurt when you piss?"

Brayden's expression tightens further. Then he nods stiffly.

"Damn. I wanna lick that," Jenner murmurs, caressing with a fingertip over the so-recently-abused opening in Brayden's dick. No sooner have the words been spoken than Jenner seems to dismiss any and all reservations and goes to one knee.

"Jenner!" Brayden quickly covers his own mouth with a hand. His eyes roll back, then close as Jenner takes a wide, greedy lick. He teases the tip of his tongue at the hole then goes for broke and wraps his lips around the whole damn thing. Cradling Brayden's softened girth in his mouth, sliding it back over his tongue, Jenner sucks him, moving in and out a few times with ample, obvious pleasure at getting to do so. Jenner lets Brayden fall wet and semi-erect from his lips. After tucking him back into his pants, Jenner stands while wiping his mouth dry.

"You fucker. Why?" Brayden demands, on edge and now uncomfortably aroused.

"Because I can," Jenner smirks.

A small but clear knock sounds at the door. Brayden and Jenner turn to each other, eyes widening fractionally.

From the hallway, a soft female voice calls, "Brayden? Is that you?"

Brayden scowls and punches Jenner's shoulder. "Yeah, Em! Just a sec."

He adjusts himself as he walks to the door, the hot, aching heaviness of his hard-on trapped snugly inside his briefs. He pauses long enough to give Jenner a dirty look from over his shoulder. Jenner only smiles without an ounce of regret.

Brayden opens the door a crack and says, "Sorry about the noise."

"'S'okay," Emma yawns drowsily. She's dressed but her hair is still mussed. She glances up at Brayden and, as she does, catches sight of Jenner lurking in the background. "Oh. I thought I heard you talking to someone, but I figured you were on the phone or something. Um, hi."

"Hi, Emma. Good morning," Jenner says pleasantly.

Brayden fits himself more snugly in the gap created by the open door, blocking Emma's view of Jenner. "We were just headed to the gym. Grabbing some stuff. I'll catch you later, okay?"

Emma raises an eyebrow at him. Brayden curses inwardly, realizing how very *not* stupid his cousin is, especially when his behavior is so suspicious.

"Yeah, okay," she agrees.

"Have fun at school."

"Yeah, right."

Brayden closes the door after Emma has retreated back in the direction of their shared bathroom.

"I like her," Jenner says with amusement.

"Let's jet," Brayden says impatiently, staying far away from Jenner and grabbing his duffel bag. "I've gotta get the hell out of here."

Eventually, they do get to the gym. Brayden gives Jenner the silent treatment for the stunt he'd pulled in the bedroom. Jenner does his best impression of a wall and blocks Brayden from view as he changes into his teeny-tiny swimsuit. When an older man walks by and tries to see what's going on, Jenner barks, "Get lost!" which Brayden tells him isn't a weird or suspicious thing to say at all.

After that, the day falls back into a more familiar routine. Brayden savors the feeling of cutting through the water in the pool, being engulfed in it, letting it wash everything else away. Jenner meets back up with him an hour later. When they get changed back into their clothes, Brayden has to convince Jenner that it would be very bizarre if he followed Brayden into the toilet and watched him urinate.

For a few mid-morning hours they go their separate ways. Brayden goes to his Nana's to shower. He packs more of his things in order to move them over to Jenner's apartment while Jenner runs errands and buys more food for the apartment. When he has a few boxes filled and ready, Brayden glances around the small bedroom that never felt like his anyway. He tries to let it sink in that he's really doing what he's doing—moving in with a male lover. It feels like running away—from Nana, Emma Leah, and his mother. But at the same time, it also feels strangely like he's standing up for himself and what he wants out of life, and everyone else's opinions be damned. It's a small, secret, lonely victory, but Brayden claims it nonetheless, proud of himself even if his family can't do the same.

Chapter 27
Difficult Choices

Before Emma Leah can return from school and make puppy-eyes at her big cousin in an attempt to keep him from leaving her, Brayden loads up his Jeep with boxes and his surfboard. Ruth watches on and offers to help, but Brayden doesn't let her. When he's ready to go, Brayden turns to her, saying, "I'll come by every day, or at least try to. After I go to the gym tomorrow, I'll come here to help you out with anything you need before my shift."

"Don't trouble yourself, sweetie," Ruth smiles, patting his arm. "Just live your life."

"Nana," Brayden sighs. "I mean it. You're important to me. Emma Leah is important to me. I'm not going anywhere. You'll see."

She scans his face carefully, taking her time with her answer.

"You're happy," she sees, her eyebrows tilting slightly with the revelation. "Maybe happier than I've seen you since you showed up."

Brayden shrugs, bowing his head to hide his expression. "Yeah, I guess so. Things feel like they're finally falling into place. They're... balanced."

"Good. That's all I need to hear." She leans in and pulls him down so that she can kiss his cheek. Then she pushes him back and pats his shoulder. "Take it easy on your back with all of these boxes."

"I can handle it, Nan."

"I'm sure you can."

"I'll see you tomorrow."

"Okay." She returns to the front porch, pulling her sweater more tightly around her to keep out the chill. As he backs out of the driveway, she waves, calling, "Love you!"

Feeling that she truly does, carrying it like a warm solidity in his chest, filling his heart, he smiles at her and waves back.

While Brayden is carting box after box upstairs to the apartment above Parrish Pub, Jenner is inside the bar on the ground floor, on the phone and talking to his brother, Callum. Jackson and Art are on clean-up duty that day, scrubbing and restocking as necessary. Behind the bar, Jenner, leans heavily on the counter and listens.

"Sunday dinner. Whad'ya say? Bring the tan blonde if you want."

Jenner represses a groan and catches sight of Brayden through the front window, his blond-streaked hair tied in a knot behind his head, bronzed skin shining in the chilly sunlight as he goes past. It occurs to Jenner that if his brother feels compelled to make repeat appearances at the Pub like he did the night before, or if he falls into conversation with their mother over living arrangements, he might find out through her that Jenner is living above the bar now. And he might notice Jenner's new roommate—an undeniably blond, very much tan, *man*. He's completely screwed himself. And he doesn't even know whether to go to the damned family dinner to do some damage control, or to avoid it and further scrutiny.

"You there?" his brother says when there's no snarky reply.

"Yeah, I'm thinking," Jenner manages.

"Wow, you *think*? Who knew? I can see it's a trial, so let me make this easy for you. I'll take your silence to be consent to show your sorry face at home on Sunday, and you can make your mother happy for once."

Rage. Pure, red and strong, swallows Jenner up. Surrounded by glass, he chooses instead to take out his wrath on something less breakable and punches the nearest wall with a closed fist. The boom it makes is loud, and everything comes to a stop in the bar. Art drops the rag he's wiping with. Jackson straightens with an opened box of napkins at his feet. Fire licks up Jenner's hand and arm as pain blossoms.

"Why do you care?!" he barks. "Go live your own goddamned life and leave me the hell alone!"

"I care because I'm a good son. I appreciate everything our parents have done for us and when I see how sad they are to be so estranged from their youngest child, to whom they have given so much, I make it my personal mission to correct that problem. You're a problem, Jenner. Stop acting like a little boy and pull on your big boy pants."

"You fucking, weasely…"

"What was that?"

"Fine. Sunday."

He hangs up and roars in frustration, knowing it to be a futile, pitiful, cowardly sort of protest, pulling the sound from the bottom of his chest, all the way down in his lungs.

"What's going on, man?" Art says calmly.

Jenner glances between Jackson and Art, blood surging, hand throbbing. He rubs his hand and grits his teeth. The skin isn't broken on his knuckles. He flexes the fingers to check for signs of any breaks, finding none.

It's bad enough Callum is the favorite, that he's so successful, so dutiful, but he's gotta constantly give me shit for all of the ways I'm not as good as him. I'm already the black sheep and they don't even know the half of it. It only goes downhill from here. Wonderful. Just fucking fantastic.

"Family issues. Excuse me."

He strides from the room, heading back to his office where he can be alone. Once inside it, he closes the door and sits in his chair, tenting his fingers in front of his mouth as his mind races a mile a minute.

Brayden, upstairs, living with Jenner; his mother, who met Brayden; Callum, who can't ever let anything go when there's even the slightest chance that the outcome might leave him looking a little more golden, especially compared to his younger brother; his father, an Army vet, who is ever watchful, silent, strong, and all-seeing—a judgmental, old-fashioned, steely son-of-a-bitch if there ever was one. Jenner has to go to Sunday dinner. There's no choice. Not anymore. And they're going to find out about Brayden. It's unavoidable.

It might not happen Sunday, but it will soon. It's become a reality.

There's a knock on the door.

"Yeah," Jenner calls.

Art inches the door open. "Bad time?"

Jenner gives his head a slight shake, jostling his curling hair. He feels it move and, bracing his head with an elbow propped on the desk, reaches up, his fingers playing with the curls.

"Lemme take a wild guess. Cal?"

"Mm," Jenner grunts.

"Wanna talk about it?" Art raises his eyebrows, holding his arms open. Jenner stares up at him, resenting Art a little for the comparative simplicity of his life, free of relationship issues. He doesn't have to try to fill impossible roles and deny key aspects of his personality and life. All Art has to worry about is holding down his job and finding a cute girl to hook up with once in a while.

"Know any tan blonde chicks I can rent out for a night? They'd have to be a good actress."

Art's eyes lose focus, and he taps his chin, thinking it over.

"I was kidding."

"No, no, gimme a sec. I might know someone. Mandy? No, Cheryl. No...."

"Brayden is moving in with me. As we speak. And my family is going to find out about him."

"So?"

"*So?*"

"Yeah, so. Who cares? You don't like Cal anyway, so who cares what he thinks. Your mom worships you. And your dad... well, okay, yeah he might present a problem, but who gives a shit? They'll love you anyway, even if they're shocked or don't approve. It's not like you're likely to magically transform into a heterosexual anytime soon. Fuckin' tell 'em."

"I'd never hear the end of it. And it's none of their business."

"They're your family. You are their business, asshole. What? You scared or something? Of *Callum?* Your *mom?* Huh? Pshh, you can take 'em. My money's on it."

Jenner smiles. It fades and he sighs.

"Or is this not about you at all? Is Brayden not good enough for you to show off to everyone? You ashamed of him?"

Jenner's gaze snaps up to Art's face. Art gestures to the ceiling and waits expectantly.

"Well? Are you? You ashamed of Brayden?"

Then Jenner can't look at Art any longer. His eyes dart to the side, and he feels it, like a pressure in the center of his chest and thick in his throat. When he closes his eyes, he can feel the old visceral response, leftover from being a teenager, how crucial it was to distance yourself from losers and outcasts, lest you be labeled as one too. In the blink of an eye, you could go from being adored and worshipped to being constantly ridiculed. Brayden was an outcast. He still is, to some degree, even though they've become adults. The imperfections like his poverty, his loneliness, his circumstances, draw criticism like flies to honey. Jenner is still respected by everyone that knows him, but if he aligns himself with Brayden, that will all change.

But then different feelings rise to the surface, and outshine the negatives. He sees Brayden's smile, the sweetness and resolution in his eyes. He feels the echo of his lips' touch and the taste of his kiss; the feel of him curled up and nestled inside Jenner's arms—a solid, trusting warmth that's his and only his. Brayden belongs to Jenner. He's Jenner's to take care of. More than anything, that's Jenner's responsibility—to love Brayden. Pride, devotion, commitment—absolute and permanent, swell inside Jenner's soul.

He imagines denying Brayden to his brother, his mother, and his father. Jenner imagines pretending he doesn't care about Brayden to the people who have known Jenner the longest, if not the best.

"Yeah. Thought so," Art murmurs, staring down his nose at Jenner. He nods once, then turns back to the door.

Before he can go, when he's halfway out, Jenner calls, "Hey!" Art pauses where he is, waiting. "Thanks."

Art glances over his shoulder. A flicker of a smile passes over his lips. With one more, small, nod, he's gone. Jenner stares at the open air where Art was, filling it up with scenes in his imagination, both wonderful and terrible.

Rubbing his temple with his aching hand, Jenner curses quietly, "Shit."

Brayden sits cross-legged on Jenner's bed. The empty apartment, filled now with both of their possessions and a small, fuzzy cat, is sprawled out around him. Brayden's surfboard leans against the far wall, and he stares at it. In an hour or so, he's expected downstairs to start his shift. In the meantime, he's trying to adjust to the reality created by the choices he's made.

The messages in his voicemail have accumulated. He listens to them sometimes. Sometimes not. Then he doesn't erase them. They simply gather there.

Andre.

Brayden draws out his phone and takes a deep breath. It shouldn't be this hard to be honest with Andre, he tells himself. Andre is the one person who really understands Brayden, besides Jenner. It feels cruel to have waited so long without calling Andre back. Subconsciously, Brayden is aware that maybe he's trying to kill the friendship, to move on and leave everyone behind. He can feel that maybe Andre wanted what they had to become more. Just because Brayden doesn't feel the same way doesn't mean he can't appreciate being wanted. But no matter how many times Andre tries to reach out, they will continue to exist in other worlds, detached and separate. That's why Brayden doesn't answer or call back. If Andre isn't connected to him, then Andre can't hurt him. Right?

"God, I'm turning into my mother," he groans to the empty room. From the living room, the cat meows in answer, as if confirming his suspicions.

But, if he makes some conscious decisions now, rebelling against his instincts, then perhaps that doesn't have to be the case. Things could be different, but only if he makes the effort and takes a few risks. Andre is a good enough friend that he's worth a risk or two, surely. Isn't he?

Thinking of Andre's laugh, of the calm, easygoing strength in his voice, Brayden curses under his breath and dials the number.

He wants to call to go to voicemail, but then the prospect of thinking of something to say to the machine is even worse.

"Hello?"

Brayden closes his eyes with a silent sigh. "Hey. It's me."

For a long, awful second, there's nothing. No response.

"I'm sorry I haven't called you back, man," Brayden starts. "I just didn't know what to say. Things got kind of complicated with us in those weeks before I left, and I wasn't sure how to carry it all over into whatever we are to each other now. You're an amazing friend to me, but sometimes it's not exactly your friendship that I'm missing, if you know what I mean. I don't know. I didn't want to have to explain myself to you, I guess."

"Explain what?"

Brayden thinks about asking if Andre spoke to Enrique, and can't. He can't do it.

"Explain what?" Andre repeats, a little more forcefully. "You know you're more than a few states away, right? So you have to gimme something, Marsha. I can't pry the truth from you except through this damn phone. Look, if you're done with me and want me to stop calling, I will. I can take a hint. Just have the courtesy to say so. Please."

"I'm not done with you," Brayden says softly, battling with his instincts and the desire to cut ties, because it's easier. "I don't regret what we did. It opened my eyes in a lot of ways, but it's like I don't even know who I am anymore some days. Talking to you, knowing you're in my corner as a friend, it definitely helps get me through, even if I'm a shitty friend in return by avoiding you so much. So, I'm sorry, okay?"

"What's going on with you, huh? Where's all this drama coming from?"

Pushing a hand back through his hair, pulling it back from his face, Brayden struggles inwardly.

"I met someone," he blurts suddenly.

There's another of those horrible silences, tense and strained, filled with Andre's physical and symbolic hugeness, before he growls, "Who?"

"I went to a BDSM club. I met him there. I thought it was an anonymous hook-up, but it wasn't. He's... he's my fucking *boss*, Andre. Now he's my Master. And my boyfriend." It becomes too much. His voice breaks and he moans, "*The things I've let him do to me....*"

"I'm coming up there."

"No!" Brayden gasps. "Please! I can handle it! I can!"

"Like hell you can."

The line goes dead.

"NO!" Brayden screams at the empty apartment. "Fuck. FUCK!"

Frantically, he redials, but the call goes right to voicemail. "Please don't do this," he begs the machine recording his message. "I know you just want to protect me, but no one knows about me and Jenner, and if you come up here looking to take him down, people are gonna *know*, and I don't want you to hurt him. I just wanted to be honest with you about why I've been dodging your calls. I *chose* this. So, please. *Please* just call me back and we'll talk. We'll talk about everything. I swear. No more bullshit. Okay? Please?"

When he hangs up, he immediately dials Enrique instead. It rings five times before it's answered.

"B-man?"

"I fuckin' told 'im, Rique. I told Andre and now he's on his way here. *What the fuck do I do?*"

Andre has plenty of cash to buy a plane ticket. He could be here by that night, or the next day at the latest.

"What do you *do?*" Enrique echoes. "You tell the gorilla to *run.*"

"Oh my god," Brayden moans.

"Your ass shoulda dated smaller men. What do you think you can do about this now? You tell him about the sex?"

"Worse than that." He imagines the things that Andre must be assuming have gone on. The sex. The sadomasochism.

"Andre is a motherfuckin' *semi-professional wrestler.*"

"Oh my *god.*"

"You listen to me. Tell the gorilla to *run.* Andre—that crazy bitch—he *loves* you and he will *take apart* anyone that he knows is doing freaky shit to you."

"No one does anything *to* me that I don't want them to. Jenner can hold his own," Brayden starts. "He's got a black belt in jujitsu."

"Your dumb ass is gonna start a fuckin' war over itself," Enrique says with amazement. "You really want them to kill each other?"

"No," Brayden laments. "Of course not."

The phone's other line beeps in his ear as a call tries to get through.

Brayden says, "Someone's trying to call. I'll call you back, okay?"

"Yeah, bro. Later."

Brayden hangs up with Enrique and takes the other call.

"You wanna talk? We'll talk. He fuck you?"

Brayden's heart jumps up into his throat.

"You might choose to forget, but *I know you*, Brayden Clare. *Did he fuck you and take it by force?*"

Deny it, Brayden screams at himself. His mouth opens and at first no sound comes out.

"No," he says, but softly.

"Liar," Andre hisses. "And you think I'm gonna let him get away with that?" Andre asks, sounding massive and murderous. "See you soon, baby."

"Andre, *please* don't. Jenner and I have an agreement. There are *rules*. We're *safe*."

"If I don't stand up for you when you won't stand up for yourself, then who will? Hmm?"

"I wanted him to do it."

"Yeah, I bet you did. I bet he's a lot bigger than you, isn't he? He probably doesn't even need to tie you down. How many bruises you got right now? Tell me none, and I won't get on that plane. But I'll know a lie. So, tell me. How many bruises?"

Brayden doesn't have to look; he can feel the aching in his body and knows the purplish yellow and brown marks that wrap his wrists, chest and ankles.

"None," he says.

"Yeah," Andre grunts. "I'll see you soon."

Chapter 28
Freefall

Jenner gets a text from Brayden asking him to come home quickly. Five minutes later, Jenner is standing in front of him, just inside the apartment's door. He can see how scared Brayden looks. When Brayden says nothing in explanation, won't even raise his eyes to meet Jenner's gaze, and only steps into Jenner's embrace, winding his arms around him, Jenner can only hold on and try to understand.

"What happened?"

"I called Andre. I've been avoiding it—telling him about us. But I didn't want to run away from things anymore. I don't want to turn into *her*. I called him to own up to my choices, and tell him about you. But he got upset. He *knows me*, Jenn. He thinks you forced yourself on me and hurt me."

I did, Jenner thinks with horror, understanding how Andre must feel without knowing who Jenner is or his intentions. They stand there, with Jenner's chin hooked right over the top of Brayden's head, resting on it.

"He's on his way, isn't he?"

"Yeah. I'm so sorry. I shouldn't have called him. I should've kept my mouth shut."

"No, you did the right thing. Actually... I have something to confess too."

Brayden tenses in Jenner's arms, but doesn't pull away, he just braces for the news like someone waiting to be struck. Feeling that tension makes Jenner hate himself a little.

"I want to take you with me to Sunday dinner at my parents'

house. I promised I'd go and I want to bring you. As my date."

Some of the stiffness drains from Brayden's form. He does pull away, but just far enough to be able to look up into Jenner's face. Chin tilted up, he gazes back into Jenner's eyes.

"You'd do that?"

"Yeah. Will you go with me? It has to be your decision. But it would mean a lot to me. I suppose I'm ready to own up to my choices, too. It had to happen eventually, right?" Jenner caresses the side of Brayden's face and places a kiss to the center of his forehead. "I love you."

"Love you too," Brayden says, still looking, still searching.

"What do you think?"

"I think I'd like to try."

Jenner smiles.

Brayden asks, "What about Andre?"

"I can handle Andre. I know where he's coming from, after all. Don't worry. It'll be okay."

"You think so?"

"Yeah."

Jenner lets Brayden see that he isn't afraid, just sad. But when Brayden pulls Jenner down for a kiss, with the heat of his mouth and the force of his devotion, the sadness melts right away.

A few hours later, Brayden is a third of the way into his shift.

"You know Mary Hendrix?" asks one of the Pub's regulars, a man named Bill. Bill lives somewhere nearby, a bachelor aged somewhere between forty-five and sixty-five. His weathered appearance and small, close-set eyes don't give much away. Most of the time, he likes to sit at the end of the bar for a few hours a night, chatting up anyone he can. Brayden figures that Bill prefers idle conversation with townies over hiding away alone at home, as he doesn't seem to have many friends. Most people he wrangles into a chat slip away quickly, with some excuse to hasten their departure. Brayden can't fault Bill for being a little overbearing. He's a nice enough guy otherwise.

Shaking his head in response to Bill's question, Brayden drags a rag over the top of the bar to clean up a few condensation rings.

"Well, Mary lives next door to me," Bill continues. "The panels of her garage door keep falling out. The damnedest thing, like someone just keeps coming past and poking 'em out with a stick or somethin', but she don't fix it. No, sir. She just sets her garbage cans in front of the holes to hide 'em, like that'll keep out the raccoons." He shakes his head. "Whole house is going to hell now that her husband's run off with that redhead. What was her name again? Eh, I forget. Anyway, hey, your mom ever do crazy shit like that with the garbage cans?"

The implied insult to his mother gets him a little hot under the collar, but Brayden just takes a deep breath and says dismissively, "I don't know, man. Get you anything else? You hungry?"

"Nah, all that fried crap Art cooks gives me indigestion. Come on, you can tell me. Everyone knows the deal with her anyway, had a few screws loose or somethin'. You've gotta have some juicy stories. Where'd she get to anyway? Africa? China?"

"Can't really say," Brayden tells him, smiling politely even if he is gritting his teeth. "How's that beer?"

Bill is momentarily distracted when the front door swings open. When he recognizes the people coming in, he calls, "Hey Steve! Over here!" Steve tries to pretend he didn't hear his name, ducking into conversation with a group in the back corner, his eyes darting over to Bill as his brow furrows with what looks like guilt. It's nothing new. Brayden has seen it all before. He wanders away from Bill to take more orders and the clock ticks steadily on.

The distraction of work has helped ease his concerns about Andre and coming out to Jenner's family, but his nerves have been jangling all day with apprehension of other things, too, like moving in with Jenner, and worry about disappointing his grandmother and cousin. Fear of Andre's imminent arrival and the prospect of being introduced to Jenner's family as a lover rather than a friend or employee are just the icing on the cake. It's also his first time at work with the knowledge that Art and Max are fully aware of the relationship between himself and Jenner. Brayden expected it to be weird, but so far Max and Art are the least of his problems and it hasn't been a big deal at all.

He takes his first break before the pre-dinner rush can hit, finding solace in being by himself in the break room. The clink, clatter and shouting from the kitchen along with the soft, constant noise from the bar fills the air.

It's the rhythm of life, the combination of the energy of each of the fifty or so people in the building. Brayden loved the beach for its open expanses, the huge breadth of the sky, infinite and beautiful above them, the limitless reaches of the ocean before them and the decadent tranquility. There is no tranquility at a bar, except maybe at the bottom of a tall glass of alcohol, but that's not what he needs. He needs the water, the feel of it engulfing him, the satisfaction of the struggle to work his body through it, the push and burn of swimming. With the balance and focus he finds with surfing, it's like he's an elemental part of the world rather than lost and floundering in it.

His mp3 player is in his bag, so he gets it out and sips from a tall glass of water. Sitting in a chair at the small table in the break room, he puts in his earbuds. He turns up some mellow, psychedelic rock, props a leg up on the edge of the table, lets his head fall back, and tries to meditate.

The music fills his head and it's good, or at least good enough. It takes him somewhere else, away from his troubles. Focusing on his breathing—in and out, in and out—he imagines the ocean flowing over him, cleansing him, filling his pores, buoying him up.

It's nice. For a small stretch of unmarked time, he begins to relax.

Then he realizes he's not alone.

That awareness is a tickle under his skin, an extrasensory understanding of his surroundings. He opens his eyes and sees Jenner sitting next to him not a foot away, watching.

It makes him feel self-conscious. Frowning slightly, trying to act like it doesn't bother him, Brayden asks, "Yeah?"

"Nothing. Don't let me disturb you."

"I can't meditate with you staring at me like that."

"I'm not staring."

Brayden's right eyebrow rises with weary disbelief.

The opened break room door is to Jenner's back. He glances over his shoulder at it, possibly realizing the danger it poses, but then he just looks back at Brayden like he can't quite bring himself to care enough to get up to close it. There's a bizarrely guilty expression flickering across Jenner's face, as if Brayden caught him in the act at something. Brayden smiles slightly despite his annoyance from being disturbed and the accrued weariness from a long day and asks, "What? Tell me."

"Nothing."

"What?" he presses, shifting in the chair. His pants leg pulls a little higher, revealing the bare, tan skin of his ankle, covered in peach fuzz until he gets around to waxing it smooth again. He's wearing short socks that don't even show above the top of his sneakers. Like his skin is a magnet, it pulls Jenner's gaze right there.

"God, I really want to suck on your ankle," Jenner says in his smooth, deep voice on the exhale.

Brayden laughs, his smile growing with his amusement.

"My *ankle*?" he chuckles, because it's ridiculous. But Jenner isn't smiling at all. His eyes are dark with lust and his gaze steady.

The feeling overtakes Brayden again, one that has become a regular feature in his life; hyperawareness of how much bigger Jenner is than himself. He's outmanned and so much smaller that any physical struggle between them would be laughable. Memories of each time Jenner has held him down and done exactly what he wanted fill Brayden's mind and senses. He feels strung out over that counter again, like a helpless, mischievous child being made to bear his punishment as Jenner's hips spank Brayden's ass while he force-fucks him.

Breath coming quicker, skin heating fast, cock swelling, Brayden asks, "Shut the door?"

"Fuck the door," Jenner says on a sigh, drawing closer, grabbing Brayden's leg and lowering his mouth to it with a low moan. Jenner's eyes flutter closed with greedy, heady desire as he seals his lips in an open-mouthed kiss to Brayden's ankle bone, then drags the flat of his tongue over the spot before doing it again, but sucking harder, his left hand kneading the muscle of Brayden's calf.

Brayden laughs a little, breathlessly, as his whole body reacts to the sudden bombardment of sensation, lighting up his nerve endings from the tips of his toes to the top of his head. Blood rushes in a torrent to his cock.

"Yeah, okay, that's kinda hot," he says around a gasp as teeth scrape lightly over bone and the tip of Jenner's tongue drags in a swirling line over the skin.

"Wanna suck every inch of you, everywhere. Suck your toes, your earlobes, your fingers. Lick your stomach, the insides of your thighs. Wanna pull your ass open and eat you out, make you scream."

Nearly panting, Brayden gets dizzy with the pounding of blood under his skin, the stiff, heavy weight of his erection, and the smooth, rolling music lilting in his ears under Jenner's low rumble of a voice, filled with temptation. Brayden doesn't protest or say a word as Jenner gets up, striding quickly to the door.

Swinging it closed, Jenner stops suddenly. There's a prolonged pause before he shuts and locks the break room's door.

Then he's on Brayden, pushing his chair roughly back from the table, the metal legs screeching over the linoleum floor. Jenner guides Brayden's thighs apart as Brayden fumbles at his fly, unfastening the button, tugging at the zipper. Easing his cock free, Brayden aligns it with Jenner's opened mouth which lowers immediately onto it, sealing with a hum of hunger around him.

Jenner knocks Brayden's hand away, taking control. He sets a steady pace, head bobbing in Brayden's lap as he sucks him raw.

Brayden lets out a long moan, knowing he shouldn't, unable to hold it in anyway. His whole body wants to curl up around the wet glove of Jenner's mouth on his dick. Grabbing a handful of Jenner's curls, urging on his pace with gentle pressure to the back of Jenner's head, Brayden gives in to it. His hips chase up off the chair, thrusting in when Jenner's mouth lowers, taking him in to the root.

Jenner's fingers yank impatiently at Brayden's jeans, getting them down farther. Then they knead at and stroke over his skin, the sides of his ass, and the undersides of his thighs. Grabbing hold of Jenner's shoulder with his left hand, Brayden scrambles for purchase. Everything in him, every thought, every drop of blood, tries to funnel down between his legs to further engorge his dick. He tries to spread wider and Jenner moans, the sound vibrating up Brayden's shaft, making him groan and buck.

It's incredible. Jenner's passion for him makes Brayden feel like he's not lost at all. The world hasn't defeated him, ripping everything of meaning away as soon as he begins to truly appreciate it. With Jenner, Brayden feels powerful, important, cherished, and most of all, lucky.

Panting roughly, pulling Jenner's head down onto him faster, thrusting up against his lips, stuffing him full of his cock, Brayden gets desperate. He doesn't care. He stops being shy and hesitant. All that matters is getting off. Jenner strokes him counter to his every suck, his fingers getting slippery with saliva, the obscene sounds his mouth make fill the air. As Brayden gets close, curling forward around Jenner's head, legs drawn up, Jenner grunts hard and twists his middle finger up through Brayden's asshole. With a startled gasp, Brayden feels it breach him. A subsequent breathless laugh turns quickly into a throaty groan. The finger slides deeper before tugging out. He clenches around it as it starts to pump in and out of him.

Eyes rolling up, Brayden's head falls back and he comes, unloading over Jenner's tongue. One of the earbuds has fallen out, allowing him to better hear Jenner's grunt as he swallows and feels the contraction of Jenner's throat working around Brayden's cockhead.

"Holy shit." Brayden gasps.

His body pulses, shuddering as he comes down, spent and blissful. Before he can fully recover, though, Jenner looks right at him and whispers, "Finger yourself. Suck on it first to get it wet. That's it."

Brayden sucks on his index finger, staring avidly at a glistening smear of semen on Jenner's lower lip. He draws the finger from his mouth and lets Jenner guide the hand down. Then, holding Brayden's hand, Jenner presses the finger slowly through Brayden's rim.

"Perfect. That's it. Hold this leg up. Good." Jenner helps Brayden get a good hold on his left leg, under the knee, with the other one braced on the floor. While Jenner keeps a hand locked to Brayden's chair so that he doesn't fall over, he pulls out his own straining erection and starts to furiously tug on it with his saliva-wet hand, staring as Brayden fingers himself. Brayden's come-slick, flaccid penis lies against his leg. It jumps as Brayden's finger moves, working in and out. Jenner grunts, stroking faster as Brayden's finger buries itself to the hilt. Closing the gap between them, Jenner kisses him, swallowing the soft gasps Brayden makes. Brayden's hand moves between them as it pumps. He tastes his come on Jenner's tongue. They kiss and Jenner beats off.

"Come inside me," Brayden gasps, speaking very softly. "Want you to."

Jenner's brow creases with a frown, suffused with such exquisite ecstasy that it makes Brayden feel like he's falling.

Ignoring the request, Jenner surges forward, kissing Brayden breathless. Brayden inhales sharply through his nose as Jenner nearly tips the chair over. Jenner's dick, hot and stiff, slides over Brayden's bared pelvis, beside where his arm juts down and his hand works busily. Jenner presses his member against Brayden, rubbing off on him. Their cocks squeeze and drag against each other. Moaning, Brayden feels Jenner climax with a hard shudder and a sharp inhale.

Catching his breath, burying his face in the side of Brayden's neck, Jenner whispers, "Didn't want to hurt you. Didn't want you to have to finish your shift with come leaking from your ass either, as awesome as that'd be for me to imagine."

They use Brayden's overnight bag and some tissues to clean up, changing their shirts as well. It only takes a minute. Then Jenner checks the area to ensure they're covered. When he unlocks and opens the door, Max is standing there hidden slightly by shadows. There's a phone in her hand, but it seems to have been completely forgotten. She stares into the break room at both of them. She doesn't say a word, but Brayden can tell by her expression that she heard everything, and stayed there so that she could hear.

With a very small, but very satisfied smirk, Jenner gives her a wink and goes past her to the bathroom to wash his hands.

Brayden is standing at his locker, retying his hair at the nape of his neck as she walks in. His skin feels too warm and covered in a thin sheen of sweat. His lips feel swollen and sore from being kissed so hard and his eyelids feel heavy, weighed down with sleepiness from his satisfied, post-coital bliss. The ghosts of Jenner's fingers, mouth and cock slide and move over Brayden's body, distracting in the best of ways, making it difficult for him to get embarrassed about Max overhearing them. Logically, he knows the room must smell of their sex, and he should care about that too, but somehow he doesn't.

"How's it goin', loverboy?" Max asks.

"Can't complain," he smiles back at her.

He tucks his shirt back in to his waistband and ties on an apron, giving her occasional upward glances as she just stands there, looking up and down his body. After a moment, she seems to remember herself and says, "'Scuse me," as she slides past him to lock her phone back inside her locker.

Seeing the hard set of her jaw, Brayden pauses before going in search of the bathroom himself. A blush creeps up Max's neck, making her cheeks pink. His voice is a low, raspy vibration in the air, mixing with the remembered echoes of his and Jenner's filthy whispers and moans as he says to her, "So, I guess you may have heard that."

Brayden may be a lot shorter than the other guys, but he's still taller than Max. She looks discomfited as he moves closer to keep the conversation private. She glances over at his body, her gaze slipping down, down, then snapping back to her locker.

A blond tendril falls beside his face, getting free of the tie. He instinctively pushes it back over his ear. The hand falls away, drawing Max's eye to a love bite on the side of his neck.

"No, really, it's fine. You're not exactly the first one to get a BJ in the break room." She claps her mouth shut, closing her eyes with mortification and a soft groan. "Sorry. None of my business."

"So, we're cool? I don't wanna make anyone uncomfortable. 'Cause I know all about uncomfortable."

"It's fine, Bray. Really," she fumbles, trying not to look directly at him while she says it. She seems to grow increasingly shyer the longer he looks at her. And the shyer she gets, the more he feels like he needs to apologize. He inches closer, completely aware of all of the flirting that they've indulged in with each other, and how that flirting might make it weird for her to be so aware of what he's doing with Jenner. *You used to think you'd be the one on your knees for me*, Brayden realizes. Max's breath quickens and she glances over at Brayden's crotch again. "It's not exactly a hardship to overhear two hot guys playing swallow the sausage."

He raises an eyebrow at her, then starts to smile knowingly, doing nothing to help dull the force of Max's blush.

"Don't look at me like that," she scolds.

"You like me, Max?"

"Yes, our unrequited love is deeply tragic." After minutes of struggle, she finally gets the damned locker opened. Tossing the phone inside, she closes the metal door and secures the padlock with a *snick*. "Get back to work, Romeo."

He doesn't go. He just stands there smirking, amused by the affect he's having on her.

"Well? Go!" She grabs him by the shoulders and turns him around. With a firm swat to his ass, she sends him on his way. "Go!"

Laughing, he heads out from the break room. In the hall, Jenner watches on, towering over them both. Brayden heads to the right, making for the sinks in the bathroom. But, before he can, Jenner catches his arm, holds him there, and asks, "Did I just see Max spank you?"

"Yes," Max says, bearing left. "And I'll do it again if you both don't stop fucking around and get back to your jobs."

"Rrreow," Jenner meows at her. "Someone's jealous."

Jenner watches her go, still holding Brayden in place, then says under his breath, "Spanking is against the rules."

"I didn't ask her to," Brayden argues. "But feel free to punish me for it later."

"Mm, bet you'd like that, huh?"

With a wanton, willing hint of a smile that's more in his eyes than on his lips, Brayden says, "Yes, Sir." He pulls free of Jenner's grip and disappears into the bathroom.

Chapter 29

Doubt

"No way I'm gonna be able to sleep tonight," Brayden laments as Jenner pulls him into their new, larger bed. It's queen-sized, and now Brayden's pillow rests atop it, directly beside Jenner's. Their clothes are stashed in the closet on shelves and hanging up, out of sight. The space remains a little sparse, but it has filled up considerably since that first night when it was empty except for a tiny single bed.

"Have you seen yourself and how exhausted you are? You look half dead."

"Gee, thanks. I mean, even if Andre finds the place in the dark and the middle of the night, we'd hear him trying to break the door down, so that's, like, warning. Right? But I think if he was able to get a flight he'd be here by now. How late do planes run?"

"Shh. We're not talking about it anymore. It's late. C'mon. There's no resisting me now," Jenner whispers temptingly. Brayden falls onto the mattress beside him and begins to try to get comfortable. He rolls onto his stomach and draws the pillow under his head, eyes already closing as Jenner pulls the covers up over them. Brayden begins to drift off as Jenner, lying on his side next to Brayden, says very softly, "So, I can put it in the closet, right?"

"Mm?" Brayden grunts, mostly asleep.

"Just agree with me. Pretend it's a dream."

"'M not sleeping."

"Of course not," Jenner scoffs gently. "So, yes to the closet?"

"What're you talkin' about, dude? Is this about the surfboard again?"

"No." Jenner chuckles, like Brayden is being ridiculous.

Brayden rolls slightly to peer up at Jenner through one cracked-open eye. "It's just a surfboard."

"It's," Jenner starts, controlling his volume masterfully, "a fucking *enormous* surfboard, painted in bright, flowery colors and standing right in the middle of my living room. There's no reason to have it out. There's not an ocean anywhere near here." "You just called me flowery," Brayden observes with amazement. "What's with you trying to shove everything in the closet? Do I need to worry about Pussy?"

Jenner breaks into a small chuckle at that before he composes his expression into a serious, tranquil one again. "Nope, way too easy. I'm passing right by that one."

"I like my surfboard. It makes me feel like I'm home, like I belong here."

Brayden gives him puppy eyes. Jenner puckers slightly, his dimples popping, and drops his gaze. "How about this? If you let me put it in the closet, I won't punish you tomorrow morning like I was planning."

Laughing, Brayden retorts, "That's your compromise? Seriously? Because I *really* didn't want you to spank me. Why don't you promise not to fuck me while you're at it?"

"Slut."

"Priss."

"Hippie."

"Gorilla."

"Gorilla?" Jenner repeats with raised eyebrows.

"Yeah, that's one of 'Rique's. Cut me some slack, I'm tired."

Jenner reaches out and brushes the hair back from the side of Brayden's face, sending it tumbling back over the pillowcase. He hooks the hand around Brayden's ear and can't help but lean in for a soft, little kiss.

"You want Andre to see that I belong here, right? That this is my home and where I want to be? I know you like things the way you like them, but if we're going to live together you have to let this be my space, too."

With a deep sigh, Jenner laments, "I can't argue with you when you have that sleepy, sexy voice."

"Mmm."

He waits a minute or two, stroking Brayden's hair as he falls asleep. Then he whispers, very quietly, "I'll let you keep it out, but in return I want permission to fuck you while you're sleeping."

"The hell is wrong with you? That would definitely wake me up!"

"Shhh, go back to sleep."

Brayden calls drowsily, "Pussy, keep an eye on this one for me," and falls asleep for good. It's not until morning has arrived in force that Brayden rouses. The bed is too comfortable. Each time he begins to surface from dreams of swimming against the tide to reach someone that's being swept out to sea, some of the low, simmering dread starts to creep in. So he pushes back into the black, preferring the battle of the dream over the battle of reality.

When a small, warm weight settles on his head, Brayden grunts and finally wakes for good. Hair tickles his nostrils, making him sneeze. The cat has curled up to lie on the side of his face, but gets startled by the sneeze. Groaning, Brayden calls, "Jenn, the cat's trying to smother me!"

"Who do you think put her on the bed?"

Brayden shoos the cat away and sits up, rubbing his eyes. "What time is it?"

"Ten. Come have something to eat. Your phone buzzed a while ago and I took the liberty of checking it. Your knight in shining armor is going to be here soon. He had an eight o'clock flight and texted you the arrival info."

"Shit," Brayden sighs. "Okay, okay. I'm up. Did he say anything else?"

"Nope."

Struggling out from the clutches of the bed's softness, Brayden is vaguely aware of Jenner looking him up and down as he staggers toward the bathroom with his morning wood at half-mast, his pants slung so low that his bare ass peeks slightly out of them.

"Damn, I'm gonna like living with you," Jenner chuckles. "I hope you thought to cover that up when you were living with poor, innocent cousin Emma."

"Hmm, what?" Brayden blinks, squinting at the sunlight.

"Never mind. I guess we can hope for her sake that she's as deep a sleeper as you and missed the regular morning show."

"You didn't fuck me while I was out, did you?" Brayden asks without bothering to turn.

"Baby, if you can't tell then I can't help you." Brayden pulls down his pants and examines his inner thighs for dried semen. In the other room, Jenner bursts out laughing. Brayden hears him sigh, "God, I love that kid."

Brayden emerges twenty minutes later. He's showered and slightly more conscious than he was when he went into the bathroom. While twisting his hair back out of his face, he calls out, "You wanna go to the gym, that's fine with me. I'd love to go along, but...."

"You're trying to foist me off on the gym?" Jenner makes a face at him. Brayden ignores it, choosing instead to make a beeline for the coffee pot and keep his head down.

"I'm trying to avoid a clash of the titans or some shit. Lemme talk to Andre. Once I explain, it'll be fine. You should stay out of it."

Laughing, Jenner follows after Brayden, standing over him and seeming ten feet tall. "It's adorable that you think there's a chance in hell I'll agree to that. You know, you haven't been completely clear with me on how far it went with him. I know he blew you, but just how familiar are you with *his* cock?"

Brayden pours coffee and asks, "What? You worried his is bigger than yours?"

"You're avoiding the question."

"No, I'm ignoring your self-esteem issues until I have some caffeine. Chill out. I like your cock better. I'm with you. Not him. Case closed. Look, when I talked to him on the phone, I felt guilty about how far I've gone with you, but now that I've gotten it off my chest, I'm cool. Andre just needs to *see* that I'm cool. It'll all be good."

"You're delusional. Okay, answer me this then. How are you going to introduce me?"

"As Jenner?"

"Who is your...."

The hesitation visibly pains Jenner. Brayden hesitates not be-cause he doesn't know what to call their relationship, but because he doesn't want to have to admit aloud, in public, to an audience, what they are. It's a lot different to look someone you respect in the eye and confess something when you're face-to-face than to say it offhandedly into a phone.

"Why do we have to categorize it?"

"Because we do."

"I think I told him you're my boyfriend." Brayden says.

Jenner argues, "Andre's not coming up here on a goddamned airplane because Braydy has himself a boyfriend."

Jenner's strong hand clasps the side of Brayden's neck. The thumb tilts Brayden's chin upwards, then the fingers slip back into his hair, wrapping in it. Moving his lips right against the shell of Brayden's ear, Jenner's low, powerful voice causes Brayden to shiv-er as he rasps, *"Who am I?"*

"M-master."

"Louder."

"Master."

"I asked you a question, slave. You need to answer it. Your body is mine now and I don't like other people touching my things. Tell me the truth."

"I used my mouth on him," Brayden admits quietly. "But it wasn't really a blowjob. Sir. That's all."

"Hands?"

The answer is written plainly in the anguish in Brayden's eyes, but Jenner apparently needs him to say the words.

"He'd restrain my hands. You know that. Or you should, Sir."

"If Nana hadn't called you up here, would you have let him fuck you?"

Brayden flinches subtly. Jenner pulls more tightly on his hair, making him gasp softly.

"Ahh, no. No, he was my best friend. That's a line I wouldn't cross."

"I was your boss first. You crossed that line."

"It's different. You're different."

"Why?"

"Because I *love* you. I want you. Just you."

Jenner kisses him quickly, frowning against the tide of emotion and need that Brayden draws out in him. Brayden gasps gently against Jenner's lips, bending under the force of Jenner's desire. Then Jenner lets him go.

"Show me."

Prove it, Brayden hears as he falls to his knees where he stands and tugs down the front of Jenner's exercise shorts to guide him free. Brayden's fingers tremble slightly, but Jenner stiffens even more at the evidence of Brayden's nervousness. Grabbing the edge of the counter with both hands, bending slightly over Brayden, Jenner curls forward around him. Hesitant, wracked with self-consciousness, Brayden starts to suck Jenner off, and Jenner moans.

It doesn't take long. Jenner gets off on Brayden's dutiful, earnest efforts to make it good. Once spent, giving Brayden a moment to recover and catch his breath, Jenner caresses through Brayden's hair. It's a quiet, decadently intimate moment. Brayden nuzzles against the heat of Jenner's groin without reservation, just seeking comfort. Once Brayden is ready, Jenner helps him up. He places a tender, soft kiss to the outer corner of Brayden's lips, drags a thumb over the wet, throbbing skin, and lets him turn to retrieve his coffee.

Jenner watches Brayden take one of his mugs from the cupboard. It's hand-painted, heavily glazed with bright colors, and therefore easily distinguishable from Jenner's plain black ones. He adds sugar first—plenty of it—and smothers it with a thick stream of the black aromatic brew. A tendril of hair escapes the knot at the back of his head. Brayden absentmindedly tucks it back over an ear.

The set of Brayden's shoulders and the weary air about him speaks of a weight that has settled upon him, one he has to bear until difficult confrontations are made. Jenner sees it all. But, more than that, he tries to see what's hidden beneath.

Brayden's past is one much more terrible than what Jenner has had to endure. With his father, whom Brayden must have deeply loved, passed away and his mother fled shortly after, Brayden is very much alone. People have disappointed him over and over again. Survivor's guilt, perhaps, along with the grief from losing his father coupled with abandonment issues from being left behind when he was still finding his way in the world. They haven't spoken of the particulars and, though Jenner wants to, he knows this isn't the time to start that conversation. Even without talking it over, Jenner suspects that those life events are what cause Brayden to need to be so tightly held during intimate moments. Tied down and trapped, there can be no chance of slipping away, whether to death, obscurity, or an even worse fate.

In Jenner's opinion, it's not Andre's place to check up on Brayden. Then again, who else is there to do it? Brayden wanted Andre to come to Robertsville. He craved the reassurance that someone cared enough to go out of their way to make sure he was all right. In lieu of the family he should have had, Brayden has begun to make his own family out of the likes of Andre and Enrique, Jenner, Max and Art, Nana and Emma Leah. Jenner watches, waits, and steps carefully, trying to reason it out, to decide on the best path to take when part of him hates Andre for having closeness with Brayden as well as some real claim on his heart.

Once his mug is half-empty, Brayden looks up with an alert, steadier, golden-green gaze. "It worries me when you're this quiet."

"No need to worry."

"Then talk to me. Tell me what you're thinking about."

"I'm thinking about what I want," Jenner confides. "I want to be at the gym, with you, watching your body cut through the water like a knife. I want to take you back to Manse. They have booths there, with walls made out of one-way mirrors where we could play, or fuck, and other men could watch. I could show them how beautiful you are when you submit to me, how much you want it. I want to take you to Sunday dinner and hold your hand and not be ashamed of that. I want to walk up to your Nana's door and kiss your cheek and not see the pain in your eyes doing that would cause. I want to call your sorry excuse for a mother and demand she explain to me how she could leave you all alone when you were still dealing with your father's death. I want to thank Andre for caring enough about you to fly up here and, after I thank him, knock him on his ass for touching you and forcing himself on you. I want to beg your forgiveness for doing the same thing myself. The worst part is, I can't guarantee it won't happen again. You make me crazy. *The things you do to me.*"

No sooner have the words passed his lips than Jenner is pulled down by Brayden who has set aside his coffee and crossed, barefoot and beautiful, over to him. Fingers sliding back into Jenner's black curls, Brayden kisses him forcefully, stretching up on his toes, drawing Jenner down until Jenner loops his arms behind him and lifts, taking Brayden off of his feet. He tastes of Jenner's spend, and sugar, coffee and life and everything that's good.

They break apart, gasping. Jenner buries his face in the light, clean scent of Brayden's hair, and the smell of soap on his skin.

"Thank you," Brayden says quietly.

"I love you," Jenner sighs, setting him down.

"I know," Brayden smiles. "And I know it's gonna be ugly. I realize that. But as long as I have you, it'll be okay. I've lost so much, Jenn, and I know I'm gonna lose more before it's done. I have to be okay with that. I'm really trying to be okay with it. I feel it, you know? The dread. The same dread would hit me when I was out on the beach, and the wind would pick up and the waves would begin to get stronger, and wilder, and there would be kids out in the water. There's nothing for it. You can't save everyone, as much as you might want to. You just take 'em as they come. Right now, it's all about trying to hold on to the good. Andre is good. He really is. And it would mean *so much* to me if you could make some peace with him."

Taking a deep breath, Jenner nods, utterly unable to deny the embodiment of his temptation, the owner of his heart. "Go get dressed."

"Yeah," Brayden agrees. He takes a last sip of coffee, sets it on the counter and walks away to get his phone.

"I might have an idea to defuse some of the tension with Andre," Jenner murmurs.

With a raised eyebrow, Brayden expresses his doubt and curiosity with a glance.

"Just let me handle it. Trust me."

"Yes, Master," Brayden grins wickedly, glancing up and down Jenner's body before retiring to the bedroom while peeling his shirt off and twisting it over his head. It gives Jenner a pristine view of the top of Brayden's tight ass and the pair of dimples right above it.

Jenner bites his tongue and keeps his feet planted, fighting against the intense urge to chase and devour his prey, possibly literally.

"That's not cute!" he calls.

"Fuck your cute," Brayden retorts.

They arrange to meet up with Andre at a café halfway between their place and the Philadelphia airport. The public setting is meant to help keep things civil and everyone comfortable. On the way there, Jenner, driving Brayden's Jeep, makes a detour that Brayden does not foresee or expect. When they pull up in front of Jenner's old place, Max is sitting outside smoking a cigarette beside Art.

"What did you do?" Brayden laments.

"Called for back-up," Jenner states simply, getting out but letting the engine run. To Max he says, "You ready?"

"Yep." She crushes the butt against the pavement.

"Hey, I'm free too if you need me," Art offers.

"Thanks," Jenner tells him, "But we don't want to gang up on him, or seem like we're trying to."

"Sure thing. I get it. Good luck, man." He waves to Brayden, who gives a weak grin through the window.

Max climbs into the back seat, slides to the middle and leans forward between the seats.

"Nervous?" she asks with a wide smile, nudging Brayden.

Brayden grunts and gives Jenner the evil eye as he gets back behind the wheel.

"You wanna sit on Brayden's lap for the ride, Maxie?" Jenner asks with blasé innocence. She stares at him, impassive, in the rearview mirror. "No? Then sit the fuck back and put on a seatbelt."

"Like you'd let my pussy get that close to *Brayden's lap*," she shoots back as Brayden hides a tired expression behind a hand.

"This just wasn't complicated enough for you, was it?" Brayden asks defensively under his breath, talking directly to Jenner.

"Max's presence is key for the simple fact that it stops this from being a pissing contest, of which you are perfectly aware. Besides, we all know Maxie's got a soft spot for you."

"You shouldn't have to do this on your own," she tells Brayden. "No judging. Promise."

But Brayden doesn't meet her gaze. Staring blankly out the windshield instead, he grumbles, "Let's just get this over with."

During the ten minute drive, Jenner itches to take Brayden's hand, but he can't decide if it would make things worse or not, so he doesn't give in to the impulse. It's a quiet trip. He can see Max trying to get a read on Brayden, and catches her eye himself once in awhile in the mirror. She gives Jenner a supportive hint of a smile, looking like she's proud of him, and it helps. He becomes more grateful that he called her.

Before they know it, they're there. Jenner finds a spot at a parking meter on the street out in front of the café. It's a sunny, mild day and people are sitting outside at little tables, though dressed in coats and layers. A warm, inviting aroma wafts into the Jeep as Brayden opens his door and swings a leg out.

"Gimme a minute or two," he asks. "I need to clear my head before we do this."

"Okay." Jenner nods. Holding himself back, he gives Brayden the space he craves even as everything in Jenner screams out for him to stay by Brayden's side, holding his hand like he should have done ten minutes ago.

The door closes heavily, leaving them in the isolated confines of the vehicle.

Max asks, "How are you holding up?"

"Swell," Jenner tells her, scanning the people milling about for a man who meets Andre's description and resembles that tiny photo on Enrique's phone.

"You're standing up for your boy. That's a good thing, Parrish."

"Yeah. I'm a great guy."

There's self-recrimination in his voice as he frowns at the sight of Brayden walking away, but before Max can call him on it his phone rings. It gives him pause, and she voices his thoughts exactly when she blurts, "Who the hell'd be calling you?"

He sees the caller I.D. flash and groans audibly. Putting the phone to his ear, he says, "Hey Ma."

"Your brother tells me that you're coming to Sunday dinner with your family."

"I am. I'm so glad that Callum is as informative as ever on my behalf."

"He's just glad you'll be there. He misses you."

That makes Jenner laugh aloud. "That's hilarious."

"Your father misses you too. I'm going to make that vegetable lasagna just how you like it. We'll open a bottle of wine and have a nice evening. I don't want to keep you, I just had to call and tell you that I was happy you changed your mind. I'm looking forward to seeing you."

"Me too, Ma," Jenner agrees, softening.

"Are you bringing anyone? I need to get a headcount so we're prepared with enough food and all."

Dread hardens in his gut. His heart beats faster. Some of his reaction must show on his face, because Max grips his shoulder and gives it a squeeze. He overlays her hand with his and makes himself say the words. "Yeah, actually I am. There's someone I've been seeing, so...."

"Good," she says, sounding pleased. "I'm glad to hear it. You've been alone for too long, sweetie. Are you going to tell me their name?"

He tries. He really does.

After a few stuttered syllables, he closes his mouth, giving up.

"Well, anyway. They're as welcome as you are. I love you, my sweet boy."

"Love you too, Ma," he manages, hoarsely.

"See you Sunday."

He hangs up and grasps Max's hand as it grips his shoulder harder. "Proud of you, Jenn," she whispers, kissing his cheek.

With effort, he gets it together. He clears his throat and rolls his head on his shoulders.

"Take your time. There's no rush," she tells him. "Breathe."

But there is a rush. Jenner sees Andre as he walks up to Brayden. Andre had been standing with his hands in his pockets at the front corner of the building, under the awning. He's a towering, massive man. His bald head is covered in a grey knit hat and he's wearing a navy woolen peacoat that only enhances his broad shoulders. He's a handsome guy, Jenner is sad to see. But he's sadder to bear witness to the huge smile that lights Brayden's face upon seeing his former roommate and lover when Andre folds him into an embrace.

Before the jealousy even touches him, Jenner is flooded with doubt and chagrin. He feels like he shouldn't be there, that he should have left this to Brayden after all. Andre grins at Brayden like an old, dear friend, touching the side of Brayden's face lovingly. Jenner's instinct is to drive away.

Max searches Jenner's face, clearly with plenty to say, but she holds her tongue. Everything that's happening out in front of the café reflects in the sadness painted over Jenner's face. He's not strong or controlling or cocky at all. He doesn't feel at all like the man he's become, who everyone expects him to be. He doesn't have it all figured out. He's not confident. He's just the type of guy who would fall in love with and rescue a tiny kitten only to hide the fact that he did out of pure shame for daring to have a heart.

Max folds her fingers over Jenner's, holding his hand since Brayden can't.

It takes him a long time. Minutes pass. Slowly, an inner battle is waged and Max is left helpless on the sidelines, a spectator. Then, like a miracle, Jenner murmurs, "He needs me," and reaches for the door handle.

He gets out of the Jeep and Max exhales her relief, saying softly, "That's my boy."

Chapter 30
Confrontation

One glance at the Jeep, with Jenner inside it and talking on the phone, tells Brayden that he has only a minute or so of respite before being faced with the dreaded introductions. He uses the time to his advantage, wanting to speak to Andre alone first. Having Andre there, big as life, smiling down at Brayden with that happy grin he knows so well, Andre's warm brown eyes twinkling –it's a balm for Brayden's aching heart.

"It's really damn good to see you, man," Brayden says, near to bursting with joy. He tries to stop smiling because his cheeks hurt from the strain and can't manage it. The side of his face tingles where Andre touched it. "You look good in a coat."

Andre laughs brightly. It's a rich, deep, rolling sound. "And here I was, worried about you. Look at'cha Marsha. I've never seen you so damn chipper."

Bouncing a little on the balls of his feet, pressing his lips shut even if he can't force his facial muscles to cooperate and ease up on the smile, Brayden lets himself enjoy the moment. Andre is really there. He came for the sole purpose of making sure Brayden is okay. It's incredible.

Andre adds, "Or is that smile just because I came to rescue you from shitty weather?"

Looking up into Andre's face, Brayden marvels at the oddity of seeing a knit hat on him. Grateful to be able to get lost in the familiar warmth of his friend's eyes, Brayden is amazed at the worry creeping in on the edges of Andre's expression—worry for Brayden's safety. It helps Brayden appreciate what he has.

He's blessed with a friend who would travel the length of the country just to make sure he's all right. He has new friends too, and a new life. There are options, support, people who matter to him, people who count on him. He sees Andre — really sees him — and what Andre wanted them to have together. But Brayden knows it never could have happened. Unlike Brayden, Andre would have wanted a relationship. He would have lost Andre's friendship and maybe broken Andre's heart in the process.

Things between them have taken the best course possible. The could-have-beens might always be there between them, but the fact is that Brayden seems to have what he's been looking for in Jenner and will get to keep Andre as a part of his life, too, if all goes well. So, he just says it. He stops being so scared, and stands up for himself for once.

"I'm in love with him, 'Dre. With Jenner. And I want you to be nice to him, because he's trying. He really is. He's not out and it's scary for him to suddenly be in a committed relationship, but this really isn't something you need to save me from." Shaking his head, still smiling that unlikely smile, his hair tickling the sides of his face where it falls over his collar, Brayden keeps bouncing slightly to keep warm and also to expend excess energy.

The mirth and humor drains from Andre's expression, too fast. People are chatting softly around them, bustling in and out of the shop with paper bags and cups of steaming coffee. Cars roll by on the street. The traffic lights change from red to green.

With a lowered voice, leaning down slightly so as not to be heard by anyone else, Andre says, "You said that shit has happened...."

"Oh, it has," Brayden allows, matching Andre's lowered volume. "Don't get me wrong. It's kind of a trip. I'm uh... I'm his slave. He gives me what I need, no matter how weird it might be, no judging, just trust, and in return, he gets to have from me what *he* needs."

Anger burns hot and bright, in the set of Andre's jaw, in his stance and the shrewdness of his gaze, so Brayden coaxes him, saying, "Go on. Be mad if you need to be, but be mad at *me*. Yes, we've had sex. Yes, I've done kinky shit. Yes, it was scary and a little out of control at first, but *I love him*. Do you hear me?"

Voice roughened, eyes prickling with tears that he tells himself are from the chill and the sun, Brayden pleads for the life he chose, because he can see Jenner getting out of the car with Max right behind him. Eyes widening slightly as he beseeches, opening himself up as much as he ever has, with anyone, Brayden asks his dearest friend, "Please, just *try*. Try so that I don't have to lose you. I don't want to lose anyone anymore."

He laughs a little as he says it, out of desperation, to keep from falling apart. It feels like he's standing on the edge of a cliff, ready to fall into the abyss and have everything that he has left ripped from him forever.

Time measures out in heartbeats as Brayden's pulse *thump-thump-thump*s under his skin, knocking out a steady, rapid rhythm inside his chest. He holds Andre's gaze and watches him try to decide what to do, knowing Brayden as well as he does, and what it all means going forward.

Each beat moves Jenner closer, his steps long and crossing the distance fast, with Max just behind, hurrying to keep up.

The pain of what it would cost Brayden to lose Andre, then and there, is a knife in his chest. It all blurs and he doesn't see it as Jenner gets to him, but he does feel the arm that slings around his shoulders, and the breath that warms his cheek as Jenner asks softly, "Hey, are you okay?"

It becomes too hard, suddenly, like it did when confronting Max and Art, but it's worse because becoming estranged from new friends is not as terrible a prospect as facing the same fate with Andre, who showed Brayden that it was okay to want what he wanted, and who has been there when Brayden sorely needed someone. Touching his forehead to Jenner's shoulder, Brayden draws strength from his nearness. Still smiling but in a heartbroken way, Brayden tries to speak; it thickens into a sob that sticks in his throat, choking him. Tears slip down Brayden's cheeks and Jenner folds him up in a hug. Brayden grasps at Jenner like a drowning man.

But then Brayden doesn't know what to do. He's lost, completely and truly, and has given all he has. There's no more courage left in him or, at least, that's how it feels. Next comes the familiar sorrow of loss, as dense and thick as fog rolling in. He's losing Andre. Someday he'll lose Jenner too. It's unavoidable.

Out of nowhere, catching Brayden entirely by surprise, he feels someone hug him from behind. Because this someone's arms wrap around under his arms, thin and delicate, he knows it to be Max.

A laugh is startled out of him, and he snorts against Jenner's coat.

"Fuck," Max *tsks*, "He's so damn sensitive sometimes! Okay, Braydy, I give! You win. I'm sorry I said that the Marlins suck donkey balls. They suck *fish* balls."

Hysterical laughter peels from Brayden as he snorts again. When he glances over his shoulder at Max, he sees she is leaning her cheek against his shoulder with a goofy, love-struck smirk.

"I love you, Max."

"Wait. Do fish have balls? I don't think I've ever seen testicles on a flounder."

Andre clears his throat. Brayden sighs, and reluctantly looks over at him. Detangling from Jenner, he shoos Max away, wriggling out of her arms when she tries to grab his ass.

"You gonna introduce me or what?" Andre asks. "Now that I've made you cry and I feel like an asshole."

"You didn't make me cry," Brayden murmurs, dropping his gaze. He cringes as he realizes that people are looking at them. "It's not easy to do this, you know. I've always sucked at confrontations. That's why I got my ass handed to me so much in school."

He'd never told Andre much about what life was like before moving to Miami, when he was just that quiet, sad kid that everyone pitied, with a crumbling support system and no secrets at all because everyone knew everything about him already. It had been Brayden's attempt at starting over, trying to move on, but no matter how many miles you travel, some things will always stay inside, waiting to come out. Standing there in front of Andre, drying his eyes, Brayden feels like he's not only introducing his new friends, he's introducing that scared, imperfect small-town boy he thought he would never have to be again.

Jenner gathers him back under the comforting, solid weight of his left arm and kisses the side of his head. The display of affection, for anyone to see, almost makes Brayden lose it again. He bites the inside of his cheek to keep the tears at bay. Once he knows his voice will be steady, he answers, "Andre, this is Jenner Parrish and our friend Maxine. They prefer to be called Parrish and Max, respectively."

Jenner immediately offers a hand and says, "Nice to meet you, Andre."

Brayden averts his eyes, bracing for whatever comes next, expecting the worst.

Andre holds back for only a second, looking Jenner over, from his dark, curly hair to his pale complexion and handsome features, his impressive build and height, but mostly his eyes, measuring him for the man that he is beyond the superficial.

Then, Andre takes the offered hand and shakes it. "Parrish. Good to meet you."

Andre turns to Max next. He takes her hand with a more gentle salutation. "And you, Max."

"Why don't we get something to eat or drink and find a table, hmm?" Jenner suggests politely, putting on a friendly grin as other patrons continue to stare.

They queue up and order scones and coffee, which they take to a booth inside the cafe where the seats and noise will give them some privacy. Max sits beside Andre. Jenner slides in next to Brayden.

Sensing that Andre hesitates to speak out of uncertainty of how much to acknowledge in mixed company, Brayden assures him, "Max knows all about me and Jenner. We're trying to be honest with people we trust for once. On Sunday, we're going to dinner at Jenner's parent's house to tell them we're together."

"What about Lara? Ruth?"

Brayden shakes his head, chewing on his lip. "But I moved in with Jenner. I'll get there, and tell them. Once I figure out how."

"It's not complicated, Marsha. You just *tell them*."

"It's not that easy," Brayden says bitterly.

"Marsha. Marsha Braydy. Huh. I like that," Max starts, trying to lighten the mood.

"Don't get *any* fucking ideas, woman," Brayden warns.

"Yeah, what're you gonna do, tough guy?" she teases.

"So, you're his Master," Andre says to Jenner, deadpan and direct.

The atmosphere turns cold as ice in an instant. The awkward tension comes right back.

"Yeah. I am," Jenner agrees, not backing down or seeming shocked, just calm and alert.

"You know what you're doing?"

"Yes. I do. We're careful."

"If you ever really hurt him, I'll fucking kill you."

"I accept that," Jenner replies with a nod.

"Cool. Are you really going to come out to your family for him?"

"Not just for him. For me, too."

Andre digests this, looking Jenner over. "Okay."

"Okay?" Brayden repeats hopefully. "Really?"

"Really. I can tell that he cares about you. I appreciate his honesty. I'd be able to smell it if there was any bullshit."

"Yeah, I totally hate bullshit. Super smelly," Max murmurs in meek agreement over the lip of her coffee cup.

Andre looks sideways down at her next to him, and she gazes up with wide, innocent eyes, lined darkly with purple eyeliner to accentuate their almond shape.

"This girl is fucking crazy. I like her," Andre chuckles.

"I hate to break it to ya, dude, but I hear you're queer," Max whispers with apparent regret. "But I'd *totally* blow you in the bathroom if you're into it. Got a thing for black dudes. *Huge* penises."

"Max!" Brayden gasps, then starts laughing his ass off. "Holy shit!"

Andre laughs with him and Jenner smiles. Wrapping an arm around Max, companionably, Andre draws her to his side.

"See?" Max says to them. "Works every time. Honesty. God bless it."

Chapter 31

Taking Control

The sit-down with Andre appears to work wonders on freeing Brayden of some stress. Jenner decides that he seems lighter for it. It also causes a definite but subtle shift in Jenner's mindset. The flirting with Max and the brief affectionate touches from Andre leave Jenner wanting to claim Brayden as his own, to remind him where he belongs.

When it comes time to say goodbye to Andre, Brayden glances to Jenner for non-verbal permission to do so with a hug. Brayden is somewhat chagrined when Jenner doesn't just give in with a nod, but instead says quietly, "Ask me."

"Jenn, come on."

"I'd like you to ask."

Andre and Max are both looking at them. Embarrassed but with heat evident behind the look he gives Jenner, Brayden asks, "Is it okay with you if I hug Andre and say goodbye?"

Jenner is unmoved because Brayden knows what Jenner is waiting for. Part of their game has always involved nudging Brayden slowly closer to where Jenner expects him to be, filling the role of the dutiful slave. For his own reasons, Brayden needs Jenner to give him that push to get there, rather than offer it willingly. So, Jenner pushes, for Brayden's sake.

"Oh my god. You're really going to make me say it?"

"I'm waiting," Jenner says impassively. "Show some respect."

Brayden lowers his eyes. Jenner almost smiles, because he can tell that Brayden is enjoying this, though maybe not consciously. But the worry and sadness over Andre's visit, over imagined possibilities and the future all seem forgotten as Brayden searches for the courage to speak the words that Jenner waits for. All of Brayden's attention is focused only on the here and now. For the moment, at least, nothing else matters.

Standing mere inches from Jenner, Brayden whispers to him, "Is it okay if I hug Andre and say goodbye, *Sir*?"

"Better. Yes, you may."

"Thank you."

"You're welcome."

Brayden turns and moves into Andre's open arms. He lingers, not letting Andre go. After all, Andre has only just gotten there. Jenner understands. That doesn't mean he has to like it.

"I miss you, man," Brayden says.

"Me too," Andre replies, caressing once over the back of Brayden's head, over his hair, before releasing him. "You should all come and visit sometime. You're more than welcome."

Jenner and Andre shake hands, and it's more than cordial enough to put a happy grin back on Brayden's face. After Andre kisses Max's cheek, they head back to the Jeep to go home.

First, they drop Max off at the house. When they get there Jenner parks on the street. Before Max is able to reach for the door handle, Jenner stops her by saying, "Wait a second."

"What's up?"

"Well, first off, thank you for coming. It meant a lot to both of us."

"You're welcome," she replies, though looking wary at Jenner's serious tone. She watches his face in the rearview mirror. Brayden must be able to sense it too, because Jenner is pleased to see that his slave's head is bowed in the picture of humble obedience.

"But I can't allow you to continue touching Brayden in a flirtatious way."

"Jenner," she scoffs, her mouth agape.

"I'm serious about this, Maxine," he says, his voice hard. "Brayden knows that one of our rules is that no one touches him but me. I won't try to regulate your conversations or the way you speak to one another, but touching is off limits. I need you to be aware of that. Twice in the past two days you've broken that rule. Brayden will face the consequences for his part in allowing it, but you need to be willing to cooperate, or else I'll have to keep the two of you apart myself."

"Wait, what do you mean Brayden will face consequences?"

Brayden groans and hunches forward even more, slouching in his seat. Jenner glances at him with a frown of displeasure, then back at Max. "Nothing to worry about. I assure you it won't be anything that Brayden won't enjoy. And you both still know what I said before. Brayden is free to go to you or Art if he needs help or wants to talk. Now, what do you say, Max? Will you behave?"

"What if I need his attention in the bar and it's loud and I have to tap his shoulder?"

"That's not what I'm talking about, and you know it. Can you respect my arrangement with Brayden or not?"

"Fine. I'll cooperate," she says, somewhat angrily. "But only if you tell me what you're going to do to Brayden."

Brayden groans. Jenner snaps, "*Silence*, slave. Okay. If that's how you want to play it. I'm going to fit Brayden with chastity devices to remind him who he belongs to, to wear at home and at work. There'll also be corporal punishment and *lots* of sex. Happy?"

"Take video for me?"

"Get out of the fucking car."

"What if I beg for you, Parrish?" She grins like a cat, and slides over to the door. "Pretty please? Pretty please with cherry-flavored lube on top? No?"

"No."

With a disappointed sigh, she gets out of the Jeep. Holding the door, she turns back to ask, "But, just to be clear, it's not against the rules for me to wank to the mental imagery, right?"

"Fantasize all you want, baby. It's a free country."

"Thanks, Parrish," she winks at Brayden and closes the door with a giggle.

"Are you fucking kidding me?" Brayden demands as they drive away.

"Silence! Until I say otherwise, you're on high protocol. I'll let you know when I want to hear your opinion. You've been very disobedient. I intend to teach you how to behave."

Brayden is quiet, his head bowed, for the rest of the short drive back to the apartment. Once they're parked, Jenner turns and says, "I don't remember giving you permission to get an erection, slave."

"I'm not—"

Jenner's hand darts out. The fingers close like a vice around the bulge in Brayden's pants. With a gasp, Brayden's hips tilt into Jenner's hand to try to relieve the pressure. His flesh jumps, enjoying the slight pain. Jenner squeezes harder and Brayden whimpers on the exhale. His head falls back against the headrest and he tries to breathe through it.

"Is this for her? Or for me?"

"Y-you, Sir."

Flattening his hand, Jenner rubs hard over Brayden's flesh. He watches his slave's mouth fall open around an unvoiced moan.

"You *will* behave for me."

"Yes, Sir."

"You'll be *punished*. You'll be *fucked*. You'll wear a collar to work *and* you'll wear a chastity belt."

"Fuck yeah. *Please*."

Jenner's fingers knead and squeeze, hard enough to draw a small, beautiful cry. "Say my name. Show respect."

"M-m-master," Brayden gasps, the honorific breaking in the middle as Brayden grabs the door handle to anchor himself. People pass by the Jeep on the sidewalk, but no one bothers to look their way.

"Again," Jenner demands, rolling the sensitive flesh in his hand. Brayden grunts softly and pushes into the touch, getting hot, getting harder, and fast.

"*Master*," Brayden moans.

"Do you want it? You want me to take care of you like this?"

"I want it. Need it. Please. *Please*."

Jenner lets him go and pulls the keys out of the ignition, tossing them in Brayden's lap. Fumbling, Brayden fishes them out from between his legs.

"Go upstairs. Take all of your clothes off and wait for me. Whenever you're in our home, if we don't have any guests, no matter the protocol or time or day, you're forbidden from wearing clothing of any kind. That's now a rule. Do you understand?"

"Yes, Master," Brayden says, his voice lust roughened, his pupils blown with desire.

Jenner grips the steering wheel and watches him go. Brayden picks out the right key, glancing around for onlookers, adjusting himself slightly when he gets to the door and turns the knob.

Chest rising and falling rapidly, Jenner tries to get a handle on it, all of it, and calm down. He imagines Brayden going upstairs and peeling off his clothes—hard, ready and willing—and basks in the amazement that he gets to have this, and that Brayden chose him to have it with. It makes Jenner feel unspeakably lucky, and very happy. Even if the dinner and confrontation with his parents is a disaster, at least he still has this. He has Brayden. It's enough. Even if his family disowns him, if they take away the bar, the apartment—all of it—they'll figure it out. Jenner and Brayden will do it together. And it'll be okay.

Smiling, Jenner gets out of the Jeep, locks it, and goes to seek out his dutiful slave.

Chapter 32

Submission

Brayden is waiting in the middle of the bedroom. His clothes have been folded neatly and set aside. The energy baking from his naked body screams out for bondage. It makes Jenner's cock so stiff, he almost moans aloud with the ache. He walks up to Brayden and grabs hold of his jaw, his fingers denting the flesh.

"We don't have as much time as I'd like, but I intend to use every fucking *second* of it. I'd love to be able to wax you first. You need it."

Jenner reaches down with his other hand and tugs on the dark brown pubic hairs above Brayden's cock, which curves up tight to his belly, hot, dark and ready.

"Do you want restraints, slave?"

"*Please*, Master."

"I love when you beg so pretty for me. You gonna beg for my cock, too?"

"Yes," he moans.

"Good. Close your eyes."

Jenner fits a leather hood over Brayden's face. It covers him from brow to chin with straps that wrap behind his head and up over the top, keeping it in place.

"I want you to focus only on what you feel me doing to you. Let me hear your safeword."

"Pussy," Brayden says, and it's muffled, but Jenner hears him well enough.

"Good. How does that feel?"

Jenner has gotten the face mask on securely. It completely covers Brayden's eyes, nose, mouth and chin, but there are nose holes for him to breathe through.

"Feels good."

Jenner moves around behind him and pulls both of Brayden's arms behind his back, folding them so that his lower arms are flush together, his hands clasping the opposite elbows. Holding them there with one-hand, Jenner drags his lips in unhurried, reverent, open-mouthed kisses over Brayden's shoulder and up his neck.

"I'm gonna walk you to the bed and get you in position, okay?"

Brayden nods and lets Jenner guide him with small steps. Hesitantly, unable to brace himself with his arms since Jenner still has them held tightly, Brayden moves to kneel on the edge of the bed. Jenner presses a hand to the center of Brayden's back to indicate that he should bend at the waist.

"Think doggy style," Jenner instructs. "I want your hands down by your ankles and legs spread. Stay nice and relaxed. You'll enjoy this. I promise."

Brayden grunts his complicity, getting into the position but letting Jenner make adjustments as needed. A metal spreader bar is placed under Brayden's ankles, with braces to hold each of them approximately a foot and a half apart. Directly beside each of the ankle cuffs, one on each side and affixed to the spreader are smaller cuffs for his wrists. Once Jenner snaps all of the locks into place, Brayden is unable to move an inch. His arms and legs are completely immobilized; his ass is up, perfectly presented and spread, ready for fucking. His balls hang heavily above the bar and when Jenner begins to fondle them, Brayden moans.

"This isn't about getting you off," Jenner warns. "This is about obedience and learning your place."

Jenner squirts a dollop of lube onto his fingers, smears it over his slave's opening in little circles before pushing two fingers into Brayden's rectum. Moaning loudly, Brayden clenches around the fingers. They coat him inside and out with lube, prodding, pressing and rotating in the snug ring of muscle. The fingers reach deeply enough to make Brayden's toes curl.

A third finger is wedged through his sphincter. Brayden grunts at the stretch but Jenner is demanding. Greedily, Jenner caresses over the rounded muscle of Brayden's buttocks as he works him open, taking his time. Brayden moans, whimpering a little, pulling at the restraints. He tries to arch his back but is unable to in such a position. He can't do anything at all but take it.

"Gorgeous. You should see how luscious your ass looks taking my fingers," Jenner teases. He presses his fingers in to the hilt and keeps them there, watching Brayden clench, feeling him push back against them with his inner muscles.

"That's it," Jenner coaxes. "Just take a minute to feel it. You're stuffed so full, but you're such a slut, I know you love it. Don't you, slave?"

Brayden grunts roughly against the mask, gulping down air. Jenner tries to spread the fingers apart, pulling Brayden open even more and sees his feet flex. The heavy breathing gets louder and Jenner scolds, "Control your breathing! Relax. You need to get used to taking anything I'm in the mood to stuff inside you. I wanna see your ass open, wet and ready to get fucked. When I let you out of your bonds and you go to work tonight, you'll be wearing a chastity belt. It'll be fitted with a steel cock ring and a butt plug. You'll wear it under your clothes. If I decide to fuck you in my office, or bring you up here, or wait until after we close, you'll cooperate and say please and thank you, and service me accordingly. It's your job to satisfy my needs, and if you're a very good, obedient slave then tonight, after work, *maybe* I'll let you orgasm."

Jenner pivots his wrist and deliberately triggers Brayden's prostate. It causes him to produce a sweetly anguished, soft cry. Brayden tries to push the fingers out but he's unable to. In response, Jenner grabs him by the balls. They're drawn up tightly to Brayden's body. Locking his hand around the base of his slave's sac, Jenner pulls on it, stretching the flesh while pushing firmly into Brayden's ass with the hand nestled there. He's rewarded for his efforts with some desperate sounds and writhing.

"Beautiful, Bray…"

Jenner's hand slowly, gradually withdraws. Brayden moans louder than ever. Empty of Jenner's fingers, Brayden's hole is pinker from the friction. Pulsing blood warms the area and it's stretched looser, ready to receive.

When Jenner finally inserts two fingers, Brayden moans gratefully. They're both of Jenner's index fingers and he pulls Brayden's ass open with them, letting him feel exposed and helpless. Brayden makes soft noises behind the mask, but tries to swallow the sounds.

"This? Is *mine*," Jenner says roughly.

Brayden moans his Master's name. It's such a sweet sound that Jenner forgives him for it immediately. For so long, Jenner has craved and dreamed about having exactly what is now presented to him—a loyal slave who derives as much pleasure from submitting and receiving Jenner's attentions as he does in bestowing them. It goes beyond the pleasure with Brayden, though, beyond the pain and the decadent escape of it all. There's a foundation of love beneath everything they do. That's a privilege Jenner never dared to dream about.

He never thought he could be this lucky.

"I want to lick you here so badly, slave," Jenner admits, "But first we need to deal with your punishment."

Brayden murmurs his assent.

"I want you to know that I punish only because I love you. To remind you of that, I'm going to fit you with your collar. The same one from before."

"Yes, Master," Brayden says eagerly. To hear Brayden wanting the punishment, the love and the collar so avidly, gives Jenner a thrill.

It only takes a moment. The leather is slipped around his neck. His long hair is brushed aside and the strap is buckled tightly.

"Thank you," Brayden sighs.

"You're welcome, beautiful," Jenner sighs fondly, kissing his neck, causing Brayden to purr with happiness.

Jenner leaves Brayden where he is while he goes to retrieve his tools, tossing them one by one onto the bed beside where Brayden is bound.

"Your ass is going to be tender. You won't be able to sit on it comfortably for a couple of days," Jenner warns. "But I want you to know *why* I'm spanking you."

Brayden grunts, his breath quickening. Sweat breaks out over his skin as his anticipation grows.

"You're being punished for flirting with Max and letting her spank you and touch you. You're also being punished for not being properly obedient with me. It might not feel like it when I'm done, but I *am* going easy on you. This is merely a *taste* of what I can give you, should I feel you need disciplining. Are we clear, slave?"

"Y- yes. Master."

"Nervous?"

Jenner plucks the long, wooden paddle from the bed and runs the flat, smoothly lacquered surface over the thick curve of Brayden's buttocks. A whimper is Brayden's only response.

The paddle slices through air and connects with Brayden's bottom, driving him forward only to yank at his shoulder joints as the restraints keep him right where he is. Another blow falls, and another, ten in total. Each one lands squarely across the thickest part of his ass, the same spot each time.

Jenner pauses, listening to Brayden gasp and grunt, then groan as the hurt radiates deeper into the muscle.

"See? You aren't going anywhere. I'm going for quantity over force here. I could hit you a lot harder, but if I was going to do that I'd restrain you differently so that you had even less room to move."

Jenner swings. The paddle is about fifteen inches long and whacks loudly against his slave's ass, cutting off all thought, leaving only stinging pain. Brayden flinches repeatedly and pulls uselessly against the spreader bar holding him in the pose.

The paddle falls in rapid succession. When he's given a brief reprieve, Brayden is grunting and whining quietly. Jenner touches him. With an opened hand, he rubs lightly over the sore, tender spot. Then, he grabs a handful of the muscle and Brayden's soft cries get much louder.

"Good. You're pinking up nicely. I can feel the blood beating under your skin. We've got a ways to go though, so get comfortable. Next you get the leather strap."

"Oh *god*," Brayden moans.

"*Then* you'll get my hand. I'm *really* looking forward to that."

Jenner tosses the paddle aside and grabs the strap, fitting the handle snugly into his palm, getting a good grip on it. The black leather strap doubles over in a loop. It makes an entirely different sound as it cuts through the air in an arc. Brayden clenches his ass and yelps at the first strike.

Jenner shifts his stance and begins delivering rapid, unceasing lashes left to right and right to left, crisscrossing to hit both sides of Brayden's reddened ass, one then the other. Though he fights it, Brayden can't escape. Nor does he use the safeword.

After twenty lashes, Brayden's ass is swelling up with welts. Jenner adjusts his angle and begins hitting the right cheek, varying his target only slightly each time.

Brayden starts to yell, bellowing out his pain. After ten more swings, Brayden's body is limp and covered in sweat.

"*Please,*" he moans deeply.

"I know it hurts," Jenner hushes, caressing the abused flesh. He scratches over it with his short nails, leaving red marks and making Brayden shout hoarsely. "But you deserve this, don't you?"

"Yes," Brayden hiccups, voice thick with tears.

Jenner pushes the strap between Brayden's legs, stroking over his erection with it repeatedly. Radiating shame, Brayden tries to thrust against the strap to get relief, but that only makes Jenner twitch his wrist, striking Brayden's dick with the leather. Brayden makes a hurt sound. Jenner draws the leather back and sees that it's wet with precome.

He bats lightly at Brayden's testicles with the strap until Brayden is growling, snarling like a dog, letting the anger replace sadness, shyness and fear.

"STOP!" he yells.

"Liar," Jenner laughs. "If you actually wanted me to stop, you'd say the safeword. *You* stop. Stop lying, slave!"

He grabs hold of Brayden's balls, yanks and delivers his hardest lash of the strap yet. Brayden gasps violently. The strap leaves a red line across the curve of his ass, on both cheeks.

Throwing the strap away, Jenner impatiently guides his cock-head to Brayden's opening. Once he's aligned, he holds Brayden's hips and pushes right in, breaching him with one determined, smooth thrust.

With a moan, Brayden takes Jenner in to the root. Restless but trapped, he yanks at his arms, tries to move his legs. He remains trapped, ass-up and spread. His bottom is so sore that when Jenner experimentally kneads his cheeks, pulling them open and squeezing the muscle, Brayden sobs into the leather mask. Jenner fucks him with abandon, setting a quick pace.

It's rough, primal and spectacular. Brayden weeps precome all over the bed beneath him. Lifting his head—the only part of him that he can move, he cries out his pleasure, yelling roughly.

Soon, Brayden is laughing deliriously through his moans and is more than ready for it when Jenner starts to spank him with an opened hand, slowing his thrusts until Brayden is begging, "More, harder, please... Master... I can't. I can't take it. *Oh god...* More! Please... fuck me harder. I need it..."

"Slut," Jenner smirks, spanking Brayden's ass raw. He sees his handprint forming atop the welts from the strap and the broad redness from the paddle.

Jenner draws the sex out as much as he can. He squeezes himself tightly, holding his climax back almost literally. Breathing through his nose, Jenner fights for control, clawing at it.

He falls to his knees and allows himself to finally do what he's wanted to do for an hour. With a deep, rolling moan of pure pleasure, Jenner extends his tongue, licking greedily up through Brayden's crease. Brayden gasps and complains loudly, "You're gonna fucking kill me, you fucking bastard! Oh *fuck...*"

Jenner moans again. He seals his lips around Brayden's rim then slips his tongue through the swollen muscle. Jenner takes a long, curling lick over the inside of Brayden's ass, humming and sucking on his rim. Cheeks hollowed out, Jenner keeps his hands wrapped around Brayden's tender ass.

"Oh fuck. *God.* Oh god. Fuck! Please. Oh god, *please...*"

Jenner tongues at him, licking around the rim, feeling the heat of him, the pulsing of the blood in the engorged tissue. He sticks a finger in and Brayden sobs, trying to hump the air, desperate. His whole body is Jenner's to play like an instrument.

When Jenner climbs back to his feet, he leans over Brayden's sweaty, exhausted body, bracing a hand on the bed beside it and reclaims his prize.

It doesn't take long. Jenner gasps, "God, Bray. So perfect. You're so exquisite... My god." Pulling out with a grunt from both of them, Jenner squeezes up his shaft twice, coming in a flood over the tortured flesh of Brayden's backside. Streaks of pearly white spunk paint starkly over tender red skin. Jenner smears it in, coating Brayden with it.

The face mask is stripped from him. Brayden is worn ragged and nearly unconscious. Jenner kisses his cheekbone, pushes tendrils of hair back from where they're stuck to Brayden's face and says, "I'll be right back. Just going to clean myself up."

There's no response. Jenner checks Brayden's vitals — his pulse rate and breathing. Everything is normal, so Jenner leaves him where he is to rest.

Brayden comes to sometime later as Jenner is unfastening the spreader bar. Brayden's limp arms and legs are guided from the cuffs and he's laid out on his back on the bed. Dutifully, unhurriedly, Jenner massages the blood back into his slave's limbs, smiling down at Brayden with a prideful, drunken sort of crooked grin. Peering up drowsily through his eyelashes, Brayden watches his Master, and winces only slightly at the pins and needles that prick at him. His cock lays swollen and hot against his pelvis. Jenner avoids coming in contact with it.

"Was I good for you?"

"Baby, you were *so good*," Jenner says with satisfaction. He pries Brayden's legs apart, letting his knees fall open widely and pushes them up to spread Brayden's ass open once again.

Producing a harness from somewhere out of sight, Jenner shows it to him. There are leather straps that buckle around the waist, and another that winds through the legs, fitted with the steel cock ring and a plug pouch to securely hold a toy.

"If you let me put this on you, I'll help you into the shower, then we'll get you something to eat. I'll have the only keys to the padlocks, so if you need to void your bowels, you'll need to ask permission first."

Lowering his eyes, licking his lips, Brayden takes a breath and nods.

"I'm proud of you, Bray. You were so incredible."

The praise swells Brayden's heart until it's ready to burst. Tearing up, smiling at his own ridiculousness, he reaches for Jenner's hand. Their fingers lace together and he holds his breath to keep from crying.

"It's okay," Jenner tells him. "Let it out. There is no shame or fear here. Only trust and love."

"I love you so much," Brayden confesses thickly. Tears slip from the corners of his eyes.

"I'm going to take such good care of you. Better than you've ever known. I swear it."

"Thank you, Jenn." Brayden smiles tiredly, chuckling at himself as the tears keep falling. He wipes them away, sniffs and holds his legs as Jenner eases the lubed plug, tapered slightly and a good six inches, into him.

"Feel okay? It's not going anywhere. The ridge at the base will keep it inside, but the strap will make sure of it. It's designed for long term use, so you should be comfortable enough. Wear your cargos and keep your shirt untucked."

"Yes, Sir. Thanks."

It feels surprisingly good to have Jenner put the plug in, and give him firm rules to play by. It makes Brayden feel like he has nothing to worry about, because he knows not only exactly what to expect, but that Jenner will take good care of him no matter what. He'll worship Brayden's body, cherish his heart, and give him anything he needs, whether it's restraints, pain or pleasure. He'll reward Brayden when he's good and punish him when he's bad. It's perfect.

Jenner helps Brayden stand to get the harness on. The buckles are pulled tight around his waist and up through his legs. His cock and balls are locked inside the ring, squeezed through it, hanging heavily between his legs. The strap holding the base of the plug is secured, pulled tight between his throbbing cheeks.

"You look so fucking hot in this," Jenner says with a smile, biting his lip, eyes sparkling with delight. "I love it. What do you think?

Be honest."

"I kind of love it too," Brayden confesses. "Is that weird?"

"No," Jenner frowns, kissing the center of Brayden's head. "It's perfect."

"Yeah." Brayden smiles bashfully and takes a bottle of water that Jenner hands to him.

"Drink up. Leave the door open while you shower in case you need me."

Brayden nods, but hesitates. Jenner waits patiently, trying to read Brayden's expression. Then, finding his courage, Brayden stretches up onto his toes and places a soft, chaste kiss to Jenner's lips, his hand cupping the side of Jenner's face.

With a brief upward glance, filled with love, adoration, devotion and joy, Brayden gives Jenner a look that reaches all the way down into his soul. Happier than he's been in his life, Brayden retreats to the bathroom to get cleaned up and ready for work.

Chapter 33

Next Steps

It's been a long, exhausting day for Brayden Clare. The confrontation with Andre was a mental trial and the punishment delivered by Jenner a purely physical one. By the middle of his shift, the only thing keeping him awake and alert is the harness hidden under his pants, binding him. The presence of the plug in his ass keeps his skin flushed a rosy pink for hours on end at the thrill of wearing such a thing while he works, and at the command of his boss. Every time he closes his eyes, Brayden sees the wicked smile that lit Jenner's face as he pushed the plug into Brayden's body. Each movement Brayden makes, whether it's to reach for a clean glass, to clear the bar-top of used glasses and empty bottles, pouring drinks, or walking to check on a customer — it causes the plug to shift and jostle deliciously in his body. Luckily, the bar is as loud as it's ever been so no one hears his soft moans through sealed lips and gritted teeth.

During his first couple of mini breaks, he seeks out the sanctuary of Jenner's office. Each time Jenner happens to find Brayden there, there is no teasing or anxiety; Jenner simply holds him, encircling Brayden in a loving embrace. Jenner caresses his slave's back, murmuring praise with adoration in his eyes.

It's perfect. Those quiet, tender moments with Jenner make Brayden feel so grateful for his life that his heart wants to burst from being so full. Sunday doesn't seem so scary anymore. The prospect of meeting Jenner's family as his date and not just an employee or roommate seems possible. It gives Brayden hope that someday, maybe, he'll be able to be just as honest with his own family, too. Maybe it won't be so bad after all.

Brayden knows he should call to check in on Emma and Nana. He hasn't spoken with them since the day before. Errand-running has become more difficult for Ruth, and Brayden knows that she would not be likely to call for his assistance unless there was no other choice. He decides that if groceries or other essentials are running low, he could always make a trip during his dinner break. As he doesn't want to slack off on his responsibilities for selfish reasons, Brayden is as determined as ever to come through for his family no matter what else he has going on.

However, that leaves him in a tough spot. How in the world can he call his grandmother while wearing a butt plug? She'll hear it in his voice that he's up to something. She'll suspect.

Brayden draws Jenner back to the office one more time and closes the door.

After Brayden explains his predicament, Jenner moves around behind him, crosses a thickly muscled arm over Brayden's lean chest. Jenner sets the phone in Brayden's hand, kisses his jaw, and waits.

"Go ahead. It's no big deal. Relax."

"Relax. Right. I've been half-hard for hours and have a toy in my butt." Jenner bites his earlobe and Brayden groans, "*Not* helping."

"Be glad I'm not fondling you," Jenner warns.

"Now I really can't call," Brayden complains, dropping the phone to his side.

"*Call.* If you can tend bar, you can ask your Nana if she's okay."

"God, I totally hate when you're logical."

"Yeah. I bet you never had that problem with Andre," Jenner smirks.

Brayden swats at him. Jenner laughs and half-heartedly blocks the smacks and thrown elbows.

With a sigh, Brayden dials.

"Hello?"

"Hey Nan. It's me. How are you? Do you need me to do a grocery run or anything tonight? I plan on stopping by around mid-day tomorrow either way. I'll drive you to the bank and we can do errands then, if you want."

"Brayden," Nana sighs happily. "I've been missing you, dear. Thank you for calling. I think we're fine for today. It's so thoughtful of you to ask. Such a good boy."

"How is Emma? Did she finish that research project for science?"

"No, she's still plugging away, but at least she's started it. Lara always used to put those kinds of assignments off until the very last second."

"Yeah, I can imagine," Brayden smiles. "Work of any kind was never Mom's thing. But don't tell her I said so."

Ruth chuckles and says, "My goodness, Brayden. You sound so much better than even a week ago. You sound so *happy*. Are you happy?"

"I am, Nan. Very much so," he admits contentedly, giving Jenner a glance. Jenner is biting thoughtfully at his thumbnail, overhearing Brayden's half of the conversation.

"So living with that Parrish fellow is working out for you?"

"You can call him Jenner, Nan. Yeah, it's been great. You have no idea."

"So, you don't regret moving up here anymore?"

Brayden frowns slightly. "I never regretted it. It was a difficult choice, but the right one. It was the right thing to do. And things are better now than they ever were in Florida. This is where I belong."

"Is that thanks to Jenner?"

Suddenly Brayden is afraid to look over his shoulder at the man in question. He feels Jenner's stare, as well as the effects he's had on both Brayden's body and his heart. With more emotion than he wishes was there, Brayden agrees, "Yes. It is."

"Then I'm glad you found him, and have him. He makes you happy."

Covering his mouth with a hand, Brayden doesn't trust himself to speak. He grunts a reply and sniffs to clear his nose.

"Sweetheart, are you crying? I never meant to make you cry…"

"No, Nan. I'm fine. I'm just… grateful. For a lot. I love you. Would it be okay if I brought Jenner by for dinner sometime? It would mean a lot to me to have you get to know each other better. You're all important to me. The three of you."

"Absolutely. Just name the day. I know you have trouble with making plans at night, so let me know when you both have a night off. Or I could always have brunch instead. And, you know, sweetie, you can tell me anything and I will always love you."

"I know. I'm trying Nan. I am."

"I can tell. You take your time."

"I, um," Brayden says thickly, getting lost in the tide again. "I've gotta go. See you tomorrow, okay?"

"It's a date. Bye bye."

Brayden hangs up and Jenner wraps him in his arms, holding on as Brayden exhales pent-up fear and joy. He's overwhelmed with everything that's happened, dreading the judgments left to befall him and Jenner both. While his tears dampen Jenner's shirt, Brayden indulges in being weak. Jenner gives him that sense of safety he craves. Smoothing Brayden's hair, radiating understanding and patience, Jenner supports his lover and lets him see that he's not alone.

"You're amazing," Jenner whispers to him.

Brayden holds on tightly and never wants to let go.

A few blocks away, Ruth Clare hangs up her phone and glances down at her granddaughter's big-eyed face. Emma adjusts her glasses on the bridge of her nose and scans her grandmother's expression. "Well?" Emma asks. "Did he tell you they're boyfriends?"

Ruth *tsks* and moves past the girl to find a seat. The nagging aches in her bones are bothering her again but not as much as the dread in her heart.

"Not exactly, hon, but your suspicions seem to be correct. He sounds happy. That's all I care about."

"He looked happy when he was here with Jenner. I've never seen him so happy as that. Jenner's cute. I can see why Brayden likes him. He's got tons of muscles."

"Emma Leah," Ruth scolds, chuckling. "You're too young to be thinking such things. Lord have mercy."

Thinking of Brayden, working every day in that bar for a man who clearly has had an impact on his life, she wonders why it never occurred to her before to go and see it for herself. She could call up some of her girlfriends and make a night of it, maybe on the night of the Pub's famous annual Halloween celebration. Emma will be spending the evening trick-or-treating with a friend, since Ruth isn't able to accompany her from house to house for hours on end. Another benefit to visiting the Pub on Halloween night is they'll likely be more than busy enough with customers that Brayden won't have to worry about working with his grandmother watching, either. It's perfect.

Ruth has always lamented that she doesn't have the closeness she desired with her daughter, but maybe, if she makes the effort to show an interest in things Brayden cares about, she can have that closeness with him.

Brayden's exhausting, unending day is capped off with a slow, luxurious, fantastic blowjob from Jenner who then proceeds to fuck Brayden's spent, utterly relaxed body into the mattress while he dozes off. After that, Brayden is out for the night and wakes up in Jenner's arms the next morning, smiling.

Breakfast is eaten standing by the counter instead of seated on a sore ass in a hard chair. Brayden multitasks, eating cereal while texting back and forth with Andre to check on how the flight home was. He also thanks Andre again for making the trip. Then, it's off to the gym with Jenner for a morning swim. Brayden wears the collar, but leaves it in his locker while he's in the water. He makes sure to ask Jenner to put it back on him as soon as they're done with their workouts.

The car ride is the worst part. Jenner sets a fluffy pillow on the passenger seat to cushion Brayden's thoroughly paddled ass. As embarrassing as it is, Brayden appreciates the gesture. Even when he tries to stay seated on the side of his butt, facing sideways, it doesn't really help. When Jenner keeps shooting sly, crooked smiles of amusement at Brayden's discomfort, Brayden restrains himself from voicing the complaints that sit ready on the tip of his tongue.

"There a problem, slave?" Jenner asks, grinning.

"Nope. No, Sir. No problem here."

"You're not *lying* again, are you? Because I'm sure the last thing you'd want is for me to take you over my knee when we get home. However, if your butt isn't as sore as I'd hoped it would be, I can always rectify that."

Brayden glares at him. They pull up to their building and park. Jenner cuts the engine and palms the keys.

"Well," Jenner sighs, "Lets head up. I'm assuming you don't have an erection you don't have permission for. I think I'll give you a choice between my hand and the paddle for the lying, and—"

"My ass hurts," Brayden blurts, loudly. "Sir. That's the problem. But it's... it's not a... oh, fuck it."

Exasperated, Brayden gets out of the car without another word. But Jenner moves faster than him and simply steps into Brayden's path as he makes for the door. Massively muscled arms like pythons are crossed over Jenner's broad chest. Brayden can see that he's pumped up and vibrantly energetic from the workout. Jenner smirks confidently down at Brayden, saying, "Excuse me? We're not done."

Ignoring this, Brayden glances up and down the road for onlookers.

"Hey. Sweetheart, eyes on me. Trust me; I'm the *only* one you need to worry about."

With effort, Brayden wrenches his gaze up to Jenner's face and, with only a little bit of prideful defiance, asks, "Can I have the harness when we go inside, Sir?"

With a nod, Jenner agrees, "Yes, you may. What did you start to say in the car?"

"I was just..." Brayden scratches restlessly at his head, then strokes the leather collar around his throat. "You know... saying that it's not a problem."

"What's not a problem?" Jenner asks, feigning ignorance.

"Goddamn it," Brayden groans. "My ass being sore isn't a problem."

"No? Good. Move it, then. Go upstairs. Now."

Brayden frowns as he hurries through the door and up the steps. As soon as he's inside the apartment, he starts to disrobe. Jenner watches avidly while closing and locking the door behind them.

With an exasperated gesture, throwing his arms widely open, Brayden faces his Master, naked.

"I can't help it! I'm sorry. It's *your* fucking fault, you know. Stop being hot," Brayden says with plenty of frustration.

Jenner works to hide a smirk and purses his lips with a pensive expression as he decides what to do. He tilts his head slightly to the side, staring at Brayden's rigid, upraised cock, which, funnily enough, only makes it swell even more.

Striding quickly, Jenner crosses to the bedroom to retrieve some things from it. Once this is done, he walks up to Brayden, grabs him by the end of the dick, and leads him by it to the couch. "C'mere. You know you want it."

Brayden's face flushes as Jenner sits heavily on the couch, spreads a towel over his lap and immediately draws Brayden down to lay draped over his legs.

Freshly showered, hair still wet, coming down from his post-exercise high, Brayden wriggles slightly as he tries to get comfortable. His bare ass is squarely over Jenner's thighs, with the rest of him stretched out on the couch cushions. The apartment is warm, the heat cranked up. Jenner turns on the TV, tosses the remote aside and begins to examine the healing welts decorating Brayden's poor ass. Stroking over them with the pads of his fingertips and the heels of his palms, Jenner gauges Brayden's reactions. With flinches and bitten-back pleasure, Brayden endures the scrutiny as his stiffened cock nudges insistently at Jenner's leg.

Grabbing the lotion that he'd brought from the bedroom, Jenner uncaps it, and squirts plenty of cream onto his hand. With rolling, kneading strokes, he begins to work it in to Brayden's enflamed cheeks. The roughness of the touch ignites pain in the bruised flesh. Brayden inhales sharply through his nose, his lips sealed tightly against any noises that might want to come out.

"That hurts?" Jenner asks.

Brayden nods.

"You have anything to say?"

Brayden shakes his head.

Jenner draws back a hand and slaps the moistened flesh. It makes Brayden cry out.

"Hands behind your head. Lace your fingers together."

Immediately, Brayden obeys with a small grunted sound of nervous anticipation. Lazily, with irregular, drawn-out smacks, Jenner peppers his slave's throbbing ass. Brayden's hips twitch against

Jenner's thighs with each blow as he clenches.

"Relax your ass, slave. If you want to hump my thigh, you have to ask first or else I'll make this hurt more." To prove his point, he delivers a much harder slap than any he'd given yet, or even the day before. Brayden shouts with the pain, his fingers clawing at his scalp.

"I'm sorry! Sorry, Master. *Fuck* that hurt. M-may I, um, hump your leg? And climax? Please?"

"Yes, baby, you may."

Freed by the permission, Brayden begins to rock his hips in a steady rolling movement that gains strength and speed. Jenner keeps kneading Brayden's ass, fondling it, smacking it lightly, tracing through the crease with a finger and playing at his hole by swirling his finger around the spot and rubbing over it lightly. After a few minutes of this, Brayden is thrusting sharply, breathing hard. His body tenses. With a shudder and a grunt, he comes over the towel and Jenner's leg beneath.

"Better?" Jenner asks, caressing up Brayden's back to his neck, rubbing that instead.

"Yeah," Brayden says woozily. "Do you have to leave and go downstairs or can we stay here a while?"

"We can stay. I've got time."

"Good," Brayden sighs contentedly, relaxing into the position again. He hums happily as Jenner pets his heated skin.

"Comfy?"

"Mm-hmm."

"Oh, there's something I keep forgetting to mention. With everything going on with Andre, and dinner with my parents, it hasn't seemed as important and I keep forgetting you're new to the bar, so you wouldn't know to expect it," Jenner says idly. "Anyway, there's this tradition at the Pub. It's been going on ever since my parents ran the place. The whole town usually comes out for it."

"What are you talking about?" Brayden murmurs.

"Halloween," Jenner grins. "Two nights from now. You don't get served if you aren't in costume. A very strict rule, and not my idea, by the way. I just do the enforcing."

"You're kidding, right? Please tell me you're kidding."

"Am I ever kidding?" Jenner retorts.

"This doesn't mean I have to wear a costume, too, does it?"

"Oh, not only do you have to wear one, but it has to be *amazing*. I realize this doesn't give you a whole lot of time to find something, but I can give you a few phone numbers and some websites to check out, places that do overnight delivery. You can charge it to my card. This is important, you know. We set the standard. The costumes are the main reason people come out for it. It's our biggest night as far as profits go. With the right costume, you can make more in tips in one night than you will for the rest of the *year*."

Glancing back over a shoulder, Brayden asks, "What are you wearing?"

"Oh, if I told you, that'd be cheating. It has to be a *surprise*."

"I hate surprises," Brayden frowns. "You know what this feels like, don't you? It feels like some 'trick the new guy into wearing a dorky outfit so that we can all laugh at him' prank. I don't do Halloween. My mom didn't give a shit about taking me trick or treating, so Dad took care of it. It was something we always did together when I was little, touring the neighborhood, collecting candy. He was the one that always helped me with my costumes and made sure to always hold my hand when we crossed the streets. When I got too old for that, we would order in Chinese food and watch scary movies together on the couch instead. Then my *life* became a scary movie, and he was dying, he was *gone* and my mom still didn't give a shit."

The pained grief in Brayden's eyes is so acute that Jenner has to look away. Head bowed, he hears Brayden say again, softly, "I don't do Halloween."

"You can have the night off," Jenner tells him. There's no option, even though he loves the thought of spending that time with Brayden, having him there so it's not as lonely an experience as it usually is for Jenner. He can't put Brayden through anything that will cause him such heartache.

Brayden nods and turns his face away, settling back down.

"I'm sorry," Jenner sighs. "I just thought it would be fun. All of the pairing up that goes on at these things... it can be a little depressing for those of us who can't indulge so easily, and the idea of having you there with me... But I won't ask you to be a part of anything you aren't comfortable with, or that will bring back painful memories."

Running a hand over Brayden's back, Jenner tries to caress some of his tension away.

"Thanks," Brayden says.

For a while, they stay there, in silence. No matter how much time slips by or how gently Jenner massages Brayden's body, tension lingers, stubbornly.

Chapter 34
No Turning Back

"You're supposed to be asleep," Jenner murmurs groggily. Brayden peers at him from the next pillow.

It's late. Brayden had the night off, spending most of it on the couch or lying in bed. Jenner worked until well past midnight. Brayden hasn't been able to stop thinking about the Halloween party at the Pub. Slowly, after hours of introspection, memories had surfaced of his mother, who had always liked to go out rather than stay home for that particular holiday. He remembers glimpsing her in costume as she was on her way out, alone. In that year or two before his father passed away, Brayden can recall mentions of a town party. *That's where Mom is*, Dad would explain. *She's letting down her hair.*

Brayden would ask if they could go with her. His father, Anthony, would say no. It was a party for grown-ups only.

Brayden would ask, *Why?*

It's held at a bar, a few blocks from here. They serve alcohol. No teenagers allowed, I'm afraid. But that's okay. We'll make our own fun. Someday, you'll be old enough, and we'll go with her.

Brayden had wanted that—to finally be old enough to go along with Lara on her adventures, for his father to be there, too, and for them all to be a family again, if only for a night of make-believe.

Now here he is, old enough, at last, to go to the party with the grown-ups, and the people he most wanted to go with have left him behind.

There's no way he can go, to be there, with part of him looking for them, the ghosts of his departed parents. It would be nothing but an awful reminder of everything he'll never have.

What he told Jenner was true, also. Showing up in costume would go against every instinct of self-preservation in him, even if, technically, he would be showing up before any customers arrived. He would have time to scope out his co-workers in advance of any public exposure. If they weren't also dressed up, the joke would still be on him, but it wouldn't be as bad as if the whole town was laughing at his expense. Not that he actually thinks Jenner would do something that cruel to him, tricking him into making a fool of himself. That's the ingrained paranoia talking, the little voice in his head that still sometimes thinks of Jenner as 'the popular quarterback'.

Brayden rolls onto his side, facing Jenner and twists a curl of Jenner's dark hair around his fingers. The beginnings of thick ringlets tumble over Jenner's forehead and spring up all over the top of his head. Brayden is completely unable to resist playing with them, winding the curls around his index finger and letting go to watch them bounce right back into shape.

"Stop doing that."

"Doing what?" Brayden asks, pulling a curl down the center of Jenner's forehead, right between his eyes. "You know, if you slicked the rest back, you would totally look like Superman. Fuck, that's hot."

"Slut."

"Do you have a suit here? And maybe, like, a royal blue shirt? That's not secretly your costume, is it? I've kind of always wanted to have Clark Kent screw me."

With a playful snarl, Jenner detangles Brayden's fingers from his hair. Twisting Brayden around, Jenner pulls him close to lay curled up in front of him. Both of them have been sleeping naked. Slowly but intentionally, Jenner begins thrusting through the crack of Brayden's ass.

"I thought you were anti-Halloween, that it brought back bad memories. How about we skip the dorky costumes and get right to the good part?"

"Oh, now where's the fun in that?" The tiredness and paper-thinness of Brayden's good humor seeps into his voice.

"You sleep at all before I got back?"

"Not so much," Brayden admits, caressing over the dark hair

covering Jenner's arm. It calms him to feel Jenner's body wrapped around his like armor. Things seem less scary when he has tangible proof of the strength of his partner, especially when he's not feeling very strong himself. Jenner's existence allows Brayden to embrace his own limitations as a beautiful thing rather than a hindrance. It's a good thing that he's not tall or as physically powerful as other people, just as it's a good thing that he craves the ability to give over the decision-making and control. It's their balance. It's how they work, not something he needs to be ashamed of or want to fix.

"I can help you relax," Jenner offers. His baritone voice softens as his hand pushes down under the sheet and between Brayden's legs.

Because he wants to give Jenner room to maneuver, Brayden gets his hands out of the way. He reaches behind himself to grasp at Jenner's thigh and over his head to run his fingers through Jenner's curls some more. Then, Brayden shifts his legs wider. He makes a soft sigh as Jenner wraps a big hand around Brayden's cock and starts to tug on it. Sliding his fingers from root to tip and back down again, Jenner whispers, "Imagine you're back in the ocean, feel the push and pull of the tide on your body."

Brayden's hands tighten their grip as Jenner pumps a little faster. Arching his back slightly, then rolling his hips forward into the hand clasped snugly around his cock, Brayden closes his eyes and imagines it, letting Jenner's deep, sexy, rough voice help him escape.

"No chlorine from the pool. No buzzing, yellow fluorescent lights. No echoing voices off the old tile walls. Just fresh air, sunshine and open space above you and nothing but the sea below. Can you feel it?"

Jenner swipes a thumb over Brayden's cockhead. "Yeah. Feels good. Damn good."

In his mind, he is back there, wrapped in the sea like he's wrapped in Jenner. Every inch of his body, everything but his face is hugged, covered by the sliding caresses. Seawater or skin, it doesn't matter. They're the same. Brayden pushes into Jenner's hand. It's his private ocean. He's picking up speed. Jenner is as huge and unyielding as the waters, demanding all of him, pulling him under. Jenner's mouth latches on to the side of his neck, sucking at him like the kiss of the tide's surge. With abandon, Brayden rides the pumping fingers like he rode the waves.

Flattening his hand, Jenner runs his fingers up the underside of Brayden's cock.

"More," Brayden gasps, breathless.

Jenner moves to lie on top of him, chest-to-chest, pressing down into Brayden's body. He draws back and thrusts forward. Their cocks, squeezed together, slide between their hips and begin to rub with delicious friction. Thick, warm fluid pulses from them, slicking the way. The harder Jenner thrusts down against Brayden, the more fervently Brayden grabs on to Jenner, pulling him down tighter, rocking up with ever-sharper movements.

With his tan fading, Brayden's skin flushes more visibly with his passion. Jenner moves against his lover and indulges in the luxury of gazing down upon him while Brayden stays lost in the fantasy. The love of wildness is there in him; that urge to delve into the untamed forces of nature and unearth the secrets of the world. It was born with him and will live in him, somewhere, even if buried, as long as he lives. As Jenner thrusts harder still, it feels like he does so to trap Brayden's spirit, keeping him there, caging him in passion and love.

Jenner is Brayden's ocean. He pulls the orgasm from Brayden. With a throaty cry, he unloads against Jenner's belly, shivering with aftershocks as Jenner rubs off against him. Grinding against his lover's come-soaked, throbbing hard-on, Jenner climaxes a moment later with a hard grunt, christening the merging of forces. Their spend mixes as he slides in rocking movements against Brayden. Jenner kisses his parted lips gently, brushing against them. Shifting off without letting go, keeping Brayden encircled with an arm, Jenner urges, "Sleep."

"Mmm," Brayden hums with a smile, and drifts off.

In a way, it's self-sabotage. He doesn't ask Jenner for those phone numbers and websites he'd mentioned, even though Brayden becomes privately more sure that he's likely to go to the Halloween party, if only to observe from the sidelines. There are a few costume rental places in driving distance which he could go to, and check out the pitiful leftovers, maybe something with a mask that covers his whole head so that he would be even more inconspicuous.

That would be the best thing to do—the easiest thing, psychologically speaking.

Which is why he gets more and more angry at himself for not getting in his Jeep and driving to one of those stores.

Because, unfortunately, he already has a costume. It's the most awful, embarrassing, humiliating thing he's ever worn, and it's buried at the bottom of one of the boxes in the closet, along with his wetsuit and all of the other things that got a lot of wear in Florida but which he no longer has any use for.

The costume has been worn too many times to count. It was tailor-made for him out of the finest materials—rich brown leather, shining metal rivets, buckles and straps that hug his form immaculately. It's not one of those cheap pieces of crap they pawn off at those pop-up Halloween outlets that appear and disappear every fall, catering to the masses and robbing them blind. Technically, it's not a Halloween costume at all.

It's his uniform.

His uniform from the last bar he worked at, in Miami, the job he hated. It was where he'd learned to flirt with customers, even if he wasn't interested. Because, of course, flirting was part of the job description. The way the staff were dressed was just one aspect of the theme of the place, reflected from floor to ceiling in the décor, the music, and, hell, even the drinks and goblets they were served in. Long hair was encouraged amongst the male employees, and was one of the reasons Brayden let his grow and grow. Bartenders and wait staff also had to be in spectacular physical shape, so he swam and exercised every day just to fill out the uniform. It was either that or quit, and the tips were too good for him to be able to quit.

The idea of wearing that outfit to Parrish Pub, with god-knows-who in attendance of such an event, brings Brayden right back to the terror he felt when Enrique showed up, but worse. It wouldn't be a question of secrets being shared. There'd be no question about it. People would stare. They would talk, and point and make comments. He would make a spectacular ass of himself just by setting foot outside the door to the apartment.

As he digs out the box, opening the flaps, reaching to the bottom and pushing contents aside, he asks himself, *What am I doing? Jenner doesn't expect me to be there. No one does. Just stay home.*

"Stay home and watch a scary movie, order in some Chinese food," he murmurs, finding the evergreen colored subligaculum. It's a canvas loin cloth that covers most of his ass, if not *all* of it. At least the groin is heavily padded. He sets it on the bed. "Pretend I'm still a child too innocent and fragile to be able to handle a *real* party, with *grown-ups*. Yeah right."

Next he finds the makeshift manacle, wraps of thick leather and cloth for forearm and wrist padding. Beneath is the cingulum, a wide, ornamented leather belt, designed to protect the waistline. The last things he draws from the box are the fascia, or leg padding, and his sandals. Because his old boss was just much of a stickler as Jenner, though much more obsessed with history — particularly that of Ancient Rome, Brayden learned all of the proper names for what he was made to wear every day. It was all crafted to appear authentic, with hidden zippers and Velcro. He has never willingly told a soul that he waited tables and bartended while outfitted as a gladiator, surrounded by gorgeous women in beautifully draped stolas. One of the few bright points about moving back to Robertsville was that he would never have to demean himself like that again, for money.

"Well, I'm not doing it for money," he sighs.

He's not doing it for a job, or even for Jenner, either. He's doing it for his father, and his mother, and because he has nothing left to be afraid of, except the cost of brutal honesty. But, if time has taught him anything, it's that nothing stays private forever and that sometimes the ones hurt most by dishonesty are those holding on to the secrets. Walking into the Pub as the man he was in Miami, and also the small town boy who has been shunned by the popular kids, as well as the person he currently identifies as — who is simultaneously a slave, a lover, a friend, a grandson and a cousin — feels like a gift he will be giving himself.

He puts on the clothing and gear, looks in the bathroom mirror, and says, "This is who I am. Maybe it's not who I intended to be, or hoped to be, but that's okay because it's the truth. Dad, if you're up there, somewhere, and you can hear me, I want you to know that I'm not lost anymore. I belong here. No more hiding in shadows. No more trying to disappear. No more lies."

As the floor thumps below his sandal-clad feet with the force of the music from the bar, the party already well underway no thanks to his hesitating about whether to go or not, Brayden thinks of all of the people he wishes were there with him—Enrique, Andre, Lara and Anthony. Then he thinks of who is there, waiting for him just downstairs. Art, Max and Jenner don't feel like a consolation prize; they feel like hope and happiness.

"I can do this," Brayden realizes, and smiles.

The last thing he puts on is the collar, *his* collar.

"Okay," he says, liking what he sees, heart pounding but confident in what he has chosen. "Here goes nothin'."

Chapter 35
Gone Too Far

For years, Jenner's Halloween has been marked only by the fevered rush and manic endeavor to host a celebration for all of Robertsville. The staff of Parrish Pub is strained at the best of times, but when they're packed to overflowing, the sheer numbers of humanity testing the law's willingness to overlook the fire code regulations, keeping up with demand is akin to torture. It's not fun, it's an endurance trial. No one gets the night off, for any reason. He even tries to bring in temporary help from friends, family and acquaintances who typically work at other bars or restaurants, promising fabulous tips if only…

A few hours into the night and it's finally dark out. Max, Art and Jackson are all angry, with good reason, at Jenner for giving Brayden an unheard-of pass. Every time he catches one of them looking his way, his reward is a cutting, accusatory glare before the rolling tide of customers breaking against the bar's counter sweeps them away again. Luckily, they're all too preoccupied for Jenner to have to defend that decision just yet.

Usually, the costume requirement is enough to take the edge off. The amusement that comes from seeing familiar faces, whether they're people he loathes, tolerates or likes, dolled up in ridiculous attire gets him through. Even if his feet are killing him and his head is pounding from the shouting and constant, high-volume chatter echoing off the walls, when slipping out the back door become more and more tempting, he can glance up and see burly John Wensley who mans the butcher's counter over at the supermarket dressed up like Little Bo Peep and have a good laugh.

Tonight it's not enough. The costumes are mostly a disappointment—a mix of slutty you-name-its for the young women and an assortment of rubber masks or pitiful attempts at zombie or vampire make-up for the men. There's no creativity, no out-of-the-box thinking. After spending so much time at Manse where the more outlandish you look, the better chance you have at being noticed and getting laid, the townsfolk's pathetic efforts are just making him sad.

There's also the matter of missing Brayden. Jenner thought that he'd be too busy to care if Brayden was absent. Things are hectic enough, but he can't get Brayden out of his mind. After so many years of thinking of the holiday as a lucrative chore, something to suck up and tolerate for the good of their bottom line, he's rather shocked to be so disappointed Brayden didn't want to be there.

It's not even about the extra help, though it would have been nice to have another set of hands pouring drinks. Jenner catches himself scanning the room, as if Brayden's smile might be found in the sea of faces, able to warm Jenner's heart in seconds and make the hard work feel worth it.

He wanted them to have this together; he's slowly realizing he wants them to have everything together. In a purely selfish way, Jenner simply wants Brayden at his side because being apart from him is a greater hardship than the year's most grueling shift. Without Brayden, Jenner feels that he is less than he could be. The shine on everything good is a little too dull and the wearying hours left to go stretch out before him like an endless ocean.

It feels just as crowded behind the bar as in front of it as the staff moves around each other, trying to do many things at once in a confined space.

Max is wearing her usual, which is cute enough, but Jenner has seen it many times before. She's dressed in a black spandex body suit with cat ears, whiskers painted on her cheeks and a fluffy tail, an ensemble affectionately referred to as 'Evil Pussy'. She'll scratch your eyes out if you aren't careful; her distaste for the comments, leering, and nightmarish collection of hours is so intense.

Art is also donning a classic, playing up his curly red hair for all its worth with a clown outfit and big red nose, though he lost the oversized shoes in the interest of efficiency.

No one gives Jenner's costume a second look, since it's the same thing he wears every year, without fail. Though he insists that everyone's outfits remain a surprise and will go on and on about how unhappy he is when his friends repeat outfits previously worn, the big joke is that he never changes his. Partly because it's his damn bar anyway, and partly because of the context of his costume, but he always gets away with it. No one ever gives him a hard time.

One strange phenomenon of being in such a crowded space is that the volume level of noise from conversation will ebb and rise as if someone is turning a knob, controlling every single voice at once. They're kind of magical coincidences, when everyone pauses to take a breath between words at once, giving Jenner's pounding headache a much-needed, yet too-brief, reprieve.

During one of these lulls, Jenner is able to detect raised voices near the entrance, clear across the room from where he is behind the bar. His gaze snaps up. People near the door move out of the way and surge toward it at the same time, both clearing space and taking it away.

Foreboding sends a sickly wave of discomfort through his body before he is even able to make out what they're saying, or who they're all looking at, because he can see it happening. He's not the only one who has stopped to stare. The lull draws out, too long. Heads turn.

"Oh my god!"

"Is that Cry Baby Braydy?"

"Jesus, look at him," some female voice laughs brightly, with malice.

Jenner's hands are on the bar, his body still as a statue, every bit of his mental focus on what's happening at the door. Nothing else matters. With tunnel vision, he lets the rest get lost in darkness.

One of the girls, dressed as what he imagines the package called 'hot honey bee', in a yellow and black striped minidress and stilettos, walks up to the person who just came through the door. Jenner doesn't even process it at first. All he sees is oiled, tan muscles, long, golden hair, leather and metal and the honey bee's hand pushing a crumpled dollar bill inside the newcomer's wide belt.

He hears laughing, focused in the rear corner, the table closest to the door, which has been packed with all of Jenner's old football buddies — Todd and Jason and Chad and all of the rest of them, claiming those seats so that they can get the first word in as soon as anyone arrives, laughing at their expense, making commentary on what they wore.

Jenner vaults the bar before Todd even stands from his stool.

Turning his shoulder in to the mass of people packed like sardines as they await their precious glasses of beer, he parts them, pushing to get there, to cross what feels like miles of distance, not looking away. Not blinking.

With both hands, Todd knocks Brayden backward into the guy who had been standing behind him. The guy frowns down at Brayden and pushes him back at Todd, from behind.

"Did you just touch my girl? Did you just touch her?" Todd sneers down at Brayden, bearing down on him, pushing him again, harder.

"No!" Brayden protests, his voice sounding fainter, slighter, getting swallowed up by the mob. "No, I…"

Jenner sees many things at once, still pushing, still trying to get there to save him in time.

He sees that his brother, Callum Parrish, is there, at a table with a date a few feet away from the action, watching it all.

Ruth Clare is there, too, over against a wall with a bunch of older ladies, diagonal from where Brayden is, and she's getting to her feet, spying her grandson, looking horrified and worried.

Art has come out from the kitchen with a tray stacked with food, wearing the stupid clown suit, seeing Brayden instantly, looking like, at any moment, the tray is going to fall right out of his hand, the burgers and fries scattering over people and the floor.

Jenner sees Brayden, too, not for the outfit he's wearing, but the wideness of his eyes and the pure, unadulterated, helpless confusion in them.

So Jenner pushes harder.

A hard shove to the center of Brayden's chest almost knocks him off his feet as Todd steps toward him, one step for every shove, moving him back toward the door like he wants to take this outside, where there's room for the real beating to happen.

And Jenner pushes harder.

"You just touched my girl, faggot," Todd bellows. It's impossibly loud in the now-quiet room. There's no mistaking it.

In his peripheral vision, Jenner sees others that are now, like him, trying to carve a path to the door, just trying to *get there*.

There's a clatter from Jenner's right — sudden and loud — but he can't look, doesn't care. Just a few more feet, peering over people's heads, trying to keep Brayden in sight as the aging ex-football stars laugh and grunt in encouragement and their girls just smile, clinging to the sides of their dates, looking at Brayden like prey, not a person. He's pushed from behind again, from the front, tossed recklessly as Todd inches him towards the threshold with nothing but black night and masked strangers beyond.

Finally, just before Todd shoves Brayden back through the door, Jenner bursts free.

Immediately, Jenner gets Brayden away from the door, putting his body between Brayden and Todd, with the table full of Jenner's old teammates behind Todd. Jenner doesn't care about the rest of the bar, the rest of the people watching — hundreds of them. All that matters is that he got to Brayden, and that Brayden is safely at Jenner's back.

Eyes locked on Todd, Jenner roars, "Get away from him! Now!"

"Jesus Christ, dude," Todd laughs, looking around at his friends to share the joke. "What's your problem? This doesn't fucking concern you."

"You don't touch him," Jenner growls, his deep voice carrying, keeping the crowd hushed, keeping all eyes on them.

Brayden is silent, but Jenner feels him there, brushing against his arm, a tense bundle of nervous energy and shrill fear that screams out to every one of Jenner's instincts to protect and defend.

"What the fuck is this?" Todd squints, stepping up in Jenner's face. "He your boyfriend, Parrish?"

There's snickering and the low murmur of comments from the table filled with the people who used to be important to him. Winning their approval used to be everything. And why? He can't remember. Why did he ever care what these people thought?

The question rings like a struck bell, and they're still laughing, still thinking this is fun, that this is all a big joke, that even if the person they had just been attacking was kicked and bleeding or worse, it was all harmless. It didn't *mean* anything.

But it does mean something. It means everything.

Jenner feels his heart beating heavily in his chest, feels the soft, warm pressure of Brayden's body against his arm and knows he's going to say it, even though he can still sense those bodies cutting through the crowd and those countless sets of eyes, watching.

There's no time for second guessing, no time to take anything back.

"Yes," Jenner says, loud enough for them all to hear, for there to be no doubt. "He is."

The whole table erupts in laughter, thinking maybe that Jenner is in on their big joke at Brayden's expense. He sees all of them — Todd, Jason, Chad, the honeybee, a few aging cheerleaders that Jenner, long ago, engaged in foreplay with just to keep suspicion off of him.

Callum appears at the edge of the mob, squeezing between two people, cursing and grumbling at them to get the hell out of the way. Then Art arrives, too.

And they're all looking at him.

Staring. Judging.

It's the culmination of a lifetime of lying, a lifetime of hiding in plain sight.

His voice loses its anger and bravado, becoming more vulnerable, less sure of itself — horribly so. He tells them, "I'm serious," and reaches out to take Brayden's hand.

Heart racing, head spinning, as soon as Jenner looks down into Brayden's eyes, seeing proof of his trust, his love, in them, it all shifts even more. The urge to fight fades away and the threatening tears rise closer to the surface, especially once he realizes what could have happened if he hadn't been there, hadn't gotten there in time. In his mind's eye he sees Patrick's kicked kitten, lying motionless on the ground, and he can't breathe.

He leans in, touching Brayden's face, asking, "Are you okay, baby?"

"He's your... boyfriend..." Jenner hears Todd saying, slowly putting it all together, just like everyone else.

Brayden nods, steadily, bravely holding Jenner's gaze, grasping Jenner's arm, leaning in to his kiss when Jenner's lips touch his forehead.

"You look amazing," Jenner tells him. "I'm handling it, okay?"

"Okay," Brayden murmurs, giving his hand a light squeeze.

All that matters is making sure Brayden is okay, and keeping him okay.

Nothing else matters.

Callum is staring at them. As is Art, and Max, and Marla the florist, and all of their regulars, like Bill and Steve, and the ex-high-school-football stars and the former cheerleaders and neighbors and everyone.

And Jenner doesn't have any fight left in him.

He's ready to go, to turn and leave and never come back — forsaking his inheritance, his legacy, his home, everything in the name of being with Brayden and taking off the masks they've been wearing for far too long.

Shattering the tense, awkward silence, Callum steps forward.

Jenner braces himself for anything, ready for the worst, wholly unprepared for what actually happens.

Callum, dressed in a pinstriped gangster suit and fedora, turns to Todd and the rest of the jocks and says, "You got a problem with my brother?"

"Or maybe," Art adds, stepping right up to Todd, intimidating him exactly the way he had tried to do with Brayden and then Jenner. "You have a problem with my friend, Brayden."

Shocked, Jenner slowly realizes that the whole bar is no longer looking at him and Brayden.

They're looking at Todd and the table full of bullies.

From the corner of his eye, Jenner sees Ruth Clare looking starkly worried and trying to approach, one of her girlfriends trying to pull her back. She calls out, "Brayden!"

"Sit down, Nan. It's okay," Brayden tells her.

"N-n-no problem," Todd tells Art and Callum, hands raised and backing off, literally. "No problem."

To a woman just beyond the edge of the crowd, Callum says, "Get me my phone, I'm calling the police."

She nods and begins to dig in her purse.

"Hey!" Todd exclaims, his voice becoming shriller, "We're cool! We're cool, right?" He glances around the table at the other guys. "See? It was just a joke. A bad joke. We didn't know."

"Apologize," Art growls, bigger than all of them, a pissed-off, enormous man dressed like a clown. It's one of the weirdest sights Jenner has ever beheld.

"S-sorry Brayden," Todd chirps. "Sorry, Parrish! No offense. I swear."

Brayden's fingers are tightly woven around his own and the feel of his body pressed to Jenner's side is everything worth fighting for, and he never knew. He never truly knew until that precise moment. But now that he does, he's never letting go.

Art turns to Jenner and Brayden, glancing between them, and says, "It's your call."

Jenner turns to Brayden, because it's not Jenner's call either.

Brayden looks at Todd, the table of grown men who used to be cruel little boys and just never grew up as much as they should have. He looks at the bar with all of the many people in it. Then he looks at Art and says, "It's fine."

Art nods, satisfied. Max smiles brightly at Brayden from a few feet away, then dashes over to give him a tight hug. Smiling, letting out a held breath, Jenner sees him lift Max clear up off the ground, both of them chuckling.

"Okay, people!" Art shouts, turning toward the masses. "Let's get this party started! What d'ya say?!"

There's an ear-splitting roar of cheering, hollering and whistling and the volume gets cranked back up. Solitary voices are once again swept up in the din. The focus shifts off of the people by the door as everyone returns to their friends and their drinks.

"Shit, this is against the rules, isn't it?" Max yells to Jenner, leaning cozily against Brayden's bare chest, letting her hand rest upon it. "Damn, I guess that means Brayden gets a spanking, right? God, Braydy, I'm *so sorry*," Max purrs with biting sarcasm, smiling wickedly.

"I'll give him a pass. Dressed like that, I expect he'll even be making the straight guys hard."

"Yeah," Max agrees. "I know, I've got a total boner right now. Where the fuck did you get this outfit?"

She plays with the leather belt, the straps wound around Brayden's arm, the edge of the leg wraps that come all the way up his thighs.

Jenner cuts in, prying her off, "All right, that's enough. The pass doesn't include full groping privileges, Maxine."

"Oh, you're no fun," she sighs, surrendering. She darts away, going back to the bar at Jackson's panicked cry, as Jackson is trying to cover in both Jenner and Max's absences.

People are swarming around everyone, jostling them, not paying Jenner and Brayden any attention anymore, even though they're still holding hands, even though Jenner just declared that they're boyfriends to the whole town.

Art has gone back to the kitchen. Callum is back with his date. The table full of hecklers are solemnly drinking their beers with their heads down, looking thoroughly reprimanded.

There's no uproar over Jenner Parrish, the ex-quarterback, coming out in front of all of Robertsville. There are no people with pitchforks and torches, chasing them out. There's barely any attention paid to them at all now that the threat of violence is gone.

He turns to Brayden, falling into his beautiful eyes, his honest smile. Jenner barely allows himself to glimpse the rest of Brayden's body — bound in leather and cloth, barely covered, displayed to perfection. But he does note the collar. Hooking his finger in it, he bites his lip and savors everything he realizes they suddenly have.

"This is quite an outfit, slave," Jenner says directly into the shell of Brayden's ear.

"So, you're pleased, Sir?" Brayden answers before Jenner pulls away, turning to kiss Jenner's jaw while he's there, in kissing range.

"Oh, I definitely am."

"Is this actually happening?"

"I have no fucking idea," Jenner laughs. "But let's go with it, shall we?"

"I'm game," Brayden grins. "Your wish is my command."

Chapter 36

Masks Off

"'Night Brayden!"

"See ya later," he shouts back, not even sure who he's saying goodbye to. There are still too many people around to be constantly sure who's talking and what's happening. People pour out of the bar, milling around on the sidewalks, lingering for a kiss under the streetlights with their sweethearts or just drawing out the night a little bit longer.

Jenner lets the last person out, then locks up. He's dressed in green army fatigues that have a good amount of wear on them—enough to make Brayden guess that they're authentic and not a costume-shop rental. The sleeves are rolled up due to the heat of the bar. At the collar, a dark t-shirt peeks out. Cargo pants and black combat boots complete the outfit. The only thing out of place is the length of his hair, too long and curly to be regulation. Something about the outfit and the confident ease with which Jenner wears it has been turning Brayden on all night, though hardly any skin is showing.

At the very least, it makes it feel less unusual to call him "Sir" in public.

With the itching and tickling of papers irritating his skin, Brayden digs out a few more stray dollar bills from inside the edges of his uniform and adds them to the wad already balled up in his fist.

When he glances back up, Jenner is there, smiling down at him.

"I seriously can't keep all of this," Brayden protests, holding up the cash. People had been sticking it inside his belt all night—men and women alike. Maybe he should have been offended, but no matter what he said or did, they just kept doing it and it added up fast.

"I told you, didn't I," Jenner says, "it's all in the choice of costume. You earned it."

"But this is hundreds of dollars! I barely did any bartending at all."

"Put it toward a trip to Florida this summer. We'll take a vacation. Or give it to Nana. Or Emma. You could start a savings fund for her."

"Huh, that's actually a really good idea," Brayden admits. He waves to someone else who had waved first, their face too hard to see in the dark. "Whose uniform is that, by the way?"

Jenner looks down at himself, "Oh, my dad's. He served in Vietnam. It's tradition. I come dressed as the person he always wanted me to be — a new and improved version of himself. The whole 'Don't ask, don't tell' aspect of it all always made me laugh. I was going to enlist, you know, but my mother forbade it. Said she wouldn't tolerate the possibility of losing me like she was always afraid of losing him."

"I know the feeling. You look really hot, you know."

"Oh please," Jenner scoffs. "You're practically a walking, breathing torture device in that, and you're calling *my* outfit hot? Where in god's name did you get that? I gave you no notice of this."

He gestures at the bar — darkened and empty. Brayden stares at it, exhaustion making him a little hazy, wondering if he'd dreamt the whole thing.

"It was *my* uniform," he answers. "In Miami. The other bar I worked at."

The change in Jenner's expression is so sudden and extreme that Brayden's heart leaps up into his throat. The urge to kneel and beg forgiveness is almost too severe to resist, so instead he bows his head, brings both arms around behind his back and holds them there, crossed at the wrists, the money wadded up in his hands.

The possessive shine to Jenner's eyes, the flex of his jaw, the curl of his lips, is burned into Brayden's brain even though his eyes are now trained on his own feet. Jenner's breath is hot on Brayden's skin and he wonders if he should apologize, even though it would be for something that happened long before Jenner had any power over Brayden's choices.

"Sir?" Brayden asks softly.

"Look at me," Jenner demands.

Brayden wrenches his gaze upward with effort. Jennner's jealousy is stark and undoubtable, but he gets it in check with effort as Brayden looks on.

After a moment, Jenner asks, "Who do you belong to, slave?"

"You, Sir," Brayden answers without hesitation, infusing the words with emotion. "Only you."

"You are not to wear this again without my permission, do you understand?"

"Yes, Sir," he says, holding Jenner's gaze. After a moment, he adds, "Thank you for what you did tonight, standing up for me like that. No one has ever done something that important for me before. It means a lot. I love you, Jenner."

Softening slightly, Jenner cups Brayden's jaw in a hand and sighs, "I love you, too."

Taking half of Brayden's cash, then claiming his hand, weaving their fingers together again, Jenner asks, "You okay?"

"Yeah, I just can't believe it, you know? Did you get to talk to your brother? My Nana?"

Jenner shakes his head.

"Yeah, thought so," Brayden sighs. He'd been too busy helping the staff, fielding questions and being sidetracked by conversations and attempts to stuff money down his pants to manage exchanging a single word with his grandmother, who had been there, listening, watching everything that went down when he'd arrived. "It's like a dream. They know. They *all* know, or they will tomorrow, once word spreads. It's what I thought I wanted, but…"

Jenner waits for him to finish, and when he doesn't, says, "Scary?"

"Yeah. I mean, this weekend. Your parents…"

"One day at a time, okay? And we kicked today's ass."

With a smile, he leans down and kisses Brayden on the lips. Somewhere nearby, someone wolf-whistles at them, making Jenner chuckle against Brayden's lips.

"We did, didn't we?" Brayden smiles back at him.

"Come on," Jenner says, leading him toward the apartment door. "Let's go home."

The next day, seated beside the front window of an Italian restaurant that's only a short walk from the apartment, Jenner and Brayden eat a modest, early dinner and sip wine in relative silence.

Looking at Brayden's faraway expression over the rim of his wine glass, Jenner thinks about how it felt to wake up and prepare to face a world where everyone knows he's gay, that he's in a relationship with Brayden Clare and that no matter how he and Brayden might feel about that, they can't undo the revelation. Now that everyone knows, there is no going back to the safety of pretending to be straight. This is their life now. The imagined spread of gossip, from person to person or phone to phone feels like an uneasy tickle he can't dispel. Even though the town's reception of the news at the Pub last night had been wildly more favorable than expected – with Callum and Art and nearly everyone else in the room showing their support, standing with Jenner and Brayden against the bullies – the hardest people to face still need to be dealt with.

Jenner can sense Brayden's unease. The good mood that traveled home with them from the Pub is fled, replaced by simmering worry. It was all well and good to know that their friends and acquaintances were fine with the homosexuals in their midst, but now it's likely that not only does Ruth know they're lovers, but Jenner's family knows, too, along with the rest of Robertsville. They didn't get to relay the news on their own terms. The cat's already out of the bag; all that's left is to show their faces and deal with the fallout.

Very literally overnight, they have left behind the trappings of childhood. The only choice now is to act like men, own their identities and see what they're left with once it all shakes loose.

He knows Brayden is afraid of losing more, as he has always lost more than he was willing to give. Not only do their families know the truth now, but their families' friends, their casual acquaintances. All of the whispering, the sometimes rude remarks that have already been made at Brayden's expense when people only suspected he might be gay will be amplified, intensified. Their families will hear it all now, too. It's one thing to be accepting of your loved one's orientation when it's a private matter. It's another to have to stand up to the threat of ridicule on a daily basis, wherever you go. Maybe their families will pull away from them to spare themselves the hassle. Maybe, eventually, they'll be left with nothing but each other.

So they sip their wine, hold hands and try to gather their courage for what's to come in mere hours.

Brayden's phone rings. He gives it a quick glance and pushes it away as he chooses to ignore it.

"Who is it?" Jenner asks.

"Nana. She's been calling but I can't do this right now, in public and over the phone like that."

Jenner understands what he's going through, as he has the same feelings of trepidation about his parents, but that doesn't mean there aren't ways to help start the conversation.

"Give it to me," Jenner tells him. Thus far, everything from Jenner has been softened and hushed so that they could enjoy a relaxing dinner together without any added pressure or stress. But this is sharper and clipped. It's an order.

"No," Brayden frowns.

"*Give it to me*," he insists. "She knows. She saw everything. There's no point in avoiding her if she's the one reaching out."

"Whatever," Brayden sighs, slapping the phone into Jenner's palm.

"Hello, this is Jenner Parrish," he says, answering. "Yes, he's not available right now but is there something I can help you with?"

Unable to hear his grandmother's side of the conversation, Brayden can only pretend to be disinterested and pick at his food.

"Yeah. Definitely. That works for us. What time? Okay. See you then, Ms. Clare. Bye."

"Oh, for Christ's sake," Brayden sighs. "What did you just agree to?"

"Dinner. Tomorrow. She asked if we might be available to come by for chicken." Jenner lowers his voice and adds, "Why, you have a problem with that, slave?"

Hiding his expression behind his wine glass, Brayden stays mum.

"Yeah, I thought so. She wants to see us. That's a good thing."

But Brayden is not so easily convinced.

After dinner, Brayden says he just wants to go to bed, so Jenner leaves him to it whilst going to finish up the night downstairs at the bar. Morning arrives. When the cat jumps up on the bed and tries to sit on Brayden's face again, he shoos her away, unintentionally waking Jenner, and goes back to sleep.

The bed shifts but it doesn't rouse Brayden as Jenner gets up. A little while later it shifts again when he comes back to bed. For Brayden it's all a sleepy blur, just as Jenner intends.

When Brayden does finally pry his eyes open, Jenner is staring at him, very much awake. Brayden, frowning with confusion, tries to puzzle out why Jenner is still in bed if he's done sleeping. For a long moment, neither of them says or does anything as Brayden waits, very obviously, for Jenner to pull him close to lay inside his arms like he usually does. It's their favorite cuddling position. But it doesn't happen, and it quickly makes Brayden grumpy, so he shifts closer on his own.

Amused by this, Jenner grins behind Brayden's back. He grabs hold of Brayden, pulling him to lie on top as Jenner rolls onto his back.

"Is this a hint?" Brayden grumbles.

Jenner's morning wood pokes suggestively at Brayden's ass. When he catches the scent of Jenner's freshly showered skin, Brayden buries his nose in Jenner's chest, inhaling deeply, dragging a few kisses there and wrapping a hand around Jenner's side.

"It's *some* kind of hint," Jenner agrees. With half-lidded eyes, Jenner gazes avidly down the length of his body at the sight of Brayden sucking kisses to Jenner's nipples, thrusting lightly against Jenner's hipbone.

"Mm, lemme use the bathroom and get washed up before we do this," Brayden says, raising his head and planting a hand on the bed beside Jenner's waist.

"Not necessary," Jenner tells him, spreading his legs, bending his knees and planting his feet so that Brayden lies between them instead. "I don't exactly give this to a lot of people. But if we're doing the whole family thing this weekend, I want you to know me as well as anyone ever has. It's kind of important to me."

Brayden's eyes widen slightly. It makes him look very young and Jenner smiles. "For real? You're letting me?"

"For *real*," Jenner agrees with sarcastic flair. They're both already naked. Brayden's hand immediately goes to caress underneath Jenner's left thigh, like now that he has permission to touch there, he can't wait to do it.

"Wow," Brayden says with amazement, lightly touching Jenner's ass, rubbing over the side of the muscle. Brayden is suddenly completely hard. Jenner can feel it. "You know I've never done this before, right?"

This doesn't seem to give Brayden much pause, though, because as soon as he says it, his fingertips are right there, circling Jenner's hole, prodding gently at it. With his bottom lip caught in his teeth, biting it as he tries to hide a pleased smirk, Brayden breaches Jenner with the tip of his middle finger and lowers his mouth back onto Jenner's chest. He sucks a kiss to the black-inked tattoo over Jenner's heart, tracing it with the tip of his tongue. Then he moves lower to kiss and lick over the dark circle of Jenner's stiffened nipple. Brayden nips it between his teeth, sucking on it.

Getting off on Brayden's eagerness in a big way, Jenner moans behind sealed lips. He lets his legs fall more widely opened, drawing them up and angling his pelvis.

"Lube, Bray," he grunts, grabbing a tube of the stuff from the nightstand and offering it to his enthusiastic virgin conqueror. "And yes, I know. I intend to claim every aspect of your virginity. It's been my life's mission since I started stalking you at the pool."

Brayden inserts his dry finger more deeply with a happy little smirk on his face. After another moment, though, he impatiently withdraws the finger. He squirts lubricant onto his hand and pushes two slicked fingers back into Jenner's ass. Once more biting intently at his lower lip in concentration, Brayden kneels between Jenner's open thighs and begins to stroke Jenner's dark, heavy erection while fingering him open.

"So this was all part of the master plan, huh? You saw me and you knew right away that you wanted to give it up to the short hippie in the itty bitty swim trunks?"

"Mm-hmm," Jenner grunts, blowing out air through his nose as Brayden spreads his fingers inside Jenner's sphincter, working the muscle loose. "Knew you'd be too eager for it to last long."

"Well, we'll see about that, won't we?" Brayden smiles. Every care is forgotten now that he's got Jenner laid out for him to plunder, Jenner is very glad to see. "Damn, I didn't think it'd be this much of a turn on to get to top you. And, by the way, I *love* having a conversation while my fingers are in your ass. Makes me feel powerful."

His eyes sparkle mischievously and Jenner loses some patience. "Yeah. Uh-huh. Less talking, Bray. Here." Jenner takes hold of his dick by the root and guides it up perpendicular to his body. He then palms the back of Brayden's head with his other hand, effectively shoving Brayden's mouth down onto his cock.

Chuckling, Brayden opens wide to let Jenner's dick slide into his mouth and wraps his tongue around the underside. He sucks, pulls off, and takes a wide lick before closing his lips around him behind the crown, sucking until his cheeks hollow out.

"Mmm, that's better," Jenner moans. "*Much* better."

Brayden hums loudly. The sound vibrates down Jenner's cock and the fingers pump inside his ass. A third one is added and Jenner's face scrunches up slightly around the burn of the stretch. With an upward glance, Brayden glances at Jenner's face. His smile grows around his mouthful. Chuckling, his expression softens as he focuses more on what he's doing.

Brayden's head moves up and down, and the suction is incredible. Just as Jenner is about to thrust up to get farther inside the soft grip of Brayden's mouth, Brayden pulls off with a loud, wet pop to confess, "I totally can't wait to fuck you."

"Yeah, well, I can tell. Less talking, more sucking."

"God, you even top from the bottom. Stop being so pushy. Just fucking lay there and enjoy it, bitch."

"Nice try," Jenner says while guiding Brayden's head back down towards the strained, reddened dick bobbing in front of his lips. "You're too adorable to pull that off. Keep sucking."

Jenner's cock slides in and out between Brayden's stretched-wide lips as he sets a rhythm. The wet glove of his throat is fantastically snug around the head of Jenner's cock. It draws a contented moan from Jenner, but, just as he starts to thrust and move right there like he wants to, Brayden pulls off again, his lips and chin shiny wet with saliva.

"I think you should say please. I mean, I *am* doing all the work here."

Brayden rubs intentionally deeper, bends his fingers and finds his target. Tapping Jenner's gland, he gets Jenner's mouth to fall open and a much sharper groan to wrench free. Jenner's head falls back onto the pillow. Precome beads at the tip of his dick. Brayden licks it away and does it again as Jenner's hips twitch, fucking the air desperately as he tries to slip his dick back into Brayden's mouth.

"Say please, Jenn," he taunts.

"Oh you are *so* paying for this later."

As a louder cry erupts from Jenner, Brayden beams with pride and says, "Why do you think I'm doing it, smartass?"

"Enough with the fingers. Come on. Lemme feel you," Jenner gasps.

"Say please," Brayden grins.

"Please," Jenner growls.

"Now that wasn't so hard, was it?"

"Will you please shut the fuck up and put your dick in me already? God, you're so chatty. I need to stock up on gags." He grabs a pillow and wedges it under his hips. Pulling his knees back with his hands, Jenner tries and fails not to roll his eyes at the wide-eyed, excited way Brayden stares at him. "Bray, stop looking at it and fuck it. Such a virgin. At least this won't take long."

"I'm just trying to savor this...."

Jenner raises an eyebrow with impatience in the set of his jaw.

"Yeah yeah. All right already," Brayden sighs. He scoots closer, aligning his dick with Jenner's opening, then presses there. Staring down between their bodies, Brayden watches as Jenner parts for him and his ass swallows Brayden's cock.

"Hell yeah," Brayden sighs with delirious pleasure. His hips snap as he moves instinctively to bury himself in Jenner, but the pressure and force of the thrust are hard to take.

"Easy," Jenner grunts. "Take it easy. My ass isn't as used to cock as yours is, slut."

But he's not even sure Brayden hears him. All of Brayden's sense seems to have funneled down to his dick with the rest of his blood. With a blank, blissful stare, Brayden bends down over Jenner, one hand braced on the bed and one gripping Jenner's thigh. His hair hangs down between them and he starts to move, undulating as he works himself in the most natural, oldest rhythm in the world.

They go slow at first. All of that silky long, golden brown hair has tumbled down to tickle Jenner's chest and obscure Brayden's face. Jenner reaches up and tucks some of it behind Brayden's ear and makes a mental note to keep hair ties handy next time because he wants to see this, and every single expression that crosses Brayden's face. Utterly relaxed, lost in lust, Brayden is nothing but his. He's Jenner's in every way. Seeing Brayden's body clench with each push, wanting to feel that, Jenner palms Brayden's bare ass, encouraging each clench of his buttocks, driving him in deeper, coaxing him faster.

Skin flushed and glistening with sweat, Brayden is exquisite. The friction and fullness of Brayden moving inside him is better than Jenner hoped it would be. It makes Jenner glad that he gave Brayden this, knowing it'll only bring them closer. Rolling his hips counter to Brayden's thrusts, pushing down against him, making Brayden frown and gasp, Jenner whispers, "God, you're beautiful."

"Love you," Brayden gasps, ducking his head as Jenner chases up, catching his lips in the middle in a breathless kiss.

Jenner's prick is squeezed between them. He grabs at Brayden's ass as their bodies grind together. Brayden, frowning, kissing Jenner with a growl, slams in hard over and over again, knocking the air out of Jenner while Jenner rubs off on Brayden's rock-hard abs.

Closer and closer Jenner gets, racing right up to the edge. His balls draw up tight, ready to blow. Wanting Brayden to come with him, Jenner moves his hand slightly, reaching under Brayden, pivoting it a little at the wrist. Brayden doesn't see it coming. Pumping into Jenner at a frenzied speed, his body locking up at the beginnings of his climax, suddenly Brayden feels Jenner's thick finger inserted in a sweat-slicked, demanding push into his ass, up to the last knuckle.

"Oh *shit*," Brayden cries. Lower lip quivering, he shoots deeply inside Jenner, coating him, making each push much wetter and easier as he slides in it.

Jenner grabs Brayden's face by the jaw and pulls him down for a kiss. While trying to swallow a sharp cry, Jenner comes hot over Brayden's taut stomach. Still pulsing, Brayden moans as Jenner wedges another finger into his ass. Each jab makes his hips pump, makes him quiver in Jenner's arms. Brayden's skin is covered in goosebumps. Gasping through his orgasm, Brayden's eyes unfocus and he looks nothing but blissfully content.

Still pushing against Brayden's cock, wanting all of it, keeping him there with the two fingers he has hooked deeply inside Brayden's ass, Jenner slowly comes down, taking his time. His whole body tingles. Chest rising and falling with each filling breath, Jenner catches Brayden's mouth in another hungry kiss, licking over his tongue, biting at his lip, swallowing each moan.

After what feels like a long time, the kiss ends. Brayden's eyes are barely open. His hair is plastered to his face in places. Brayden's nipples are stiff so Jenner can't help but play with them, thereby burning off the last remnants of sense left in Brayden's head. Brayden makes no move to pull out of Jenner and go.

"That was really, really good," Brayden slurs.

"Yeah it was."

"No, I mean it. It was *really good*," Brayden insists.

Jenner chuckles. His inner muscles clench in flutters around Brayden, making him groan softly and push against him in a needy thrust.

"Does that mean you don't want to bottom anymore, then?"

"Are you kidding? No, I'm gonna stay right here and wait for my dick to recover so I can fuck you again. But this time I'm gonna make sure you don't come so I can climb on and ride you when I'm done. And I want the collar. Oh, and handcuffs. Definitely handcuffs. And maybe a butt plug cause the thing with the fingers was great. I liked that a lot."

"Bray?"

"Hmm?"

"Shut up and kiss me," Jenner says lovingly, pulling him in.

"Okay," Brayden nods, humming happily against Jenner's lips.

An hour later, Brayden is sat upon Jenner's dick, rolling his hips in tight circles as Jenner grabs hold of the cuffs keeping Brayden's hands bound behind his back. Curled up into a seated position, Jenner tugs Brayden's over-stimulated left nipple with his teeth and gasps through his second orgasm as he unloads into Brayden's ass. He's been fondling Brayden's spent, come-soaked cock, making him writhe and moan.

"So good, Jenn," he mutters dazedly, his head rolled back on his shoulders, body given over to Jenner in every sense.

"You're getting the harness today," Jenner warns. "And tonight, after we get home, I'm gonna take you again, but I'm not gonna let you come. You want that?"

"*So good*," Brayden moans.

Chuckling, Jenner rolls them. Brayden pulls off with a small grunt and falls down onto his face against the bed. Jenner unfastens the cuffs and kisses his cheek. "Take a nap."

"Whut?" Brayden grunts, half asleep already.

Jenner gives Brayden's ass a hard slap and struggles to get off the bed, his legs wobbly. Pulling the sheet up over Brayden, Jenner gives him a long, fond look before going to get cleaned up.

Chapter 37

Hold What You Have

They walk up to the door to Ruth Clare's house. When Jenner takes Brayden's hand, it's because of the many ways that the world has failed and saved him that Brayden folds their fingers tightly together and doesn't let go.

It scares Brayden to face his grandmother and Emma Leah, and it makes him feel sad in a profound way that not many people his age get to experience, so he holds Jenner's hand. And, because when he looks at Jenner, Brayden sees that making love to him has changed their dynamic permanently, he holds Jenner's hand.

This is what Brayden has. He has Jenner Parrish and he has pride, courage and responsibilities. He has a good man at his side, loving him, and a family that has asked them to dinner. And that's enough.

Brayden rings the doorbell and, as a figure approaches from within, keeping his own hand fitted inside his partner's hand is one of the bravest things Brayden has ever done.

The door opens. Ruth smiles at them like she wasn't entirely sure they would show up. Glancing between them with that same triumphant grin, she seems to let go of a heavy weight that had been pressing her down and says, "Good. Good. Welcome. Both of you."

She doesn't say anything about what happened at the Pub. She doesn't have to. It's all written on her face and in her eyes, and in Brayden's eyes too. When his Nana opens her arms to him, Brayden steps forward and gives her a hug.

Hugging him back tightly, she sniffles a little and pats his hair. "Such a good man you've become. I'm proud of you."

Brayden is buoyed by the words and steps back, lighter as well.

"Ms. Clare," Jenner says in greeting. "Thank you for inviting us."

"Oh please. We've already been through this, haven't we? It's Ruth. My goodness." She beckons to Jenner and draws him in for a hug as well. He's almost twice the size of her. Brayden smiles to see the sight of Jenner bending almost in half to hug his grandmother. "Come on in. The food's just getting finished up so you can set the table while Emma helps me get it sorted."

"Brayden!" Emma squeals happily when she sees him.

"Hey, squirt," he grins, drawing her in for a one-armed hug as she beams up at him with something akin to relief.

"Nan let me pitch in with making the chicken," Emma says proudly. "I did the breading and mashed the potatoes."

"You did a great job, it looks amazing. I'm starving."

Emma gives Jenner a shy glance.

"Hey, Emma," he smiles.

"Hi," she squeaks.

"Go on upstairs to wash up for supper," Ruth tells her. Emma flies past, running to the stairs. With a chuckle and shake of her head, Ruth directs Brayden to the cupboard with the plates.

They sit down around the kitchen table with the food laid out between them, the aroma of the freshly fried chicken making their mouths water.

"This all looks incredible, Ruth," Jenner tells her.

"Thank you, Jenner," she replies. "Top-secret family recipe. I'll share it with you later."

Jenner nudges Brayden's foot under the table. Brayden smiles with sincere, powerful happiness.

"Hey," Brayden says suddenly. "That's my scarf!"

Emma pulls the brightly-colored scarf wrapped around her neck up to cover her mouth. Only her big, shining glasses and her mop of golden brown hair stick out the top. "I found it in the laundry room. You can have it back, but only if you give Jenner a kiss," she giggles.

"Emma Leah," Ruth gasps in feigned shock.

Jenner puckers up his lips and turns them toward Brayden while keeping his eyes locked on Emma. It makes her giggle even more. After a couple of smooching sounds from Jenner, Brayden gives it up and turns to give Jenner a quick, chaste peck.

"Yay!" Emma squeaks.

"Oh my god. I think it was a bad idea to introduce the two of you," Brayden groans as Jenner puckers up for another kiss and Emma giggles even more helplessly. She begins to unwind the scarf, since Brayden did what she asked and kissed Jenner. "No, you can keep it," he tells her. "It looks good on you."

"Yay," Emma says with quiet delight from under the ridiculously big scarf wound around and around her tiny neck.

"Yay," Jenner mimics, making Emma snort with mirth. Brayden smiles.

Once dinner is done and they're walking back home, Brayden is more genuinely contented than Jenner has ever seen him. That contentment adds a spring to Brayden's step and lets his cheerful spirit shine out brightly.

The new patterns of his life have been revealed to Brayden. The next morning, he wakes up revived, showers, dresses and cooks breakfast all before Jenner stirs. They go to the gym and burn off pent-up energy. Brayden goes to watch Jenner practice jujitsu with some other men and women, smiling proudly. It goes unspoken but they both realize that today it's Brayden's job to be the strong one for Jenner, and be there for him in whatever way that's needed. That Jenner truly needs him seems to help ground Brayden and give him purpose.

The day flies by. Dinner is scheduled early at the Parrish household. Jenner assures Brayden that he's fine. Max and Art call to check on them, and Jenner tells them much of the same.

But Brayden seems to detect the jittery undercurrent of panic in Jenner's every movement and the hard shine of his eyes, as he braces for something truly awful, expecting it. If he expects it, maybe, Jenner thinks, it'll be easier to survive the pain. Jenner's strain makes it hard for Brayden to stay positive and maintain his tough exterior.

Even though Jenner tries to internalize as much of his trepidation as he can, it's no use. The two of them are too connected not to sense one another's unease.

By the time they're walking up the steps of the front porch at Jenner's parents' house, Brayden has become very quiet. There's an air rich with sadness about him like a dense fog. He seems to shrink in on himself as he smoothes out his white button-down shirt and khakis, and fusses restlessly to keep his hair neatly tied back at the nape of his neck.

It becomes incredibly difficult for Jenner to take those last couple of steps and knock on the door. Maybe it is too much. Maybe it's not fair to ask this of Brayden so soon.

Jenner hesitates, bringing Brayden to an abrupt halt.

"Come on." Brayden pulls him by the hand toward the door.

"I don't know," Jenner says quietly.

"I do. It's fine. We're here aren't we?"

But it's not as simple as that. Jenner clenches his jaw and doesn't move an inch. Glancing up at the house he grew up in, Jenner doubts his ability to risk losing so much after witnessing how much it has hurt Brayden to give up the same thing. Brayden's parents are gone, and their absence changed him. Their abandonment made every part of his life harder.

Thus far, Jenner has done everything possible to keep his family and friends at safe distances. He's built walls and kept secrets. When he has let people close after putting them through trials to test their trustworthiness, loyalty and value—like Max and Art—it felt like he was giving them a gift by allowing them the privilege of knowing him, beyond all of the fortifications. The many slaves he's tried to pair with, and found to be less than satisfactory, failed the tests he laid out for them. It was their loss, in the end. Not Jenner's.

But witnessing all that Brayden has endured, giving up so much, so freely, and for only the sake of others, has opened Jenner's eyes. Brayden knows loss. While Jenner has gotten satisfaction out of causing others' loss, Brayden has had to learn to live through it, to cope with it. He's been stronger than Jenner ever has, falsely, believed himself to be.

Because, maybe all of this time, Jenner has been the one losing out. In denying others, he has only denied himself possible joy.

Maybe following Brayden's lead and bravely, openly trusting is the path to true reward.

Laying a hand on Jenner's chest, over his tattoo, Brayden says, "Hey. I love you. I know it's hard, but you can do this. Okay?"

Taking a deep breath, Jenner closes his eyes and gives Brayden a soft kiss. Their foreheads touch as he struggles to gather courage, preparing to take steps he never thought he would.

Then, he hears, "You boys coming in sometime tonight or you gonna keep smooching on the porch? Just let me know, so I know whether to wait or go keep the lasagna from burning to a crisp."

"Oh my god," Jenner moans with horror. "Ma...."

He stands up straight; stops touching Brayden and backs up a step with a guilty expression like a child caught stealing cookies. With a sideways glance, Brayden grabs Jenner's hand and purposefully weaves their fingers together.

"If I burn that lasagna, Jenner Parrish, it's *your* damn fault," his mother scolds, shaking a finger at him. "In or out. Come on."

"Bette, it's good to see you again," Brayden tries.

"Oh, and you too, Brayden!" she smiles happily. "Do you see what I've been dealing with for almost half of my life? Stubborn as a mule, this one. You can pull all you want, but he just ain't goin' if he doesn't want to go."

Brayden smiles.

"But—" Jenner sputters. "I don't... I mean, you— You don't exactly seem *surprised.*"

"You noticed that, huh? Do you think I was born yesterday, child? I am your mother, in case you've forgotten. I do know you. My goodness. You still haven't answered my initial question, you know. I smell that good food going over."

"Okay, okay. Damn, Ma."

"It's about time," she sighs, holding the door open for them. "Wouldn't blame you if you wanted to stay out, though. He is a cutie, isn't he?"

Before Jenner can collect his senses, his mother is kissing Brayden's cheek, then giving Brayden a squeezing hug before turning to her son and giving him a kiss as well. With that out of the way,

Bette turns and jogs back down the hall to the kitchen, leaving them both there, befuddled.

Jenner is utterly speechless and completely confused. For a moment he just stands there, shocked.

When he turns to Brayden to see his reaction, it's not what Jenner expects. He's faced with the sight of Brayden, stock-still and heartbroken, and it hurts Jenner deeply. Brayden's expression is mostly blank but tears slip silently down his cheeks as he tries, somehow, to recover from the sting of bittersweet regret from witnessing Bette Parrish's love and unquestioning acceptance when Lara Clare isn't capable of giving her child such comforts.

With a sigh of lament, Jenner gathers Brayden up in his arms. Jenner holds Brayden's face against his shoulder. The fabric of his shirt gets damp from Brayden's tears and Jenner feels Brayden's arms wind around his waist. The grief has him and it's pulling him under.

"This was a bad idea. I'm sorry, it's my fault. I should've known better," Jenner apologizes, jolted into action now that he knows Brayden needs him.

"What's wrong?" Bette asks with shocked concern, reappearing from the kitchen with a dishtowel in her hands. "What happened?!"

"Later, Ma," Jenner starts.

Embarrassed, Brayden dries his eyes. Bette fetches a box of tissues and brings it over to him.

"Thanks," he murmurs. "I'm sorry for making a scene."

"Oh please," she says, dismissing his concern. "I hope this isn't because my son hasn't been treating you as he should."

"No, Jenner's been incredible. He's really done a lot for me." He looks up at Jenner, and another tear falls. Jenner brushes it away with the pad of his thumb.

"I know what this needs," Bette says seriously, planting his hands on her hips. "*Wine.* Lots of wine. Excuse me."

Brayden laughs despite himself and starts to get it together even as Bette's kind understanding almost makes him fall apart again. One shared look communicates this to Jenner, clearly. Jenner kisses his partner's forehead and smiles supportively.

"Thought I heard you come in," Callum Parrish says loudly, strolling into the front hall and popping an appetizer into his mouth.

Jenner tenses instantly, reflexively, after a lifetime of coping with his brother's every insinuation by putting up walls, not knowing what to say or what to expect after what Callum did for him at the Pub.

"'Bout time you dragged your sorry ass to family dinner," Callum continues, speaking around his mouthful of food. "Friggin' slacker. You know, since you told everyone you're queer, I like you a heck of a lot more. The whole air of pissy defensiveness makes a lot more sense now."

Jenner can't even respond. He has no idea what to say. Then, from the next room comes a gruff voice shouting, "It's unnatural!"

"You shut your mouth, you old fart!" Bette calls angrily from the kitchen.

"Yeah, Pop," Callum agrees with plenty of volume. "Give it a rest already! Don't be a jerk. You wanna eat dinner out with the dog or with the adults at the table 'cause you know Ma will kick you out. You're just sore you won't get lots of grankiddies."

Mr. Parrish harrumphs loudly and mutters something about homosexuals taking over the world. Callum flaps a hand in his father's general direction and shakes his head with pity. "Don't mind him. It's Brayden, right? The tan blond?"

While Jenner's face colors with guilt, Callum, smiling, offers a hand and Brayden shakes it.

"Yeah. It's Brayden."

"Cool. I'm Callum. You can call me Cal."

"Who are you and what have you done with my brother?" Jenner asks.

"Oh, get your head out of your ass. Maybe if you hadn't been lying to your family for so many years, you wouldn't be such a miserable bastard all the time, huh? Brayden, come give an opinion on the wine."

Brayden starts to follow Callum with a surprised shrug back at Jenner who is too stunned to do anything but stand there and watch them go.

While Callum lets Brayden sample a few bottles of wine that they have opened, Jenner snaps out of it with effort and goes to his mother at the stove. He pulls her aside, into the dining room.

The room has already been readied for their arrival with the table set and candles lit. In the relative seclusion, Jenner explains briefly to Bette about Lara and Anthony and the reasons for Brayden's emotional instability.

The farther he gets into his explanation, the harder his mother presses her lips together. As soon as he reaches the part about Brayden leaving his life in Miami behind in order to take care of his grandmother and cousin, since his absentee mother had given him no other choice, Bette snaps.

With a frustrated, angry huff, she stalks past Jenner, through the kitchen and right up to Brayden.

Holding Brayden at arm's length, she holds his gaze and says fiercely, "Now you listen to me. If I know my son, and believe me, *I know my son*, he wouldn't have gone through all of the hubbub of bringing you here and showing us at long last what I've known or at least strongly suspected for a long time if he didn't care about you very much. And seeing how he acts with you only confirms that for me. You're a part of the family now, Brayden, and I don't want to hear any of this nonsense about you not having a mother. You have one and she's right here. From now on, you call me Ma. Everyone else does anyway. So, let me hear it. Come on. That food's not going to walk itself to the table."

Brayden stifles a smile, glances at Jenner's flabbergasted expression over Bette's shoulder, and tries, "Okay. Ma."

"Better!" she says happily, throwing her hands up in the air in triumph. Clapping once, she turns to the counter and yells, "Food's ready to go out! Pop, get your behind in here and be helpful!"

Jenner, beaming, returns to his place at Brayden's side. He takes Brayden's hand and gives it a squeeze.

"Now I know where you get your bossiness from," Brayden laughs.

With a small smile, Jenner shrugs and grabs a dishtowel from the counter. He twirls it and snaps it against Brayden's ass as he goes to assist with the food.

"I saw that!" Bette calls sharply. "You be nice to him, Jenner Parrish! He's smaller than you. Don't be a bully!"

Brayden laughs brightly.

Jenner deflates and mutters a dutiful, "Yes, Ma."

Chapter 38

On Display

"Don't even think about it," Jenner warns.

It's a few weeks later and a Friday night. Manse is having a beach bonfire party. The bonfire is out on the front lawn, and the beach is inside. Bubbles and foam are sprayed over the amassed crowd, floating through the air, gathering at their feet. Brightly colored lights flash, highlighting bronzed, waxed, mostly bare male bodies. Even though it's freezing outside, the heat of the bonfire and the collective warmth of many bodies packed into a small space is making them sweat.

The dress code is swimsuits only. Brayden is in his itty bitty trunks as well as his collar. All night long, men have been ogling Brayden from near and far. Jenner has been bristling impressively with a case of raging possessiveness.

They both had debated wearing masks but, in the end, had realized that they have nothing to hide. Not anymore. However, allowing the many horny hardbodies surrounding them to get a good look at Brayden's lithe swimmer's body and adorable face has proved to make them extra grabby.

"The next person to touch your ass is getting kicked in the balls," Jenner growls.

"This was your idea, tough guy," Brayden laughs. He rubs a hand over the firm swell of Jenner's pectoral muscle and the tantalizingly inked skin. "What d'you say? We could dance... or go upstairs... or get a booth...."

"Well, first off," Jenner starts. "I don't dance. Secondly, if I wanted to fuck you in private, I'd have just stayed home. Last time we went upstairs together we barely had security watching us, let alone an actual, captive audience."

"So, the booth it is," Brayden grins wickedly. "You know, I'm probably still wet and stretched from the plug. It'd be really hot to know people were watching you stuff me full of your cock."

"Yeah," Jenner says eagerly. "I bet you'd love that, cockslut. Gonna let me pull out your dick? Give 'em a comeshot, too? I'll let you orgasm if you follow orders. How many days has it been, anyway?"

"Five. *Five* fucking days," Brayden says roughly, glancing quickly around at everyone nearby them, watching them and listening in. He wonders if Jenner's elusive mentor, David, is nearby, keeping an eye on them. Maybe Jenner warned David they were coming. Maybe David is one of the men right beside them, groping him, and Jenner is simply pretending they're all strangers. Or, maybe David is waiting by the booths, on the other side of the glass, for the show to start and for his old apprentice to display his new prize.

"You know, for all the tough talk, I don't think you could go through with it," Jenner teases. "You're too shy. Shy little Braydy."

"Try me. I dare you."

Brayden's heart is practically beating out of his chest with anticipation as his breathing quickens. The front of the skimpy speedos tents, straining the fabric. Jenner grabs a handful and squeezes. It makes Brayden gasp and lean in for a kiss. When Jenner slips a hand under the waistband with people all around them, bumping into them, staring at them, whispering about them, and wraps his fingers around Brayden's dick, that decides him.

"Let's go," Brayden says breathlessly, extricating himself, yanking Jenner along.

The booths are down a hall and farther from the crowds. There are three booths in a row and none of them are taken. Jenner and Brayden pick the first one. They go inside and close the door behind them. Three of the walls are drywall, but the fourth is one-way glass. All they see is mirror, but they know that on the other side, people are probably watching from the secluded room where they can enjoy the show.

"Hands on the glass. You move 'em, I stop," Jenner warns.

Brayden plants his hands on the glass, staring at his reflection, and watches as Jenner pulls down Brayden's trunks. His dick springs up, curving in a hot, thick line between his legs. The skin all around it is bare and recently waxed smooth by Jenner.

Stroking Brayden slowly, root to tip, until his dick starts to weep precome, Jenner sucks a mark on his slave's neck then pushes the thumb of his other hand in through the wet, ready hole between Brayden's cheeks.

"Come on, I'm *ready*," Brayden begs.

"Not yet. Be patient. We gotta give 'em a show first, don't we? I want them to see how badly you need me to fuck you."

The glass reveals nothing to Brayden but the hunger and determination in Jenner's eyes from over Brayden's shoulder. He wonders how many people are out there, staring, and becomes more certain that David is among them.

Jenner holds up two fingers, pressed together. Then he drops the hand behind Brayden's back, between their bodies, and twists the digits up through his hole, pumping them in smooth, long strokes a few times. It makes Brayden breathe heavier, his fingers tensed on the mirrored glass. Jenner tugs his hand back out and leans closer to Brayden.

"Look at me."

Brayden turns his head, and glances back over his shoulder. Their eyes meet. Jenner lowers his head and begins to passionately kiss his lover's lips. They break and Jenner feeds him the fingers instead, working them in and out. Brayden sucks them, wrapping his tongue around the fingers and helplessly making sweetly desperate, somewhat nervous, soft sounds.

"That's it. Good, slave. You gonna be dirty for me?"

"*Yes*," Brayden gasps as the fingers slip free. They rub over his slightly swollen lower lip on the withdrawal.

Suddenly Jenner is right there, pressing up behind him, their bodies flush together. Jenner breaches Brayden with a sharp thrust. The force, sudden fullness and the stretch make Brayden cry out with a moan, clawing at the slick glass which hides nothing. Nothing at all. Jenner slides all the way in and Brayden gasps for air.

Bowing his head, Brayden grows shy, his back arching as Jenner withdraws slightly. Sticking out his ass in invitation for the next thrust, Brayden moans even louder when Jenner slowly presses back in, giving him every inch again. They hold like that for a few moments, catching their breath. Then, Jenner's hand reaches around to wrap Brayden's hard-on, stiff and heavy between his legs. Fondling it, sweeping his thumb back and forth over the head, Jenner waits until Brayden whimpers for more, then starts to jack him fast and hard while fucking him at a steady, slow pace.

It makes Brayden crazy, not knowing whether to chase the hand or push back onto the cock. Tossing his hair back over his shoulder, back bowed beautifully, panting, flushed, sweaty, impaled on Jenner and trapped inside his hand, Brayden cries out raggedly.

They've only started and he's so close already. Sensing Brayden's imminent climax, Jenner stops jerking him off. The hand that was just manipulating his cock drags lazily up the length of Brayden's torso instead to sharply twist one of his nipples.

Lips parted and wanton, Brayden pushes back against Jenner's next long thrust. He does it again and again, fucking himself back onto Jenner's throbbing, steely shaft. Jenner's fingers twist Brayden's nipple the other way and Brayden comes suddenly, untouched, shooting over the glass, splattering come in hot streaks over himself as well.

"Touch me," he pleads as he pulses again. "Master, please...."

Jenner shifts his angle, adjusting Brayden's pose with hands locked on Brayden's hips. The next pointed thrust draws a desperate little shout as Jenner's cock drags over Brayden's sweet spot. More come pulses from his slit and Brayden almost drops his hand to stroke himself.

"Don't," Jenner warns sharply. "Don't you dare, slave. Keep 'em on the glass."

"Shit," Brayden hisses. He fucks the air a few times, shuddering with aftershocks and stimulation, his eyes rolling back as Jenner takes his time reaming out Brayden's ass.

Soon, Jenner pulls out completely and strokes himself, unloading over Brayden's bare, well-fucked ass.

"Hands behind your head. Do it," Jenner says gruffly, groaning through the effects of his orgasm. "Good, now turn and face me."

"Oh my god," Brayden moans.

"Do it, slave!"

Brayden turns, putting his back to the glass.

Semen runs down in thick trickles over his butt cheeks, down his crack and over the backs and insides of his thighs. Jenner steps up closely to kiss him and rubs greedily through the mess, working it into the skin, leaving it as a film covering it. With two fingers he pushes some of the warm fluid into Brayden's stretched and tender hole. Then he spreads Brayden's cheeks with both hands, letting their audience see.

"Who do you belong to?" Jenner asks.

"You," Brayden swears. "I belong to you, Sir. Always."

Jenner pulls the snug trunks up to cover Brayden and glances at the glass with countless unknown faces hidden beyond it.

Caressing the side of Brayden's face, smiling as he turns into the touch, Jenner whispers, "You're the best thing that's ever happened to me. I'm so proud of you. Love you, Bray. Now let's get the fuck out of here and go home."

They exit the booth. The noise of the crowd is like the whistle of wind, the cry of seagulls and the pulse of life. But for Brayden, Jenner is the sea. He's the home ever sought and the elusive dream that for so long hovered just out of reach, like sunlight shining on rippling water.

But now Jenner is all around him and in him, filling every void. Brayden surrenders to fate, to nature and he drowns, but he drowns in Jenner who claims him, body and soul, transforming him. Fear and uncertainty are left behind. Freedom brought by possession and devoted love takes their place. Coming out on the other side, Brayden is reborn. He takes his first, filling breath and smiles.

If you enjoyed this story, you can sign up for a free membership at
ForbiddenFiction.com and discuss it with other readers
and the author at the *Bound by Lies* story page
at http://forbiddenfiction.com/library/story/LK1-1.000109.

We do our best to proof all our work, but if you spot a text error we missed, please let us know via our website Contact Form at http://forbiddenfiction.com/contact.

Author's Notes

When I was in seventh grade, I attended a small school in a small town. There were approximately 20 kids in my entire grade level. One day, the principal called me into her office. I'd been the victim of a lot of bullying and she wanted to give me a pep talk of sorts. She sat me in a chair across from where she sat behind her desk and told me I was an ugly duckling who would turn into a swan. Now, I know her intentions were pure, and I knew what she meant, but all that stuck with me were those words and the realization that even the principal of the school, a figure of great authority in my life, saw me as an ugly duckling, and I never forgot it. Looking back, my entire life almost feels like one big statement of, "I'm more than that, damn it."

This book was inspired in part by that day in the principal's office. Brayden is someone who had lots of people telling him he was an ugly duckling, too, and the thing about being stuck with that label is how do you know when you've become the swan? Is it a gradual transformation or does it happen overnight? And, even after you've become the swan, do those around you notice or are they so used to seeing you as the ugly duckling that they'll never be able to see you as anything else?

I wanted to explore those questions through Brayden, and also help him find the love needed to strengthen his convictions. This story picks up after Brayden has gone through most of his transformation. He's only beginning to be able to see himself as the swan, so when he's thrown back into the small town where he's only Cry Baby Braydy, he flounders and questions everything.

Being able to take Brayden, who I identify with so much, on this journey of self-acceptance was intensely fulfilling. But this isn't just Brayden's story. Living in a small town, everyone struggles with the way those around them feel they already know everything about you there is to know, and the constant, relentless curiosity whenever new information or occurrences come to light. It's a balance of living as the person you're thought to be, living as the person you know you are, and trying to carve out some semblance of privacy, even if it takes lying or misdirection to attain it. Though this story grew from Brayden, Jenner is the one who haunts me most. Once Jenner began to flesh out in my head, I couldn't shake him off. While Brayden only wants to be wanted enough for someone to keep him, Jenner is the romantic. He sees Brayden first as the swan, and even when he discovers how Brayden used to be an ugly duckling, it only draws Jenner to him more. Jenner falls first, long before Brayden, and fights it, trying to resist, or do the right thing, then lying to protect the one he loves. Both Brayden and Jenner have their "Who am I?" moments, for different reasons. Whereas Brayden is overcoming perceived personal limitations, Jenner is trying to break free of the comfort of an assumed identity. Initially, they both let everyone else tell them who they are versus being brave enough to own who they are, come what may. They become each other's reasons to step forward, inviting judgment and chaos, to say, "No, *this* is who I am."

I found great joy and personal satisfaction in writing this story. I worked on it while writing other, darker, stories and every time I came back to it, it felt like my happy place. It's my hope that the characters' flaws only help you relate to them more, and give you more reason to cheer them on as they struggle, stumble and persevere. Thank you my editors, Rylan and Dany, for giving me the guidance needed to take this story where it needed to go. I couldn't have done it without you. During the editing process, entire storylines, entire characters were removed and added, but each change lifted the story higher than I thought it could go. A special thank you to my dear Leyanne who lent much needed support from the beginning, when this was called *When the Sun Breaks Through* and it felt like all of my hopes and dreams were wrapped up in it. And thank you to my readers. It gives me great pleasure to introduce you to Brayden, Jenner, and all their friends. I hope you enjoy their journey as much as I have.

$-Lynn$

About the Author

Website: http://www.lynnkelling.com/

Lynn Kelling began writing in order to tell stories that weren't afraid of the dark, didn't hold anything back and always strived to be memorable, forging lasting attachments between character and reader. Her inspiration comes from taking a closer look at behaviors and ideas lurking at the fringes of life — basically anything that people may hesitate to speak of in mixed company, but everyone wonders about anyway. Her work is driven by the taboo in order to expose the humanity within it. Lynn is an artist, designer and lover of any form of creative self-expression that comes from a place of honesty and emotion, whether it's body art or opera. She has had multiple novels published, has written over fifty works of erotic fiction of varying lengths, and always has several novels in progress.

About the Publisher

ForbiddenFiction.com is a publisher devoted to writing that breaks the boundaries of original erotic fiction. Our stories combine intense sexuality with quality writing. Stories at ForbiddenFiction.com not only arouse readers through sensations, but also engage them emotionally and mentally through storytelling as well-crafted as the sex is hot.

ForbiddenFiction.com is also designed to be a social reading environment. You'll have fun even if just reading the latest post each day, yet you will have the chance for so much more. Readers and authors can be part of ongoing discussions of specific works and individual authors as well as more general topics.

Sign up for a FREE Membership today at <u>ForbiddenFiction.com</u>